Vasily Aksenov

THE STEEL BIRD

AND OTHER STORIES

translations by Rae Slonek, Susan Brownsberger,
Paul Cubberly, Greta Slobin, Helen C. Poot
& Valentina G. Brougher

ARDIS

Vasily Aksenov

The Steel Bird & Other Stories.

Copyright © 1979 by Ardis.
ISBN 0-88233-295-3 (cloth)

Published by Ardis, 2901 Heatherway,
Ann Arbor, Michigan 48104

Manufactured in the United States of America.

THE STEEL BIRD

TABLE OF CONTENTS

INTRODUCTION:
THE LIFE AND WORKS OF AKSENOV

John J. Johnson, Jr.

Vasily Pavlovich Aksenov was born on August 20, 1932 in Kazan. His mother, Eugenia Semenovna Ginzburg, was a history instructor at Kazan University who later became a well-known writer for her prison-camp memoir *Journey into the Whirlwind* (1962). His father, Pavel Vasilievich Aksenov, was a leading member of the Tartar Regional Committee of the Party, a professional Party man and revolutionary.

Previous to the Stalinist incarceration of his parents in 1937 Aksenov lived in a happy home that in addition to his parents consisted of his older brother, Alyosha, who died in the blockade of Leningrad, an older sister, Mayka, presently a Russian language teacher at Moscow University, a nurse, Fima, and his paternal grandmother, who was glowingly described by Ginzburg in her memoirs. Although the memoirs mention young Vasily as a two-year-old, he was actually four years old when his mother was arrested in February 1937, and almost five when his father was arrested later that year. Eugenia Ginzburg spent two years in Yaroslavl, followed by sixteen years in the Far East region of the Kolyma River, first at Magadan, then Elgen (the Yakut word for "dead"), then back in Magadan, "farther from Moscow than California," Aksenov once said, with an average temperature of -4 degrees Centigrade. His father ended up on the Pechora River in Siberia, 10,000 kilometers from his wife.[1]

In 1948, at the end of his eighth year in school (on a ten-year system), Aksenov joined his mother, who was by then out of the camp and living as an exile in Magadan. (His father had not yet been released.) In 1950, still in Magadan, he completed his elementary education. He then returned from the Far East to Leningrad where in 1956 he graduated as a doctor from the First Leningrad Medical Institute named after I. L. Pavlov.

From August 1956 until October 1957, Aksenov worked in the quarantine service of the Leningrad seaport and then in a hospital for water transportation workers located in the village of Voznesenye on Lake Onega, which is still in the Leningrad administrative district. In 1957 Aksenov met his future wife, Kira, in Leningrad, at a dance. He once recalled how he used to love to "rock to Bill Haley at university parties." Kira was from Moscow, and he followed her there after their marriage at the end of 1957.

From December 1957 until June 1958 he was a staff physician in the TB clinic located in the village of Grebneva in the Moscow area. Then until September 1960 he was a specialist in adolescent tuberculosis in a Moscow TB clinic. In July of 1959 *Youth (Yunost')* magazine published two stories,

"Our Vera Ivanovna" and "Paved Roads," which announced him as a new and interesting writer. Then in June and July of 1960 his novel *The Colleagues* was presented in two issues of the same magazine. Controversy immediately pushed him into the foreground, and he left medicine to write full time. In the same year his only child, Alyosha, was born.

Much of Aksenov's early work is autobiographical or heavily drawn from a familiar environment. "Our Vera Ivanovna" is set in a hospital much like the one he knew in Voznesenye. A government minister from Moscow finds himself hampered by a possible heart condition and a doctor who treats him as she would a regular patient. A flash flood forces him to help evacuate the hospital and then help look for the doctor, whom they so badly need. In admiration he now invites her to Moscow to have a plush job. Typical of Aksenov's early stories, the moral is meant to be obvious, and so she refuses because the people need her more.

"Paved Roads" is much more significant because it is an early example of the "youth story" genre on which Aksenov's controversial name was built. As a twenty-six-year-old writer he felt close ties to the young and to their highly colloquial speech. He chose to portray the generation that he saw and heard as they really were, not as the political theoreticians had hoped they would be. In this story twenty-five-year-old Gleb Pomorin returns from the army and tries to make a smooth transition back into civilian society. He runs into an old friend, Gerka, who seems to be living quite well: smoking foreign cigarettes and driving his own car. Slowly the new immorality of his old friend unwinds. "Work! That's a laugh! People go to work, save their money, dream of the future, but I want it all now: a dacha, a car, a good suit, women. That's happiness!"[2] Further revelations show that Gerka is a *fartsovshchik* (black market operator), and because of his relative wealth he has managed to coax Gleb's former girl-friend into a living arrangement with him. At the end, as Gerka runs from formerly fleeced road-pavers, the morally indignant Gleb notes: "He won't get far: the earth will burn under his feet. Our roads aren't for the likes of him." Clearly, here and in later works the moral message of Aksenov is to show that all young people are not alike, that they cannot be condemned as a generation. Yet his insistence on revealing the problem side of the young generation bore a mixed blessing—popularity with some, infamy with others. While the first group was large and representative of the reading public as a whole, the latter group was in power.

Aksenov's attitude toward young people is more thoroughly developed in *The Colleagues*. Here three young people, recent graduates of medical school, Maximov, Karpov and Zelenin, are faced with their mandatory postgraduate assignments. Maximov and Karpov accept work as shipboard doctors because of the promised travel and excitement. Zelenin opts for more dedicated work in a village.

One scene in the novel highlights Aksenov's main argument in this period. The three young men, out for a walk, encounter an invalid from the war who sizes them up by their clothing and hair-length and then proceeds to verbally abuse them as "hippies." The argument against the older generation's prejudice is immediately evident by the fact that these are doctors about to serve society in positions of responsibility. In their work they cross all kinds of realities, mostly unheard of in Soviet literature but well-known in real life. Karpov's girl friend marries a local laboratory researcher to avoid an unattractive post-graduate work assignment. The ship doctors find bribery and corruption in the port service. Zelenin finds alcoholism, violence and inhuman living conditions in his remote village location. But morality wins again, i.e., the girl is forever miserable, the doctors expose the corruption and Zelenin joins the dedicated local authorities in building a new order.

The controversy that sprung up following this novel posed questions far beyond the scope of the book or the writings of Aksenov as a whole. Writers and critics paired off into camps either attacking or approving of the new presentation of reality, of the new image of youth which was referred to as the "youth-theme" genre.

Because of the success of *The Colleagues* Aksenov left medicine at the end of 1960 and dedicated his life to writing. In an article which might be interpreted as an announcement of his intentions, he attacks the anti-youth attitude of the critics and the older generation as a whole. "We're talking about people who don't believe in youth, who consider them a generation of 'hippies' and pretty bourgeois. Not to believe in youth is to not believe in our future."[3] His intention was to write about youth as he saw them, as he felt they really were. While his intention seems to have been logical and worthy of pursuit, it clashed in principle with the make-believe world of socialist realism and inflexible Soviet rhetoric.

The problems of youth and their solutions are even more sharply drawn in Aksenov's most famous work "A Ticket to the Stars" (1961). "The heroes of this work seek answers to the questions: how should I live and for what purpose? They do not want ready answers, relieving them of their responsibilities. They seek their own solutions."[4] Aksenov, in fact, has caught the most characteristic psychological feature of young people in those years—striving for their own, personal answer in their relationship to life. The key difference in "A Ticket to the Stars" is that he delivers his message from the view-point of seventeen-year-old high school students just when they are graduating and learning to cope with the world. When the older generation attacks them they can not yet claim to be doctors and responsible citizens. Where Aksenov showed the attacks in *The Colleagues* to be purely an *argumentum ad hominem* and not logically directed to the philosophical beliefs of the young, he now strips his heroes of that defense. The basic story is that upon graduation four young people decide not to go on with school right away, nor to go off to work, but instead to head for the Baltic Sea beaches and enjoy life. When their money runs out they take jobs in a fishing collective, and in the end they are better people for it. However, this moral improvement did not prevent violent attacks on the novel by critics who were fearful of the example of freedom of action that it set for young people.

During 1961 a stage version of *The Colleagues* was produced in numerous theaters throughout the Soviet Union. In August 1962 it was performed by Moscow's Maly Theater Company at an international festival in the Paris Theater of Nations. 1962 was a year of travel not only for Aksenov's works but for Aksenov himself. The mandatory first trip to socialist nations sent him to Poland; he then joined a delegation to Japan and relaxed in India on his return home. Meanwhile his first movie *My Younger Brother* (1962) based on "A Ticket to the Stars" was finally on the screens at home, having been held up nearly a year for ideological reasons.

Following his success with longer works Aksenov composed a number of short stories most of which were published for the first time much later in collections. "The Ejection Seat" (1961) shows certain narrow-minded types, here military airmen, who have little respect for other people until they establish a strange and artificial liaison (a "granfalloon" in Vonnegut's terminology) that bonds them together—here the bond is having been catapulted from an ejection seat. "Changing a Way of Life" (1961), which is translated here, is about a hard working businessman who takes some time off at the beach for a change in his life-style. The real change comes when he reevaluates his relationship with his girl friend and the reader is left to believe that he may finally marry her. "The Lunches of '43" (1962), also found here, may be thought of as one of Aksenov's early experimental works. The story takes place on a train with the hero certain that he has recognized a traveling companion as a friend from his childhood. Through the use of erratic time changes and flashbacks he tells the full story of their relationship, concentrating on the school lunches that he was forced by the bully to hand over in 1943.

The experimental nature of the time sequence in "The Lunches of '43" was new to Aksenov but used not long before by Valentin Kataev, one of Aksenov's early mentors. Kataev was editor of *Youth* magazine in the period that Aksenov began to submit manuscripts and is known to have reworked the entire first part of *The Colleagues*. What is especially interesting in "The Lunches of '43" is the psychological portrayal of the hero. Aksenov seems to portray this character in a very personal and internal world somewhat reminiscent of Dostoevsky's humiliated men. For political reasons the hero is not as humiliated nor as pessimistic as with Dostoevsky's heroes, but the literary connection, if not the intention, is there.

In 1962 Aksenov was already thirty years old and an internationally known writer for two years. Naturally he found it difficult to continue to identify with teen-agers and young street types, and as his circle of friends and life-style changed, so did his stories.

Highly representative of this maturing yet still young hero is thirty-two year old Sergei, the chief character of the significantly successful short story "Papa, What Does it Spell?" (1962). Sergei is a former soccer player who never made it to the big leagues as he dreamed and now feels the emptiness of his present life. We slowly learn that the things which he holds in esteem—his work, his sports, his family and his friends—are all eroding in value under the banality of everyday life.

Sergei's wife, Alla, must attend a conference at her institute, so he must watch Olga, his daughter, on a day when he had planned to meet his friends and take in a soccer game. What appears to be a mild conflict at the outset soon develops into a serious disruption of his various relationships: his friends see him for the first time as a family man; Olga has no interest in going to the game and insists upon going to a park instead; his daughter, surprisingly seems to know one of his friends very well, explained by frequent, hitherto unknown, meetings with Alla, meetings which imply an adulterous relationship. A phone call to the institute reveals that there is no conference that day and Alla is nowhere to be found.

Sergei is therefore forced to review his life and relationships, portrayed with obvious sympathy from the author. Almost instant maturity is accompanied by a growing concern and feeling of responsibility for his daughter.

> "... he thought about how his daughter would grow up, how she would be eight, fourteen and then sixteen, seventeen, twenty... how she would go away to pioneer camp and come back, how he would teach her to swim, what a fashionable little lady she would become and how she would neck in the stairway with some hippie or other, how they would sometime or other go off somewhere, maybe to the sea."[5]

Aksenov ends the story on this thought, a bond of unity with his daughter against all else in the world.

"Half-way to the Moon" (1962) is probably Aksenov's most internationally known short work. He was inspired in this effort by a real-life character who got on an airplane with him in Khabarovsk. When this worker, straight from the taiga, took off his outer coat, the stewardess offered to take it from him and hang it up. "He was so stunned by this" Aksenov later explained in an interview "that he gasped dumbfoundedly: 'Do you believe that? She took my coat for me!...'." The effect of this kindness on the worker can apparently be compared to the effect of art or music on the savage beast. The story derived from this event is described by one critic as a "variation on the theory of moral self-perfection."[6] What this critic describes is a "Jack London device: 'a wild' worker meets a heavenly creature—a girl of 'the highest order'... and his soul, dedicated to beauty, finally sees the light!" (p. 209)

The story which is included in this collection received much praise for its aspects of contemporaneousness: it is a jet-age search for love covering half the distance to the moon. However, if moral awakening is accomplished then the import of the story should be seen instead in the internal distance traveled by the hero.[7] Clearly a new emphasis and a more mature hero were evident in Aksenov's work by 1962.

In general 1962 had been a year of literary hope and advancement. Solzhenitsyn had been published by order of Khrushchev. In November Aksenov was made an editor of *Youth* along with Evtushenko and Rozov. "The hopes of 1962 were perhaps best expressed by the poet Alexander Tvardovsky: 'In art and literature, as in love, one can lie only for a while; sooner or later comes the time to tell the truth.' "[8] But in this hope and openness, in this very push for the truth were to be found the roots of the oncoming reaction. "The mood of the artistic and literary intelligentsia in 1962 can perhaps best be gauged from [Leonid] Ilichev's complaint that 'in certain intellectual milieux it is considered unseemly and unfashionable to defend correct Party positions.' "[9] The mood of the neo-Stalinists, then, was to put an end to the literary liberalism.

In December Khrushchev drew the attention of the world by attacking an art exhibit at the Manael Riding Stables. His personal attack on Boris Birger, Ernst Neizvestny and others was thought to be a warning to the proponents of the new creativity in all arts. The attack, however specific and personal in form, was indeed a declaration of war by the old-school realists (i.e., socialist idealists) on the representatives of alternative art forms (i.e., emancipatory realists, modernists, abstractionists, etc.).

But by 1962 Aksenov was not writing the offending "youth stories," at least not exclusively. He no longer felt close to younger people. He felt that a generation change had taken place and that the characteristics of his early heroes, so heatedly denied by official party critics, were no longer to be found in young people. His new novel of January 1963, *Oranges from Morocco,* which had been released at the beginning of the attack, was instead about workers in the Far East. Aksenov explained that as a writer he did not feel himself limited to youth problems. However, not everyone was pleased with the descriptions of these workers in "Oranges."

The story is simply an event and various people's reactions to that event. The event is the arrival of a ship loaded with oranges from Morocco. The reactions are not complimentary, however honest they might be. An American reader could be easily confused by what truly seems to be an exaggerated portrayal. Life practically stops for hundreds of miles around while all available personnel and means of transportation are directed toward the port. The fallacy here is in comparing two remotely different cultures, for although an orange brings very little attention in America and is available throughout the year, everywhere, the same humble orange was then rarely seen in the Soviet Union in winter except in large cities and in the southern climates. At the time that the story was written oranges commonly sold on the black market for more than a dollar apiece. It is then consistent with known realities about the supply system and the attitude of Soviet citizens toward the arrival of such goods to assume that the apparent exaggeration is, in fact, responsibly close to the mark.

Perhaps because of this disparity in cultural reactions to oranges the novel has never been well received abroad. Its scope compared to the "youth themes" may be justly considered excessively provincial. Regardless of Aksenov's movement away from the polemical stories which instigated the attack on his ideological correctness, the unfriendly description of greedy and coarse workers riding their tractors into town for oranges and not off into a socialist sunset led to further attacks.

The journals in February and March were filled with attacks on the "young" writers, Aksenov often being singled out, like Socrates, as an example of a corrupter of youth. On March 8, 1963, a meeting of intellectuals was called in the Kremlin. Khrushchev and Ilichev elaborated the correct party position and called for renouncements of former ideological errors. The first to do so were Simonov and Shostakovich. They were soon followed by Neizvestny, Rozhdestvensky, Voznesensky and others. Another meeting was called by the Writers' Union to escalate the attack. A writer named Vladimir Firsev delivered the following message:

> What compliments were not showered upon Evtushenko, Akhmadulina, Aksyonov! . . . But have we re-educated comrades Aksenov, Evtushenko, Voznesensky by continuously letting them go on foreign trips, by putting them on editorial boards, and by publishing their works in enormous editions? It is they who have been 'educating' readers during that time, and often they have educated them in such a way that it will take us a lot of work to liquidate the consequences of their educational efforts.[10]

The threat of this official speech, then, was clear—they were subject to losing their travel abroad, their positions on journals and their normal publication rights. Evtushenko recanted on March 29. Aksenov who had been conveniently out of town during the writers' meeting returned and, like Galileo, recanted.

April 3, 1963, in *Pravda,* he said that under the threat of imperialism Soviet writers must recognize their responsibility. They must be prepared to answer for every line which could be misinterpreted in the West. "I, like any writer," he added "am trying to create my own, unique, positive hero who would be at the same time a true son of his times—a man with strong bones and a normal circulatory system, a decent, open soul, with a concept in mind concentrating into one thought all the magnitude, optimism and complexity of our communist era."[11]

His promise here to create a positive hero "of his times" in a normal human being was in a sense, a reworked description of his heroes as they might be described in communist propaganda. By this interpretation one could suggest that he actually meant real-life people who live in this contemporary world with all its problems and who reflect not the weak official optimism which he always rejected by the "complexity of our communist era" which is what he always wrote about.

As Thomas Whitney has pointed out, world influence and opinion had an effect on the events of 1963 in the Soviet Union. China had played up the ideological controversy that year and the Stalinists found themselves in a more important battle than controlling the "young writers." The western communists had, moreover, taken a stand against the new literary policies outlined above. Even Soviet bloc nations such as Poland had reacted critically to the literary repression. The result was a letup in the clampdown of early 1963.[12]

1963 also saw the release of a film, *When the Bridges Go Up*, written by Aksenov in 1962 and identified in the press as "based on the short story" although no such story ever existed. The same year his earlier film *The Colleagues* was shown at Mar-del-Plata, Argentina at a film festival which he also attended as a member of the delegation.

A travel article, "Japanese Jottings" (1963), which is translated in this book, was written in a form that seems to repeat itself often whenever Aksenov wishes to relate his various impressions of a foreign land. It is an enigmatic rendering of witty statements and allusions inteded to give an overall view by its juxtaposed dashes of color. On canvas it would be called impressionism. Amazingly its experimental form has never drawn criticism from the old-school Socialist realists.

Previously, form took less of a role in Aksenov's work than content. "I think about form" he said once, "when I'm not writing. When I write, I don't think about it."[13] However, progress in literature for Aksenov often meant the ability to go off in any and all directions. As the force of his "youth themes" genre was slowed by time and by criticism, he began more and more to experiment in form.

In 1964 a novel written by Aksenov in 1963 was serialized in the journal, *The Young Guard*. *It's Time, My Friend, It's Time* (1964) was an attempt to supply the positive hero which he had promised in his recantation. This positive hero is Valya Marvich, a driver attached to a movie crew which is shooting a film in Estonia. In the manner of Aksenov's earlier "youth stories," and this may be chronologically the last example of that genre, Marvich questions his life and the direction it is going. Since Marvich is no longer young, this mature hero is given an appropriate adult complication to his search—he is additionally confused about the renewal of feelings from his former marriage. Another new feature found here that becomes typical for the mature hero in Aksenov is that he is always a loner: always aloof, an individual in the collective. The strength of the novel lies in Marvich's internal psychological conflict between his ideals and his failure to realize them within his circle of friends and loved ones. Marvich is a very real, atypical for Soviet literature, positive hero, who searches for truth and his ideals in a real world filled with negative activities and people. The credibility of both the positive hero and of the author is maintained.

From 1964 to 1966 Aksenov wrote a number of short stories that were to appear in collections of 1966 and 1969 as well as in literary journals individually. These stories are significant in so far as they reveal both a new interest and a new emphasis in his creations, completing the break with "youth themes" begun in 1962. His works of this period involve the growing importance for Aksenov of fantasy and imagination. They emphasize exaggeration and irony in style, deviance and ill-adjustment in characterization.

One of the best of these stories and a good example of his new style and characterization is "The Odd-Ball" (1964). Far from a "youth" story, it is about two old men, one of whom, Zbaikov, is an old bolshevik revolutionary and victim of Stalinism, as was Aksenov's own father. The other, the "odd-ball" from Zbaikov's childhood, has never left his village except to shop in a neighboring village. As the old friends meet and talk, the reader is struck by the tremendous differences in the fates of these two men. "Odd-ball" complains that they would not take him in the Red Army and was even passed up in the Stalinist excesses of the 1930s. " 'Ye-ah' drawled Odd-ball, 'I didn't even get to go to prison.' "[14] There is a tacit agreement that Zbaikov, even with his horrible experiences of war and prison, has lived a better life than a man whose life has apparently been no better than a farm animal's.

Then in the closing pages the irony sets in. "Odd-ball" ends up to be an engineering genius who has built himself a radio by means of which he is in constant touch with cities from London to Honolulu. He then decides to show his old friend his secret machine. His machine is a *perpetuum mobile* which has been running for many, many years. " 'What is it then, a perpetual motion machine, or what?' 'Seems to be,' he whispered. 'Seems to be.' " (p. 32)

Another classic example of the deviant in Aksenov's works is Uncle Mitya from "Comrade Smart-hat" (1964). Uncle Mitya is a taxi driver and perhaps more basically a capitalist "hustler" in a communist society. In this story his illegal activities are in jeopardy because of police surveillance in general and because of the special attention of officer Ivan Yermakov, whom he calls "Comrade Smart-hat." Uncle Mitya plots to encourage Yermakov's interest in his daughter assuming that once they are married he will have *carte blanche* in his business. However, the irony is that after the marriage the local police redouble their efforts to keep Uncle Mitya, their new relative, in line.

In this same period a "youth" story of sorts does crop up, but with some interesting experimentation. "Local Troublemaker Abramashvili" (1964) is the story of a life-guard at the Gagra beach area in Soviet Georgia.[15] The impression presented at first corresponds to the Soviet stereotype for such a situation. The reader is prepared to learn how the local "hot-blooded" native boys seduce the "fair-skinned" Russian girls on vacation. Ironically, it is eighteen year old Gogi Abramashvili, who is seduced by the northern Alina in her hotel room. " 'Well, you've had a pretty good day' she said tenderly, 'your first cigarette, your first woman'."[16] Gogi falls in love.

The following night he tries to talk to her at a dance and learns that her husband, who Gogi did not know existed, has unexpectedly arrived, as a result of which she does not want anything more to do with him. Gogi reacts angrily and is led out by the *druzhinniki*, the voluntary, civilian patrol. Several days later the town bulletin board, maintained by the *druzhinniki*, bears a picture of Gogi and the message that girls are forbidden to dance with the "local troublemaker Abramashvili."

What is unusually experimental in this story is not at first clear to the western reader. Sex in the West is a normal part of literature even to the point where critics refer to the "mandatory sex scenes" of a best seller. On the other hand sex is at best considered underground literature in both the Russian tradition and the Soviet present. While there are no sexually explicit scenes in the story, there are numerous implications and references to the contemporary sexual norms of Soviet youth. Soviet sociologists are only now, fifteen years later, dealing with the reality described in circumlocution by Aksenov in this story.

A basis in autobiographical fact which was found in Aksenov's earlier works is also found in "Little Whale, Varnisher of Reality" (1964). "Little Whale" is in fact Aksenov's son, Alyosha whom he actually nicknamed "Whale" and who was born in 1960 making him the same age as the young hero of the story. The story which is included here is, in essence, a study of what is reality and what is imagination—a subject that Aksenov was to explore in many of his future works. Stories from this period that are also included in this volume are, "It's a Pity You Weren't With Us," "The Victory" and "Ginger From Next Door." "It's a Pity You Weren't With Us," a short story written in 1964 is also the name of a collection of stories published in 1969. The story is an unusual, thought-provoking assessment of the lives of some very unusual people. "The Victory" (1965) is one of Aksenov's most successful stories. Outwardly it is the story of a grand master at chess playing a game on a train with a chance passenger. The ironic ending is one of the best in Aksenov's works.

"Ginger From Next Door" (1966) is, like "The Lunches of '43," a chronologically disconnected remembrance of childhood. This time it is more clearly Aksenov's own remembrance, as he refers to his one-time home in the former residence of industrial engineer Zherebtsov, in Kazan. The chief difference is that his fantasies change in this period from mental exercises to actual occurrences, in a fictional form, of course. Aksenov, by this period, already refused to make a clear distinction between "acceptable" descriptive fiction and his creative fantasies in prose. At a much later time he clarified his stance, somewhat:

> The imagination of an artist is, after all, also reality. Fantasy is perhaps no less real than the rustle of leaves... I sometimes think that real events which surround us, such as sunsets, river currents, stones, birds and sand are not any less mysterious than fantasy is... The artist only gives a name to the yet unknown, he penetrates into another dimension and gives a name to previously unseen bodies, gives them form, color and sound. He substitutes them for life in the opinion of some people. I suggest that subjects of art do not substitute for life but that they become new states within it, that is, they refurbish life and expand its horizons.[17]

Therefore there are no clear lines as to where the reality of the traditinal, practical sort blends into the emancipatory reality of the Aksenov philosophic idealism.

Another story that returns to his life in the former residence of industrial engineer Zherebtsov, in Kazan, is "On the Square and Beyond the River" (1966). On the surface it is a memory of the last day of World War II. But then there is the addition of a Gogolian or Hoffmannesque fantasy tale which is given at an ambiguous moment that allows it to be interpreted as a dream, or as one critic called it, a nightmare. When the message comes over the radio declaring victory over Hitler's Germany, the square becomes filled with jubilant people including a circus troop, which because it is real yet somehow imaginary, sets up the dream sequence which is imaginary yet somehow real. The dream sequence begins with the appearance of an unknown man seeking refuge. The young hero senses an evil creature and begins a chase onto the square and beyond the river. The creature flies off making sounds like a metallic bird and plunges into a lake. It is the symbolic death of Hitler.

Strange symbolic birds making metallic sounds were not new to Aksenov. In 1965 Aksenov had already written one of his most successful fantasy tales with these same characteristics, called *The Steel Bird* (1965). For over a decade he attempted to get the text published in the Soviet Union, but to no avail. A short excerpt called "The House on Lamplight Alley" (1966) was published in *The Literary Gazette* but since it only concerned one of the minor characters of the story, it was irrelevant to the main plot. The Russian text was published by Ardis last year in the inaugural issue of a new Russian-language literary almanac and the first English translation is available in this volume.

Anatoli Gladilin, a close friend of Aksenov and a writer who is mentioned in passing in the text of *The Steel Bird*, has written in the Western press about the first reading of the short novel. In those days a group of short story writers would meet regularly in the Central Club of the Writers' Union in Moscow to preview and critique the members' newest works. The reading of *The Steel Bird* attracted a "standing room only" audience and instead of reading only the thirty or forty pages scheduled, Aksenov was encouraged to read the entire work of over a hundred pages which required several hours and set a new time record for such readings. "Everyone was absolutely certain," wrote Gladilin, "that the story would, naturally, be published, the disagreements arose only concerning the literary journal: where to send it— to *New World (Novyi mir)* or to *Youth*?"[18] However neither journal, nor any Soviet journal for that matter, dared to take that step.

The editors felt, perhaps justifiably, that the allegory was dangerous, that the satire on Soviet society was too clear. Aksenov felt that the satire was not on any specific society but on mankind as a whole and more specifically on the nature of man in a totalitarian society. He challenged the decision against printing the work on the grounds that to see Soviet society implied was to take the position that Soviet society was totalitarian and oppressive. Aksenov and Gladilin both have expressed the attitude that the work should be considered "pro-Soviet," that it points out the pitfalls of the improper path to communism, the cult of personality, and is not critical of a properly run Soviet government. The editors apparently saw something in their society that Aksenov hoped was not there and in rejecting the work gave support to that impropriety by refusing to expose it.

The story itself was inspired by poetic lines which are repeated in the book as the theme of a cornet-a-pistons: "reason gave us steel wing-like arms/ and instead of a heart, a flaming motor."[19] The name, *The Steel Bird*, came later from the text of a 1930s aviation song that included the following stanza (in my translation):

There, where the infantry can not pass
Where there are no rushing armored-trains
No heavy tank crawls through the grass
That is where the steel bird reigns (p. 27).

The book opens in Moscow on Lamplight Alley in the spring of 1948 with the appearance of the ultimate of Aksenov's deviants, Veniamin Fedoseevich Popenkov. Popenkov is bearing two sacks from which something dark continues to drip. Because he understands the metallic language of the cornet-a-pistons which the housing manager plays, he is able to convince the manager to let him move into the elevator of the house at number 14 Lamplight Alley. At first he only occupies the elevator after all the residents are in bed, hiding in dark corners during the daytime. Significantly, all the residents get used to his presence and they begin to accept him. As the book progresses, there are constantly hints that he can fly, that he is not really human, that he speaks a strange metallic language and that he is changing from a weak "street rat" to a strong commanding "man of steel."[20] One night Popenkov goes into convulsions in the elevator. As he is nursed back to health, the residents vote to shut down the elevator for his comfort. Gradually he takes over the entranceway and the staircase is blocked off. The residents accept this and get used to using the emergency stairwell to the rear. Popenkov gains more and more power until he has a number of the residents working for him, making counterfeit French tapestries. The wife of a Vice Minister who lived at number 14 leaves her husband for Popenkov and brings her apartment full of antiques to his vestibule residence. By this point his power becomes seemingly immense.

The doctors now decide that he is not a human, not exactly an airplane, nor a bird but a combination: a steel bird. Then in 1953, when Stalin dies, Popenkov somehow is among the close, privileged mourners. However his private plans for the house at number 14 Lamplight Alley are to get everyone involved in work, to forget their sadness by labor. His new wife does not approve of his using Tsvetkova, her former husband's mistress, for such productive work.

> "Ha-ha-ha, you need Tsvetkova do you?" patronized Popenkov with laughter. "Take her, baby."
> "Thank you," mysteriously smiled Zinochka.
> "What do you want to do with her? Fuchi elazi kompfor trandiratziyu?" asked Popenkov.
> "Fuchi emazi kir madagor" said Zinochka.
> "Kekl fedekl?" laughed Popenkov.
> "Chlok buritano," giggled Zinochka.
> "Kukubu!" exclaimed Popenkov.[21]

His wife who now spoke his language learned that there were steel birds all over the world but that he was the head of all of them. In the night he flies off to digest the metal statues of the world, from the Bronze Horseman to Abraham Lincoln. He is symbolically now in control of history: "There will not be a past, there will not be a future and I've already eaten the present," he announces (p. 39). The weight of his body increases (caused by his midnight snacking) and the house at number 14 begins to tilt. When the walls begin to crack, the residents finally revolt, eventually conquering the steel bird. At this point the housing manager returns like the cavalry on a white steed to announce that the residents have been given a new apartment building. It should be noted that it is not the infantry, nor an armored-train, nor a heavy tank that penetrates the realm of the steel bird but a horseman. The new building that he promises will be almost entirely glass and plastic, with light-blue bathtubs, garbage disposals, swimming pools for everyone. So the residents leave. A few moments later the house at number 14 collapses, leaving only the elevator shaft upon which sits the steel bird. Months later he alights from his perch and flies over Moscow. Behind him stretch two dark trails, like the earlier droppings from his sacks, which are then scattered in the wind.

Clearly Aksenov means to say that human beings must avoid accepting and getting used to their oppression. He clearly is saying that such criticism is not only of Soviet society but of all totalitarian societies. There are steel birds everywhere, perhaps the image of Hitler in "On the Square and Beyond the River" is one of them. For the present time it seems that the Soviet one is the chief one. Popenkov is not Stalin, as some would guess, but in the tradition of Stalin. Popenkov mourns the death of Stalin but goes on to oppress his people and to establish his own cult of personality. Technology has helped him to bolt down the fates of men. Stalin once called the true Soviet man a screw in the machine of society. Man's emotions and his spiritual side have in this way, and by this type, been neglected, while reason and technology have turned his arms into steel wings, his heart into a flaming motor. He has judged his progress by trips to the moon and steel birds in the sky, leaving human beings to be dominated by computers and mechanical men. A computer language is, perhaps, no more intelligible to the soul than the ravings of the steel bird. Aksenov has every right to be disgusted that such a work can not be printed in all countries, for it is written for the sake of all human beings in all political systems.

Ironically one of the several things that Aksenov had published in those years included "The Dotted Line of Progress" (1966) which is a short statement praising the progress of man when the Soviet apparatus *lunakhod* was landed on the moon.

Less ironically and more tragically Aksenov was among the protesters arrested in 1966 on Red Square. The group had been against the unveiling of a bust of Stalin which now marks his grave-site behind Lenin's mausoleum. Many of those who suffered needlessly due to the cult of personality, as Aksenov's family did, felt that the raising of any monument to Stalin was a symbolic gesture, beginning an attitude of acceptance of his crimes.

There were also some good events in those years such as the release of *The Journey* (1966), a film based on three short stories by Aksenov: "Papa, What Does It Spell?," "The Lunches of '43" and "Half-way to the Moon." He also traveled a great deal: Rome, to a writers' conference, and Yugoslavia in 1965; Japan, Austria, Switzerland and Munich in 1966; Bulgaria and London in 1967. This last trip would prove to be his last chance to travel to the West for eight years. Another good event was the award of first prize in a literary contest sponsored by *Trud* newspaper. The story that won was called "The Light-blue Sea Cannons" (1967). It is a story told from the point of view of a young boy concerning his uncle's ironical service during World War II.

In the same period as these stories Aksenov wrote three plays which he labeled as "satirical fantasies." Although they remain unpublished one of them, *Always For Sale* (1965), ran for a long time at the Contemporary Theater in Moscow. The play was very controversial and has been called a number of things from "Philistine fantasy" to "the study of Man." Speaking of this play, a critic said: "The question of his 'grown-up' generation has become for Aksenov the question of *man*. His heroes now live not only in a defined slice of history but in the history of mankind as a whole."[22]

One light, humorous story of this period concerned one of Aksenov's sporting passions: boxing. "A Poem of Ecstasy" (1968) tells the story of a young boxer who becomes convinced by the example of Muhammad Ali's poetry that the fine arts, especially music and poetry, are the key to modern boxing success. In the amateur championships he is victorious thanks to his construction in the ring of a "symphonic poem of ecstasy."

A much longer story, "The Overloaded Packing-barrels" (1968) is, according to the subtitle, a "tale with exaggerations and dreams." In many respects it is the logical culmination of Aksenov's fantasy stories. It is an example of the Russian literary tradition of viewing the normal in a fresh, new, but inevitably strange way *(ostranenie)*. Consistent with this appraisal the tale has been compared to the work of Bulgakov, Olesha and Gogol. The unconventionality of his point of view caused much misunderstanding, confusion and even anger.

The external plot of the story begins with the need to move a load of barrels from the village general store to the regional center. Various people who do not know each other, yet need to go to the regional center, end up on the truck as fellow passengers. There is a scholar from Moscow who is the world's foremost expert on the country of Haligaliya (cf. Eng. Hully-gully, a dance which in Russian is called hali-gali) to which he is unable to get a visa. The old timer, Mochenkin, specializes in complaints, recommendations, requests and other official forms. The teacher, Irina Valentinovna, who is going on vacation, is a beautiful young lady with no admirers except a fourteen-year-old schoolboy. The sailor, Gleb, is returning to his Black Sea assignment. The driver is Vladimir Teleskopov who is the boy-friend of Sima the woman in charge of the barrels. Sima does not travel with them but continues, nevertheless, to be a character throughout the tale. Along the way other people are added and subtracted from their group.

As these people travel with the packing-barrels, several unusual things happen. The sailor and the teacher become romantically involved. All of them, even the driver, fall asleep and their dreams are presented. At first they are all individual dreams, unified only by the appearance for each of them of the "Good Man" approaching in the morning dew. The sleep of the driver ends in a minor accident which is followed by an airplane crash caused somehow, it is implied, by the eyes of the teacher in her new powerful role of blossoming woman. They arrive in a village to learn that they are not on course and spend the first night there. The scholar learns that Teleskopov, the driver, has been by accident to Haligaliya and they are united by a love for the same girl who lives in this distant fairy-tale land. In the second round of dreams the new-found friends become characters in each other's dreams. Among the several days they spend completing this short trip, one is spent in a town where Teleskopov is thrown in jail by a former suitor of Sima's. His sentence is reduced to a fine for the sake of the packing-barrels. The fine is then cancelled by a kiss from Irina Valentinovna. The most important development is that they all become bonded together by mutual love and respect for the barrels. When the depot refuses the barrels for being overloaded, they all reboard the truck and drive off together. In the final, mutual dream, the barrels float off to sea, singing gaily on their endless journey. Somewhere on an island, the "Good Man" waits for them, forever.

What all this means is a subjective decision similar to the interpretation of a symbolic poem. There are some factual observations that deserve note, however. The "Good Man" represents an ideal, a noble goal for each and every one of them. But just as people in general use indefinable abstract words to communicate concepts such as "God," "freedom" and "truth," these people use the "Good Man" as a variable concept: for each one of them the goal is as individual and different as they are one from the other. They all are dreamers,a fact which extends their "truths" to emotional and spiritual concepts beyond the realm of the material and the physically possible. Aksenov's concept of reality, as has been shown above, is liberating and stretches beyond the boarders of Soviet reality and of all human reality in free-flying thought waves. Lastly, the barrels begin in a normal, though overloaded, form and become first metaphorically humanized, then literally on their own, loved and respected by the people around them. "We," one of the characters says, speaking for the group, "are simply people of different views and different professions, voluntarily united on the basis of love and respect for our packing-barrels."[23]

Perhaps, in speculation, these people are then symbolic of the people of the world and the barrels are the "teeming" overloaded populations of humanity as a whole. Humanity to the individual is sometimes animate, sometimes remote and seemingly inanimate. The more people strive for the ideal, the "Good Man" as each individual interprets him, the more love and respect each has for humanity, whether that humanity in its overloaded, overpopulated mass is acceptable to others or not. The planet Earth bearing humanity, like an uncontrollable truck, goes on its way wherever it wants to, whenever it wants. "I don't know when we'll see each other again," Teleskopov writes to Sima, "because we are going where our dear packing-barrels want to, not where we want to. Do you understand?" (p. 58) Its goal in its random course is not always in conjunction with the ideal, and so people must unite and help each other bring it there. If this is impossible, then they, with the wisdom of the philosophies of the East, must accept their fate and ride along.

Also in speculation note that there are corrupt officials in this story who use their power to jail the innocent (Teleskopov). However the corrupt are here eventually softened by *philos*, love for humanity (the barrels) and set straight by *eros*, love for an individual (Irina Valentinovna). Note also that the pilot who spreads manure on the earth (a propagandist of any political view) is brought down by *eros* and *philos* together. In his dream sequence there is a hint that even *agape*, love for God (the angel), may be involved as well. Remember he never rides with the people (he is towed behind in his plane) and so he is never more than remotely connected with the people and with humanity. In time, without having learned from humanity, he returns to the skies to fertilize the earth with his manure.

Another excellent story and one of Aksenov's favorites is "The Rendezvous" (1969) published in 1971. It is the story of a most popular and talented individual: a poet, hockey star, mathematician, a Soviet Renaissance man and jet-setter. Feeling unloved, he goes off on a mysterious rendezvous that puts an end to his search but only at the price of his life.

During the next several years Aksenov experimented with various types of prose. He also wrote a number of humorous feuilletons for *The Literary Gazette* which included several stories about a character called Memozov. Memozov is a playful character device Aksenov likes to refer to as his anti-author.

One type of genre which he tried was the "chronicle novel" which was a popular form of writing in the early 1970s. For a series on famous revolutionaries he was asked to provide a book on Leonid Krasin, an electrical engineer and bolshevik revolutionary. The novel, *Love For Electricity* (1971), uses actual documents from the period intertwined with fictional embellishment. Even though it is basically about the tragedy of the revolution for the intellectuals who started it, that fact is generally misunderstood and so it is currently on the list of recommended books for school children.

A less serious experiment was an adventure novel, *Gene Green-The Untouchable,* which he participated in with two other authors. The book is the story of CIA agent No. 014 (twice what 007 was!). The pseudonym given as author, Grivady Gorpozhaks, actually represents a combination of the names of the three authors together who are identified only as translators of individual chapters. Of the thirty-two chapters, Aksenov wrote eight and collaborated on another four.

Another type of prose which he attempted is the children's book. *My Granddad the Monument* (1972) and its continuation, *The Box in Which Something Rattles* (1976), are highly adventurous tales based around the Leningrad Pioneer (like a Boy Scout) Gennady Stratofontov.

In 1975 Aksenov came to America as a Regent Lecturer for the University of California. After a long series of lectures at UCLA he made a short lecture tour to Stanford and Berkeley, and then visited the University of Michigan and Indiana University on his return to New York City. On his way back to Moscow he also spent time in London, Venice and Milano. From this prolonged stay abroad came the shorter works "The Asphalt Orangery" (1976) and "About That Similarity" (1977) and a long work about his impressions of America called *'Round the Clock Non-Stop* (1976). This last work which includes the anti-author Memozov is an important work in that it sums up and explains many of his previous writings.

Meanwhile in 1976 one of his older stories was dug from the files and printed. "Swanny Lake" (1968) is an autobiographical piece with little "Whale" and his father joining "Whale's" grandfather, obviously based on Aksenov's real-life father, for a day at the lake. The internal thoughts of the three generations are artistically interwound to provide a charming yet meaningful message.

Two other short stories of that year "Out of Season" (1976) and "The Sea and Tricks" (1976) are actually parts of a longer work, *In Search of a Genre*, which was published in full in January of 1978.

Recently Aksenov has traveled a great deal in Europe, to Germany, Paris, Corsica and Bordeaux. He presently lives in Moscow with his wife Kira, his son Alyosha, who is no longer "little Whale" but an eighteen-year-old art student, and his dog Ralph Emerson Klychin. He recently began filming *A Center From the Skies,* a filmscript he wrote about a basketball player. Currently he is translating E. L. Doctorow's *Ragtime* into Russian.

NOTES

1. The separation proved unbearable and Aksenov's father remarried. A half-sister, the result of this second marriage, Antonina Aksenova, is now an actress in the Leningrad Comedy Theater.

2. "Asfal'tovye dorogi" *Junost'* 7 (1959), p. 60.

3. "Goriachii sneg v rukakh," *Literaturnaia gazeta* (December 1, 1960), p. 3.

4. L. Lazerev, "K zvezdam," *Voprosy literatury,* 9 (1961) p. 22.

5. "Papa, slozhi!" in *Katapul'ta* (Moscow: Sovetski pisatel', 1964) p. 115.

6. Larisa Kriacko, "Puti, zabluzhdeniia i nakhodki," *Oktiabr'* 3 (1963) p. 208.

7. In September 1962 an interesting parody of "Half-way to the Moon" was published in *Literaturnaia gazeta.* In this version Shlakoblochenko (literally "Mr. Cinderblock" a variant of Kirpichenko, literally "Mr. Brick") falls in love with the ticket machine on a streetcar and spends his month vacation riding back and forth buying tickets.

8. Patricia Blake and Max Hayward, eds., *Half-way to the Moon* (New York: Anchor Books, 1965), p. x.

9. Leopold Labedz, "Soviet Art Must be Beautiful," *Partisan Review* 30 (Spring, 1963), p. 101.

10. As quoted by Leopold Labedz, ibid., p. 106.

11. "Otvetstvennost' " *Pravda,* April 3, 1963, p. 4. To quote an unrelated though, perhaps, appropriate statement written by Aksenov much later and here cited deliberately out of context: "Maybe I should make something up? More simply, maybe I should lie? For a writer such a life-saving idea can be reassuring." (*Kruglye sutki, Non-stop, Novyi mir* 8, 1976, p. 107).

12. Thomas Whitney, *The New Writing in Russia* (Ann Arbor: Univ. of Mich Press, 1964), pp. 42-43.

13. "Molodye—o sebe" *Voprosy literatury* 9 (1962) p. 118.

14. "Dikoi" in *Na polputi k lune* (Moscow: Sovetskaia Rossiia, 1966), p. 29.

15. Aksenov often writes about the sea and the beach because it is quite often the

area he is in while writing. It has long become normal procedure for him to gather ideas at home and then go off to the seaside to relax and write.

16. "Mestnyi khuligan Abramasvili" in *Na polputi k lune,* op. cit., p. 55.

17. *Kruglye sutki, Non-stop,* pp. 75-76.

18. A. Gladilin, "Stal'naia ptitsa" *Kontinent* 14 (1977) p 358.

19. V. Aksenov, *Stal'naia ptitsa,* in *Glagol* 1 (1977) p. 65.

20. "Man of Steel" has sometimes been suggested as a translation of Iosif Vissarionovich Dzugashvili's chosen name of Stalin.

21. Aksenov, *Stal'naia ptitsa,* op. cit., p. 73.

22. Yu. Kagarlitskii, "Simpatii u nas obshchie" *Teatr* 9 (1965) p. 38.

23. "Zatovarennaia bochkotara" *Yunost'* 3 (1968) p. 50.

THE STEEL BIRD

THE STEEL BIRD
A Tale with Digressions and a Solo for Cornet.

> Where the infantry can't pass
> Nor armored train race by
> Nor heavy tank crawl through
> The Steel bird will fly.
> (*Battle song of the thirties*).

Enter the hero, and an attempt at a portrait.

It would appear that the hero of my tale appeared in Moscow in the spring of 1948, at any rate that is when he was first observed on Fonarnii[1] Lane. It is possible that he had inhabited the capital even earlier, no one denies it, maybe even a number of years, there are plenty of blank spots on the city map, after all.

A sharp smell of mold, of filthy damp underwear, a mouse-like smell struck the folk crowded round the beer vendor opposite No. 14 Fonarnii as the hero walked past. Their nostrils were invaded by decay and foul weather, disintegration and putrefaction, by the twilight of civilization. Even seasoned veterans who had marched from the Volga to the Spree were stunned, so out of keeping was this smell, this sign of preposterous destructive forces with the Moscow spring evening, with the voices of Vadim Siniavskii and Claudia Shulzhenko, with the peaceful lowing of captive BMWs and Opel-Admirals, with the abolition of ration cards, with reminiscences of retreats and advances, with the beer, the rust, but astonishingly tasty sardelle,[2] with the wife of Deputy Minister Z., whose charming hands had fluttered the first-floor curtains literally one minute earlier.

The smell conjured up something that not even the most desperate times had produced, that a normal person would never dream of, not even hell, something far worse.

The stunned episodic characters stared mutely at my hero's frail back, and at this moment he stopped. Even ex-paratrooper Fuchinian, a man of snap and precise decisions, was taken aback by the sight of our hero, his pale, somewhat hairy hands, with their two string bags and the scraps of yellow newspaper poking out of the holes in these string bags. The string bags dripped something dark onto the asphalt. Even so, Fuchinian resolved to rouse the crowd with a joke, to terminate the oppressive situation, to get his cronies in formation for the rebuff.

"Now here's a little rat," he said. "If I were a cat I'd gobble him up, and that would be the end of him."

His cronies were about to roar laughing, were just about to line up, but just then my hero turned to them and choked off their laughter with the inexpressible sadness of his eye-sockets, deep and dark as railway tunnels in scorching Mesopotamia.

"Could you please tell me, Comrades," he said in an ordinary sort of voice which still gave each of the beer-drinkers the shudders, "how to get to 14 Fonarnii Lane."

The episodic characters were silent, even Fuchinian said nothing.

"Would you be so good as to indicate No. 14 Fonarnii," said the hero.

"Something is dripping from your bags," pronounced Fuchinian in a hollow jerky voice.

"No wonder," the hero smiled meekly. "This one is meat," he raised his right arm, "and this one is fish," raising his left arm. "Omnea mea mecum porto" he smiled again and there was a gleam of light in the Mesopotamian tunnels.

"No. 14 is across the street," someone said. "That entrance there. Who do you want there?"

"Thanks," said our hero and crossed the street, leaving two dark trails behind him.

"I've seen him somewhere before," said one.

"I've met him too," said another.

"His snout is familiar," said a third.

"Enough!" cried Fuchinian. "You know me, I'm Fuchinian! Whoever wants a beer had better drink, anybody who doesn't, needn't. Everyone knows me here."

And notwithstanding the terribly edgy atmosphere they all began drinking beer.

The doctor's recollections and a more detailed portrait.

The history of his first illness and my part in it is a mystery to me to this day. Firstly, I don't understand how I, an experienced clinician and generally acknowledged diagnostician, was unable to make a diagnosis, or even a working assumption, on the nature of the illness. I have never seen anything like it—there was nothing to kick off from, not the slightest starting point for the development of a medical thought, nothing to catch on to at all.

Before me lay the naked body of a comparatively young man; the subcutaneous fatty layer was a little wanting, but in general near average; the cutaneous coverings were pale, dirty and unhappy, (I remember going cold with horror when I made mental use of this highly unmedical term, but later things got much worse), breathing was even, there was no wheezing, all I could detect was the alveola's fussy whisper and the soft twitter of the hemoglobin absorbing oxygen; the heart beat was distinct and rhythmic, but it became quite clear to me while I was listening that this was a suffering

4

heart (we doctors laugh at a lyrical term like "suffering," for anyone with the slightest education knows that spiritual sufferings develop in the cortex of the large hemispheres, but in the given instance it was a spiritually suffering heart, and again I was overcome with fear). The stomach was soft and smooth to the touch, but the sigmoidal intestine showed signs of a strange playfulness (this threw me completely); the peripheral blood vessels were examined on the extremities under a layer of skin, and suddenly on the right thigh I read the blood formula, just as if it were typed on a form from our hospital: L- 6500, ROE - 5mm/hour, NV-98, (the formula was normal);—that is, an objective examination yielded no sign of physical suffering, and only in his eyes, in their deep sockets, in the ancient cave city, raged pneumonia, military tuberculosis, syphilis, cancer, tropical fever all rolled into one.

In the first place there was all that, and in the second place I have no idea why I didn't send him to a clinic but instead leaped outside into the night and ran all over the place rousing my colleagues in my hunt for penicillin, which was very scarce those days.

When I got back, I bent over him with the syringe containing the precious penicillin, and one of the countless women surrounding his bed babbled behind me:

"Doctor, it won't hurt him very much, will it?"

My own hands were trembling with pity for this creature, and the paltry injection I was planning to give him seemed almost like a laporotomy, but nevertheless I remembered my medical calling and ordered:

"Turn over onto your stomach."

He instantly rolled onto his stomach, I couldn't even work out which muscles were exerted to make this movement possible.

"Pull down your pants," I said.

He pulled down his pants, baring buttocks of a very unpleasant appearance, resembling the edge of a forest where stumps had been grubbed out prior to a forest fire coming through.

"Poor thing!" gasped the women from behind.

When the needle entered the upper outside square of the right buttock my patient began to tremble, at first gently-gently, then his whole body began vibrating violently, something popped and gurgled inside him, something whistled, sweat stains spread across the pillow, but this lasted no more than a minute, then all abated and he was calm.

"What is this?" I thought, slowly pushing forward the plunger of the syringe. "What secret chains have suddenly forged me to this horrible behind, this transcendental being?"

When the procedure was over the patient immediately turned over onto his back, and his eyes lit up bright yellow, like the headlights of approaching trains. He smiled meekly, even humbly.

"When will we be having another jab, Doctor?" he asked me.

"Whenever you want, my friend, any time of day or night, the first beckoning of your hand, the first call, no matter where I am," I replied in all seriousness.

"Thank you, Doctor," he thanked me simply, but I immediately felt warm inside.

"Thank you, dear Doctor, you have saved him," whispered the women, closing the circle. We all fell silent in order to remember for ever the majesty of this moment.

Nevertheless I couldn't resist measuring some of his body proportions with a tape measure. For years I kept this data secret, but recently it was codified by the Committee for Coordination of Scientific Research.

Chapter 1.

Nikolaev, Nikolai Nikolaevich, manager of the houses[3] on Fonarnii Lane, was busy sorting out a dispute which had flared up between the occupants of Flat 31, No. 14, Samopalova Maria and Samopalov Lev Ustinovich.

The case was simple enough both in essence and ramifications, but savage and militant, with no foreseeable reconciliation.

Maria and Lev Ustinovich had once been husband and wife, but had separated some ten years before the war on account of an extreme rupture at the cultural level. The house manager understood this well and sympathized with Lev Ustinovich and respected his resolve and strong will, because for a quarter of a century now he himself had been oppressed by the low cultural level of his better half.

That was long ago and long forgotten, and now, of course, the former couple didn't even remember that they had once twined in tender embraces and forgotten themselves in fits of unrestrained mutual passion. Now they sat before Nikolaev and looked at one another with heavy stale ill-will. Maria, a cottage-industry worker, was stout and dark-faced, whereas Lev Ustinovich, manager of a hair-dressing salon, was the exact opposite—desiccated and fair.

At that time, ten years before the war, Samopalov had brought into the house one Zulphia, a woman of eastern origins, and begotten of her four boy-devils, and all those years Maria had battled along with Samopalov's first-born, her daughter Agrippina, whom she kept, raised and made into an assistant in her difficult domestic trade.

The essence of the dispute came back to Lev Ustinovich's complaint that Maria, who had formerly earned her living by inoffensive embroidery, had now acquired a loom, whose rattling did not create any conditions whatsoever for relaxation for Samopalov and his family. The arguments on both sides had already been exhausted, except for the main trumps which were kept in reserve, and the two sides were merely exchanging meaningless retorts.

6

"You're a slob, Lev Ustinovich," said Maria.

"And you, Maria, are a self-seeking, a narrow egoist," countered Samopalov.

"Your Sulphidon makes more noise than my loom when she's bashing your head against the wall."

"My God!" choked Samopalov with indignation. "What slander! And I have forbidden you, Maria, to call Zulphia Sulphidon."

"And what about your kids bawling at night?" Maria wasn't letting up.

"The floors shake the way your Agrippina walks!" shouted Samopalov, stung.

"My Agrippina is like a turtle dove, as for you, Lev Ustinovich, you might pay attention to people's protests, clearing your throat of a morning in the toilet and making such noises it's impossible to go past into the kitchen."

"That's not true!"

"It is so!"

"Children!" called Samopalov, and instantly his four swarthy boys, the best gymnasts in No. 14, ran into the house manager's office.

"Agrippina!" shouted Maria and into the office swayed her incredibly plump fair-haired daughter, the dead spit of Samopalov.

"It's a disgrace, Lev Ustinovich," she blabbed, "the way you victimize Mother and me in communal matters, it's beyond endurance."

Samopalov's children by Zulphia, Ivan, Ahmed, Zurab and Valentin surrounded Agrippina, yelling, and the House manager Nikolaev couldn't make out a single word.

The irresoluble situation which had arisen in Flat 31 depressed Nikolai Nikolaevich beyond words, this great storm of passion merely saddened him, but God forbid that he should give the slightest indication of sorrow or alarm, after all he was the administrator, the law and the terror, the word and deed of Fonarnii Lane. How could he help these people, what could he rouse them to? At that time the term "peaceful coexistence" did not exist. The only thing he could do was put one of the Samopalovs in prison, but strange as it may seem, that didn't even enter his head. What could be done, what initiatives taken, on whom could he lean? As everybody knows, the role of the public at that time was reduced to zero: it was necessary to act alone, to administer, divide and rule, with the whip and treacle cake, or whatever.

"Quiet, everybody!" he commanded softly, and the Samopalovs fell silent, because they knew that for all Nikolai Nikolaevich appeared slow moving, he could be tough and occasionally capricious.

"I order you from this day to cease dissension and quarrels," said the house manager severely, adding in a gentler tone with an inward smile. "After all, you are relatives."

"But what about that loom? The loom should be smashed!" burst in the hot-headed Ivan, but he was restrained by the more rational Ahmed.

"Comrade House Manager," began Samopalov, bringing out his hidden trump, "the loom, as I see it, is a typically capitalist means of production, and in our country, as I see it..."

"Oooh, Lev Ustinovich! Oh, you so and so!" Realizing the point of his speech, Maria let fly, "and you don't hold on to your means and take clients at home, why, you shave the deputy minister in his flat, you rake it in on the side, and you want to do the dirty on a poor widow!"

"Just a minute, what sort of a widow are you?" retorted an outraged Samopalov. "I seem to be still alive. None of my wives have been widows yet."

"Mama has a certificate from the co-op for the loom," wailed Agrippina, in floods of tears.

"I won't give up the loom, certificate or no," declared Maria. "I'm a Soviet citizen and I'm not going to give up my beloved loom. I'll write to Stalin, our father."

"Don't you dare!" shouted the House manager at this juncture with unfeigned anger. "Don't you dare take Generalissimo Stalin's name in vain! What is this? As if Josif Vissarionovich could be bothered with your squabbles and your idiotic loom."

The quarrel subsided and the Samopalovs abandoned the office.

Nikolai Nikolaevich, brushing away melancholy thoughts, established some basic order in his place of work, closed the office and set off home. He too, like the Samopalovs, lived in No. 14, which had been built in 1910, and so was faced with tiles that gleamed in the sunset. The house had six stories, one main entrance with a bizarre canopy overhead, a working, if pre-revolutionary lift, central heating, telephones and other such conveniences. There were 36 flats in the house and 101 accountable tenants. In a word, this house was the pride of Fonarnii Lane, and indeed remarkable for the whole Arbat[4] area.

When he had finished his supper, read the "Evening Moscow" and fed his superb goldfish, Nikolai Nikolaevich sat down on the ottoman, drew the cornet—a-piston, out of its case and called to his wife:

"Klasha, lock up!"

His wife, accustomed to such commands, locked the flat entrance without demur and fastened the chain. Nikolai Nikolaevich raised the instrument to his lips and softly, most tenderly began to produce the melody "... And squadron by squadron, the cavalry-men tighten the reins and fly into battle."[5]

At this point Nikolai Nikolaevich's small secret had better be revealed. Before the war he was soloist in the Gorkii Park woodwind orchestra, and in the war years, despite breaking his neck to get into the front lines he was assigned to the orchestra at the front. Cornetist Nikolaev's playing won many a military commander by the purity of its sound and its major key quality, and so by the end of the war he had earned the rank of major. Guards major. On leaving the service he realized there was no way back, a Guards major couldn't, had no right to be a frivolous cornet-a-piston player, even in the C.P.C.R. or the orchestra of the Bolshoi Theater. Having blotted out his past, Nikolaev appeared before the Raikom[6] and requested an administrative job. And so he became a House manager. Naturally, none of the inhabitants of Fonarnii Lane knew about Nikolai Nikolaevich's past, and those of them who heard the pure major notes of an evening assumed it was the radio.

True, occasionally Nikolai Nikolaevich would begin to stray into a minor key: such was the nature of the work, it would dispose anyone to melancholy reflections, even to philosophy. And then these very secret evening rehearsals became the source of Nikolai Nikolaevich's melancholy, a source of recollections of a bright, happy life, of that animated collective labor to which the rank of Guards major prevented him from returning.

Nikolai Nikolaevich was a high class musician and had achieved such a degree of unity with his instrument that sometimes the cornet-a-piston would begin to express those deep thoughts and feelings of its master to which House manager Nikolaev did not normally give rein, and which he at times did not even suspect in his make-up.

And so now it was with the aim of distracting himself from sorrow that Nikolai Nikolaevich began rendering the rollicking cavalry song, but slipped without noticing it into a queer and none too jolly improvisation.

"How did it happen, how can it be, why is there discord in the Samopalov fam-i-ly?" sang the cornet. "Poor, poor Stalin, my unhappy leader, beloved father, dear heart of iron."

It should be observed at this juncture that Nikolai Nikolaevich, in addition to the prevalent filial respect for Stalin and worship of his qualities of genius, experienced the most ordinary pity for the leader, i.e. he felt almost fatherly towards him, as he would toward a child of his own torn from its parents by inhuman destiny, or towards an orphan. Sometimes he had the feeling that the leader was tormented by his comrades-in-arms and ministers, and by the 220 million Soviet people plus all progressive mankind. Of course he was afraid of these feelings and suppressed them, but now and again they would break out via the cornet-a-piston.

"Dear people, you are not crocodiles, why then do you shun friendship and love? Aunty Maria, run your wretched loom a bit quieter, don't disturb others. Dear barber Samopalov, remember how tenderly you once caressed Maria, remember the child, share your living space,[7] always keep the laws of society. Don't write to Stalin, dear Maria, don't hinder the poor man thinking and creating. Have pity, my dear, on the standard-bearer of peace, our dearly beloved son and father,"—sang the cornet.

"The theme of the leader is magnificent," said someone behind Nikolai Nikolaevich.

It would be difficult, no, impossible to describe Nikolai Nikolaevich's state the following instant. His physical movements were extremely unbecoming: firstly, he dropped the cornet, secondly, he fell to the floor, thirdly, he farted, fourthly, he attempted to hide his instrument under the ottoman bolster and only fifthly and finally did he turn around.

Before him in an indecisive pose stood a man holding two string bags. Something dark dripped from the latter onto the parquet floor.

"What? What did you say?" exclaimed Nikolai Nikolaevich.

"Don't worry," said the man, "I merely said that you gave a very moving and original rendition of the leader theme. I have never heard it treated like that before."

"How do you know what I was expressing? What kind of paradox is this?"

"I just happen to understand and love music," replied the man with the string bags very seriously.

"Then you understand my cornet?" Nikolai Nikolaevich was still conducting this dialogue in rather high, almost falsetto tones.

"Yes."

"Are you a composer?"

"No."

"Who are you then?"

"Benjamin Fedoseevich Popenkov."[8]

Nikolai Nikolaevich was silent simply staring at the newcomer.

The latter stood before him, frail, unclean and stinking, in a soiled frayed lounge suit, which was however made of good pre-war "Champion" cloth, a field shirt under the jacket, minus a single medal or decoration, but wearing two pre-war badges—a "MOPR"[9] and a "Voroshilov gunner"[10] Nikolai Nikolaevich pinched himself hard on the behind, but all in vain, it was solid reality.

"Please understand," the silence was broken by the man called Popenkov, "what you were playing was very close to me. It was my life, my feelings, my sufferings. Take the Samopalovs, to whom the cornet appealed so movingly, I don't know them, but they must be wonderful, wonderful, *Wonderful* people!" he cried, "but can't they really come to any agreement? And what you were playing about Stalin, that's right here,"—his chin nodded towards the area of the heart.

"Something is dripping from your bag," said Nikolai Nikolaevich gloomily, all the strings in his soul ajangle.

"No wonder," Popenkov smiled meekly. "This one's meat"—he raised his right hand, "and this one's fish"—he raised his left hand. "Omnea mea mecum porto, or translated, all I have I carry with me."

"Are you just out of prison?" asked Nikolai Nikolaevich. He still hoped for salvation.

"No," replied Popenkov, "I haven't had the slightest connection, not even family connection, with enemies of the people."

Nikolai Nikolaevich felt crushed, pitiful, almost naked, almost a slave.

"What can I do for you?" still frowning, grasping for his position, he asked.

"Nikolai Nikolaevich, Comrade Nikolaev," began Popenkov piteously, "I come to you not only as a man, not only as a musician, but as to a House manager. You are a wonderful, wonderful, *Wonderful* man!" he barked.

Here he squatted down and looked up at Nikolai Nikolaevich from the deep hollows of his eyes, and Nikolai Nikolaevich was touched by the desert heat, so powerful was the sorrow in these eyes. The next instant Popenkov, leaving his string bags behind on the floor, leaped high into the air, even too high, rubbed his hands madly and landed.

"Nikolai Nikolaevich, I am asking for refuge, cover, a roof over my head in one of the houses entrusted to you."

"But you know about the passport system," mumbled Nikolai Nikolaevich plaintively, "and then where could I put you, even so they are occupied beyond capacity."

"Nikolai Nikolaevich, I'll lay my cards on the table, I'll tell you everything," Popenkov began hastily. "I have walked a long way here, I have been through a lot, I flew here, driven by loyalty and love for a certain person. For a year now... that is, I beg your pardon, for a week now I have been living down amongst the foundations of the Palace of Soviets. And now I have finally worked up the courage to come to him. My cards are on the table—I am talking about Deputy minister Comrade Z.! The fact is, dear Nikolai Nikolaevich, that I saved Z's life several times. I sacrificed myself for his sake, and he said 'Benjamin, come and live with me, you'll be my friend, my brother, a part of my very self.' And here I am, and what do I see? A wife, a young beauty, beauty, a *Beauty*!" he cried, "antique furniture... I was very happy for him. But Z. didn't recognize me, more than that, he was even frightened of me. I don't understand how anyone can be afraid of me, a small pitiable man. In short, Z. showed me the door. Believe me, I am not judging him, Z. is a marvellous, marvellous, *Marvellous!*, he cried, "man, I see his point—responsible position, mental and physical hypertension, a young wife, and so on, but what am I to do now, because that was my last hope."

Popenkov squatted on his heels again and looked up at Nikolai Nikolaevich from below, and if the House manager had had any concept of the geography of our planet he would have compared the sorrow of his eyes to the ancient sorrow of Mesopotamia or the sun-scorched hills of the Anatolian peninsula. But since he had no such object of comparison, the intangible sorrow of the eyes affected him more powerfully than any learned geographer or historian.

"You say that you have suffered, that you have lived down in the foundations, and I still don't know where to put you," said Nikolai

Nikolaevich in a shaky voice. "Of course you realize that I can't very well lean on Z., he's way above me."

"Yes, yes, me too," concurred Popenkov.

"He only lives here, you know, out of a sort of eccentricity, and because his wife likes the pre-revolutionary molded ceilings, essentially he lives here in Fonarnii Lane only out of democratism and I don't know what to do about you, Comrade Popenkov," Nikolai Nikolaevich was completely nonplussed.

"Don't feel awkward about it," Popenkov said encouragingly, "I'm not fussy, you know. Any left-over space would do. Your entrance, for example, is spacious and just fine..."

"The entrance would be impossible, the district inspector is very severe, you know. The yard-keepers I could manage, but the district inspector..."

"A-t-t-t-t- A-t-t-t-t-" Popenkov began thinking, clicking his tongue loudly, "A-t-t-t-t-... The lift! Your excellent spacious lift! It would suit me just fine."

"The lift..... is for general use," muttered Nikolai Nikolaevich.

"Well, of course," agreed Popenkov, straightening up, "Believe me, I won't disturb anyone. You can give me a camp-bed and I'll set it up in the lift only when I have checked that all are present, that all the birdies are in their little nests, and I'll be on my feet at six a.m. and the lift will be at everybody's disposal. In the event of any extreme nocturnal need, first aid, or say, a visit from our comrades from the organs[11] I will free the lift immediately, flit straight out. How about it? Well, Nikolai Nikolaevich? I can see you've come round already. Well, one last effort. Remember, dear friend, what the cornet-a-piston was singing. Dear people, you are no crocodiles, why then do you shun friendship and love..."

"Well, allright, I'll give you a camp-bed, but be so good as to remember that the lift is for general use," growled Nikolai Nikolaevich, who always growled like that when meeting someone half-way. "Let's go, Comrade Popenkov."

"Wait a moment!" exclaimed Popenkov. "Let's have a few moments silence. Moments like these should be captured."

Nikolai Nikolaevich, in a complete trance, as if he were under hypnosis, silently captured the moment.

Having done this, they went out into the hall. Klavdia Petrovna glanced out of the kitchen and froze, her mouth wide open, seeing her husband scramble up to the top cupboard after the camp-bed. Popenkov looked at her sorrowfully from the top of the ladder.

"Here is your camp-bed," growled Nikolaev. "But take note, it's only meant for one: the springs are weak."

"Nikolai Nikolaevich, you are a wonderful, wonderful, *Wonderful!* man," Popenkov began his descent with the stretcher under his arm.

"Tell me, how did you get in?" Nikolaev asked after him.

Popenkov turned round.

"The usual way. Don't you worry, Nikolai Nikolaevich, I won't let on about your cornet. Not a whisper, silent as the grave. I understand that each of us has his little secrets, I for example..."

"Thank you, you needn't let me in on your secrets," said Nikolai Nikolaevich gloomily, looking askance at the string bags, which were still dripping something.

When he had shut the door he got stuck into Klavdia Petrovna.

"Why on earth don't you shut the door, mother, when you're asked?"

"Kolia, dear, have a conscience, I locked it the moment you began to play, and fastened the chain."

"Then did he fly in the window or what?"

"That's true," gasped Klavdia Petrovna, "it couldn't have been through the window. Perhaps I forgot, got caught up with things in the kitchen. I'm getting old, Kolia, sclerosis... Who was he?"

"From the organs," growled Nikolai Nikolaevich to stop further questioning.

His wife was well-trained and said no more.

That evening on their way past into the lift several of the tenants noticed a sorrowful figure with two string bags and a camp-bed in the dark corner of the entrance hall, but some passed by without noticing. Popenkov acknowledged the tenants with a submissive nod. When the last tenant, the flighty Marina Tsvetkova, having adroitly given the slip to the officer who had seen her home, had taken the lift up to her floor, and when the officer had stopped capering around the entrance, railing against Maria's treachery, Popenkov brought the lift down, set up his camp-bed in it, ate a little meat, a little fish, and assumed a horizontal position. In this position he thought with a feeling of deep gratitude, about the House manager Nikolaev, with kindly feelings about Maria Samopalov, whom he as yet knew only from the cornet song, with slight reproach about Deputy minister Z., with some agitation of the latter's young wife, with a touch of playfulness about the fleet-footed Marina Tsvetkova, and then he sank into dreams.

His dreams were unchecked, almost fantastic, but we won't enlarge on them just yet, let us just say that if for most people sleep is sleep with or without dreams, for Popenkov sleep was a sort of orgy of dreams.

In the morning, at six sharp, Popenkov cleared out the lift and took up his position in the corner, submissively greeting the inmates as they left the house. So it was on the following day, on the third, the fifth and the tenth...

Naturally all kinds of rumors, conjectures, speculations got about, but they eventually got back to the house office and stopped there.

A conversation something like the following took place between Nikolaev and Deputy Minister Z.

13

"Listen here, Comrade Major," said Z., "this type from the entrance, he hasn't said anything to you about me, has he?"

"He said that he saved your life more than once," replied Nikolaev.

"There are a lot of people who have saved my life, but I don't seem to remember this one," mused Z., "no, I definitely don't remember him."

"Perhaps he'll save it yet," suggested Nikolaev.

"Do you think so?" again Z. was thoughtful. "He couldn't be dangerous, could he? I'm not a nervous type myself, you know, but my policeman is agitated."

(Police sergeant Yurii Filippovich Isaev was on permanent guard on the Deputy Minister's landing.)

"I don't think he's dangerous," said Nikolaev, "what's dangerous about him? An unfortunate man, sensitive, understands... er... art."

"Then that's all right," Z. dismissed it with a wave.

Well that's about all, this is where the first chapter ends. It should only be said that everybody soon got used to Popenkov, and many were even inspired to sympathy. Soon he was admitted to some of the apartments. He was a good listener, he sympathised with people and a fair number of the inhabitants opened their hearts to him. True, the working class, headed by diver Fuchinian, looked askance at Popenkov and wouldn't let him anywhere near them.

The building inspector's report

The double door to No. 14 opens outwards, is 3 meters 52 centimeters wide and 6 meters 7 centimeters high. The door is manufactured from the wood family known as "oak," has copper handles in the form of a reptile, "the snake," on both sides.

Above the door hangs a light in a colored metal grid, the grid has 24 cells, the bulb (100 w.) is working.

Note. The oaken surface of both sections of the door has a carved representation of the fruit of the vine, seriously damaged in the lower parts. Three centimeters from the external handle a three-letter inscription[12] carved out with a sharp instrument has been concealed by three parallel strokes by order of the house office, however can be deciphered under close examination.

Passing through the door we have before us an oval-shaped area, known as the main entrance hall, measuring approximately 178.3 meters. The figure is approximate, since it is as difficult to measure the square area of an oval as of a circle. The height of the dome-shaped ceiling of the "main entrance" is 16.8 meters at its highest point. The floor consists of a tiled mosaic of oriental, or more precisely Mauritian character (consultation at the Oriental

Institute). The tile stock of the floor has been damaged, about 17.2% of the total number of tiles.

A light fitting in the form of an ancient Greek amphora with handles hangs from the ceiling by a metal cord (consultation with the A.S. Pushkin Museum).

This is not functioning and represents a danger to life and limb, on account of the worn nature of the cord, but in view of the absence of the requisite ladders (12m.) in the houe office, it cannot be removed for transfer to a museum.

Lighting of the "main entrance" is effected by means of four light fittings, two on each side, each having three light sockets. Of the twelve bulbs eight are functioning. The light is diffuse, dull yellow. The far right plafond is damaged (broken) on the left corner, thus directing the light into a niche on the left side of the door, about 1.25 meters from the latter. The niche has an arched top, is 2.5 meters high, 1.5 meters wide. Formerly the niche housed a hollow cast-iron sculpture of Emperor Peter I, of which only the 1.1 meter high boots, known as Wellingtons, remain. (consultation with the journal "October").

Color of the walls to a height of 1.6 meters is dark blue, oil paint mixed with turps. Above this point and all over the dome are fragments of badly damaged frescoes (1914 A.D.), that is curls, extremities, folds of garments, female mammary glands, etc., elements of Greek mythology (consultation with the journal "October")'

Note. To the right and the left on the dark-blue background of the walls are chalk inscriptions and drawings, erased by order of the house office, although the said inscriptions and drawings were not harming anybody.

Daytime lighting of the "front entrance" is effected by means of six windows with colored glass, three windows on each side. The windows rise to a point, are 4.5 meters high, 0.5 meters wide, situated 0.7 meters off the floor at a intervals of 0.8 meters from one another. The panes on the left side reflect an oriental, more precisely a Japano-Chinese subject, that is: geishas, rickshas, water-carriers, tea-houses, gun-boats (consultation with the Soviet-Chinese Friendship Society).

The windows on the right hand side reflect a medieval Franco-Germanic subject, that is: knights, minstrels, fair ladies, animals, horses, side-arms (consultation with the Soviet-French Friendship Society). The lower section of the second left pane is reinforced by a sheet of ply 0.5m x 0.7m, the lower section of the first pane on the right is reinforced by a sheet of cardboard 0.5 x 0.9.

The area is heated—four central heating radiators, with three sections each, set along the walls.

At the far end of the oval-shaped area is a lift shaft housing a working lift. On the doors of the lift are four enamelled white plates 0.2 x 0.4 c with black letters. The signs say: "Look after the lift—it preserves your health," "unload children first, then yourselves," "Dogs prohibited," "the lift is not a lavatory!"

The inside of the lift is a box, area 4 sq. m., 2.5m high, painted brown, containing a square mirror, unevenly broken in 1937.

To the right of the lift begins the first flight of a white-marble staircase, numbering thirty-eight steps, of which sixteen are damaged. At the very base of the stairs is a hollow cast-iron figure 1.25 high, absolutely unidentified by the specialists. In the figure's right hand there is a lamp, which several of the inhabitants attempt to use as a rubbish bin, when they know quite well that the lamp is fixed solid and can't be tipped up and what will happen if the rubbish reaches the top?

Part for cornet-a-piston

Theme: Goodday, capital, goodday, Moscow! Goodday, Moscow sky! These words are in everyman's heart, no matter how far away he is... Improvisations: Poor unfortunate, he lay in the foundations, suffered long years. He saved the Deputy Minister, only to be cast out by him, where then is gratitude? There is no justice, there is no justice, they can ruin the fledgling. Poor stinking wretched transient, who are you? Have you a residence permit,[13] have you a mother, have you a passport? Terrible fledgling, live in your lift, only keep tight about me. If you should tell, it will be dreadful for me, I shall be silenced for ever. The terrible burden of authority oppresses night and day. A post in management is a great thing, a terrible thing...

Sudden end to the part: Morning meets us with coolness, the river meets us with the wind, curly head, why then do you not welcome the gay whistle's song?

Chapter 2.

What had happened? What was wrong? There was banging and shouting on every floor, a noctural working bee in No. 14 Fornarnii. Sergeant Yurii Filippovich, stupefied with terror, pounded at Z's door, fell into the flat and began trembling in the Deputy Minister's arms.

"What's the matter, Yurii Filippovich?" asked Z., back only half an hour from a night conference. "What's happened?"

"I don't know, blessed father, I don't know, blessed mother... The banging and the shouts," muttered Yurii Filippovich.

Leaving his guard to his spouse, Z. dived for his cherished Browning.

Samopalov's children came spilling down from the sixth floor. Maria in her fright threw herself on Lev Ustinovich's neck. Zulphia clutched at him from the other side. Only Agrippina, duffer though she was, immediately armed herself with a coupling bolt ready to defend her mother's loom.

Doctor Zeldovich from the fifth floor emerged onto the landing already dressed in an overcoat and warm scarf, carrying a suitcase. His family likewise made ready in the space of a few minutes.

It had all started with that flighty Marina Tsvetkova galloping down four flights of the marble staircase like a frightened antelope and all but tearing off its hinges the door to Nikolai Nikolaevich's flat. At this time, it being the dead of night, Nikolai Nikolaevich was sitting in the lavatory, concealed from his family, and was playing his cornet. On the sly, almost inaudibly. The cornet piece was interrupted by unbelievable god-forsaken banging and crashing.

"Comrade Nikolaev!" yelled Tsvetkova.

"Him. Your! protege! there! in the lift!.."

"What's the matter with him?" roared Nikolaev like a bear.

"In.. convulsions!" shouted Tsvetkova, opening wide her already huge eyes.

"Save him, good people!" roared the cornet-player in a panic.

The whole house was roused and everybody streamed downstairs, some in pajamas, some in dressing-gowns, some in underpants, in whatever came to hand. In one minute the vestibule was crammed with a buzzing crowd, resembling the Roman forum. Those who pushed nearer to the front could see Popenkov writhing on his camp-bed through the open doors of the lift.

"Doctor! Get a doctor! Comrade Zeldovich!" shouted people in the crowd.

Doctor Zeldovich steered a course through the corridor that had formed to the lift, and here the convulsions ceased, Popenkov lay quiet, his arms stretched out along his sides.

This unpleasant occurrence (the convulsions, the sharp attack) took place several months after Popenkov moved into the lift. Until then the life of the house had flowed comparatively peacefully, calmly, almost without a hitch, at any rate without any overt troubles.

As has already been stated, the inhabitants quickly got used to the submissive figure with the camp-bed, patiently standing in the darkest corner of the vestibule near the radiator. And the figure meanwhile was adapting to its new place of abode.

Above all he had to master the vestibule, to interpret its secret nocturnal life. In the dead of night Popenkov observed things very closely, silently, not interfering until he had completely got to the bottom of their contradictions.

The fact is, the oriental ornament was in direct and irreconcilable conflict with the ancient Greek amphora hanging directly above it. It would clink its tiles at night, changing the figures of its mosaic in order to create an indecent word, thereby offending the ill-mannered amphora for good, and the frescoes too, all these lumps of unbridled flesh, in short, the whole ancient world. Alas, all the ornament's efforts were in vain, either there was not enough time, or something else, just as with the ceiling's nightly attempts to organize the scattered parts of the body into one whole.

And there was ferment in the stained glass panels, a restrained simmering of passions. A flat Gothic figure, perhaps Roland or Richard the Lion Heart, being seated with fair ladies, was sending kisses to the geisha on the other side, who in turn had turned to the knight the enticing triangle of her naked back and was smiling over her shoulder, scorning utterly the samurai and water-carriers.

"Ojo-san, tai hen kirei des' ne," whispered the knight in Japanese.

"Arigato," replied the geisha, gently as a little bell. "Domo Arigato."

An enigmatic figure on the staircase (it would have been Diogenes, were it not for some likeness to Aladdin) kept straining to go out for a walk, but at his first movement the snake on the inside stretched and hissed, and the one on the outside beat its head furiously against the door.

Then naturally they were all devilishly interested in the luckless amphora, nobody knew what was inside it. The knights and samurai assumed that it was wine, and what man doesn't dream of wine? The fair ladies and the geishas were convinced the amphora contained a sweet-smelling substance and dreamed of massaging themselves with it. By morning speculation on the amphora had gone to extremes.

Only Popenkov knew for certain that there was nothing in the amphora but half a century of dust, thirteen desiccated flies, two spiders dying of starvation, and a "Herzegovina Flor" cigarette butt—goodness knows how that got there.

On the whole, this noctural life was not to his taste. He had some reason to suspect that if it went on much longer, there would be a general shift, and the samurais would dash for the fair ladies and the knights would get in amongst the geishas; the gun-boats would land the "tommy" troops, the lad with the lamp would got out on the town, the ornament finally form its cherished word, the amphora would naturally be broken open; the snakes, God forbid, might find their way into his camp-bed and the world he intended to rule by virtue of being animate might collapse altogether. So one day, in the heat of the vestibule orgy, that is at five a.m., he sprang out of his camp-bed, scattered the already maddened ornament and leapt into Peter's boots.

Naturally everybody took fright, gasped, began whispering in corners as to who and what, what kind of a bird this was, but Popenkov hushed them, jumped up (somewhat strangely, since he jumped together with the boots), tore down the Greek amphora, smashed it to smithereens on the floor, and, back in his niche, proclaimed:

"There's your despicable filthy dream, there's nothing in it but dead flies and half-dead spiders, and I'll finish smoking the butt, "Herzegovina Flor" doesn't lie around the floor. Is it understood now, who's boss?"

With these words he jumped out of the Wellingtons, picked up the butt and puffed away on it for a good hour, lying in the camp-bed.

They all fell silent and froze for ever and ever, even before his specific instructions, only the ornament arched obsequiously and attempted to crawl up and lick him on the foot in gratitude for his having dealt with the amphora, but Popenkov brushed it away with his heel and wouldn't let it near him.

In the morning Maria Samopalov was first down, she was off to the co-op to deliver her work.

"Well, well," she said when she caught sight of the broken amphora. She thought about it and gasped.

"The cord wore out, Maria Timofeevna, what can you do, time erodes even the most solid metal," remarked Popenkov philosophically.

"It could have come down on my head," Maria calculated.

"According to the probability theory, quite likely," concurred Popenkov.

"It could have slammed Lev Ustinovich," Maria screwed up her eyes.

"Easily," nodded Popenkov. "Imagine, one minute there was Lev Ustinovich, and the next he was finished."

"It could have crowned Nikolai Nikolaevich...."

"Not only him, it could even have been Deputy Minister Z," Popenkov entered in enthusiastically.

"Yes, if one of the top bosses came to our house it could have crashed down on him," Maria went on speculating.

"Exactly. That would be a right disaster," Popenkov grew sorrowful.

"Anybody at all could have been killed," said Maria, summing up.

"You are quite right," agreed Popenkov.

"And what about you, you weren't hurt, Benjamin?" enquired Maria.

"I got by, Maria Timofeevna. I was sleeping peacefully, Maria Timofeevna, when suddenly I heard a crash, practically an explosion! Shades of the war, and I began shaking with horror. Surely not again? Surely the imperialists couldn't do it again... Do you understand?"

"I wouldn't put anything past them," growled Maria. "The light should have come down on Churchill's head, or Truman's."

"I subscribe to your sentiments," said Popenkov, opening the door for Maria. "It looks as if you are on your way to the co-op, Maria Timofeevna?"

"I am delivering my work," replied Maria importantly. "It mightn't be much, but I do my bit for the state, not like your barbers. At a pinch a man can get by with a beard, but he can't manage without textiles. The other day I was walking past Kindergarten No. 105, they've got a bit of my embroidered linen on their window, it's real heart-warming."

"Permit me to have a peep at your work," asked Popenkov.

They went outside and Maria, for all she was very suspicious, unwrapped her bundle and showed him part of the linen. Popenkov, his arms folded on his breast, stared at the cloth.

"Why don't you say something?" Maria was surprised. Popenkov brushed that aside.

"Of course we are only handicraft workers, invalids," whined Maria, "we're a long way off these..."

"This is art!" suddenly exclaimed Popenkov fervently. "It's real art, Maria Timofeevna. You are a talented, talented, *Talented* person," he cried out.

"Spontaneity, expression, fi-li-gree. You ought to go further. You could produce," —his voice dropped to a whisper, "old French Tapestries."

"What tapestries? Are you out of your mind, Benjamin? You'll get me into a predicament," Maria was getting anxious.

"Don't worry, I'll explain everything. Let me come with you," he seized the bundle with one hand and Maria with the other. "I'll help you, I'll get the reproductions, and you and I will make tapestries. I don't need any kind of remuneration. I would just like people to have beautiful old tapestries."

He led Maria along the winding Fonarnii Lane, persuading her to take up old tapestries, simultaneously going into raptures over the charms of the lindens in flower, the flight of swallows, (a keen dagger-like glance above), and the clear June day. From time to time he would jump into the air, rubbing his hands excitedly. Maria merely groaned under his pressure.

The reader is quite right to ask who is this Benjamin Fedoseevich Popenkov, where he came from, his cultural level, what he is by profession and so on and so forth. If he isn't given this information the reader is within his rights to assume the author is leading him by the nose.

I could fall back on some naive mystification and really lead the reader by the nose, but literary ethics above all, so I am forced to declare that I know nothing about Popenkov. Water in clouds is dark. I have the feeling that in the course of the narrative some kind of a portrait of this character will emerge, however approximate, but the story of his origins and various other data are most unlikely to ever float to the surface.

The first tapestry was naturally sold to antique-lover Zinochka Z., young wife of our good Deputy Minister. The tapestry was beautiful, although of course it had suffered from the effects of time, whatever you say, almost two centuries have gone by since it was produced by anonymous craftsmen in Lyons. A pastorale was depicted on it, slightly reminiscent of Bouché.

Zinochka actually gasped when Popenkov brought her this tapestry. So did the Deputy Minister, when he learnt what it cost.

"It's unthinkable!" he said, immediately calculating in his head that

20

about two months wages would go on the acquisition of this object. "Zinochka, it's unthinkable, it smacks of bourgeois decadence."

"What are you talking about, darling?" said Zina in astonishment and came towards him, her shape visible through a transparent negligee.

The Deputy Minister immediately flew into the abyss, the tenth wave closed over his head, a typhoon raged.

"Mind you, it's very valuable," he said, when some time had elapsed.

After the sale of the tapestry friendly relations were established between Popenkov and Zina. The Deputy Minister was hardly ever home, he lived for his department, and Zina naturally was bored, and in need of live human company. Occasionally in a state of misanthropy she would despatch Yurii Filippovich to walk the dog and summon Popenkov up to talk about life, the sad nature of human existence.

"For goodness' sake, Benjamin Fedoseevich," she would say, reclining on the sofa in her dressing gown, with Popenkov sitting on the edge, "Here I am, young, beautiful... I'm not ugly, am I?"

"How can you ask! How can you?" said Popenkov indignantly.

"No, I'm not fishing for compliments," Zina dismissed his protest with a wave of the hand, "it's only lack of confidence in myself, doubts, anxieties.. You understand, I am young and not ugly, I've got everything— a beautiful apartment, money, my own car, foodstuffs, why should I be so unhappy, why aren't I satisfied with life? Perhaps I am a superfluous person, like Pechorin?"

"I understand you Zina, I am familiar with all that," said Popenkov sadly, gazing at the floor, "it's as if we were the same person. We are drawn to the heights. We are superior beings, Zina," —for an instant he raised his eyes and scorched Zinochka with the fire of Mesopotamia.

"In 43 I gave myself to a pilot," said Zinochka, "He was the first, he took me savagely, inhumanly. It happened on the river bank in a downpour, but he was like a tiger, like.."

"Like an eagle,"prompted Popenkov, "after all, he was a pilot."

"He was a pilot then, now he's a Deputy Minister," nodded Zina sadly. "He's a friend of my husband's, he visits and drinks vodka with Z., he's changed."

Popenkov would get up, pace the carpet nervously, rub his hands, turn sharply to Zinochka... Ooh, how she appealed to him, ly-y-ing there unafraid.

Then there would be Yurii Filippovich's cough and the dog's bark. Zinochka would get up off the sofa, tell Popenkov all sorts of trivia to do with the delivery of antiques and see him to the door. Because of Yurii Filippovich and the dog, their meetings began to take on a sort of unnecessary ambiguity.

At night Popenkov would command the frescoes on the dome to move, to piece together the scattered parts of the body. He didn't give up hope of assembling Zina's tempting figure, but kept getting freaks, sympathetic enough to look at, but "typically not the real article."

Two people were much later than the rest coming home, No. 14's number two charmer Maria Tsvetkova and the Deputy Minister himself. In those days, as everybody knows, the windows in the ministries and departments shone all night in the center of sleeping Moscow.

Z. always entered the house energetically, slammed the doors hard, crossed the vestibule in military strides, waking Popenkov as he went.

"How is life for the young, Savior?"

Popenkov jumped up, opened the lift door, refrained from answering this question, which hurt his pride, but would ask humbly:

"Will you take the lift?"

"It won't be required," Z. would say and fly up to his first floor apartment on strong legs.

Tsvetkova would tap with her wedge-heeled shoes, the current season's model. She wore a white woolen coat, like Claudia Shulzhenko, and had a "Marika Rokk" hair-style.

In the war years a girl like Tsvetkova was the dream of all the warring countries, that is, of all civilized mankind. She had something that disturbed and inspired hardened fighting men, that connected them with normal human life, and if this was symbolically labeled "Ludmilla Tselikova," "Valentina Serova," "Wait for me, and I will return,"[14] and on the other side "Marika Rokk," "Zarah Leander..." "Lili Marlene," and in the sands of the Sahara and in the Atlantic "Diana Durbin," "Sonia Henie," "It's a long way to Tipperary," in real life it was Maria Tsvetkova.

The war years were for her a time of tender power, of romance, sorrow and hope. Her boys, her beaus, were flying over Königsberg in night bombing raids, tramping the highways of Poland and Czechoslovakia, surfacing in submarines in the cold Norwegian reefs. By one such hero, actually the only one she had really loved, Tsvetkova had a daughter. The hero didn't return, he died after Germany's capitulation, somewhere near Prague.

Tsvetkova was still lovely in 1948, but her style had altered a fraction, almost imperceptibly. She continued to accept the attentions of officers, because their shoulder-straps and decorations reminded her of the not-too-distant past, and because "youth was passing," but as for civilian dandies in long jackets with box shoulders—they got zero attention and a pound of scorn.

The officers would see Tsvetkova home, she would get into the lift with bouquets of flowers, and tap one wedge heel as they went up, hum "The night is short, the clouds slumber," barely notice the camp-bed with Popenkov, and never react in any way to his compliments regarding her figure and general charms.

Whereas Popenkov added Tsvetkova to his dreams, practiced black magic on his dome and ornament, and in general, if we are to be quite honest,

22

experienced great anger towards the human race.

That night Tsvetkova entered the vestibule tipsy and gay, covered in dahlias, poppies and other flower-buds.

"Permit me a sniff," requested Popenkov and buried his face in the bouquet, almost touching Marina's breast with his bony nose.

"You really should visit the bath-house, Popenkov," said Marina, "you smell most unpleasant. Would you like thirty copecks for a bath? Here's a thirty copeck note, and a peony for good measure."

"How am I to interpret your gift?" asked Popenkov, stuffing the flower and the note into his bosom. "As a sign of interest or a sign of pity? If it's pity, then I shall return it; pity lowers a man, and man has a proud ring about him."

"Are you a man, then, Popenkov?" Tsvetkova showed naive surprise and pressed the button for her floor.

Popenkov shuddered with proud and powerful feelings he himself didn't fully understand.

"You are a flighty creature, Marina, I know everything about you," he said, getting a grip on himself.

"You don't know anything about me," Tsvetkova suddenly grew sullen, "and I'm not at all flighty, I'm very down to earth, and you don't know a thing about me."

They went up.

"I do know," said Popenkov.

"Ha-ha," said Tsvetkova, "you don't know anything. For example, you don't know who I'm in love with, which man I have adored from afar for a long time, I love Deputy Minister Z., so there!"

The lift came to a halt and Tsvetkova attempted to get out, but Popenkov pushed the ground-floor button, and down they went.

"What do you think you're doing?" asked Tsvetkova.

"Just this," giggled Popenkov. "But what about Zinochka Z.?"

"Zinka, that so-and-so heifer!" cried Tsvetkova. "When Z. moved into our house he liked me better than Zinka, but I dropped him, because he was a Deputy Minister so he wouldn't think that I loved him just because he was a Deputy Minister. Fool that I am!" she burst into tears and pressed the button for her floor.

Up they went.

"Curious, curious," pronounced Popenkov. "So you were seeing Z. then?"

"So we were seeing one another, what of it, so we went on trips together, but we haven't been seing one another for a year now, and I don't want anything from him," Tsvetkova was still crying.

"Don't cry, my dear," said Popenkov, putting his arms around Tsvetkova and unobtrusively pressing the ground-floor button, "don't cry, unhappy, delightful, *Delightful* woman," he cried, opening his eyes wide.

"Unrequited love, how well I understand it, that's the story of my life, we are creatures with a similar destiny..."

Down they went.

"Let go of me, you foul-smelling fellow!" Tsvetkova suddenly came to and pressed the button for her floor. "Have you gone mad or what?"

She tried to struggle out of Popenkov's embrace, but his arms were like steel. She felt the incredible superhuman strength of his arms and was even afraid.

"Let me go!"

Down!

"And if it is exposed... haven't you thought?... the excesses?.... Zinaida's wrath... and if it were made public?... What if I take it around the various departments... eh?"

Up!

"Let me go, you wretch! You nut... miserable booby," and slap across the face, "idiot ... let me go, I won't be answerable for what I do... I.. I work on the newspaper... as a secretary... I'll write a piece about you.. What a scoundrel you are... let me go! ... that's it..."

Down!

"In misfortune I... kreg, kreg, karusers chuvyt... hemoroids... how can I see?... fit, fit, rykl, ekl, a?"

Up!

"You nothing... you scourge, you animal! My tears are not over you! My lover was a pilot, a hero twice over! Get out of the way!"

Down!

"In the paper.. about me?.. chryk, chryk,.. grym firaus ekl... in brackets... why not take pity... I ekl buzhur zhirnau chlok chuvyr... kuri-kuri... a weak organism..."

Up!

"Are you out of your mind? You're quite mad! Ha-ha-ha-ha-ha-ha-ha-ha-ha-ha-ha-ha-ha! You can't fool me!"

Down!

"Lyk bruter, kikan, kikan, kikan..., pity and love... I thirst like an eagle... order... liton fri au, au... we'll fly away... fit, fit, rykl, ekl, a?... over the ruins, over the houses... Flowers, Marina... ekl..."

Down, down, she was no longer in control of her arms, her laughter had died away and her tears dried up, whereas the lift was as full of electricity as a Leiden jar, and kept falling, falling, then rocketed upwards into thick blackness, into a wretched sky, and she felt as if she herself.. any minute.. just like her beloved pilot or tankman.. the one who hadn't returned.. any minute would meet her end, but just then Popenkov crashed onto the camp-bed and went into convulsions.

The women of No. 14 set up a rescue committee and organized a roster by the patient's bedside.

In the morning they brought semolina, cream and cottage cheese from a neighboring kindergarten.

Comrade Z., under pressure from his wife, sent a doctor from the Kremlin hospital and the latter held a consultation with Doctor Zeldovich. Yurii Filippovich ran to the chemist. Alarming the pharmacists with his uniform and the inscription *cito!*, he got the medicines without having to queue.

Lev Ustinovich shaved the patient gratis, and his children made no noise in the entrance, on the contrary, they tried to amuse Popenkov, reading him verses and singing him oriental songs.

Maria and Agrippina draped the lift with clean and artistic canvases.

"What will we do about the lift?" asked Nikolai Nikolaevich at a general meeting of the tenants.

"What about the lift? What is a lift, when there's a sick man in it? Damn the lift!" replied the tenants as one man.

"So that's settled—the lift is out of action!" Nikolai Nikolaevich summed up, and his usually stern eyes softened.

And so in No. 14 Fonarnii Lane the lift was put out of action. On that we could end the second chapter.

Recollections of Mikhail Fuchinian, a diver.

Everybody knows me, I'm Fuchinian, and anybody who doesn't, soon will, and anybody who doesn't want to know me can leave, and if they don't leave, they'll get to know me, and these here are my friends, they're first rate young men and lads. Bottoms up! Away, lads!

Well, O.K., if anybody's interested, I can tell you about this type. Only mind you don't interrupt, those who are going to interrupt had better leave right away, or they'll run into trouble.

In short, here is my arm, check it yourselves, if you want. Well, how is my arm, in order? Biceps, triceps, all in place? The left one's the same, see! In short, before you is my whole humeral belt. On the whole, as you see, no weakling!

One evening the lads and I were sitting in the yard playing dominoes. Tolik, he was a driver at the Central Fish Cannery, had that very day scored about six kilo of dried fish, so as it turned out, we sent the boys for some beer. The boys dragged in two cases of beer and it was turning out a nice quiet evening. We were sitting normally, having knocked off the same, we're gorging the dried fish, washing it down with beer and swapping experiences from the Second World War.

Then this booby Benjamin Popenkov appears. He squats down, picks away at the fish, someone poured him a beer, he's sitting there saying nothing. Nice and clean, not like in '48, smelling of "Flight" eau-de-cologne,

25

in a tie, boots, no worries.

I disliked this little rat from the very beginning—if I were a cat, I'd have gobbled him up and that would be that, but I didn't show my feelings, because it's my principle to live and let live, the lads will tell you that.

But here I began to get mad just looking at him. Oh you unfortunate fellow, I thinks, you wretched, homeless creature, everybody's feeding you, everybody's sorry for you, they all throw something your way, and meanwhile you're making yourself comfortable, you damned rook. I just thought God grant that everybody set himself up as well as this wretch. True, he hasn't got a flat, but then he's got the whole of the vestibule at his disposal, he's put in screens there, the tenants have only got the narrowest passage from the stairs to the door, and I don't even mention the lift. Next question: our poor unfortunate has taken himself the best stacked woman in the whole lane and has a ball with her behind the screens, and how!—the whole house rocks. Next: Here am I, a diver, a highly paid worker, well, for my two-hundred and fifty I squirm around on the bottom of the Moscow River like a crab, while that bastard walks around up top in a suit the like I've never dreamed of, and the smells in the vestibule are so gastronomic, there's never anything like them in my place. If you look at it this way, there's an unfortunate devil walking around looking at everybody as if they all owed him something. It's a sort of hypnotism, like with magicians, such as the Kio brothers or Cleo Dorotti.

Well anyway, I got mad and I took a sharp turn towards trouble. Tolik Proglotilin was just recounting an operation on Tsemissk Bay, and Popenkov kept humoring him, nodding away with his beak. Here I interrupt Tolik and say:

"Why don't you share your war-time experiences, Popenkov? I suppose you were defending Tashkent? No doubt you struck a blow to the dried apricots?" He smiles, the cad, smiles a mysterious, contained, incredible smile.

"Ah, Misha," he says to me, "you know nothing about my war. Your war is over, but mine isn't. My war will be more terrible than yours."

Everybody fell silent, sensing there was going to be trouble, everybody knows I don't like my fighting past being insulted.

"Who could you fight, you sparrow, you chicken feed," I say, with my voice raised. "Women? You wouldn't have the strength for anything else, you tom-tit!"

But he keeps on grinning away, and suddenly he fixes his orbs on me, so that a blast of heat comes my way, like out of a ship's furnace.

"In the first place, Misha, I'm no sparrow or tom-tit, and in the second place, not everybody knows his real strength. Perhaps I am stronger than you, eh Misha?"

So. Like that. That's how it's going to be.

Then I lift my right arm, this very arm you see before you, and put my elbow on the table.

"O.K., strong man, let's put it to the test."

It's a real laugh, but he too places his wasted paw on the table, his pale, moderately hairy paw. The lads are bursting with laughter, because I am the champion at this caper, not just in Fonarnii Lane, but in the whole of the Arbat district, and for that matter I don't know who in the whole of Moscow could pin my arm to the table, except perhaps Grigorii Novak.

So we engaged, and gently, almost without trying I bent his paw down, but about ten centimenters from the table it somehow jammed. I doubled my pressure, to no avail. I trebled it, but it was no go. It was as if my arm were resting on solid metal, practically tank armor. I looked into his eyes, with their yellow fire. On his lips was an amiable smile. I quadrupled my efforts and at this point my arm, as if it didn't belong to me, moved upwards, and then down under the force of a pressure that just couldn't be human, it had to be mechanical, and there it was stamped to the table. Everybody was silent.

"He beat you by sheer nerve, Misha, sheer nerve," whispered Vaska Axiomov. "Have another go. Flex your muscles..."

"Quite right," says Popenkov, "It wasn't my muscle power that beat Misha, it was the superiority of my nervous system. If you like, we could have another go..."

We tried again—the result was the same.

We tried a third time—no go.

Here to tell you the truth, my temperament got the better of me—as you know, my father is of Armenian origin—and I leapt on Popenkov. I rolled him, I pummelled him, I spun him, I bent him, and suddenly I was pinned down by both shoulder blades, touché, and above me yellow fires, ugh!, his damned eyes.

"Nerves," said Tolik Proglotilin, "he's got nerves of steel. We've all got weak nerves, but they," indicating Popenkov with respect, "they've got nerves of steel."

A gentleman acknowledges defeat, and I did so, I slapped Popenkov on the shoulder (he practically collapsed) and sent for vodka.

Popenkov sat quiet and modest, I must say he didn't brag at all. We drank. To smooth it over the lads began singing songs of the war and pre-war years, different marching songs.

> Where the infantry can't pass
> Nor armored train race by
> Nor heavy tank crawl through
> The Steel Bird will fly.

"Here's our steel bird," said Vaska Axiomov, embracing Popenkov, "our very own real steel bird."

27

"Steel, all metal," continued Tolik Proglotilin affectionately. And a new version was composed.

> Where Axiomov is not outstripped
> Where Proglotilin can't race by
> Nor Fuchinian crawl through
> The Steel Bird will fly.

Well, naturally, they all roared laughing. You only have to hold a finger up to our boys and they guffaw.

And here, brothers, something very strange took place, just like they describe in novels. Popenkov jumped up, began waving his arms around, just like a bird, his eyes burning feverishly, he became pretty terrifying, and began telling in some half-intelligible language:

"Kertl fur linker, I knew it, at last! Yes, I am a Steel zhiza, chuiza drong! Aha, we've got.. fricheki, klocheki kryt, kryt, kryt! In flight—the whistle and claw of their percators!"

We were all dumb-founded, looking at this freak, then suddenly he was silent, got embarrassed, smiled gently and squatted down.

"Not a bad trick I played on you, eh? A funny one, eh?"

Everybody breathed a sigh of relief and burst out laughing—"What a card! A Steel bird, all right, what a nervous system!"

But he called me aside.

"Actually, Misha, I was after your hide," he told me softly.

I began to shake, and resolved to resist to the end, defend to the death.

"You couldn't help me to install some furniture tomorrow, I suppose?" he asked. "I can't manage alone, and my wife, you know, is a weak woman. You see, we have decided to furnish the place, as it is, it's like being on bivouac. It would be nice to have furniture for when our relatives come."

"Sure, Steel Bird," I said, to tell the truth relieved that my hide hadn't been required after all, "Sure, Steel Bird, we'll do whatever we can. I'll be along tomorrow with Vaska and Tolik." So that's how it was, chaps! We went on with what we were doing. Bottoms up! Salute. Oh yes, we carried the furniture in for him, and that evening he nailed up the main entrance. Since then the tenants have been using the back entrance.

The doctor's recollections.

I treated him many times, each time as if I were blind-folded, each time the diagnosis was completely unclear to me. In the finish I began to think it was nothing to do with my treatment, the antibiotics or the physio-therapy that made him get better, it was just his own will, the same way as he got sick.

Each summons to him was agony for me, a concentration of all my spiritual strength, that is, all the strength of my higher nervous system. In the first place, I sometimes began to think that there was something powerful and mysterious about him, in his organism, something of the sort that completely contradicts my outlook as a Soviet doctor. In the second place, I noticed each time that this secret force plunged me into a state of absolute abulia, i.e. the absence of any voluntary reactions, into the torpid state of a domestic animal, merely awaiting orders and the lash.

One day he asked me to admit one of his relatives to hospital for two weeks. This relative was a strapping seed bull, like a blacksmith. I examined him and naturally refused to hospitalize a perfectly healthy man. What on earth for, I thought, after all even the hospital corridors were crammed with critically ill patients, really in need of treatment.

"Try to understand, Doctor," Popenkov wheedled, "this man has traveled a long distance, he has spent a month in the foundations of the Palace of Soviets, he'll die if you don't save him."

"Not at all, Comrade Popenkov," I objected. "Your relative is in fine working condition. If he is tired from the journey, he can rest at your place. I observe that your vestibule has turned into a fairly comfortable apartment." At this point I permitted myself a grin.

That was in a very difficult time for we medicos, the winter of 1953. Just a short while before a group of professors had been arrested and charged with terrible crimes. All my life I had admired these scholars, in point of fact they were my teachers, and I couldn't understand their logic. How could they leave the high road of humanism for the path of crime against humanity? Naturally I kept my thoughts to myself.

It was all aggravated by the fact that the crimes of these scholars ricocheted on all of we honest Soviet doctors. Some folk even developed a distrust of anything in a white coat. In the polyclinic where I conducted consultations once a week I had occasion to meet such instances of suspicion and also insulting comments, can you imagine, apropos of my nose. I never would have thought that a nose was anything to do with medicine.

One night as I lay in bed I heard the lift coming up. The lift in our building hadn't been used for several years, so this unusual and unexpected sound put me on my guard.

"You can't fry an omelette without breaking eggs," I thought and quickly got up and put on warm clothes.

There was a soft knock at the door, I calmly opened it, and on the landing stood Popenkov.

"I wanted to have a word with you, Doctor," he said, "I can't understand what's going on. Two days ago you gave me some medicine for my ears, and my liver played up. Forgive me, but for some time I have been noticing some strange things, fuchi melazi rikatuer, you prescribe something for the heart, and there's a sharp pain in the ureter, kryt, kryt, liska bul chvar, your vitamins cause severe vitamin deficiency. What is it all about? Can you give me an explanation?"

On my word of honor, he said all that to me.

"Yes, I see," I replied, "I am sorry, it won't happen again."

Next morning I took his relative to the hospital.

The doctors' consilium, having taken place in the summer of 1956.

"Yes, we must look the facts boldly in the face. There is still much in nature that has not been studied..."

"You will excuse me, comrades, perhaps you will think me mad, but..."

"Why did you stop? Go on!"

"No, wait a bit."

"Let's compare our data once more with the anthrocometry and the test data and x-rays of a homo sapiens."

"Nonsense, colleague! Perhaps you are assuming that normal anatomy and physiology can have somehow changed recently."

"Comrades, you will think I'm mad, but..."

"You've stopped again? Say it."

"No, I'll wait a bit."

"However our data is so astonishing, that one inevitably begins wondering..."

"Doctors, let us remain within the bounds of science. Miracles don't happen."

"No, but that way we will never get out of the impasse."

"Comrades, I must be mad, but..."

"Well, say it!"

"Go on, say it!"

"Have your say!"

"... but could we not surmise that we have before us an airplane?"

"Imagine, the same thing occurred to me, but I couldn't bring myself to say it."

"Colleagues, colleagues, let us stay within the bounds..."

"... and yet I am convinced that before us is no homo sapiens, but an ordinary steel airplane."

"Let's not be too hasty, let's call in a construction engineer. I'll ring an engineer I know."

....

Tupolev arrived and was acquainted with the data.

"No, this is not altogether an airplane," he said, "although it has many features in common with a fighter-interceptor."

....
"Comrades, perhaps my train of thought will seem strange, but...??"

"... but would it be impossible to assume we have a bird before us?"

"I wanted to suggest it myself, but couldn't bring myself."

"Let's not rush to conclusions, Doctor, let's call in an ornithologist."

....

Academician Bukhvostov arrived and was acquainted with the data.

"Although it has some similarities," he said, "it is not a bird. It can't be a bird with such obvious features of a fighter-interceptor."

....

"Might we not, Comrades,—of course, this may throw us way off,— but might we not, considering all the statements and summing up the opinions of authoritative specialists, and likewise the nature of the subject's behavior, his somewhat frequent use of sound combinations as yet unknown on earth, might we not assume, with all due caution, naturally, could we not tentatively assume that we are dealing with a completely new species with a unique combination of organic and inorganic features, could it not be assumed that in this given instance we are pioneers, might we not be dealing with a Steel Bird?"

"I ask you all to rise, I ask you all to remember that the records of this consilium are absolutely confidential."

Part for cornet-a-piston

Theme: We were born to make fantasy fact, overcome distance and space... Improvisation: The doors are nailed up with rusty nails, what are we tenants to do about him? It's hard to get through the dirty back way, but still if we must, we will go that way. As long as there's concord, peace, and splendor, and the fire regulations are observed. End of theme: ... Steel arm-wings gave us reason, and in place of a heart a combustion engine.

The barber's recollections

Our downstairs neighbor from the vestibule pinned me to the wall. "I beg your pardon," I say, "what's going on?" And he says:

"kryt kryt, fil burore liap," that is, in some foreign language. "And what if I have a go at you with the cut-throat? Snap and the razor snapped. Let me through," but he doesn't. "And what if I have a go at you with scissors?" Snap, and the scissors snapped. "And what if I give you a blow-wave?" "That—by all means," he says. "And what if I freshen you up with 'Flight' eau-de-cologne?" "By all means," he says. "And what about a face massage with nourishing cream?" "By all means," he says, and lets me through.

Chapter 3.

The dreary necessity of battling on with the plot obliges me to try to re-construct the chronological sequence of events.

In 1950, or maybe the year before or after, a quarrel of unusual force blew up between the Zs. It started, of course, on account of old French tapestries and other such objects from the time of Mme. Pompadour. The Deputy Minister was becoming impoverished terrifyingly fast, his wardrobe was wearing out, the food was deteriorating daily, all his salary and extra allowances, and even a certain portion of their rations went on antiques. It reached the point where Z. began botting on his guard Yurii Filippovich for a "North" cigarette. That's what it had come to—descending from "Herzegovina Flor" to "North," somebody else's, at that.

"You know, Zinaida," said Z., "it's high time to put a stop to this. Our apartment has turned into a second-hand shop. It's bourgeois deca-dence and cosmopolitanism."

"You've no sensitivity, you're a ruffian, you're rusty," sobbed Zinaida. "I get no understanding from you, no flicker of interest. All you want to do is to wink at that vulgar Tsvetkova. I'm leaving."

"What has Tsvetkova got to do with it? Where are you going? Who to? God, what's going on?" wailed Z. The thought that Zinochka might deprive him of her embraces seemed incredibly awful, quite hellish. Incidentally he thought of the unpleasantnesses at work, of explanations in the party, of the whole complex of unpleasantnesses associated with a wife's departure.

"I am going to a man who speaks my language. To a man whose es-thetic views concord with my own," announced Zinochka.

And she went downstairs, to the vestibule, to Popenkov, who had for ages been jumping in wild anticipation all over the squares of the ornament.

"Will you have me?" she asked dramatically.

"My love, light of my eyes, kuvyral lekur lekuvirl ki ki!" Popenkov danced in delight.

"How about that! I've toppled the Deputy Minister," he thought, beside himself with joy and animal optimism.

There was an immediate division of property, after which Z. was left in his rooms alone with a camp-stretcher, a bed-side table, a battered ward-robe and a few books in his speciality. He was standing there at a complete loss, almost prostrate, when in walked Popenkov with the aim of delivering the final blow to k.o. the ungrateful Deputy Minister.

"As a man and a knight," he addressed himself to Z. "I am obliged to intervene on behalf of the unfortunate woman you have tormented and in addition to everything else accused of cosmopolitanism. Zinaida is not a cosmopolitan, she is a true Soviet citizen, whereas you, Comrade Z. would do well to remember those peculiar notions and doubts which you shared with your wife after disconnecting the telephone and tucking up in the blankets. Remember, I am in the know. By the way, Zinaida asked me to bring down this little cupboard. A woman can't exist without a wardrobe, and you'll get by without it. Adios."

Effortlessly lifting the huge wardrobe and shaking out Z.'s last few things, he departed.

All night long the vestibule was noisy, with the squeak of springs, incomprehensible throaty utterances, while on the first floor landing Z. and Yurii Filippovich suffered bitterly over a demi-liter.

"We have been orphaned, you and I, Filippich," wept Z. "We are alone, Filippich... How shall we bear it?"

"Shut yourself off, Comrade Deputy Minister," advised the sergeant, "withdraw into yourself and think only of work..."

Quite understandably, from that night Z.'s career took a sharp downward turn.

Popenkov and his young consort gradually normalized their surroundings. Relatives frequently arrived to do their bit. Relative Koka helped with his hammer, relative Goga with his paint brush, relative Dmitrii turned out to be good at everything.

The vestibule was partitioned, creating two rooms, alcoves, boudoirs, and sanitary areas. Peter the Great's boots ended up in Popenkov's study. The Japanese theme adorned Zinochka's boudoir, intimately and yet delicately. The knights, Vikings and Novgorodians finished up in the sitting room, which must have greatly inspired visiting relatives as they frequently sang war-like songs together there.

Their diet improved constantly, Zinochka grew kinder, succulent, with milky-waxy, sugary-creamy ripeness. Her life was complete harmony, her inner world was ruled by sub-tropical calm, splendor, and magnificent peace.

Popenkov would appear in her boudoir always suddenly, purposefully, throwing from the threshold a dagger-like glance into the blue lagoons of her eyes, fling himself in, drown in delights, boiling furiously.

"You are my geisha!" he would cry out. "My courtesan! My Lorelia!"

In the winter of 1953 an important event took place in Moscow,— J.V. Stalin died. The nation's grief overwhelmed No. 14 Fonarnii Lane too. Hollow groans could be heard there for several days. Up on the first floor two lone wolves, Yurii Filippovich and Deputy Minister, wept bitterly at night. The shrill desperate notes of the cornet-a-piston penetrated every apartment, taking advantage of the tragic freedom of those days.

Nikolai Nikolaevich Nikolaev all but perished in the scuffle on Trubnaia Square. Misha Fuchinian, Tolik Proglotilin and Vaska Axiomov just managed to drag him out of the sewerage hatch. These men organized a battle unit and somehow or other rescued the tortured inhabitants of Fonarnii Lane from the Trubnaia. So not one of them pushed through into the Hall of columns.

Nobody, that is, except of course, Popenkov, who without himself knowing how, perhaps by supernatural means and without special effort or bodily harm found himself in the "holy of holies," saw everything in the greatest detail and even brought back as a souvenir a scrap of the mourning crêpe from the chandelier.

The whole day after that he was preoccupied, absorbed in himself, he repulsed the relatives and even Zinochka, he stood in Peter's wellingtons and thought and thought.

Well, he decided towards the end of the day, here is the result of half measures and running on the spot. The sad result, the consequence of an unnecessary masquerade. Fuchi elazi kompror, and kindly lie in a coffin. No, we will take another route, ru hioplastr, ru!

Then he took his lift up to the fifth floor and went into Maria Samopalov's flat, rattling his iron boots.

As he anticipated, Maria and Agrippina were sitting grief-stricken by their idle loom. Folding his arms on his breast, Popenkov mourned with them several minutes in complete silence. Then he said his piece.

"Maria Timofeevna and you, Agrippina! Our grief is boundless, but life goes on. We mustn't forget our nearest, we mustn't forget the thousands waiting on us for joy, light, desirous of daily worshipping art. We must work. We must respond with labor!"

At this, Maria and Agrippina roused themselves and set the loom in motion. Popenkov stood for a while watching the next masterpiece emerge then left quietly so as not to disturb the creative process.

Maria and her daughter had worked all these years, barely sleeping a wink. They understood perfectly the importance of their job, after all Benjamin Fedoseevich's relatives, those disinterested culture-peddlers, were spreading antique French tapestries throughout the Far East and in Siberia, the Ukraine, the Trans-Caucasian and Central Asian republics.

Popenkov took the barber on himself, had a chat with him, expounding the importance of Maria's work. He had a chat with Zulphia, too, who soon afterwards set on her husband, demanding a small tapestry for their apartment, and forcing Lev Ustinovich to loosen the purse-strings.

After this purchase the Samopalov family's attitude to Maria became very respectful, moreover over the years all the members of the family had grown accustomed to the noise of the loom which now was perceived by them as something dear and familiar.

House manager Nikolaev marvelled: the squabbles in Flat 31 had stopped and so had the scandals and constant appellations to himself and Stalin. Mind you, the latter addressee, as everybody knows, soon dropped out of the picture, having tasted very little of the quiet life.

Nikolai Nikolaevich lived in constant terror. He was afraid Popenkov might unmask him to the tenants, show him up as a common cornet-a-piston player, a frivolous musician, not a manager.

When they met he would adopt a superior dourness and show interest in the organization of his quarters.

"Well, how is it? Are you getting organized? Can you cope with the discomfort? Can I send you a metal worker?"

Popenkov would smile understandingly, tip him a wink and turn around conspiratorially.

"And how about you, Nikolai Nikolaevich? Are you still improvising? I'm keeping mum."

And Nikolai Nikolaevich would be lost, drop his domineering tone and crumple before Popenkov like a delinquent schoolboy before the headmaster.

"I put up with the discomfort, of course, Nikolai Nikolaevich. You know for yourself, the flat is like a thoroughfare. My wife's nerves are in a bad way."

And Popenkov would adopt his favorite pose, squatting on his haunches and looking up at Nikolai Nikolaevich with his burning gaze.

"But what can be done, Benjamin Fedoseevich, I can't think of anything, it's an entrance hall, after all," said Nikolaev.

"Hulo marano ri!" Popenkov exclaimed, jumped up and rubbed his hands wildly.

"What did you say?" Nikolai Nikolaevich began to tremble like an aspen leaf.

"I beg your pardon," Popenkov feigned embarrassment, "I meant to say that it will be no great misfortune if we decide to do away with the unnecessary extravagant vulgar so-called main entrance which was once used by jurors and other servants of the bourgeoisie and direct the stream of tenants through the so-called back entrance, which is really quite convenient and even a more expedient entrance."

"That of course... is of course reasonable," mumbled Nikolaev, "but the so-called back entrance is terribly narrow. With my size I can only squeeze through with a great effort, and in the event of somebody buying a piano or somebody's death, how would you carry in a piano or a coffin?"

"What are the windows for?" exclaimed Popenkov, but recollecting, burst out laughing. "But what am I saying—the windows are quite unacceptable to you... Wait, wait the windows could easily be used for raising a piano or lowering a coffin. A bracket, a pully, a strong rope, that's all! Do you follow me?"

"A bold... a bold.." muttered Nikolaev, "a very bold solution to the problem, but.."

"You needn't worry about the rest, dear Nikolai Nikolaevich, I'll handle the tenants' reaction. Don't you worry yourself over anything, just keep on quietly making music, ha-ha-ha! Yes, I understand, I understand, I won't say a word, not a word!"

And so the main entrance was nailed up and the white marble staircase was walled up. Relative Goga made a really aristocratic candelabra for Zinochka out of the snake door handles. In the beginning the windows were used for getting in and out of the fashionable apartment, but later, when the tenants were used to the new regime, the front entrance was re-opened, but only for the Popenkov family's private use.

And so the first stage was completed, and although it had taken quite a number of years, Popenkov was satisfied, went around serene and proud, but his eyes betrayed their former heavy yellow heat, the ancient dream and longing of Tamerlane.

Sometimes at night he would interrupt his delights and put a question to his spouse.

"Are you content with your fate, Zinaida?"

The fabulously magnificent Zinaida would stretch in servile languor.

"I am almost content, 99.9 per cent content, and if you were to.."

"I understand your restless soul. I understand the magnitude of that .1 per cent," he said and began to boil furiously, and then a little later asked again, "but do you understand me?"

Zinochka, now 99.99 per cent content, replied:

"I think I understand you and the beauty of your dream. You, like a mighty spirit, have transformed this foul vestibule into a majestic palace, an esthetic temple to our fatal passion, and you are different from the grey drab men, the Deputy Ministers, and policemen, doctors, barbers and divers that I knew before you, you are a hurricane of fire and steel, a powerful and proud spirit, but sometimes, Benjamin, I am bewildered, I still cannot understand your mysterious words..."

"Which words....?" Popenkov laughed excitedly.

"Well, for example, the words which you utter in an excess of passion— bu zhiza hoku romuar, tebet felari..."

".. kukubu?" cried Popenkov. The dialogue was temporarily interrupted.

"Yes, those words, what do they mean?" Zinochka asked weakly afterwards.

"Ha-ha," Popenkov was euphoric, "but you know I am no ordinary man, and some of my characteristics are even different from those of a bird. I am the Steel Bird. That's our language, the language of steel birds."

"Oh, how fascinating! How exciting! A *Steel* Bird!" breathed Zinochka.

"Kukubu!" cried Popenkov.

Once more there was an interruption in the conversation.

"But are there any others? Are there more in the world like you?" Zinochka renewed the conversation.

"Not many yet, but not so few, either. Earlier attempts unfortunately fell through, in my opinion because of half-measures and running on the spot. Chivi, chivi zol farar, do you understand me?"

"Almost."

"For the time being we are forced to get around in jackets and shoes and lisp English, French or Spanish. And I have to use the great and wonderful, truthful and free,[15] damn it, chuchumo rogi far! But never mind, the time will come! What strength I feel! What predestination! You know," he whispered, "I am the chief Steel Bird..."

"You are the chief! The chief! The chief!" breathed Zinochka.

"Kukubu!" cried Popenkov.

"Let me in on your plans, my Steel Bird," Zinochka cooed tenderly after a short pause.

Popenkov ran out of the boudoir and returned with the iron boots on his bare legs.

"I can do anything," he said, striding around the bed, "I shall arrange everything as I want it. First I shall complete my little experiment with this puny six-storey house. I'll sit them all at looms, all these intellectuals. They'll all be weaving tapestries for me, all these Samopalovs, Zeldoviches, Nikolaevs, Fuchinians, Proglotilins, Axiomovs, Tsvetkovas..."

"Tsvetkova too?" Zinochka inquired drily. "I think Tsvetkova should be treated differently."

"Ha-ha-ha, you want to deal with Tsvetkova?" Popenkov laughed patronizingly. "By all means, pet."

"Thank you," Zinochka smiled secretively.

"What do you want to do with her? Fuchi elazi kompfor trandiratsiu?" asked Popenkov.

"Fuchi emazi kir madagor," replied Zinochka.

"Kekl fedekl?" Popenkov roared with laughter.

"Chlok buritano," giggled Zinochka.

"Mugi halogi ku?"

"Lachi artugo holeonon."

"Burtl?"

"Holo oloh, ha-ha-ha!" shrieked Zinochka madly, like a mare.

"Kukubu!" cried Popenkov.

A pause and silence, desire and lust, scuffling and profanation, loathing, rotting, rebirth and self-generation, quivering, swallowing, absorption, expulsion, smothering, annihilation of a live, light, good person with the gait of a calf, the eyes of a young deer, with apple-breasts, with emerald eyes, with a little orange of a heart and a mysterious soul, annihilation.

And meanwhile the chapter comes to an end, and the years pass, certain individuals are growing old, some are growing up and see love and college, records, fame and earthly goods on soft pillows and sweaty fists, and nobody sees death, on the contrary, everybody sees scenes from life, and nobody hears in his sleep the soft rumble of the apparently nonfunctioning lift going up and down, even Doctor Zeldovich sleeps soundly now, his warm things hidden in a trunk with naphthalene till winter.

The Night Flight of the Steel Bird.

a) Address to the Bronze Horseman.
Whence did you think to threaten the Swedes?
Tut-tut. And this city you founded to spite
an arrogant neighbor? Tut-tut. Were all your deeds
the fleet, Poltava, a window on Europe?
Well, do you know who stands before you? I am
the Steel Zhiza Chuiza Drong! I
need no monuments, I myself am
a flying monument. If I want,
I devour, if I want, I pardon. I shan't
pardon you, don't expect it. I will gobble you up, Peter Alexeevich.

b) Address to the monument to Yurii Dolgorukii.
I shall devour your horse, make shashliks
of your horse. To the "Aragva" with your
horse, to the kitchens! You I have already devoured.

c) Address to the monument commemorating a Thousand years of Russia.
What a date—a miserable thousand!
What sort of creatures are these in cassocks, in
cloaks, in armor, in jerkins, in
frock-coats? I'll smelt you all and make
a porridge of bronze, and here will be a monument
to bronze porridge! and I will eat it.

d) Address to the monument to Abraham Lincoln.
"Don't look down your nose, Abe! You freed
the negroes? Nothing to be proud of.
No protests! to the rubbish heap!

e) Address to the monument to the Warsaw ghetto.
Well, no need for discussion here! Everyone
into the oven, and I've already eaten Mordechai Anilewicz.

f) Conversion to Earth Satellite and address to all mankind.
This is Earth Satellite the Steel Bird
speaking. All your artificial satellites
I have already devoured. Honored comrades, a great

38

surprise is being made ready,
a big purge, a purge of the planet from
the monuments of the past. There will be no past,
there will be no future, and I have devoured the present
already. Honored comrades, eat up monuments
disciplinedly! Now you have one monument—the charming satellite, the Steel Bird. Make ready
perches, a perch from each city, or I
shall eat you up.

The Doctor's Recollections.

He came to see me and complained about his appetite. His stomach
actually was swollen and covered in blue lines. My appetite has disappeared,
he said. Then take the matter to the police, I advised boldly. What about the
digestion tract, he asked. Some rivets in the gut really had worked loose,
there were bolts rattling around, and some welded seams had come apart.
When all's said and done I'm no engineer and we're not living in some science
fiction novel, but in ordinary Soviet reality, I announced to him and washed
my hands of it. Very well, Zeldovich, you'll end up in here, he said and
slapped his swollen belly. I opened the window and suggested he vacate the
flat. He flew out of the window. His flight was heavy, sometimes he would
fall, like a plane in air pockets, but then he would suddenly soar and disappear. Of course I realize I'll have to pay for my boldness, but the prospect
of ending up in his stomach, in that steel bag, I tell you straight, I don't relish
in the least.

The Building Inspector's report.

In the course of the years due to the rebuilding of the ground floor,
and likewise due to the almost incessant rhythmic shaking in the right-hand
corner of the former vestibule the foundations of No. 14 are collapsing and
the right-hand corner sinking after the fashion of an Italian tower in Pisa
(Consultation with U.S.S.R.—Italian Friendship Society). Sewage from the
new autonomous sewerage system is vigorously washing away the soil.
    The situation is catastrophic, one could say, Help, good people! A
representative for the foundation, the corner stone, declared in a private
conversation that they can't hold out more than two months.
    I hereby give warning and take this opportunity to state, on the basis
of the above, that in the continuing absence of measures to organize a re-
prieve for No. 14, which I love and adore, I relinquish my commission as
building-inspector and in a state of spiritual disharmony will put an end to

myself by means of a hemp rope.

Part for Cornet-a-piston.

Theme: A smell of crisp crusts floats out the windows, and a flutter of hands behind the curtain....
Improvisation: The foundations are collapsing, clouds are gathering, it leans like a willow, our dear home. It has inclined like the tower in Pisa, it leaks, sewage at that. Young tenants, old heroes go on living in it, unsuspecting. There will be a disaster, my heart is thumping, my arms hang loose, there is grief in my gut...
End of theme: Help, good people!

Chapter 4.

Coming back to a strictly chronological narrative, I must inform you that exactly eighteen years have passed since the beginning of this story. Every reader is aware of the changes that have taken place over that period in the life of society, so there's no need to elaborate on them. I shall continue my dreary task and weave the web of the plot, the web in which my heroes have been trapped without realizing it, and in which for the time being they are basking, their emerald tummies turned upwards to the caressing May sun.

One wonderful May evening the barber Samopalov's eldest son Ahmed, by now a very famous, almost fantastically famous young writer, one of those idols of the young that drive around in small "Zaporozhets"[16] cars and have the habit of turning up exactly where they are least expected, well, this same Ahmed Lvovich Samopalov was going to his home in Fonarnii Lane. Ahmed had recently smashed his "Zaporozhets" and sold it for scrap, so he was returning home on foot. He was excited by his battles in the Central Writers' club and was still passionately engaged in mental polemics with his opponents.

"It didn't come off, the old man didn't die," he thought. "Well then, alright, you're aligning, you come along, you vipers, sit and snigger, you crawl, and interfere with the game, right? And to finish it off you pit against me one of your well-trained scum, right? You think that he's got a strong attack and a good defense, don't you? You've got Ahmed Samopalov already buried, haven't you? I'll show you, I only need two serves to find his weak points, I see quite clearly that he won't get a twister into the right hand corner of the table. First I serve him a couple of strong hits from the right, he gets them, I fore-shorten, he gets it, then I smash one into the right corner and even if by some miracle he gets it I immediately cut in from the left and he's done for, the point goes my way. Fine activists and geniuses when they can't even hold a racket correctly, poor little pricks!"

Here Ahmed suddenly gasped, shuddered, clutched at his heart, then his pulse, next closed his eyes, opened them again, and then pinched himself on the leg.

In the shadow on the other side of the street, in the blue marine ozone strode along a rare specimen of the human race, a long-legged, blue-eyed, tanned, sexy, fair, provocative girl. Ahmed began drumming to himself a militant literary anthem, because this specimen was the ideal, the idol, the clarion call of 1965 young Moscow prose, the secret dream of all "Zaporo-zhets" car owners, starting with Anatolii Gladilin.[17]

I don't know what it will be in the printed text, but I just numbered this page 88 in my manuscript. This was completely fortuitous, but significant, since 88 in the language of radio operators means love, as was proclaimed by the poet Robert Ivanovich Rozhdestvenskii.

Ahmed Lvovich drummed the anthem and darted purposefully forward.

"Ninochka! What a surprise! Have you been back long? Did you see anyone from home?" he cried, feigning unprecedented and absolutely platonic delight.

"Hello, Ahmed Lvovich," said the girl awkwardly, slowing her pace, reddening and lowering her eyes.

"Popularity, blasted popularity, monstrous fame," raced wildly through Ahmed's head.

"Well, how are the folks there? How brown you are, how you've grown, you're a grown woman," he burbled affectionately, taking her by the elbow. "Have you been back long, Ninochka?"

"I beg your pardon, Ahmed Lvovich, but I'm not Ninochka, my name is Alia, I'm Alia Tsvetkova from across the landing," lisped the girl, "And I saw your folks this morning, Lev Ustinovich and Aunti Zulphia, and Auntie Maria, and Auntie Agrippina, and Zurab took me for a ride on his motorcycle... But I haven't seen *you* for about five days, Ahmed Lvovich."

It was quite understandable that she hadn't seen him for so long. Ahmed Lvovich hadn't slept at home for five days, he had been hanging around the literary scene, playing dice, "buru," "preference," "Fool," "King," "nines,"[18] ping-pong.

"Good God, so you're Alia then, Marina's daughter!" cried Ahmed. "What has happened to you in the last five days?"

"I've no idea what's happened," replied Alia. "You can see how I've changed in the last five days. Men won't leave me alone, and your brother Zurab takes me for a ride on his motorcycle every morning. Last week he wouldn't let me near his motorcycle, he wouldn't let me lay a finger on it," she sobbed.

"There, there, there, Alia, Alia, Aliechka, Aliechka," muttered Ahmed thinking: "If Zurab gets in the way I'll wrap his motorcycle around his head!"

41

They were already in Fonarnii Lane, and destiny herself skated towards them in the form of a jolly, purposeful old man on roller skates with a perky turned-up goatee, and with a long pole, by means of which he was lighting the luminescent lamps, as if they were the gas lanterns of blessed 19th century memory, and the lanterns lit up in the sun, which, like destiny, was sitting on the chimney of No. 14., dangling its thin legs in striped stockings, smoking and winking away, and the sky was blue, like their bright blue destiny, and without a single cross, a single fighter plane, an antediluvian blissful sky with small orange corners.

"Well, have you read any of my books?" Ahmed suddenly remembered his position in society.

"Of course I have," replied Alia. "We did them in school. Brovner-Dunduchnikov, our literature teacher, analyzed your books and really ran you down, but I told him I loved you."

"What?" exclaimed Ahmed, giving Alia's elbow a tight squeeze.

"I did, that's just what I said to him. I love Ahmed Samopalov's work because it treats the problem of alienation very interestingly. And then we had a joint conference about your work with Soft Toys Factory No. 4, and all the girls at the factory said that you give an interesting treatment of alienation, and Brovner-Dunduchnikov couldn't say anything. You might say it was only because of this common interest that I went to work at Soft Toys Factory No. 4 after I left School."

For the fourth time Zurab Samopalov's motorcycle dashed by, minus its muffler, expressing its indignation with the most dreadful din. Zurab himself ran after it in utter despair, in a state of dreadful oriental jealousy.

"So you love me?" Ahmed asked insinuatingly.

"On the whole, as a writer," said Alia.

With these words, they entered the yard.

In the yard two members of the pensioners' council were sitting in the blazing sun—the former Deputy Minister Z. and Lev Ustinovich Samopalov, along with the janitor, Yurii Filippovich Isaev. They had for hours been discussing matters of literature and art.

"What I think about these abstract artists," said Yurii Filippovich, "is if you can't draw, then don't try, don't muck about. Personally I love painting and understand what's what. I used to draw myself once. I love Levitan's "Eternal Peace," now that's an outstanding water-color. Have you ever noticed, comrades, how well it portrays vast expanse? And now we are conquering that expanse, that's why the painting is so good. Now your Ivan, Lev Ustinovich, is a real abstractionist, a formalist, an unreliable element. I don't know which way Nikolaev is looking, what he's thinking about in the House Office, when there are abstractionists under his nose spreading their rotten influence on spiritually ripe young people."

"That's not true, Filipich, my Ivan is a figuratist!" objected Lev Ustinovich heatedly. "Of course, he does distort, he filters, so to speak, nature

42

through his imagination, through his fantasy, but that's not formalism, Filipich, that's a search for new forms."

"A figuratist, you say?" Yurii Filippovich was indignant. "Just recently I posed for him, and how do you suppose he depicted me? A tiny forehead, a face like a fat blister, and a blue knife drawn on from the side, now what was that in aid of?"

"You shouldn't take offense, Filipich, he was portraying your inner self, not printing a photograph."

"Then my inner self is a fat blister?"

"That's right," concurred Samopalov.

"They should be pulled out by the roots, your figuratists!" bawled Isaev. "In other days they would have been struck down at the root and that would be that. Isn't that right, Comrade Zinoliubov?"[19]

"You must have Belinsky's times in mind, Yurii Filippovich? The times of the violent Visarrion?" Z. smiled gently.

"That's right, Comrade Zinoliubov! Precisely those times!" yelled the janitor.

"Not so loud," said Z., "a bit more gently, delicately. Don't forget, Yurii Filippovich, you have to tread carefully with talent, not all at once."

"What are you ranting about, Filipich," said Samopalov. "What are you cursing for? Why should you be losing sleep over my sons? We're all going to die soon, we'll be grains of sand in the stream of the universe."

"Philosophically correct," remarked Z.

"What did I say? You think I don't agree? Of course we'll soon be grains of sand in the philosophical whirlwind of the universe," said the janitor. "That's why we should let a few of them have what for before it's too late, strike at the roots of this whole fraternity."

"Easy, easy, Yurii Filippovich, gently, gently, be more cultivated," Z. admonished his former bodyguard.

And so the pensioners sat for hours on end, discussing issues of literature and art. Every week these issues were put on the agenda of the Pensioners' committee meeting, where opinions were recorded for posterity.

Meanwhile at the bottom of the yard, the dominoes had been cast aside, and Fuchinian, Proglotilin and Axiomov were discussing questions of literature and art.

"Today I started up the machine, got a book, and I'm reading away," Vasilii Axiomov was telling the others. "Well, I'm reading this little book. Up comes the chief engineer. 'What are you reading, Axiomov?' I turned the book over and read the title. It turns out this book was written by our Ahmed Samopalov. *Look back in delight,* it was called. 'Do you like it?—' asks the chief engineer. 'Pretty powerfully put together,' I say, 'the way he rips through the full stops and commas.' 'Crap!' yells Mitia Kosholkis from his machine. 'I know the book inside out,' he yells, 'it's utter crap.' Well, then all the boys begin talking at once. Some of them are shouting: 'he's out of touch with the people!' Orthers that: 'he *is* in touch with the people!' You can't make head or tail of it. The chief engineer says: 'Opinions are divided. Let's have a discussion. Stop the machines.' We stopped the machines and began discussing Ahmed's book. Our foreman Shcherbakov spoke from the synopsis. The director came and joined in. We've got a fiery director, he's easy to get going. We argued till lunch-time."

"I've read that book," said Tolik Proglotilin. "Yesterday the controller gave it to me together with my roster. Something funny happened. I'm driving down Sadovy Street, reading. I nearly went through a red light. I look around and the sergeant is sitting in his box reading. What are you reading, Sarge? I ask. He holds it up—it's *Look back in delight*. Pretty, good, isn't it? I yell. Not bad, he says with a sour smile, you can see Bunin's influence, Robbe-Grillet's too. Just then a semi-trailer ran into the back of me. The driver got carried away with the book too. So we had a lightning reader's conference."

"I've read that book too,"said Fuchinian. "Yesterday we were repairing a cable under Crimea Bridge, so I put it in my diving-suit. I put it inside my mask, in front of my eyes, I'm repairing the cable and reading away. To tell you the truth, chaps, I was engrossed. I didn't notice that the air tube broke. Ahmed really deals well with alienation of the individual."

"That's true. What's true is true," agreed Axiomov and Proglotilin. In short it was a peaceful warm spring evening. In three windows people were playing violins, in five more—the piano. One window was transmitting a number for cornet-a-piston via the radio. Furniture movers were unhurriedly hoisting up another two pianos on pulleys, one of them dangled for the moment at third floor level and the other was crawling up to the sixth. From Maria Samopalov's window the incessant tap of a loom floated down. Agrippina had hung several new Old-French tapestries in the yard and was beating the dust of labor out of them. The artist-figuratist Ivan Samopalov displayed his latest portrait in his window, the likeness of a man-bird shot with burnished steel, product of the figuratist imagination. A still captivating Marina Tsvetkova was training a mirror on ex-Deputy Minister Zinoliubov through the wild ivy shading her window.

Well, what else? Yes, the junior footballers were neatly hitting the ground floor windows. And a furious motorcycle burst into the yard. Zurab had finally got it saddled and begun circling the yard, from time to time shooting up onto the fire-proof wall. And then the youngest Samopalov, Valentin, entered the yard in Texan jeans, flippers, and a mask, with an aqualung on his back, a transistor on his chest, a movie camera in his pocket, a guitar in his hands, playing big beat,[20] whirling a hula hoop and shooting an amateur movie through his pocket. And last of all, to everyone's surprise, Ahmed was kissing young Alia Tsvetkova under the arch, punctuating the kisses with vows of eternal love.

Doctor Zeldovich appeared under the arch. Catching sight of Ahmed kissing, he addressed him:

"Good evening, Ahmed. Good evening, Alenka. Here's a sweetie for you. You know, Ahmed, during an operation today we got to arguing about literature. We opened up an abdominal cavity and somehow got talking. Well naturally we remembered your *Look back in delight*.   The theater sister was reading it in the theater and said she was mad about it. I gave you your due too, Ahmed, although I confess I did criticize certain shortcomings. Our anesthetist was completely on your side, but the patient we were operating on said that the book might well be interesting, but that it was harmful."

"He should have been given an anesthetic," said Ahmed disapprovingly.

"Just imagine, the strange thing was he was talking under anesthetic," said Zeldovich. "Anyway, we got into a discussion and decided to conduct the operation in two stages. The patient said he would marshall his arguments together with quotes for the second stage. But I beg your pardon, I am disturbing you. All the best. Every success."

Zeldovich was about to whisk through the back entry, but he bolted straight back out because Benjamin Fedoseevich and his wife Zinaida were coming out towards him.

Popenkov had changed little over the years, he had merely acquired stability, a slight heaviness and distinct imperiousness in his gaze. Zinaida reminded one of a festive cake. The instant they appeared the radio went off on the fifth floor and into the yard ran a breathless Nikolai Nikolaevich, pulling on his braces as he ran. Apologizing for being late he joined the Popenkovs and walked after them, just a little behind.

A tense silence immediately settled on the yard, if you ignore the kisses and intermittent whispering under the arch, the clatter of the motorcycle, the cries of big beat and the lowing of the frivolous artist.

"Cut off the Samopalov's water and power for the disrespectful formalist caricature," Popenkov threw over his shoulder.

Nikolai Nikolaevich made a note of it.

"How will we manage without water and power?" gasped Lev Ustinovich. "I've got a large family, Benjamin Fedoseevich, you know yourself, it won't be possible to have a shave or a hair-cut.."

"Why kumni tari huchi cha?" shouted an enraged Popenkov.

"What?"

"Why doesn't your son want to put his talent to the service of the people?" translated Zinaida.

"Benjamin Fedoseevich, what about my application? Have you looked into it?" he was addressed by Zinoliubov.

"The Marriage to Tsvetkova?" grinned Popenkov.

"Chichi michi kholeonon," Zinaida whispered into his ear and burst out laughing.

"Quite so, marriage to Marina Nikitichna Tsvetkova," affirmed Zinoliubov. "The realization of an old dream. At one time you used to say that you had saved my life on several occasions, Benjamin Fedoseevich, and on one occasion you saved it in deed," with a sideways glance at Zinochka. "Now you have yet another opportunity."

"Kukubu with Tsvetkova? Chivilikh! Klocheki, drocheki rykl ekl!"

"Marriage to Tsvetkova? Never! In the event of insubordination we will cut off your power, water and sewerage," translated Zinaida, adding on her own account, "The sewerage, understand? Do you understand what that smells of, Comade Zinoliubov?"

"He is forgetting Russian altogether, this Steel Bird," said Ahmed to Alia.

"Oh, damn *him,*" said Alia. "Kiss me again please, Ahmed Lvovich."

The tour of the yard continued. Popenkov stopped in the center and began examining the walls and open windows of the building very carefully.

"Benjamin Fedoseevich, I meant to tell you yesterday," began Nikolaev carefully. "The fact is, Benjamin Fedoseevich, they have begun taking an interest in you."

"What? How? Where?" cried Popenkov. "Where have they begun taking an interest in me?"

"Up there," said Nikolaev significantly, indicating the sky with his thumb.

Popenkov dropped onto his belly and began crawling, twisting his head round like a guilty dog and poking out his tongue. Then he jumped up and slid around the yard on tip-toes, to tragic music that only he could hear.

"Assa," he whispered to himself, "assa, a dance to feast the eyes, oom-pa, oom-pa, oom-pa-pa!"

The whole yard followed with interest Popenkov's pirouettes, his jumps, the tragic clapping and dislocations of his hands, his fiery smiles, bows and equivocation towards the spectators, the top-like gyrations quivering to a stop.

Nikolai Nikolaevich, at first bewitched by the dance, almost expired with fright when Popenkov lay down on the asphalt. He ran to him, lay down alongside and whispered:

"Benjamin Fedoseevich, get up, my dear man! Don't torment me. They want to put you on the commission for decent living. They acknowledge your experience, Benjamin Fedoseevich, your grasp of the subject, your taste..."

Popenkov quickly jumped to his feet and shook himself.

"Why not, I'm willing!" he exclaimed. "I'll join the commission gladly. It's high time they put me on the commission, shushi marushi formazatron!"

"I'll introduce order into life," translated Zinochka.

"By the way, Nikolaev," Popenkov made a slow tour around the yard and motioned to the Zhek chief to follow him. "By the way, rufir haratari koblo bator..."

"Please, speak Russian," begged Nikolaev.

"It's time you understood," said Popenkov in irritation. "Very well. Well, it's like this. Tomorrow my relatives want to remodel the roof, make a hatch so I can get straight out of the lift onto the roof."

"What for?" asked Nikolaev in panic.

"What do you mean, what for? You know I occasionally use the lift to... to go for a ride. Sometimes I feel like having a sit on the roof."

"Of course I understand that," said Nikolaev, "I understand your desire, but the fact is, Benjamin Fedoseevich, that our building is in a very precarious state, almost a state of collapse. The building inspector gave me a report on it today, and I am afraid that an opening in the roof may finally shatter the foundations."

"Rubbish. Panic-mongering. It's high time the building inspector passed on to the next world," said Popenkov. "In short, the discussion is closed. Tomorrow my relatives make the hatch."

Suddenly a cry resounded over the yard.

"Citizens!"

And everybody looked up to see the building inspector standing on the fifth floor ledge. He was waving his hands to balance himself, like a large butterfly beating against an invisible window.

"Citizens!" he cried. "This is the third night I am unable to sleep, I can't eat, my teeth have worked loose, my strength is ebbing away... Citizens, our building is in a state of collapse! Take a look, can't you see it has become like the Italian tower in the city of Pisa? The foundations can't hold for more than a week. He told me that himself! Citizens, urgent measures are called for! Citizens, all my reports just get shelved!"

To stop himself falling the building inspector was making circular movements with his arms, but he didn't look like a bird, rather like an unfortunate butterfly, because he was wearing his wife's vast floral dressing gown, from under which his bare legs poked out.

Nobody noticed how Popenkov appeared on the ledge, they only saw him quickly sliding towards the building inspector.

"Citizens!" called the building inspector for the last time and was just then seized in the steel grasp of Popenkov, quick as a wink crushing the bold fabric of the dressing gown.

"Did you see the madman?" barked Popenkov to those below, scattering bolts of lightning from his burning eyes, dragging the limp body of the building inspector. "Citizens, he is mad! Nikulu chikulu gram, ous, suo!"

"There is no place in civilized life for madmen and panic-merchants!" cried Zinaida.

Popenkov clambered up the water pipe with the speed of light with the building inspector's body, clattered across the roof and disappeared through the dormer window.

The tenants, stunned and aroused, crowded round Nikolai Nikolaevich. What was it all about? What had happened? Was there any reason to evacuate? What had set the building inspector off?

"Citizens, remain calm, remain in your places," Nikolaev admonished them. "Of course there are certain grounds for concern, the foundations are in a pretty tense position, I talked to him, too, but disaster is projected only in the long range, somewhere at the end of the quarter, no sooner. Citizens, tomorrow I go to the regional housing office[21] to do battle, I shall return either on my shield, or with my shield. I would like your thoughts and hearts to be with me at that moment."

"What was that we heard, Nikolai Nikolaevich?" shouted Proglotilin. "Is Popenkov intending to smash the roof?"

"That way we won't make it to the end of the quarter, the shanty will collapse!" screamed Axiomov.

Fuchinian, his muscles flexed, jumped into the center of the circle.

"Fuchinian is here!" he shouted. "Everybody knows me—I am here! I will not permit it. The roof shall be whole! And we shall break the Steel Bird's wings. Vaska, Tolik, am I talking sense?"

"We'll carve the Steel Bird up into hair combs!" cried Vaska.

The tenants were in an uproar.

"Nikulu chikulu gram, ous, suo!" cried Zinaida Popenkova in a panic. "Nikolai Nikolaevich, what is going on? Crowd hysteria?"

"Citizens, quiet! Citizens, order," admonished Nikolaev. "The removal of part of the roof does not threaten instant disaster. Citizens, you must understand Benjamin Fedoseevich, enter into his position. Citizens, quiet. Citizens, let's talk it over."

But the crowd grew even noisier, aroused by the belligerent and assertive appearance of Fuchinian.

"It's all Popenkov's fault!" people shouted.

"He shakes the building in the most incredible fashion all night!"

"Evict him!"

"Open up the front entrance!"

"We're sick of it!"

"Away with the Steel Bird!"

"Citizens, I'll try to see Benjamin Fedoseevich on this matter," entreated Nikolaev. Nobody recognized the stern administrator, "I'll try to beat him down. Citizens, I practically promise that the roof will remain whole."

The sun set, the shadows thickened, but the tenants still did not disperse and in the buzzing crowd there was the flash of matches, the flicker of cigarette-lighter flames, cigarettes and eyes, the whole dark yard was an uneasy volatile flicker. Fuchinian, Proglotilin and Axiomov climbed up onto the roof via the fire escape. They had resolved to save it by means of their vigilant roster and readiness for any kind of battle, even to the death. The

48

young Samopalovs, Zurab and Valentin, blockaded the back entrance. Ahmed and Alia Tsvetkova were called on to keep watch in the garden. Comrade Zinoliubov took up an observation post in Tsvetkova's apartment. Maria Samopalov and Agrippina declared a strike and went to bed for the first time in eighteen years. Lev Ustinovich got his cut-throat ready and armed Zulphia with the scissors. In a word, all the tenants did what they could in the collective protest against Popenkov's arbitrariness.

The night passed uneasily, people slept in bursts, kissed feverishly, smoked, and smoked, some of them drank, others made ready to evacuate, nobody knew what morning would bring.

Fuchinian, Proglotilin and Axiomov sat on the ridge of the roof, knocking over a bottle, they were elated, remembering by-gone battles on the vast expanse between the Volga and the Spree. Several times it seemed to them that a dark body passed over them with a quiet reactive whistle, blocking out the stars, and then they regretted not having anti-aircraft artillery at their disposal.

The sun rose high, dragged itself out of the city's ravines, and hung over Moscow. The roof immediately got scorching hot.

At eight o'clock in the morning the self-defense brigade got the feeling there was someone below them in the attic. They quickly assumed their battle positions, tensed themselves, ready. Out of the dormer windows crawled Popenkov's relatives—relative Koka, relative Goga and relative Dmitrii. They were armed with axes, hand saws and hammers.

"Hello, lads! Sun-baking?" said relative Dmitrii to the self-defense brigade. "We are getting an early start to work."

"Now then boys, back down without any fuss!" commanded Fuchinian and advanced.

"Look Mitia," said relative Goga, looking down at the pavement, "it's a big drop. If anyone should accidentally get pushed, he'd be squashed flat as a pancake! What do you think?"

"He'd be like jelly," suggested relative Koka sadly.

"Liquid," relative Dmitrii summed up and began sawing the roof.

"Now we'll test out what would happen," said the self-defense brigade and rolled up its sleeves. The roof swelled and cracked under their first heavy step.

The relatives, abandoning their jests, also flexed their muscles and advanced. Their tattoed muscles swelled up to such an extent it seemed as though this was not three men moving, but a series of terrifying balloons; in a flick the narrow strings of pocket knives leaped out of their fists; bared gold teeth reflected the sun; so did signet-rings, bracelets, pendants, earrings and rings. In the blazing light of the morning sun bright, joyous death advanced on the self-defense brigade in foreign waist-coats and jack boots.

"Vaska, you get the one on the right! Tolik, the one on the left! And I'll get Goga the bad!" yelled Fuchinian and dashed forward.

There began the self-defense without arms. The relatives' Argentinian pocket knives swished through the air, but collected nothing. Fuchinian, Proglotilin and Axiomov, remembering their street fighting days, pulled at the relatives' legs and punched them on the noses. The relatives' tears and snot rose like fountains to the blue sky, but nevertheless knives are knives, and blood flowed, and they drove our lads to the edge of the roof.

Suddenly there was a crash to the rear of the relatives. The four Samopalov brothers were crawling along the roof, the writer, the artist, the motorcyclist and big beat.

"Retreat!" ordered relative Dmitrii and jumped off first. Relative Koka and relative Goga flung themselves off after him.

The self-defense brigade leaned over in horror, imagining the conversion of these powerful organisms into a pancake, jelly and liquid respectively. However, the relatives landed unharmed and took to their heels in different directions.

At eight hours thirty minutes the first crack appeared on the northern side of the building. Maria Samopalova leaned out through the crack and shouted to the whole of Fonarnii Lane:

"Fight, good people!"

At eight hours forty-five minutes all the inhabitants of No. 14 had gathered by the front entrance, as had the sympathetic occupants of neighboring buildings. Domestic animals, cats, Pomeranians, fox-terriers, dogs jumped out the windows onto the pavement. Siskins, canaries and parrots, that had been released from their cages, soared above the crowd. The emerald water of aquariums ran out of the water pipes, carrying veiltails, redfins and loaches. Shutters flapped, draughts blew through empty apartments, overturning pots of everlastings. There were groaning sounds. The tenants sighed over abandoned possessions, over everyday articles and expensive and cherished knick-knacks.

The building inspector bustled about in the crowd in his wife's billowing dressing-gown.

"Citizens!" he cried. "I have done some calculations. The building can hold another twenty-seven minutes. It's still possible to save a few things! We only need to open up the front entrance! Clean out the vestibule!"

"Open the front entrance!"

"Break down the doors!"

"Bugger them!"

"But the suite, my good fellows, we've just bought it! We saved seven years for it, we hardly ate or drank!"

"Break it down!"

The doors were already bending under the force of the crowd, but inside Popenkov was calmly tying his tie, pinning a diamond into it, polishing his nails and getting into his iron boots.

"You'll think of something, won't you?" Zinaida was dashing about, bouncing like a push-ball. "You'll find a way out, my darling, my love, mankind's genius, my gigantic steel bird?? Zhuzho zhirnava zhuko zhuro?"

"Noki murloki kvakl chitazu!" replied Popenkov calmly. "Are you afraid of this crowd, my Lorelia? This pitiful crowd, these lice. Ten minutes work for a cyclone. Filio drong chiriolan!"

And wrenching out all the nails in one go, he flung open the door and stood in front of the tenants.

Silence fell. The building inspector, remembering yesterday's treatment, hid in the crowd.

"What are you all here for? What do you want?" asked Popenkov, his arms folded on his breast.

"We want to throw you out, Steel Bird," replied the bandaged and altogether heroic Fuchinian.

"Throw me out?" grinned Popenkov. "Now hear out my conditions." And his eyes kindled with a distant secret and terrifying fire, sounds like a jet's exhaust issued from his throat. "Drong haleoti fyng, syng! Zhofrys hi lasr furi talot..."

"We don't understand your language!" cried voices from the crowd. "Leave, comrade, while you still can!"

Popenkov switched to Russian with a visible effort.

"These are my conditions. Everybody returns to his apartment, is to get a loom, the looms will be here by evening and... to work! Is that understood? Naturally some sacrifices will have to be made. Some of you will be subjected to chiziolastrofitation. Chuchukhu, klocheki, drocheki?"

"If you want to take us on a 'get it—got it' basis," said Fuchinian "then we want to take you on a 'get it—got it' basis. Got it?"

He advanced again, and they all advanced, and Popenkov suddenly actually realized that he was going to come off worst: the circle tightened, and the damned tin awning hung directly over him. Of course it would be possible to break through it, but in that instant somebody would grab him by his iron legs. There was practically no way out, and he almost burst into tragic laughter inside at such a ludicrous end to his great cause.

At one point there was suddenly complete silence, and in this instant the staccato clatter of approaching hooves reached them. The sound of hooves in Moscow is an out-of-the-ordinary occurrence, so they all turned round and saw a galloping white horse at the end of Fonarnii lane, and on it Nikolai Nikolaevich Nikolaev, head of ZhEK. It was nine hours fifteen minutes, Nikolaev was returning from the regional housing commission with his shield, and to boot on a white horse with a wide breast, round powerful croup, cunning pink eyes, a fringe fluttering like a holiday flag. Galloping unhurriedly, the horse recalled to mind an old-time caravelle, merrily sailing across a fresh sea beneath billowing white sails.

Drawing near and seeing the crowd at the entrance, the wide-open windows and branched cracks in the walls, Nikolai Nikolaevich pulled out from under his shirt a cornet-a-piston which glittered in the sun, and raised it to his lips.

"Dear citizens, sisters and brothers!" sang the cornet triumphantly. "'The regional housing commission has allotted us a building! It's eight stories high, practically all glass, practically all plastic, I assure you! In a fabulous experimental area, a palace being erected for all to admire! Blue bathrooms, adjacent lavatories and waste disposal units await you! A solarium each, a dendrarium each, a dining-room each, a swimming pool each! Make ready, citizens, sisters and brothers, we are going to trot off towards happiness in a piebald caravan!"

"Hoorah!" the tenants all shouted, and, forgetting Popenkov, they dashed into their disintegrating dwelling for their belongings. Popenkov managed to dive into the lift.

At nine hours thirty minutes a wagon train, sent by the regional housing commission, drew up at the entrance. They were shaggy lively ponies, perkily chewing on their figured bits, pounding the asphalt with their strong little hooves. They were harnessed into small, but capacious carts, decorated with carved folk motifs.

At nine hours thirty nine minutes the loading of goods and chattels was completed and the wagon train trotted cheerfully off down Fonarnii Lane. The hooves clattered, the little bells rang, colored ribbons and flags fluttered, harmonicas, guitars, transistors were playing, and at the head rode Nikolai Nikolaevich on a white horse with his cornet-a-piston. The long caravan wound through Moscow streets, headed for a new life, to New Cheriomukhy.[22]

At nine hours fourty four minutes No. 14 collapsed. When the brick dust had cleared the few who had stayed behind in Fonarnii Lane saw that only the lift shaft rose above the ruins. Soon after, the lift began ascending out of its depths. In it stood a completely withdrawn Benjamin Fedoseevich Popenkov. When the lift stopped at the top of its shaft, Popenkov opened the door, squatted on his haunches and froze, fixing his lifeless gaze on the boundless expanse. Nobody knows what he was thinking or what he saw in the distance. Nor is it certain whether he saw Zinaida bouncing like a push-ball along Fonarnii Lane.

For long months he sat on the carcass of the lift shaft quite motionless, like one of the chimera of Paris' Notre Dame cathedral.

One day bull-dozers appeared in Fonarnii Lane. Hearing the officious rumbling of their engines, Popenkov roused himself, jumped and flew off over Moscow, over the lanes of Arbat, the blue saucer of Moscow's swimming pool, the big Kamennyi bridge... Two dark trails stretched out behind him. Then the wind dispersed them.

The End.

The Steel Bird's farewell monologue.

Rurrro kalitto Zhiza Chuiza Drong! Chivilikh zhifafa koblo urazzo! Rykl, ekl, filimocha absterchurare? Fylo sylo ylar urar!

Shur yramtura y, y, y! Zhastry chastry gastry nefol! Nefol foliadavr logi zhu-zhu? Uzh zhu ruzh zhur oruzh zhuro oleozhar! Razha!

Faga!

Lirri-otul!

Chivilokh zuzamaza azam ula lu? Luzi urozi klockek tupak! Z fftshch! Zhmin percator sapala! Sa! Pa! La! Al! Spl! Vspyl sevel fuk zhuraru! Refo yarom filioram, otskiuda siplstvo any yna! Any, yna, any, yna, any yna, any! Pshpyl, pshpyl, pshpyl—vzhif, vzhif karakatal!

Chorus

and notwithstanding the flowers bloom and childhood lives on in every head and old age asks for a hand some depart thereto with a kiss and merge in passion in order to meet in heaven and butter on a fresh bun and berries in the morning dew in a jumble of shining dotted lines where can one find a cunning little face with berries on its lips in the streets the sentries evoke love with a guitarrr frost on the pavement morning voices promise us milk in the latest newspaper the usual reports of the doings of dolphins younger brothers in the light surface layers of the ocean tend for us shoals of tasty and delicate fish and each dreams of a ticket on an ordinary thousand-seater airplane to fly over the ocean with a greeting for the marine shepherds and later return to their old folk to their cunning little kids falls asleep so as to gallop on his creaky wooden horse through the forest across the clearings in the gleam of the spring morning of the spring summer and the autumnal winter of the summer spring and the wintry autumn of the wintry summer and the summery winter of the wintery spring and the summery autumn of the spring winter and the autumnal summer.

Translated by Rae Slonek

July 65

Kalda farm.

1. In Russian Fonar means a lamp.

2. (small) fish.

3. Manager of ZhEK, the local housing office which is reponsible for maintenance and oversight of a number of blocks of flats, perhaps a whole street or square.

4. A central district of Moscow.

5. From one of the songs of the Civil War.

6. Raikom: the Regional Party Office, the highest instrument of local government.

7. Each Soviet citizen is entitled to a minimum amount of living space, currently 9 square meters for the head of a family, or single tenant, and 6 square meters for every additional member of the family.

8. Based on 'popa,' euphemism for 'arse.'

9. International Organization to aid fighters for the Revolution, founded in 1922 at the 21st Communist International Congress.

10. Voroshilov gunner. Voroshilov, a cavalry commander during the Revolution, was People's Commissar for Defense 1925-1934. With the militarization of sport in the thirties senior school students, tertiary students and young workers learned to shoot in Voroshilov Shooting Clubs. The "Voroshilov gunner" badge was awarded to those who attained a certain score in shooting competitions.

11. The K.G.B.

12. The Russian word for 'prick.'

13. Each citizen must obtain a residence permit and have the address stamped in his passport before taking up residence in a flat.

14. Famous war-time poem by K. Simonov.

15. Reference to Turgenev's well-known poem in prose on the Russian language.

16. The smallest Soviet-made sedan (a four-seater).

17. One of the fashionable young writers of the sixties, depicting positive Soviet youth. Also notable for innovative style, (collage), using colloquial language and drawing on newspaper cuttings, excerpts from radio broadcasts, etc.

18. Card-games.

19. Means 'Zina-lover.'

20. In English in the original.

21. The office responsible for issuing accommodation, and to which the ZhEK office is subordinate.

22. New area of Moscow with intensive housing development schemes.

VICTORY — A STORY WITH EXAGGERATIONS

In a compartment of an express train a grandmaster was playing chess with a chance companion.

The man had recognized the grandmaster immediately when the grandmaster had entered the compartment and he was immediately consumed by an unthinkable desire for an unthinkable victory over the grandmaster. "So what," he thought, casting sly knowing glances at the grandmaster, "so what, he's just a runt, big deal."

The grandmaster understood immediately that he was recognized and sadly resigned himself: can't avoid at least two games. He immediately recognized the man's type. He had often seen the hard, pink foreheads of people like that through the windows of the Chess club on Gogol Square.

Once the train was moving, the grandmaster's companion stretched with an expression of naive cunning and asked indifferently:

"How about a little game of chess, comrade?"

"Oh, I suppose so," the grandmaster muttered.

The man stuck his head out of the compartment, called the conductress, a chess set appeared, he grabbed it with an eagerness that belied indifference, scattered the pieces, selected two pawns, clenched them in his fists and showed the fists to the grandmaster. On the bulge between the thumb and the index finger of his left hand there was a tatoo: "G.O."

"Left," said the grandmaster and cringed slightly, imagining blows from these fists, either the left or the right.

He drew white.

"We've got to kill time, right?... you can't beat a game of chess on a trip," G.O. chattered as he arranged the chessmen.

They quickly played the Northern Gambit, then everything became confused. The grandmaster looked at the board attentively making small, insignificant moves. Several times, all the possible checkmate moves of the queen appeared like lightning before his eye, but he extinguished these flashes by lowering his eyelids slightly and submitting to the weak inner drone of an irritating, plaintive note, like the buzz of a mosquito.

"Khas-Bulat, you are bold, but how poor is your hut..." G.O. hummed tunelessly on the same note.

The grandmaster was the embodiment of neatness, the embodiment of simplicity of dress and manner, so characteristic of insecure and vulnerable people. He was young, he wore a gray suit, a white shirt and a simple tie. No one but the grandmaster himself knew that his simple ties bore the label "House of Dior." This small secret had always been, somehow, a source of comfort and warmth for the young, reticent grandmaster. His glasses too, had served him often, hiding the uncertainty and shyness of his glance from strangers. He regretted his lips which had the habit of stretching into pitiable little smiles or quivers. He would gladly cover them from the eyes of strangers but this, alas, was not accepted in society as yet.

G.O.'s playing shocked and hurt the grandmaster. The pieces on the left flank were crowded together forming a bundle of cabalistic charlatan symbols. The whole left flank stank of the bathroom and chlorine, of the sour smell of barracks and wet kitchen rags, with a whiff of the early childhood smells of castor oil and diarrhea.

"You are the grandmaster So-and-So, right?" G.O. asked.

"Yes," confirmed the grandmaster.

"Ho, ho, ho, what a coincidence!"

"What coincidence? What coincidence is he talking about? This is just incredible! How could this have happened? I refuse, accept my refusal," the grandmaster thought quickly in panic; then he guessed what was the matter and smiled.

"Yes, of course, of course."

"Here you are, a grandmaster, and I fork your rook and queen," said G.O. He raised his hand. The knight-provocateur hung above the board.

"Fork in the behind," thought the grandmaster, "Great little fork! Grandfather had his own fork and nobody was allowed to use it. Ownership. Personal fork, spoon and knife and a personal phial for phlegm. Also remember the 'lyre-bird' coat, the heavy coat of 'lyre-bird' fur, it used to hang at the entrance; grandfather hardly ever went out on the street. A fork on grandma and grandpa. It's a shame to lose the old folks."

While the knight hung over the board, the phosphorescent lines and dots of the possible pre-checkmate victims and raids flashed again before the grandmaster's eyes. Alas, the dirty-lilac flannel sticking out on the knight's neck was so convincing, that the grandmaster shrugged his shoulders.

"Giving away the rook?" asked G.O.

"What's one to do?"

"Sacrificing the rook for the attack, right?" asked G.O., still hesitating to place his knight on the desired square.

"Simply saving the queen," muttered the grandmaster.

"You're not baiting me, are you?"

"Oh, no, you are a strong player."

G.O. executed his cherished "fork." The grandmaster hid the queen in a quiet corner behind the terrace, behind the semi-crumbled stone terrace with the slightly rotted carved little pillars, with a pungent smell of rotting maple leaves here in the fall. Here, one can sit it out squatting comfortably. It's nice here; in any case, the ego does not suffer. He got up for a moment, peeked from the terrace and noticed that G.O. had removed the rook.

The intrusion of the black knight into a senseless crowd on the left flank and his occupation of (b-4), in any case, demanded further thought.

The grandmaster understood that in this variant, on this green spring evening, the myths of youth would not suffice. It is all true, there are jolly fools wandering in the world—sailor Billy, cowboy Harry, the beautiful Mary and Nelly, and the brigantine is raising its sails; but there comes a moment when one feels the dangerous and real proximity of the black knight in square (b-4). Ahead was the struggle—complicated, intricate, entrancing and calculating. Ahead was life.

The grandmaster took a pawn, got out a handkerchief and blew his nose. The few moments of complete solitude, when both lips and nose were hidden by the handkerchief, put him in a banal-philosophical mood. "So you keep striving for something," he thought, "and what then? All your life you are striving for something; victory comes but it does not bring happiness. Take, for example, the city of Hong Kong. It is distant and quite mysterious, but I have already been there. I have already been everywhere."

The loss of a pawn did not upset G.O. much; after all, he had just won a rook. He responded to the grandmaster by the move of the queen, which brought on heartburn and a sudden attack of migraine.

The grandmaster surmised that there were still some joys in store for him. For example, the joy of the prolonged moves of the bishop along the whole diagonal. Dragging the bishop lightly across the board could substitute, to a degree, for a headlong glide in a skiff along the sunlit and slightly stagnant water of a Moscow pond, from light to shade, from shade to light. The grandmaster felt an overwhelming, passionate desire to conquer square (h-8), that square, that mound of love, with transparent grasshoppers hanging above it.

"That was clever, the way you got my rook and I missed it," said G.O. in a bass voice. Only the last word betrayed his irritation.

"Forgive me," the grandmaster said quietly, "perhaps you should return the moves?"

"No-no, no favors, I beg of you," said G.O.

"I will give you my sword, and my horse, and my gun..." G.O. began to hum, deep in considerations of strategy.

The tempestuous summer holiday of love in the field failed to please and, at the same time, disturbed the grandmaster. He felt that the externally logical but internally absurd forces would accumulate in the center very soon. As before, he would hear cacophony and the smell of chlorine as in that damned memory of the distant corridors on the left flank.

"I wonder: why are all the chess-players Jewish?" G.O. asked.

"Why all?" said the grandmaster, "for example, I am not Jewish."

"Really?" said G.O. with surprise and added: "Please, don't think that I mean anything. I have no prejudices on this account. Just curious."

"Well, take you, for example, you are not Jewish."

"How could I be?" muttered G.O., sinking back into his secret plans.

"If I do this, he'll do that. If I take one here, he'll take one there, then I go here, he responds like this... Anyway, I'll finish him off, I'll break him down, anyway. Big deal, grandmaster-cheatmaster, your muscle still can't match mine. I know your championships: prearranged. I'll squash you anyway, let your nose bleed."

"Well, I've lost quality," he said to the grandmaster, "but that's O.K., it isn't evening yet."

He began the attack in the center and of course, as expected, the center immediately turned into an arena of senseless and terrible actions. This was non-love, non-meeting, non-hope, non-greeting, non-life. The chills of flu and, again, the yellow snow, the post-war discomfort, the itching all over the body. In the center, the black queen kept croaking like a raven in love, the raven love and, besides, the neighbors were scraping a tin bowl with a knife. Nothing proved the senselessness and the elusiveness of life as definitely as this center position. It was time to end the game.

"No," the grandmaster thought, "there is still something besides this." He put on a large cassette of Bach's piano pieces, calming his heart with sound, pure and even, like the splashing of waves. Then he went out of the summer cottage and down to the sea. The pines were rustling above him and there was a slippery springy floor of pine needles under his feet.

Remembering and imitating the sea, he began to analyze the position, to harmonize it. His soul suddenly felt pure and light. Logically, like the Bach coda, came the checkmate to the black. A dim and beautiful light lit the opaque position, now complete, like an egg. The grandmaster looked at G.O. He was silent, bull-like, staring into the furthest positions of the grandmaster. He did not notice the checkmate to his king. The grandmaster was silent for fear of destroying the magic of the moment.

"Check," said G.O. quietly and carefully, moving his knight. He could barely contain his inner bellow.

... The grandmaster let out a scream and began to run. After him, stamping and whistling, ran the landlord of the summer house, the coachman Eurypides and Nina Kuzminichna. Ahead of them all, catching up with the grandmaster, bounded the unleased dog, Duskie.

"Check," repeated G.O., moving his knight and swallowing air with painful lust.

... The grandmaster was being led along a passage in the midst of a silenced crowd. Someone was following him, barely touching his back with some hard object. A man in a black overcoat with S.S. insignia on the lapels was waiting for him in front. One step-half-a-second, another step-a second, another step-two... Steps leading upward. Why upward? Such things ought to be done in a ditch. One must be brave. Must one? How much time does it take to put a stinking burlap sack over one's head. Then, it got completely dark and difficult to breathe, and only somewhere very far off an orchestra was playing with bravura "Khas-Bulat, the Bold."

"Checkmate," G.O. shrieked like a copper horn.

"So, you see," muttered the grandmaster, "congratulations!"

"Ugh, ugh, umph, I'm all sweated up, just incredible, it happened, god damn it! Incredible, slapping a checkmate on a grandmaster! Incredible, but a fact!" G.O. broke out laughing. "I'm quite a guy!" He patted himself jokingly on the head. "Oh, you grandmaster, my dear grandmaster," he buzzed, putting his hands on the grandmaster's shoulders and squeezing them with familiarity, "my dear young man... The poor little nerves gave out, right? Admit it!"

"Yes, yes, I broke down," the grandmaster confirmed hurriedly.

G.O. swept the pieces off the board with a wide free gesture. The board was old and cracked, the polished coating was lost in places exposing yellow tired old wood, with fragments of round stains left long ago, here and there, by glasses of railroad tea.

The grandmaster stared at the empty board, at the sixty-four absolutely dispassionate squares which were capable of accommodating not only his personal life, but an infinite number of lives. And this endless pattern of light and dark squares filled him with adoration and quiet joy. "It seems," he thought, "that I haven't committed any really treacherous acts in my life."

"Suppose I were to tell about this, nobody would believe me," G.O. sighed.

"But why shouldn't they? What's so extraordinary about this? You are a strong player with will power."

"No one will believe it," G.O. said. "They will say I am lying. What proof have I got?"

"Allow me," said the grandmaster, somewhat hurt, staring at the hard, pink forehead of G.O. "I will give you convincing proof. I knew that I would meet you."

He opened his briefcase and took out a gold medal as large as his hand. An inscription was engraved beautifully upon it: "The bearer of this defeated me at chess. Grandmaster So-and-So."

"It remains only to add the date." He removed a set of tools from his briefcase and engraved the date, also beautifully, in the corner of the medal. "This is pure gold," he said, presenting the medal.

"You don't mean it?" G.O. asked.

"Absolutely pure gold," repeated the grandmaster. "I ordered a lot of these medals and I shall replenish my stock continually."

Translated by Greta Slobin

HALFWAY TO THE MOON

"Can I bring you some coffee?"

"Sure."

"Turkish?"

"Huh?"

"Turkish coffee," the waitress sang out ceremoniously and floated off between the tables.

"Forget it, she's nothing special," Kirpichenko consoled himself as he watched her go.

"Forget it," he thought, grimacing from a headache. "Fifty minutes left. Any second now they'll announce my flight, and it'll be like I'd never been in this town. I've had it with this town anyway. Not much of a place. It's not Moscow. Maybe some even like it, but personally I can't say much for it. Well, screw it. Maybe another time it will appeal to me."

Yesterday there'd been some heavy drinking going on. Not so much that anyone was out on his ear, but pretty close to it. Yesterday, the day before, and the day before that. All because of that bastard Banin and his dear little sister. Boy, they really soaked you for your hard-earned rubles.

Kirpichenko had run into Banin three days ago at the Yuzhny Airport.[1] He hadn't even known that their vacations coincided. In general, he had very little to do with Banin. At the forestry complex they were always making a great fuss over him, and crying all the time: "Banin-Banin! Be like Banin." But Valeri Kirpichenko didn't pay him any special attention. Naturally, he knew the name and the face was familiar—Banin, the electrician—but by and large he wasn't the kind of guy you would notice, in spite of all the hoopla that was raised around him on holidays.

"That's the way, Banin! Now look, that's Banin for you."

There were fellows at the forestry complex who worked as well as Banin, and perhaps even gave him a run for his money on all counts. But, you know, the administration is always like that—when they latch on to a man, they make a big fuss over him. There's no point in envying these fellows, you have to pity them. There was a certain Sinitsyn in Bayukly,[2] who, like Kirpichenko, also ran a small locomotive. Reporters took a fancy to him and made a terrible fuss over him. At first the fellow collected newspaper clippings, but later he couldn't stand it any more and took off for Okha.[3] But Banin didn't mind; he put up with it. He walked around so neat and clean, so spiffy. Such an ordinary sort of fellow, whom you hardly noticed or heard a peep out of.

Last spring two hundred young girls were brought from the mainland to the fish cannery—seasonal workers whose job it was to clean fish. The fellows were getting ready to visit them; they were shrieking, making noise...

They look and there sits Banin in the back, in a corner, so quiet that you didn't notice him or hear a peep out of him.

"Say, Banin,...."

At the Yuzhny Airport Banin threw himself at Kirpichenko as if the latter were his best friend. Literally choking with joy, he shouted loudly that he was terribly happy, that he had a sister in Khabarovsk,[4] and that she had girl friends—great gals. When he began to describe all this in great detail, Kirpichenko grew dizzy. From the time the young girls had left the fish cannery, Kirpichenko had seen only two women the whole winter, or to be more precise, two old crocodiles—the timekeeper and the cook.

"Oh, you, Banin-Banin."

On the plane he kept shouting to the pilots: "Hey, pilots, throw on more coal!" Such a clown—you simply couldn't recognize him as the same fellow.

"I've cast more than a few favors your way, Banin!"

The house in which Banin's sister lived barely peeked out from behind the snowdrifts. The humpbacked street had evidently been cleaned by special machines, but the piles of snow had not been cleared away and almost hid the tiny houses from view; it was as if the tiny houses lay in a trench. Blue puffs of smoke hovered in the crisp frosty air above the chimneys, and antennas and poles for starling boxes stuck out at different angles. It was a perfect village street. It was even difficult to believe that on the hill a trolley bus ran along the avenue.

Kirpichenko went a little wild even at the airport when he saw a long stream of cars with green lights and the glass wall of a restaurant, through whose frosty patterns a band playing subdued jazz could be made out. He really let himself go at a food store on the main street of town. He kept pulling out green fifty-ruble bills, laughing loudly, stuffing bottles into his pockets and scooping up canned goods. An overjoyed Banin laughed even harder than Kirpichenko, and simply kept grabbing cheeses and cans. Later he entered into negotiations with the department manager and managed to get a whole ring of sausage. Banin and Kirpichenko drove up to the house in a taxi filled to overflowing with various foods and bottles of Chechen-Ingush cognac. All in all, they didn't come to his sister empty-handed.

Kirpichenko entered the room wearing a shaggy fur hat which almost touched the ceiling. He put the goods down on the bed, which was covered with a white piqué coverlet, straightened up, and immediately caught sight of his thin, red, cross-looking face in the mirror.

Lariska, Banin's sister, such a plumpish little nurse in appearance, was already unbuttoning his overcoat, repeating: "Any friend of my brother's is a friend of mine." Then she put on her overcoat and boots and clumped off somewhere.

Banin wielded the corkscrew and knife while Kirpichenko looked around. The room was nicely furnished. There was a sideboard with a mirror, a chest of drawers, and a radio-phonograph. Above the chest hung a pre-war portrait of Voroshilov,[5] without epaulets and with his marshal's stars on the lapels; alongside hung a framed citation: "To an outstanding marksman of the Internal Security Troops for his achievements in combat and political training.--The Administration of the North-Eastern Corrective Labor Camps."

"That's dad's citation," explained Banin.

"So your dad was a labor camp guard?"

"Was, but he split," sighed Banin. "Died."

However, he wasn't sad for long. He began to play old, familiar records—"Rio-Rita" and "The Black Sea Seagull." But one was some sort of French record—three guys singing in harmony and so wonderfully, as if they had been around the whole wide world and seen such things as you'll never ever see.

Lariska walked in with a girl friend named Toma. Lariska began to clear and set the table; she kept running back and forth to the kitchen, carrying some sort of pickles and mushrooms. In the meantime, Toma sat in a corner with her hands on her lap, not budging an inch. Kirpichenko did not know how far he would get with her and tried not to look at her. If he so much as looked at her, he felt dizzy.

"Our hands have froze, our feet are ice; a nip or two would sure be nice!" Banin exclaimed with nervous gaiety. "Please come to the table, ladies and gentlemen."

"I can see I didn't get you enough cigarettes, Banin."

Kirpichenko was smoking long cigarettes called "Forty Years of the Soviet Ukraine," smoking and blowing smoke rings. Lariska was laughing loudly and threading them on her little finger. It was stuffy in the low-ceilinged room. Kirpichenko's feet had gotten damp in his felt boots and steam was probably rising from them. Banin was dancing with Toma. The latter hadn't said a word all evening. Banin was whispering something to her, and she was smiling wryly with her tight-lipped mouth. The girl was well-built; pink underwear showed through her nylon blouse. The walls, Voroshilov's portrait, and the little elephants on the dresser were dissolving in dark orange circles, and the smoke rings which he had blown bobbed up and down. Lariska's finger was tracing some kind of unintelligible signs in the air.

Banin and Toma went off to another room. The spring lock quietly clicked behind them.

"Ha-ha-ha," Lariska laughed loudly. "Why weren't you dancing, Valeri? You should have danced."

The record ended, and it grew quiet. Lariska was looking at him, wrinkling her slanting brown eyes. From the next room stifled squealing could be heard.

"From you, Valeri, all's production and no seduction," giggled Lariska. Kirpichenko suddenly saw that she was almost thirty and that she had been around.

She walked up to him and whispered, "Let's go dance."

"But I'm in my felt boots," he said.

"So what, let's go."

He got up. She put on a record and, in a room smelling of tomatoes and Chechen-Ingush cognac, three French fellows began to sing in harmony about how they had been around the whole wide world and had seen such things as you'd never have a chance to see.

"Only not that one," Kirpichenko said hoarsely.

"Why not?" Lariska retorted loudly. "It's a great record. It has real style."

She began to twirl around the room. Her skirt danced about her legs. Kirpichenko took off the record and put on "Rio-Rita." He then strode over to Lariska and grabbed her by the shoulders.

It always seems, when fingers are stroking your neck in the dark, that these are fingers of the moon, no matter what cheap girl is lying next to you... it's all the same afterwards, when fingers are touching your neck... you ought to slap her hands, but it seems that these are the fingers of the moon, who is herself high up in the sky, resembling a runny egg-yolk through the frosty glass... but this never happens, and don't kid yourself that it will ever happen... you're already twenty-nine and all the good and bad times, your whole fantastically beautiful life with its intense and dull moments, no matter what your life has been like, when fingers stroke your neck in the dark, it seems that...

"What year were you born?" asked the woman.

"In '32."

"So you're a driver."

"Uhuh."

"Earn a lot?"

Valeri lit a match and saw her round face with its slanting brown eyes.

"And what's it to you?" he muttered gruffly and lit up.

In the morning Banin shuffled around in quilted underwear. He squeezed the juice from some pickles into a glass and threw their shrivelled little bodies onto a dish. Toma sat in a corner, neat and quiet, just like yesterday. After breakfast she and Lariska went off to work.

"We had a proper good time, didn't we, eh, Valeri?" Banin laughed ingratiatingly. "Well, all right, let's go to the movies."

They saw three films in a row, and afterwards stopped at the food store, where Kirpichenko again really let himself go. He kept pulling out red bills and dumping cheeses and canned goods into Banin's arms.

And so it went for three days and three nights, but this morning, when the girls had left, Banin suddenly said:

"It looks like we're related now, aren't we, Valeri?"

Kirpichenko choked on the pickle brine.

"Wha-at?"

"What do you mean, 'what?' " Banin suddenly roared. "Are you sleeping with my sister or not? Come on, tell me when we're going to have the wedding or else I'll notify the authorities. Got it, you immoral bastard?"

Kirpichenko struck him in the face all the way from across the table. Banin flew into the corner, but jumped up right away and grabbed a chair.

"You son of a bitch!" snarled Kirpichenko and headed for him. "If you have to marry every cheap girl...."

"Jailbird!" Banin screamed. "Convict!" And threw a chair at him.

But here Kirpichenko showed him what's what. When Banin grabbed his sheepskin coat and ran into the street, Kirpichenko, grinding his teeth in anger, frenzy, and wild anguish, dragged out his suitcase, threw his things in, put on his coat and his sheepskin coat, pulled from his pocket a photo of himself (wearing a tie and his best checked sportshirt), and quickly wrote on it: "To Lariska, in fond memory. Without words, but from the heart." He put it in Lariska's room on her pillow and cleared out. In the yard, Banin, spitting and swearing, was untying a ferocious dog. Kirpichenko kicked the dog away and went through the wicket gate.

"How's your coffee?" asked the waitress.

"Not bad, it's having some effect," sighed Kirpichenko and stroked her hand.

"Now-now," smiled the waitress.

At that moment his flight was announced.

With a light heart and big strong steps Kirpichenko headed for the plane. To get far away from here, as far away as possible. You don't take a vacation once in a blue moon to hang around in a stuffy shack eating mushrooms and gouda cheese. There are fellows who while away their whole vacation just like this, but he's no fool. He'll arrive in Moscow, buy himself three suits and Czech shoes in GUM,[6] then onward, onward to the Black Sea—"Seagull, Black Sea seagull, my dream"—he will eat chebureki[7] and stroll about in just a jacket.

He saw himself at that moment as if from outside himself—a big strong guy in both a cloth coat and a sheepskin coat, in a muskrat hat, in felt boots— just look at him strutting along. One woman with whom he'd had an affair the summer before last said that he had the face of an Indian chief. This woman was even the head of a geological expedition, how's that! Such a fine woman, that Nina Petrovna, a lecturer or something of the sort. She wrote him letters, and he answered her: "Greetings, my dear Nina Petrovna. This letter is being written by Valeri Kirpichenko who is known to you," and other such pleasantries.

A large crowd of passengers had already gathered at the turnstiles. A little ways off, jumping up and down in her boots, was Lariska. Her face was white and almost blue from the cold, and her lips were bright red. And the brooch on her collar, with its running reindeer, looked awfully stupid.

64

"Why'd you come?" asked Kirpichenko.

"T-to see you off," Lariska barely got out.

"Come on, knock it off"—and he cut her off with a wave of his hand. "OK, you and your brother have been soaking me for all I'm worth for three days, but there's no point in harping on about love."

Lariska began to cry, and Valeri got scared.

"There, there, now...."

"Yes, we've been using you," Lariska babbled... "Sure, that's true... OK, fine, I know what you think of me... that's just the kind of girl I am... so, can't I love you anyway?"

"Oh, knock it off!"

"Well I won't, I won't!"... Lariska almost screamed. "You, Valya," she drew close—"You're not like anyone else..."

"I'm just like everyone else, only perhaps..." and slowly breaking into a smile Kirpichenko uttered a gross, ugly phrase.

Lariska turned away and began to cry even harder. Her whole pitiful little body shook.

"Come on, there's no reason to cry...," Kirpichenko said bewilderedly and stroked her shoulder.

At that moment the crowd streamed onto the airfield. Kirpichenko went also, without looking back, and thinking of how sorry he was for Lariska, how he had come to feel comfortable with her. But, for that matter, he eventually comes to feel comfortable with every girl he spends time with, that's his stupid nature. And then you forget and everything's back to normal. Back to normal, and period.

He walked along in the crowd of passengers, looking at the huge glistening plane awaiting him, and very quickly forgot everything, all the rottenness of his three-day sojourn here and the fingers of the moon on his neck. You can't buy him at that price. You never could. You can't buy him and you can't break him. Not just cheap women had come his way. He'd had some really fine women, too. The lecturer, for example, was a really fine soul. They all fell in love with him, and Valeri understood that this happened not because of his cruelty but because of something else entirely, perhaps because of his silent nature, perhaps because each wanted to be a real find for him, because they apparently felt in these moments that he was like a blind man groping along with hands outstretched. But he always said to himself—"You can't buy me for those little favors, you can't change my ways. We had our affair, and that's that. And everything's back to normal. Back to normal."

The plane was frightfully large. It was huge and heavy, like a cruiser. Kirpichenko had never flown on such a plane before, and now admiration simply took his breath away. That's one thing he loved—machinery. He went up the high gangplank. The stewardess in her dark blue uniform and cap looked at his ticket and told him where his seat was. It was in the first section, but some strange fellow had already taken it, some guy in glasses and hat.

"OK, beat it," said Kirpichenko as he showed his ticket to the guy in glasses.

"Couldn't you take my place?" asked the man. "I get sick in the tail section."

"Beat it, I tell you!" Kirpichenko barked at him.

"You could be a little more polite," said the man in an insulted tone. For some reason he didn't budge.

Kirpichenko tore off the man's hat and threw it toward the back of the plane, in the direction of the man's assigned seat. He really showed him where to go—as if to say: "Beat it, take the seat you paid for."

"Citizen, why are you causing a scene?" said the stewardess.

"Take it easy," said Kirpichenko.

The man in glasses, completely unnerved, went hunting for his hat, and Kirpichenko took his assigned seat.

He took off his sheepskin coat and put it at his feet, establishing, so to speak, his right to the reserved place.

The passengers were entering the plane, one by one, and it seemed that there was no end to them. Light music was playing inside the plane. Sun-drenched icy vapor poured into the hatch. The stewardesses, one and all wearing blue uniforms, were fussily running down the aisle. They all had long legs and had on extremely high heels. Kirpichenko was reading the paper. About disarmament and Berlin, about the championship game in Chile and about snow-cover for crops. A peasant woman wrapped in a shawl sat by the window and a ruddy sailor took the seat next to Kirpichenko. He kept cracking jokes.

"Hey, lady, have you written your will?"

And then he yelled to the stewardess: "Ma'am, to whom does one submit a will?"

It was always Kirpichenko's luck to meet such jokers.

Finally the hatch was slammed shut, and the red sign went on: "No smoking, fasten your seat belts," and something in English, maybe the same thing, or maybe something else. Maybe, the other way around: "Please smoke. You don't have to fasten your seat belts." Kirpichenko didn't know English.

A woman's voice made an announcement over the loudspeaker: "Attention, please. The ship's captain would like to welcome the passengers on board Soviet liner TU-114.[8] Our jumbo jet is en route from Khabarovsk to Moscow. We will fly at an altitude of 9,000 meters at a speed of 700 kilometers per hour. Total flight time: 8 hours and 30 minutes. Thank you for your attention."

And in English: "Koorli, shoorli, lops-drops... Syenkyu."

"There, that's the way," Kirpichenko said with satisfaction and winked at the sailor. "Everything's hunky-dory."

"So what else would you expect," said the sailor, as if this plane were his very own, as if he himself had arranged everything, the announcements in the two languages and all the rest.

The plane taxied onto the runway. The peasant woman was sitting tense with anticipation. Airport buildings swam by the window.

"May I take your coat?" asked the stewardess. It was the same one who had rebuked Kirpichenko. He looked at her and melted. She was smiling. Her smiling face and hair bent over him. Her dark hair—no, not black, but dark and undoubtedly soft hair—was neatly done up and looked like fur, like fleece, like nylon, like all the treasures of the world. Her fingers touched his sheepskin coat. You've never seen such fingers. No, all this happens in magazines, and of course not only there, but it never happens that you find all of these things at once: such a smile, and the voice of the very first woman on earth; such things don't happen.

"Did you see that? She took my coat," said Kirpichenko, smiling stupidly to the sailor. The latter winked at him and said proudly: "They're a sharp crew, aren't they? You bet."

She returned and took the peasant woman's short fur coat, the sailor's leather coat, and Kirpichenko's coat. She pressed the armful to her heavenly body and said:

"Fasten your seat belts, comrades."

The motors began to roar. The peasant woman was paralyzed with fear and secretly kept crossing herself. The sailor, mimicking her with relish, kept casting side glances to see if Kirpichenko was laughing. But the latter was craning his neck, watching the girl take the coats somewhere. And then she appeared with a tray and offered everyone candy, perhaps not really candy but gold, gold nuggets, or heart pills. And then later, when they were in the air, she offered everyone something to drink, soft drinks and mineral water, that very same water which flows from the highest and purest waterfalls. And then she disappeared.

"Do you play preference?" asked the sailor. "We could get enough hands to play."

The red sign went off, and Kirpichenko realized that he could smoke. He got up and went to the fore section, to a nook behind a screen from which clouds of smoke were already pouring.

"We'd like to give you some information about the flight," the loudspeaker announced. "Our altitude is 9,000 meters; our speed is 750 kilometers per hour. The temperature outside is -58 degrees C. Thank you for your attention."

Down below, very far away, floated a jagged, rocky, lifeless expanse, which concealed death in every fold. Kirpichenko actually shuddered when he imagined that in this icy expanse over a harsh and desolate earth floated a metal cigar, filled with human warmth, courtesy, cigarette smoke, muffled talk and laughter, the kind of jokes that weren't worth remembering, mineral water and drops from a waterfall in some fertile region. And here he is, sitting and smoking, and somewhere in the tail section, or perhaps even in the midsection, a woman is promenading about, the likes of which don't really exist, and who are as far away from you as the moon.

He began thinking about his life and remembering. He had never thought about the past before, except when forced to say something, and then he would spin some sort of tall tale. But now it suddenly dawned on him: "I'm traveling across the entire country for the fourth time, and this is the first time I'm paying my own way. What a ball!"

All the previous trips had been at government expense. In '39 when he was still a very small child, their entire kolkhoz suddenly expressed the desire to move from Stavropol[9] to the Far-Eastern Maritime Territory.[10] The resettlement took a long time. He could remember bits and pieces of this trip—sour milk and sour cabbage soup, his mother doing the wash in a corner of the heated train car and hanging it outside to dry; it flapped outside the window like flags, but then, stiffened by the frost, it would begin to rattle, while he sang: "The pilots are soaring in planes that are roaring; and while they all fly, they look down from on high...." His mother died during the war, and his father died a hero's death in '45 in the Kurille Islands.[11] Valeri had finished grammar school in an orphanage, then on-the-job training in a factory, then he worked in a mine and "gave his country coal, soft coal, but lots of it." In '50 he went into the army, and again they transported him across the entire country, this time to the Baltics. In the army he became a qualified driver, and after his discharge he and a friend took off for Novorossiisk.[12] Within a year he was arrested. Some bastard had ripped off spare parts from the garage, and the authorities didn't spend too much time looking into the matter; they put him in jail as the person "materially responsible." He got three years and was sent to Sakhalin. He spent a year and a half in the labor camp, and then he was freed for consistently overfulfilling his work quotas; and later they even struck the conviction from his record. From that time on he had been working at the forestry complex. He liked the work and the pay was really good. What he did was tow trailers up a mountain pass and then down with all brakes on. He drank, went to movies, and in the summer went to dances at the fish cannery. He lived in a dormitory. He had always lived in dormitories, barracks, or some kind of temporary housing. Bunks, bunks, single and double, plank beds, storage chests to sleep on.... He didn't have any close friends, but knew lots of "fellow countrymen." People were somewhat afraid of him; jokes didn't go over well with him. He wouldn't think twice about punching you and making you see stars. But on the job he was a pace setter. He loved machinery. He remembered the vehicles he'd had to drive as other people remember their friends. There was "Ivan-Willys" in the army, then a tractor, and then a one and-a-half ton truck, a "Tatra," and the diesel he had now. In different towns—in Yuzhno-Sakhalinsk, Poronaisk, Korsakov, he would sometimes stop on a street corner and look at the windows of the new apartment houses, at the stylish lamps and curtains, and this would fill him with anxiety. He hadn't thought about how old he was, and only recently realized that in a few days he would turn thirty. Better not think about it! In Moscow he'd by three suits, a green hat, and then go south, like some big-shot engineer. He had traveler's checks sewn into his underwear—a freightcar load of money. He was sure going to have a good time in the south. Everything was fine, fine, and that's all there was to it!

He got up and went to look for her. Where could she have gotten to? As a matter of fact, the passengers were dying of thirst, and she was standing and jabbering in English with some capitalist.

She was chattering away, screwing up her eyes, smiling broadly; it was apparent that she enjoyed talking on and on in English. The capitalist was standing right next to her; he was a very tall and thin man, and although he had a gray crew cut, he was in fact young. His jacket was open, and a thin gold watch-chain extended from his belt to his pocket. His voice rumbled; and his words thundered in his mouth as if they were crashing against his teeth. We all know what these little conversations are like.

He: "Let's go, darling, to San Francisco and drink whiskey there."

She: "You're presuming too much."

He: "In banana-lemon Singapore... Get it?"

She: "Do you really mean it? When banana trees are bending in the wind?"

He: "Let's take off for the 102nd floor; there boogie-woogie jazz is blaring."

Kirpichenko went up to the capitalist and pushed him aside with his shoulder. The latter was taken aback and said: "I am sorry," which meant of course:"Watch it, buddy, you're cruisin' for a bruisin'."

"Take it easy," said Kirpichenko, "peace—friendship."

He knew his politics.

The capitalist said something to her over Kirpichenko's head, probably: "Take your choice, me or him, San Francisco or Bayukly."

And she answered him with a little smile:

"I know this comrade. And now leave me alone; I am a Soviet."

"What's the problem, comrade?" she asked Kirpichenko.

"It's just that my throat is dry," he said. "Got anything I can wet my whistle with?"

"Come on," she said and went ahead of him, like a little goat, like in the movies, like in a dream. Oh, how he had longed for her while he had been smoking in the fore section.

She was walking ahead of him, like I don't know what, and brought him to what looked like a snackbar, but which perhaps was her own home, where there was no one, and where the sun on high shone peacefully and indomitably through the plane window, or perhaps, through a window in a new home on the ninth floor. She took a bottle and poured the bubbling water into a small glass cup. She picked up the cup and it began to sparkle in the sunlight. But he was looking at the girl, and he wanted to have children with her. But he couldn't even imagine that it was possible to do with her what people do when they want to have children; and this was the first time he had felt this way, and a new, unexpected feeling of happiness suddenly consumed him.

"What's your name?" he asked with the same feeling which he had each time he made it across the mountain—frightened, yet knowing everything is behind him.

"Tatyana Viktorovna," she answered. "Tanya."

"Well, then, I'm Kirpichenko, Valeri," he said and extended his hand.

She gave him her fingers and smiled.

"You're not a very reserved fellow."

"I am a bit...," he said, crushed.

For a few seconds they looked at each other in silence. She could hardly keep from laughing. She struggled with herself and he too, but suddenly he couldn't contain himself any longer and he smiled as he had probably never smiled before in his whole life.

At that moment someone called her and she ran off. She looked back and thought: "Boy, what a face!"

"How strange," she thought as she went down to the lower deck of the plane. "He looks like a thug, but I'm not afraid of him. I wouldn't even be frightened if I met him in the woods all alone."

Kirpichenko walked back down the aisle and saw the guy in glasses who had been trying to grab his assigned seat. The fellow was stretched out in his seat with his eyes closed. His pretty face was like smooth unblemished marble.

"Listen, friend," Kirpichenko tapped him on the shoulder, "take my place if you want." The fellow opened his eyes and smiled weakly:

"Thank you very much, I'm fine here...."

He had flown on such planes more than once and knew that they don't shake, even in the tail section. He had taken a seat in the fore section not because he was afraid of a rough trip, but because he wanted to watch the cockpit door open and see the pilots scratching themselves, smoking, laughing, reading newspapers, and occasionally glancing at the instruments. This had a calming effect on him. He wasn't a coward; he simply had a well-developed imagination. Someone had told him about streaming air currents in which even large planes like this begin to turn somersaults and sometimes even fall apart. He very vividly imagined what this would be like, although he knew perfectly well that it wouldn't happen. Over there were the stewardesses, so young and constantly flying; this was their job. And there was the ship's captain, fat, smoking a pipe. And there was even this rude fellow who had insulted him, wandering up and down the plane.

Tanya began to serve dinner. She brought Valeri a tray as well and looked at him out of the corner of her eye.

"And where do you live, Tanya?" he asked.

"Tanya, Ta-nya, T-a-n-ya."

"In Moscow," she answered and walked away.

Kirpichenko ate, and all the while it seemed to him that his steak was thicker than everyone else's, his apple bigger, and that she had given him more bread than the others. Then she brought tea.

"So you're a Muscovite?" he again asked.

"Uh-huh," she answered ever so brightly and left.

"You're wasting your time, chum," the sailor smirked. "Some smart fellow is probably waiting for her in Moscow."

"Relax," said Kirpichenko with a steady and strong feeling of his own well-being and happiness.

But, by God, these flights don't go on forever, and from aloft, from such heights, a plane does have the special characteristic of coming down. And shifts come to an end, as do professional duties; and you get your cloth coat back; and delicate little fingers bear you your sheepskin coat, and eyes already have that far-off look, and everything slowly winds down, like the mainspring in a toy; and everything becomes flat, like a page out of a journal. "Aeroflot—your air travel agent"—this marvel—all these manicured hands, and high heels, and smart hairstyles.

No, no, no, nothing is lost, nothing becomes dull and flat, although we are already landing. And as for those other fellows, you can punch their faces in, that's just the way it is. What a commotion has begun—and the cap far off somewhere.

"Don't hold other people up, citizen...."

"Let's go, pal...."

"Moscow's staring us in the face...."

"It makes your heart throb to see the place...."

"Well, move on for Pete's sake...."

Still not understanding what was happening to him, Kirpichenko left the plane with the sailor, walked down the gangplank and got on the bus. The bus headed for the terminal and the "Soviet Liner TU-114, jumbo jet," the flying fortress of his incomprehensible longings, quickly disappeared from view.

The taxi flew along a super-wide highway. There was three-lane traffic. Trucks, vans, and dumptrucks squeezed into the right-hand lane, while passenger cars moved at great speed, overtaking them as if they were standing still. And here the wooded area ended, and Kirpichenko and the sailor saw the pink, thousand-eyed buildings of the South-West.[13] The sailor began to fidget and put his hand on Valeri's shoulder.

"The capital! Here we are, Valeri!"

"Listen, is our plane going to fly back now?" asked Kirpichenko.

"Naturally. They leave tomorrow."

"And with the same crew?"

The sailor let out a derisive whistle. "Knock it off. What's so special about her—she's just another stylish, modern girl. There are a million like her in Moscow. Don't be silly."

"Oh, I'm just talking," mumbled Kirpichenko.

"Where to, boys?" asked the driver.

"Head for GUM!" snapped Kirpichenko and immediately forgot all about the plane.

The car was already racing along Moscow streets.

In GUM he bought three suits straight off—a blue, a gray and a brown. He kept the brown one on and rolled up his old one, made four years ago at a tailor's in Korsakov, and left it in a lavatory stall. The sailor got himself some gabardine for a raincoat and said that he would have it made in Odessa.[14] Then they drank a bottle of champagne apiece at the food counter and took a tour of the Kremlin. Then they went to the National Hotel and ate God knows what—something called julienne—and drank "Soviet Cognac." There were a lot of girls here who looked like Tanya, and perhaps Tanya herself had dropped in; perhaps she sat with them at the table, pouring him some more mineral water and then running to the kitchen to check on how they were doing his steak. In any case, the capitalist was there. Kirpichenko waved to him and he stood up and bowed. Then they went out on the street and drank yet another bottle of champagne apiece. On Gorky Street[15] Tanya was more and more involved in frenzied activity. She was hopping out of trolleys and running into stores; she was strolling with dandies on the other side of the street, and then smiling from display windows. Kirpichenko and the sailor, hanging heavily onto each other, walked along Gorky Street, smiling. The sailor was humming: "Ma-da-gaskar, my country...."

It was that time of day when dusk is descending but the streets lights are not yet lit. Yes, at the end of the street, on the horizon, spring burned scarlet and green. They wondered why girls were keeping away from them.

Later, there were closed doors and lines everywhere, and it was impossible to get in anywhere. They began to think seriously about a place to sleep and took a taxi to Vnukovo Airport.[16] They took a double room at the airport hotel. As soon as he saw the clean sheets, Kirpichenko realized how tired he was. He tore off his new suit and collapsed on the bed.

The sailor woke him in an hour. He was running around the room, shaving his cheeks with a "Sputnik" electric razor, squealing, cackling, choking:

"Rise and shine, Valeri! I've just met some girls here you wouldn't believe... Boy! Get up, let's go visit them. They live in a dormitory here. It's a sure thing, pal, they won't string us along.... I have a nose for this kind of thing... Get up, get out of bed! Ma-da-gaskar!..."

"Why are you cackling like you'd just laid an egg?" said Kirpichenko, taking a cigarette from his bedside table and lighting it.

"Are you coming or not?" asked the sailor, who was already at the door.

"Cut off the light, will you?" asked Kirpichenko.

The light went out and immediately the moonlit square of the window, cut by the window frame and the swaying shadows of the bare branches, was imprinted on the wall. It was quiet; somewhere far off a radio-phonograph was playing. In the next room somebody asked "Anybody got a six?" and a slap on the table could be heard. Then a plane landed with a roar. Kirpichenko smoked and imagined her lying with him, their lying together afterwards, and her fingers stroking his neck as if they were the fingers of the moon. Yes, this was the real world, not any make-believe one, but the real thing... and her long naked body was really the flesh of the moon, because everything incomprehensible which happened to him in childhood, the times when his whole body was covered with goose bumps, his youth, hills silhouetted against the rosy fire of dawn, the sea in darkness, melting snow, weariness after work, Saturday and Sunday morning—all this is in fact she, Tanya.

"So that's the way things are," he thought, and again he was seized by a steady and strong sense of his own well-being and happiness. He was happy that this had happened to him; he was wild with joy. Only one thing frightened him—that a hundred years would pass and he would forget her face and voice.

The sailor came quietly into the room. He undressed and lay down, took a cigarette from the night table, lit it and began to sing sadly: "Ma-da-gaskar, land of mine, here as everywhere, it's now springtime..."

"How long have you been a sailor?" Kirpichenko asked.

"Since '57," answered the sailor and again began to sing:

Madagaskar, land of mine,
Here, as everywhere, it's now springtime.
We're people like you
We love like you do,
Tho our skin be black, our blood is red, too...

"Write down the words," requested Kirpichenko.

They turned on the light and the sailor dictated the words of this delightful song to Valeri. Kirpichenko really liked such songs.

The next day they confirmed their tickets: Kirpichenko for Adler,[17] the sailor for Odessa. They had breakfast. Kirpichenko bought a book of Chekhov and a copy of "New World"[18] at the kiosk.

"Listen," said the sailor, "she has a really nice girl friend. Maybe we can make a quick trip to Moscow with them?"

"Oh, I don't think so," he said. "You two go on, and I'll just sit here

73

and read what these books have to say."

The sailor gave a nautical signal: "Got it, wish you luck, am setting course."

Kirpichenko loafed around the airport all day, but didn't see Tanya. In the evening he saw the sailor off for Odessa. They drank a bottle of champagne apiece and then he escorted the sailor's girl friend to the dormitory and returned to the airport. He went to the ticket window and bought a seat on a TU-114 jumbo jet, flight No. 901, Moscow-Khabarovsk.

On the plane everything was the same as before: announcements in two languages and all the comforts, but no Tanya. On board was a new crew. There were girls, just as young and just as pretty, who resembled Tanya, but none of them were the first; Tanya was the first; it was after her that this whole breed developed, mass production, so to speak.

In the morning Kirpichenkov found himself in Khabarovsk, and in an hour again took off for Moscow on a different plane. But again, there was no Tanya.

In all he made seven trips there and back on TU-114's, at an altitude of 9000 meters, at a speed of 750 km. per hour. The temperature outside fluctuated between -50 degrees and -60 degrees C. All the instruments functioned normally.

He already knew by face almost all of the stewardesses on this run and some of the pilots as well. He was afraid they would remember him.

He was afraid they would take him for a spy.

He kept changing his suit. He made one flight in the blue, another in the brown, a third in the gray.

He ripped open his underwear and transferred the traveler's checks to his coat pocket. There were fewer and fewer traveler's checks.

There was still no Tanya.

There was a fiercely bright sun on high; there were sunrises and sunsets above the snowy cloudy desert. There was a moon which seemed close. And it really wasn't far away.

It reached the point where he confused time and place and stopped resetting his watch. Khabarovsk seemed to him to be a suburb of Moscow, and Moscow, a new section of Khabarovsk.

He read a whole lot. Never in his life had he read so much.

Never in his life had he done so much thinking.

Never in his life had he cried.

Never in his life had he rested in such first-class fashion.

Spring was coming to Moscow. Drops from those same high pure waterfalls fell on the back of his neck. He bought a black and gray checked scarf.

In case he met Tanya he bought her a present—a perfume set called "May First" and a length of cloth for a dress.

I met him inside the Khabarovsk air terminal. He was sitting in an

74

armchair with his legs crossed, reading Stanyukovich.[19] A net bag filled with oranges hung on the arm of the chair. On the bookcover a clipper ship skimmed along, its sails billowing in a storm.

"Are you a sailor, by any chance?" he asked me after glancing at my leather jacket.

"No."

I stared at this strange, unsettling face, but he read a few more lines and again asked me:

"Aren't you sorry you're not a sailor?"

"Of course I am," I said.

"I'm sorry too," he grinned. "I have a friend who's a sailor. Here's a cable he sent me from on board ship."

Then he showed me the cable.

"Aha," I said, and he asked, using the familiar right away:

"And you, when were you born?"

"In '32," I answered.

He beamed broadly.

"Hey, we were born the same year!"

The coincidence really was phenomenal, and I shook his hand.

"I bet you live in Moscow, don't you?" he asked.

"You guessed it," I answered. "In Moscow."

"I bet you've got an apartment, don't you? A wife, a kid, right? And all the other trappings."

"You guessed it. I've got all those things."

"What do you say we go have breakfast?"

I was about to go with him, but at that moment they announced my flight. I was flying to Petropavlovsk.[20] We exchanged addresses, and I went to board my plane. I walked on the airfield, hunched over from the wind and thought:

"What a strange fellow, what amazing coincidences."

And at that moment he glanced at his watch, took his netbag and walked out. He took a taxi downtown. He and the driver barely found that hunchbacked village street because he didn't remember its name. The little houses on this street all looked alike, huge dogs were barking in all the yards, and he got a bit confused. Finally he remembered the right house. He got out of the car, hung the bag with the oranges on the fencepost, camouflaged it with newspaper so that neighbors or passers-by wouldn't rip off his treasure, and went back to the car.

"Step on it, boss! I don't want to be late for my plane."

"Where are you going?" asked the driver.

"To Moscow, to the capital."

He saw Tanya two days later in the Khabarovsk airport when he was already on his way back to Sakhalin, when he had already used up all his traveler's checks, and when he had only a few red bills left in his pocket. She was wearing a belted white fur coat. She was laughing and eating candy out of a little sack, and she was treating the other girls, who were also laughing. He immediately grew weak and sat down on his suitcase. He watched Tanya take the candies and undo the wrappers, and watched the other girls do the same thing. And he didn't understand why they were standing there and not going anywhere. Then he realized, that spring had come, that it was a spring night, and that the moon over the airport looked like an orange; that it wasn't cold now, and that you could stand just like that and simply look at the lights and laugh and get lost in thought for a moment with candy in your mouth...

An engineer who worked in a neighboring mine-pit and who was also coming back from vacation touched Kirpichenko on the shoulder. "What's with you? They've already announced our flight."

"Manevich, do you know how many kilometers it is to the Moon?" asked Kirpichenko.

"It's obvious that you overdid it on your vacation," Manevich said angrily and turned to go.

Kirpichenko grabbed him by the coat-tail.

"But you're a young specialist, Manevich," he said pleadingly, looking at Tanya. "After all, you have to know...."

"Oh, 300,000, maybe," said Manevich, as he pulled away.

"That's not far," thought Kirpichenko. "No sweat." He looked at Tanya and imagined how he would remember her as he headed for the mountain crossing, and yet at the crossing how he would suddenly forget—that wasn't the place for it—and afterwards, at the bottom of the slope, he would again remember and would continue to remember the whole evening and night, and in the morning would wake up with thoughts of her.

Then he got up from his suitcase.

1965

Translated by Valentina G. Brougher and Helen C. Poot

NOTES

1. Yuzhno-Sakhalinsk is the capital of the Sakhalin Region of the RSFSR; located in the southeastern part of Sakhalin Island, which is a heavily forested island off the coast of Siberia. The island was noted during czarist times as a place of exile. It has been colonized extensively, and the native population has been reduced to a minority. The most important industries are lumber and herring fishing.

2. A small town on Sakhalin Island.

3. A town on the northernmost part of Sakhalin.

4. An important transportation center of the Soviet Far East, located on the south bank of the Amur River (not far from Manchuria) where the Trans-Siberian Railway crosses it; capital of the Khabarovsk Territory of the RSFSR.

5. Voroshilov, Klimet Ye. (1881-1969): Soviet military leader and statesman. He helped organize the secret police after the Bolshevik Revolution, served as a Red Army commander and police chief in south Russia and the Ukraine during the Russian Civil War, and served as war commissar from 1925 to 1940, when he was made a USSR vice-premier. During World War II he briefly commanded the Baltic Front, but suffered many defeats and was removed to a nominal post at general headquarters. When Stalin died in 1953, he became Chairman of the Presidium of the Supreme Soviet, but was removed from this post by Krushchev in 1960.

6. GUM: main department store, located on Red Square.

7. Large "pirozhki" (pies) made of finely rolled unleavened dough, stuffed with ground mutton or lamb and onion, then fried. Common in the Caucasus and Crimea.

8. Tupolev (TU) 114: an immense Soviet passenger aircraft (the largest, in fact, until the advent of the Boeing 747); it evolved from a bomber model, the Tupolev 4.

9. A city in the Kuybyshev Region of the RSFSR, located about 250 miles west of the Caspian Sea on the left bank of the Volga.

10. A territory of the USSR on the southeast coast of Siberia bordering the Sea of Japan; its capital is Vladivostok.

11. A chain of approximately 30 large islands and many smaller ones, extending for a distance of 730 miles from the tip of the Kamchatka Peninsula of Siberia to within a few miles of the coast of Hokkaido (the northernmost island of Japan). Earlier a territory of Japan, the islands were occupied by the USSR pursuant to the Yalta agreement of 1945 and became part of the Sakhalin Region in 1947.

12. Seaport city situated on the northeast shore of the Black Sea in the western part of the Krasnodar Territory of the RSFSR.

13. One of the new housing districts in Moscow, consisting of miles of identical prefabricated apartment buildings.

14. Third largest city in the Ukraine and the most important Black Sea port.

15. Gorky Street: the main thoroughfare of Moscow, leading from Leningrad Highway to Red Square. A wide street lined with numerous shops, hotels, cafes, etc.; many of Moscow's major attractions are located on the sidestreets which diverge from Gorky Street. Formerly known as Tverskaya; renamed in honor of Maxim Gorky.

16. Moscow's main airport, located 15 miles southwest of the city.

17. A resort on the Black Sea.

18. *Novy Mir*—New World—is the most important "thick" journal published within the Soviet Union. Founded in 1925 as an organ of the Writers' Union, *Novy Mir* was conceived as the mouthpiece for the fellow-travelers, those writers who sympathized with the Revolution and its goals, but who were not Party members. The journal has had a history marked by the high quality of its material; many of the most controversial works of Soviet literature were published in it, including Solzhenitsyn's *A Day in the Life of Ivan Denisovich* (1962).

19. Stanyukovich, Konstantin Mikhailovich (1843-1903): a novelist of the late nineteenth century and an adherent of the populists. Although he wrote a number of tendentious novels, most of which are forgotten, he is best remembered for his series of *Sea Stories,* published in the 1880's and 1890's, which were entertaining accounts of Russian naval life.

20. Capital of the Northern Kazakhstan Region of the Kazakh Soviet Socialist Republic.

LITTLE WHALE, VARNISHER OF REALITY

"What's that thing you brought home?" Whale asked me.

"It's a cap."

"Let me see."

He seized my new leather cap and wonderingly began to look it over. Within seconds his curiosity had reached such a fierce pitch that he was trembling. He let out a shout: "Daddy, what is it?"

"Just a funny kind of a cap," I grunted.

"A cap to fly in?" he shouted, more fiercely still, and began leaping about with the cap in his hands.

I was willing to play along. "Yes, to fly in. We'll fly to the North Pole in this cap, you and I."

"Hooray! To see the polar bears?"

"Yes."

"The walruses?"

"Yes, and the walruses."

"And who else?"

My head was splitting: I'd had words with several people at the office that day, taken a dressing down from the manager, and made several mistakes. I was in a god-awful mood, but still, I racked my brains to recall the scant fauna of the Arctic Ocean. "The sharks," I said in desperation.

"That's a lie," he retorted indignantly. "They don't have sharks there. Sharks are evil, and all the animals at the North Pole are good."

"You're right," I agreed hastily. "Well then, we'll go and see the polar bears, the walruses..."

"The whales," he prompted.

"Uh-huh, the whales and the... er..."

"The limpedooza!" he shouted rapturously.

"Now what's a limpedooza?"

He stopped in confusion, laid the cap on the divan, went off to the far corner, and whispered from across the room. "A limpedooza is a kind of an animal."

"Right you are," I said. "How could I have forgotten? The limpedooza! A kind of slithery, clever little animal, right?"

"No! He's big and fluffy!" said Whale with conviction.

My wife came into the room and said to Whale, "Let's go tend to our business." They went out together, but my wife came back and asked, "Did you call him?"

"Who?"

"Don't pretend. You had all day and couldn't make a phone call?"

"All right, I'll do it now."

She went out, and for the first time that day I was left alone. Listening to the unusual stillness, I might have been taking a bath or a shower, a shower of solitude after a work day filled in all its dimensions with clamorous people, some of them friends, some strangers.

I sat down at the empty desk and laid my hands on it, felt with pleasure its cool empty surface, devoid of any business or papers, serving now only as a prop for my heavy hands.

Outside the window the sun, having noiselessly surmounted the thickety yellow garden next door, was rolling toward the corner of a multistory apartment house, a gigantic up-ended parallelepiped, dark now and seemingly lifeless.

In the courtyard below, some demonic ten-year-olds were tearing around on the toolshed roof. From their wide-open mouths, I could imagine what a ruckus they were raising their outside our window panes.

A proper little old lady came timidly around from the front yard and, watchfully as a doe, turned toward the toolshed. As soon as they spotted her the boys leaped down from the roof.

This little old lady, who came out to the courtyard every evening for a breath of oxygen, with an inflatable rubber pillow to put under her meager seat, was a constant target of evil small-boy tricks. She was long since used to them and patiently endured the antics of these courtyard terrorists, so puzzling to her, so crafty and fleet—patiently endured them, but was nonetheless afraid of them, always afraid.

Now the boys had turned the janitor's hose directly across her path; they were having a wonderful time, leaping wildly about with their mouths open in laughter, while the old lady stood there patiently waiting for them to tire of their game. The janitor's wife appeared, a friend of the old lady's, and rushed to the attack, opening her mouth wide and waving her arms as she ran.

This whole scene, had it been wired for sound, would surely have roused me to anger or pain, but now it passed before my indifferent gaze like the frames of an old silent film.

And so, the old lady successfully traversed the courtyard, while the terrorists raged on the toolshed roof, mindless that the old lady's death, even now impending, might bring about the first desolation—a slight one, to be sure—of their own souls.

Striving to maintain my indifference and providential languor, I pulled the phone over and began to dial that damned number, as if paying no attention, as if it were nothing for me to call him, but by the third digit my insides were already knotted up, my heart, my liver, my spleen had contracted into one madly pounding lump, and only the short quick beeps delivered me. Busy!

I pictured him sitting in an easy chair, or maybe lying on the divan, but in any case fiddling with his spectacles, twirling them on one finger while he talked to someone. To whom? Sadovnikov? Voynovsky? Ovsyan-nikov?

I swore, and at that moment I heard Whale's shout from the kitchen. He was acting up, for no good reason. Something comes over him sometimes.

"Go away!" he roared at the top of his lungs. "Go away!" he shouted to my wife. "We don't need you!"

I could hear my wife's indignant voice and then the click of the light switch. Sanctions had been applied to Whale—he was left in the kitchen, in solitude and darkness. He immediately quieted down.

My wife went off to the bedroom to sulk. She takes it very hard when she has a tiff with her Whale-child, with this baby boy, our sweet little male-child, this Tom Thumb of a man just over three years old.

I got up and started for the kitchen, stomping the parquet elephant-style, trumpeting gaily and sternly, "Too-roo-roo! Here comes the Elephant Dad! Out of the depths of the jungle, Bimbo the Elephant himself! Too-roo-roo! Daddy himself! The one and only! In person!"

A feeling of tranquillity and love sprang up in my heart like a whirl-wind.

In the kitchen I saw his round head silhouetted against the dusky window. He was sitting on the potty whispering something, his finger raised toward the window, where the lights were already beginning to come on in the building across the way.

I'm almost used to Whale now. More and more seldom am I visited by that strange sense of illusoriness when he runs into the room or wheels in on his tricycle. The reverence before mystery, and the fear, that I felt the first few months of his life are almost gone. Now it's "Oh, there's Whale"—and that's it. Small boy, sweet son, magic marvel whale-fish beside the Humpback Horsey sits... He's the stuff the old rhymes are made of.

He was six months old when I named him Whale. The two of us, my wife and I, were bathing him in a little tub; he wiggled in the soapy water, his toothless mouth gaping. I held up his head and kept stuffing the bits of cotton back in his ears as they fell out. From time to time he lifted his blue gaze to me and smiled a sly little smile, as if in foreknowledge of the intricate relations we have now. First off it struck me he looked like a sausage in bouillon, and I told my wife so: "A sausage in bouillon, that's what he is."

After a moment's reflection my wife observed that this was scarcely an elegant comparison. Then I thought of the three whales that used to hold up the world in olden times:

"He's a baby Whale."

My wife was silent.

That evening, after the bath, I went out to Vnukovo airport and boarded a huge plane for the East. Then in Sakhalin, traveling around the little ports they have there, I would take out his picture in hotels and tourist homes and find myself thinking, "How's that little Whale of mine?"

Not that I didn't give him plenty of other nicknames later on. He was Bullyboy for a while, and Cupkins, and once he acquired this elaborate surname: Plumpkins-Bumpkins-Rumtumtumpkins-Sleepygrumpkins-Lunch-kins-Munchkins. Yet little by little these nicknames all faded away and were forgotten, until there remained but one, the big one—Whale.

"Well, what happened, Whale?" I asked, as I settled myself on the kitchen stepstool and lit up a cigarette.

"Look," he said, pointing out the window, "pretty little lights!" He set about counting them: "One, two, three, eighteen, eleven, nine... Look!" he exclaimed suddenly, "the moon!"

I turned toward the window. A pale moon with its side eaten away hung over the houses.

"Yes, the moon." It upset me, somehow, and I flicked my ash on the floor.

"Tolya, Tolya, we do have an ashtray," said Whale in his mother's tone of voice.

"You're right," I said. "Sorry."

We fell silent and sat for a while—I on the stepstool, he on the potty—in absolute stillness, broken only by my wife's sighs from the bedroom and the rustle of the pages of her book. Whale's eyes shone mysteriously. The lull was evidently to his liking.

"Y'know"—he suddenly roused himself—"Gagarin the pilot flies to the moon."

"Yes," I said.

"Y'know," he said, "Gagarin doesn't, and Titov doesn't, and Teresh-kova doesn't, and John Glenn doesn't..." A thoughtful pause.

"What?" I asked.

"And Cooper doesn't—they don't breathe anything into their mouth or nose," he completed his thought.

My wife came into the kitchen and lifted him off the potty. "You didn't do anything. Sit down again and try. You aren't trying at all."

"Tolya, do you try when you sit on the potty?" asked Whale.

"Yes," I said. "Bimbo the Elephant tries."

"And Tumba the Mama Elephant?"

"She does too."

"And Kuchka the Baby Elephant?"

"Sure he tries."

"And who else tries?"

"The dolphin," I said.

"Is the dolphin good?" he asked.

"Did you call him?" my wife asked.

"It was busy," I said.

"Then call him again."

"Listen here!" My temper flared. "This is my business, right? It's my business, and I'm the one who knows when to call."

"You're just chicken," she said scornfully.

I jumped up from the stool.

"Go take a walk, the both of you!" she said sharply. "Get dressed, fast! Out!"

Whale and I went out of the house and walked down our street toward the boulevard. It was already dark. Whale took big, business-like steps, his soft baby hand firmly clasping mine.

"So what about it?" he asked.

"What?" I was lost.

"Is the dolphin good?"

"Yes, of course he's good. Sharks are evil, but the dolphin is good."

How does he picture the sea, when he's never laid eyes on it, I thought. How does he picture the depth and boundlessness of the sea? How does he picture this city? What does Moscow mean to him? He doesn't know anything yet, at all. He doesn't know that the world is split into two camps. He doesn't know what it is, the world. We have already labelled... it's been catch as catch can, but we've managed to put a label to practically all the phenomena in our environment; we've built ourselves up this real world of ours. But right now he's living in a world strange and wonderful, not in the slightest like ours.

"And who bit off the side of the moon?" he asked.

"The Great Bear," I blurted, and at once felt alarmed, realizing how long it would take me to explain all that to him. I could tell from his tiny hand that once again he was quivering all over with curiosity.

"What do you mean, Tolya?" he asked carefully. "What kind of a bear?"

I picked him up in my arms and pointed to the sky. "See those little stars? Those right there—one, two, three, four, five, six, seven... In the shape of a dipper. That's called the Great Bear."

What are they, the stars? What is the Great Bear? Why has she hung over us like this since time immemorial?

"Yes, the great bear!" he cried happily, shaking his finger at her. "She's the one that bit off the side of the moon! Tch, tch!"

The ease with which he had grasped these fictions emboldened me. "And up a bit higher there," I said, "there's a Lesser Bear too. See the little small dipper? That's the Lesser Bear."

"Where's the Daddy Bear?" It was a reasonable question; he was trying to set up a bear family.

"The Daddy Bear..." I muttered, "the Daddy Bear..."

Whale came to my aid. "He's gone hunting in the woods, hasn't he?"

"That's it." I let him down from my shoulder.

We came out on to the boulevard. The benches here were all taken by old men and nannies, but promenading along the mall were packs of fourteen-year-old girls, followed by packs of fifteen-year-old boys. It was bright and bluish here: flourescent lamps cast their light on a Humpback Horsey the size of a dinosaur; a Firebird that looked like a giant turkey; an enormous Puss-in-Boots, tall as two men, with a depraved expression on his round visage; another cat—this one with a totally corrupt look—on a golden chain by the curving sea; King Guidon, the Swan Princess, a rocket, the Queen of the Fields, Gulliver...

It was Fantasy World, a children's book fair set up on our boulevard. At this hour the stalls were closed; only here and there did a yellow light gleam through the cracks in the fabulous plywood giants—the vendors were inside counting their take.

Whale was overwhelmed. He did not know where to run first—the Cat, the Prince, the Swan. For a moment or so he stood as if struck dumb: he just rolled his big eyes and whispered soundlessly. Then he tugged at my hand and let out a squeal, and practically skipping we took off for the stalls. I fought off a barrage of questions and was a long time telling him what was what, who was good and who was evil.

As it turned out, nearly all the figures stood for goodness and light, wisdom and the native wit of the people; there was only the wretched kite, hovering over the Swan, to represent the forces of evil, and Guidon's arrow was already aimed at him.

At length my Whale got tired and leaned heavily against the Hump-back Horsey.

"Let's go, Whale," I said. "We should be getting home."

"Tolya, listen, let's take them all with us."

"But they're so big, how can we?"

"Who cares, we'll take them anyhow." He swatted the Horse with his small palm: "This one's taken!" He ran over and swatted the Cat: "And this one!"

Thus he captured them all to have with him at bedtime and after that departed for home—quite tranquil now—without a backward glance.

At the turnoff from the boulevard he was lagging behind. I stopped; what now?

"Look, Tolya," he said. "Look what a pretty lady."

And what should I see but a pretty lady, who was coming our way. Her gait called to mind a restrained, or rather a scarcely restrainable, dance. With each nudge of her marvelous knees she flung open the skirts of her marvelous coat, and the umbrella, incredibly sharp and slim, which she held under her arm was plainly nothing less than a spare inner pivot for her gyrations, and her eyes, secret and subtle, flashed brilliantly at the sight of us. It was three days since I had last seen her, this lady, and now a dismal, anxious mood came over me, as always when I saw her or thought of her. The more so now, with Whale there.

"Oh," said she, "so this is what he's like, your little Whale. How delightful!"

She bent down to him, but he touched the umbrella and asked, "What's this? An arrow? A gun?"

"It's an umbrella," she exclaimed, and in a trice she had it open. With a faint flip it unfolded over her head, lending her whole figure a supplemental buoyancy, an airiness almost of the circus.

"Let me hold it!" shouted Whale.

She handed him the umbrella.

"It is a pleasure, Signor, to see you engaged in such peaceful pursuits," said she to me.

"And you, Mam'selle, are a joy to behold," said I.

We really could have done without the fatuous badinage customary in our circle and plunged right into serious talk about whatever had lately been on our minds; but it was the thing to do—one had to start by displaying his sense of humor in this or some more felicitous manner—and neither she nor I could break with the custom.

Whale was circling about on the great umbrella, and we were able to talk in peace.

"Tolya, why so sour?"

"Am I offending you?"

"You're sick of me, aren't you?"

"How come?"

"You think I'm crowding you—"

"Do you have to play games?"

She said she was not playing games, we shouldn't have to quarrel, after all we hadn't seen each other in three days, she understood that I had a fox gnawing at my vitals, she understood all, I was always in her thoughts, and maybe that was helping me.

She was lying and not lying. How neatly the female heart combines sincerity and subtlety, I thought. Everlasting peace and the senseless, disgusting inner turmoil of vanity. They have it easier later on, pretty women do, I thought; they have no fear of death, never give it a thought, their only fear is old age. Silly things, they're afraid of old age.

I had the further thought, as she went on being sympathetic, that I'd better not enter into her world again; I wasn't up to it, I had nothing in my head but turmoil, I was in no mood for adventure just now and no mood for romance; how I yearned for tranquillity, yet only once that whole day had I been tranquil, amid the plywood monstrosities of Fantasy World.

"Darling," said the pretty lady to me, "I know how humiliating it is, but pluck up your courage and make that phone call. You *must* clear things up once and for all, and even if it turns out for the worse, it will still be for the better, I assure you."

She lifted her hand and put the palm of this hand to my cheek...

stroked...

Just then Whale came squirming in between us. He tugged the pretty lady by the sleeve: "Hey, take your old umbrella and don't touch Daddy. He's my Daddy, not yours."

We parted from the pretty lady and started home. Ever so slightly false, affectedly amiable, possibly bitter, her laughter lingered a few seconds in our ears.

Along the way we stopped at the gate of the bus depot. Enormous buses kept driving in through the gate, and middle-sized ones, and micro-buses.

"Daddy Bus, Mama Bus, Baby Bus," said Whale, and laughed.

And so we returned home. While Whale had supper and told his Mama about the walk, I hung around in the livingroom, glancing at the phone from time to time, and got myself too upset to do anything at all.

I hate that instrument. It amazes me the way my wife can talk to her girl friends for hours on end, the way she can achieve a cordial intimacy with people by means of a telephone. Could it be that her affection for her friends is transferred to the telephone receiver, and all those hours it's really the receiver she's so fond of?

I do waste a lot of time out of dislike for the phone. Rather than pick up the receiver and make some gaffe, I drive clear across town, a waste of time and money. Maybe it's because I aspire to a life of realism, while any voice you hear in the receiver seems like make-believe, always make-believe, never the real thing.

Perhaps that's what I should do this time? Perhaps not call him today, but go over tomorrow and have this talk face to face. Once we are face to face I can use the art of mime, delicate, barely perceptible mimicry, to show him I'm not all that simple, it's not all that simple to humiliate me; give him to understand that I'm no milktoast but a man of courage, that this visit of mine, too, is an act of courage, and I care not a fig for him. A conversation over the phone gives him an enormous advantage, over the phone I might just as well be conversing with a supernatural power.

The phone rang. Jangled, the ugly thing! I picked up the receiver and heard the voice of my old pal Stasik.

"I'm mad at you, you're mad at me, I'm a skunk, you're a skunk," babbled Stasik.

With the overture out of the way, I asked what he was calling for.

"I'll tell you what for: don't be a fool, call that party immediately. You know yourself how much depends on him. I saw Voynovsky today, and he'd run into Ovsyannikov, who'd spoken to Sadovnikov yesterday; all of them feel you *must* do it. I'm about to call Ovsyannikov, and he'll try and get in touch with Sadovnikov, and Sadovnikov will be calling you. You wouldn't know Voynovsky's number?"

I hung up. The plungers clicked nastily. For fifteen minutes, sitting by the now silent instrument, I had an almost physical awareness of the telephonic hurry-scurry my friends had set in motion—pictured their words, sleek as mice, darting cleverly into the cables and slithering along in convergent streams.

Then Sadovnikov called, promising to hurry and get in touch with Ovsyannikov, who would give him Stasik's number, and Stasik would help him contact Voynovsky.

"Did you get through to him?" my wife asked as she came into the room.

"There's no one home," I lied.

"Of course not. You're just a man with no answers."

She left. I was in a state of complete confusion and disarray when in came Whale, smiling, his arms piled with books.

"Read me a story, Tolya?"

There were works by Marshak, Jacob Akim, Eugene Rein, and Henry Samgir, as well as an assortment of folk tales. We took up the folk tales. Whale leaned against me and listened attentively, pulling on my ear at tense moments.

The Indian story of the little elephant he rejected, however. When we came to the part where the crocodile seizes the little elephant by the trunk, Whale gave a shout, snatched the book, and hurled it to the floor.

"It's a lie!" He even flushed red. "That didn't happen! It's a bad story!"

"Now look, Whale," I said, "the story is a good one. It has a happy ending."

"No it's not. It's evil! Read this one here."

What he pulled from the pile was "The Wolf and the Seven Little Goats." My God, I thought, here too we have dramatic happenings—a dreadful act, the devouring of the baby goats—and even though it all ends happily, how am I going to read it to Whale, my baby fact-varnisher?

Whale, meanwhile, was leafing through the book, scrutinizing the crude illustrations.

"Here's the Mama Goat," he said, "bringing milk. Here are the little goat-children, playing."

The delightful idyll unfolded before us, and it gladdened Whale. Naive as he was, and ignorant of the laws of dramaturgy, he turned calmly to the next page, where a garishly ferocious wolf was taking the poor little white kid into his fearsome maw. I froze.

"And here's the nice Daddy Goat," said Whale, pointing to the wolf. "He's playing with the baby." He had set up the goat family in a most peaceful fashion.

"Whale, you're mistaken," I said cautiously. "That's not the Daddy Goat, it's the nasty gray wolf. He's about to swallow the little goat, but everything turns out all right, the wolf will be punished. This is Dramaturgy, my little Whale."

"No!" he shouted, on the verge of tears. "That's not a wolf! It's the Daddy Goat. He's playing. You don't understand anything, Tolya!"

"My mistake," I said hastily. "You're right. It's the Daddy Goat."

"Ivan dearest, time for bed," called his mother, and off he went, taking with him into his gentle dreams the family of heavenly bears, the "bus family," and the nice family of goats, the pretty lady's umbrella, the good monstrosities of Fantasy World, and my cap, which would of course grow overnight to the size of an airplane and which he would fly to the North Pole, to the kingdom of good animals.

When she had tucked him in my wife returned and sat down in the armchair opposite me. We lighted cigarettes. Normally these were happy moments, when we smoked together at the end of the day, but tonight it was no good.

"Who's the lady Ivan was telling me about?" asked my wife.

"Someone from the main office. A consultant on legal problems."

"Is that so," she said. "What do you intend to do now?"

"I don't know."

"Is that so," she said.

"My God, I wish it were winter!" I burst out.

"Why winter?"

"Winter's when I have vacation. I'll go skiing."

"But of course," she said caustically. "You're a great skier."

"Don't."

"No, it's true. You *are* a first-class skier. Everyone knows that."

She bit her lip, ever so slightly, to keep from breaking into tears. Whereupon I pulled the phone over and dialed that damned number at one fell swoop.

While the long slow tones rang in the receiver, I pictured him swinging his feet down from the divan and leisurely walking to the telephone, reading from one of his books on the way. Maybe he was rubbing his back or his seat, maybe thinking, "Who can this be? Most likely that sad sack with his fatuous requests." Here he was, picking up the receiver.

He spoke to me gently, confidingly. "Listen, my friend, they tell me you've had trouble bringing yourself to call me. I've been waiting for your call a long time. Come now, why the rigamarole and apprehension? Apparently it's all been due to a misconception. When last we met I wondered whether you hadn't misunderstood me. I do believe everything will be favorably resolved. Sleep in peace. With all my soul I am for you, and by its every fiber and by my every nerve, my heart, my liver, and my spleen, by my virtue and my honor, my fidelity, my sincerity and my love, by all that is sacred to humankind, by the ideals of all generations, by the earth's axis, by the solar system, by the wisdom of my best-beloved writers and philosophers, by history, geography, and botany, by the red sun, the blue sea, and the high and far off kingdom I vow to be unto you a faithful servant, your armor-bearer and your page."

Drenched in sweat, I hung up the receiver.

"There," said my wife to me, "that wasn't so dreadful, was it? You just have to make a wish, and..." She smiled at me.

I got up, went into the bathroom, washed, and then stopped by the bedroom for a look at Whale. He slept like an infant hero, arms and legs flung wide. The creases of his baby fat had not quite faded away; they still marked his wrists, his dimpled paws. In his sleep he smiled a sly little smile, evidently busy completing various droll and delightful turnabouts in his kingdom.

When I look at him I am filled with gladness, goodness, and light. I feel like drinking to the long, happy life of the Seven Little Goats.

Translated by Susan Brownsberger

"Oh yes, there is such a theory, or rather, hypothesis. They think the satellites around Mars—Phobus and Deimos—are slowed down a little by the atmosphere of the planet. Therefore, they're hollow inside, you see. And hollow bodies, as everyone knows, can only be created... how?"

"Only... only..." stammered the first lady, like a schoolgirl.

"Only by artificial means."

"Goodness!" exclaimed the second lady, who was a bit quicker.

"Yes, artificially. So, they were made by some sort of intelligent beings."

I looked at the man telling these interesting stories and racked my brain to recall where I had seen him before. He was sitting opposite me in the train compartment, his knees elegantly crossed, swinging his foot. He had on a smart but not flashy blue suit with a tie to match, and an impeccably white shirt. Everything about him indicated a man who had not let himself go and had no intention of doing so; besides, he wasn't all that old, thirty-five at most. A certain fullness to his cheeks made his face simple and likeable. None of this gave me the slightest reason for supposing I had met him anywhere before. It was only the oddly familiar way he sometimes curled his lip, and the far-off, familiar intonations flickering now and again in his speech, that compelled me to stare at him.

"Recent discoveries in the Sahara and Mesopotamia give us reason to think that in far-off times the Earth was visited by strangers from outer space."

"Perhaps these same Martians?" The ladies oohed and aahed with one voice.

"We can't rule out that possibility," he said with a smile. "We can't rule out the possibility that we are direct descendants of the Martians," he concluded brightly, and, leaving the ladies in a state of confusion, he took up his newspapers.

He had a lot of different newspapers, a thick stack of them. He looked through each in turn and, when he had finished, put it on the table, pinning it down with his elbow.

Beyond the window, pine trees and young undergrowth rushed past, bright sunlit glades flashed by us. The forest was warm and peaceful. I pictured myself walking along in the forest, parting the bushes and getting tangled in ferns; an unseen forest cobweb would land on my face, I'd come out into a bright glade, and the squirrels would look at me from every side, inspiring me to kind, simple-minded thoughts.

All this was somehow a most decisive contrast to whatever I shared with the man who had taken cover behind the newspaper.

"May I have a look, sir?" I asked, and gently pulled a paper from under his elbow. He started, peered out from behind his paper, and at that I remembered him instantly.

I had been in the same grade with him in school during the war, in a remote, overcrowded Volga town coated with dirty yellow ice. He had been kept back three times, and I caught up with him in the fourth grade in 1943. I was then a puny little boy. I went around in a heavy woman's jacket, over-sized boots, and the dark blue trousers that had been my authorized share of the American gift packages. The trousers were tough heavy-weight denim, but by that time I had already worn them through, and my seat was adorned with two patches, round like eyeglasses, made of a different fabric. Nonetheless I continued to pride myself on my trousers—patches were nothing to be ashamed of then. Another thing I prided myself on was a fountain pen, a trophy my sister had sent me from the field army. But I didn't have long to be proud of the pen. He took it away from me. He took everything from me, everything that held any interest for him. And not just from me but from the whole class.

I remembered two of his comrades, too: a hunchbacked guy named Leo and a thin, pale Cossack with burning eyes. At night the three would be outside the Electro Cinema selling cigarettes to wounded men and amazingly big huge women. I was friends with Abe Ziperson; he and I often went to the movies together—wormed our way in through the coal chute and made ourselves comfortable on the balcony near the projection booth. My God... *Let George Do it*, and my funny soldier-hero Antosha Rybkin, and that pathetic Hitler, always playing the fool—if you just came up and let him have it between the eyes he was done for. But the real Hitler was not like that, we knew, and sitting in the darkness near the projection booth we used to concoct tortures for the real one. Put him in a cage and drag him around to all the cities for people to spit on and pelt with cigarette butts. No, better drop him into molten lead. And then in China there's the fine torture they call "The Thousand Small Pieces."

When we came out of the theater we invariably encountered them. They'd be hopping from one foot to the other, bawling, "Hey, flyboys! Cigarettes here!"

Abe and I would try to avoid them, take cover in the shadows, but they never even noticed us. By night they didn't recognize us, as if we weren't in the same class with them, as if they didn't take our school lunches away from us every day.

Lunches were handed out to us every day at school—doughy rolls made of rye flour. The monitor carried them up on a big platter, while we stood on the upstairs landing and watched this miraculous dish float towards us from the cold bowels of the school, float up from its mournful depths.

"That's an interesting business, don't you think?" I said to him, and pointed to an account in the paper.

He glanced at it, smiled, and began to tell me the details of the affair. I kept nodding and looking out the window. It was hard for me to look into his blue eyes, because they had met me every day around the corner of the schoolhouse.

"Hand it over," he'd say, and I'd hold out my roll, still dented with my fingerprints.

"Hand it over," he'd say to the next guy. Leo and the Cossack worked right alongside him.

I'd get home and wait for my little sister. Then together we'd wait for my aunt. My aunt would come back from the market bringing a loaf of bread and some potatoes. Sometimes she didn't bring anything. She struggled on our behalf with a resigned fury that had already become habit. Every morning, getting ready for school, I saw her pass beneath my windows, broad-shouldered and squat, her nose bulbous but her lips compressed in a thin line.

Once she said to me, "Nina brings her lunches home, but not you. Rustam brings his home, and all the boys next door, but you eat yours up yourself."

I went out into the yard and sat on a broken-down iron cot by the terrace. In the darkening gray sky, rooks were circling over the lime trees. Beyond the fence there walked the girls of wartime. "As long as the boy could be seen through the haze, the girl kept the lamp in her window ablaze." What do rooks eat? Bugs, worms, air? They have it good. But perhaps even for them there's someone like that, someone who takes everything for himself? The weathervane on top of our house creaked harshly. Flying low over the city came the dive-bombers. What would become of me?

All night my aunt did laundry. Water flowed behind the screen, splashed, gurgled. Whirlpools darkened, waterfalls thundered, Hitler in funny striped shorts choked in the soapy water, my aunt crushed him in her gnarled hands.

The next day an incident occurred. The rolls had been spread with a thin layer of lard and sprinkled with powdered egg. I tore a leaf from my notebook, wrapped the roll in it, and put it in my bookbag. When I rounded the corner—quivering with valor—I grabbed him by the shirtfront and punched him. Abe Ziperson did the same, and some of the other guys too. In a matter of seconds I was lying in the snow, the Cossack was sitting astride me, and Leo was stuffing my own lunch down my throat.

"Here, be a he-man, take a bite!"

"There you have it, the whole story," he said. "I know because a close friend of mine had something to do with it. But in the papers you get just the bare facts; the details often slip away. It's only natural."

"Of course," I said, and thanked him. "Much obliged."

Nearby the ladies kept up a sweet twitter. They were treating each other to cherries and talking about how you couldn't call these cherries, now in the south there were real cherries, and unexpectedly it developed they were both from Lvov, for goodness sake, and had practically lived on the same street, and apparently had gone to the same school, and there turned out to be so many coincidences that in the end the ladies flowed together into one enormous whole.

Next day, when the last lesson was over, I put my notebook in my bag and glanced at the back row. The Cossack, Leo, and he were sitting together on the same desk, grinning as they looked at me. Apparently they could tell by my face that I was going to try and fight for my lunch again. They got up and went out. I purposely sat at my desk and waited until everyone had left. I didn't want to get Abe and the other guys mixed up in this stupid business again. When everyone had left I checked over my slingshot and shook a supply of tin bullets out of my bookbag into my pocket. If they were going to be standing around the corner again, I'd give them three rounds, hit each of them smack in the kisser, and then with a neat and easy maneuver like Antosha Rybkin I'd seize one of them by the leg, maybe Leo or the Cossack but better yet *him,* and flip him over on his back. Well, and then come what may. Let them beat me up, I'd do it every day.

I went slowly downstairs, fingering the tin bullets in my pocket. Someone jumped on my back from above, and ahead, *he* came looming up in front of me. He grabbed at my face with his five fingers and squeezed. From below someone jerked at my feet. I heard light, scornful laughter. The job was soon done. They dragged my boots off and unwound all the stuff I had wrapped around my feet. Then they hung all those foul-smelling rags out on the stairs and started down.

"Keep your boots, he-man!" he shouted, and my boots, tumbling crazily, came flying up. Laughing merrily the gang went their way. They had forgotten to cop my lunch.

"May I invite you to join me in the dining car, sir?" I said to him.

He put down his newspaper and smiled. "I was just wanting to do the same for you," he said. "You anticipated me. Allow me to invite you."

"Oh no," I cried, gripped with a mighty agitation. "As children say, first dibs! Do you understand me?"

"Yes, I do," he said, looking intently into my eyes...

I started to cry. I gathered up the foot-rags my aunt had labored over, and cried. I felt that now I was utterly beaten and it would be a long time before I could hold up my head, and many years would pass before I could forget that light scornful laughter and the fingers squeezing my face. The bell rang. I heard the swelling tramp of many feet, and down the stairs past me rolled a giggling avalanche of upperclassmen.

I went out to the street and crossed it, climbed through the iron palings, and walked in the old overgrown park. Down at the end of the path there was a bunch of upperclassmen tearing around. I dawdled along behind them; I sort of wanted to watch them play soccer.

There, next to the summer reading room—which had been half torn down for firewood—our school had trampled out a playing field. The upperclassmen, who had split up into two teams, raced up and down it, now this way, now that. Every offensive was shattering, no matter which side it was aimed at; it was headlong and wild, with the inevitable losses and a howl of triumph. Waves of sweat now surged, now receded, while I sat at the edge of the field and great strong legs, felt boots, leather boots skimmed by me; and, as if wanting to instill in me confidence in my own strength, they fought ever more violently, more bitterly for possession of the ball—they, the upperclassmen.

Plunging up to my waist in the deep snow, I fetched them the balls that went out of bounds into the park.

So I don't even know whether this was a defeat or a victory. Sometimes they—the Cossack, Leo, and he—stopped me and took my lunch, and I didn't resist; but sometimes, I don't know why, they didn't touch me. I'd bring home my roll, and in the evening we'd have gluey slices of rye dough for a snack with our tea.

We walked down the aisles of the cars, and I opened doors for him and let him go first; when he went first, he opened doors for me and let me go first. I was in luck—it was I who opened the door to the diner.

Somehow they found out that Abe Ziperson's mother worked in the hospital.

"Listen, Stick-in-the-Mud, how about getting some glucose off of your old lady?"

Abe put them off for a while but then, when they "divvied up" his briefcase into shreds, he brought them a few ampules. They liked the glucose; it was sweet and nourishing. From then on they had a new name for Abe: "Glucose."

"Hey, Glucose," they would say, "come here."

I don't know which caused Abe more suffering: the fact that he had to steal, or the fact that they gave him such a catching, shameful nickname.

Whichever it was, I did see him fighting with them once. I rushed to his aid, and they beat us both up badly. Each one of this trio was stronger than anybody in our class. They were three years older than we were.

Of course we could have banded together and jointly given them what they had coming, but the school code said that we could fight only one to one, and till first blood. In our small-boy logic, we did not see how a guy could beat up on someone who was clearly weaker, how three guys together could beat up on one, or how the whole class could beat up on three guys. This was the whole point: they were struggling for food without sticking to the code. And too, they didn't argue, just took it. They were older than we were.

"But why doesn't he recognize me?" I thought.

The dining car was empty, pleasant, and clean. The little tables shone with starched white linens, and only one, evidently just vacated, bore the traces of a lavish banquet.

I did the ordering. I spared no expense. Cognac—"Select," the best. This was no time for me to scrimp and save. If ever there was a time to go all out, this was it. Too bad that when it came to food I had to settle for the usual dining car fare—solyanka soup, Caucasian kabobs, and plum compote.

I carried on a simple, amicable conversation with him about the changing seasons and looked at his hands, at the fine reddish hair showing from under his watchband. Then I raised my eyes and recalled yet another item of interest.

His heart was not on the left side but on the right. Somewhat later I learned that this phenomenon is called "dextrocardia." Generally speaking, the people who have it are few and mighty far between in this world.

At the very beginning of the school year, before they turned to the forcible expropriation of surplus groceries, he used to bet with us on that score. He'd bet for a lunch.

"I'll bet you my heart is on the wrong side," he'd say, and proudly unbutton his shirt.

Later on, when everyone already knew about this peculiarity of his, he turned to extortion by force.

"Make a bet?" he'd ask. He'd sit down beside you and twist your arm. "Is it a bet or not?" And he'd unbutton his shirt.

Lub-dub, lub-dub—evenly, peacefully, there was his heart beating away on the righthand side.

The heavy, radiant surface of the soup was agitated by the diner's steady jolting. Amber drops of fat trembled, gathered around the small pieces of sausage floating on the surface, and in the depths of this slop lurked the devil knows what—scraps of ham, and cucumbers, and bits of chicken.

"What awful food!" I said. "But remember what food was like during the war?"

"Yes," he said, "the food was pretty bad then."

I plucked up my courage and looked him in the eye. "Remember our school lunches?"

"Yes," he said firmly, and I understood from his tone that he was still plenty strong.

"Rye rolls, sort of doughy?"

"Oh yes," he smiled, "those were some rolls."

I was itching to make my move. No, I couldn't do it yet. No, no... Let him eat up. I was even enjoying watching him eat. Let him sate himself, and I would pay.

"Lard and powdered eggs, right?" I asked with an easy grin.

"The second front?" He matched my tone and smiled.

"But what we loved best of all then was the caked dregs of sunflower seed oil."

"That was a delicacy," he laughed.

Dinner proceeded in a splendid flutter of smiles.

The French have a way: they pour the cognac, spit in it, and dash it in the guy's face. Guys like this, collaborationists.

"Shall we have a drink?" I said.

"To your health," he replied.

The kabobs were served.

As I chewed on the succulent, nicely done meat, I said, "Of course this isn't the Aragvi Restaurant, but..."

"It's not bad at all," he took me up, nodding his head as if listening to the movement of his inner juices. "The sauce, of course, is not a Tkemali, but..."

At that I was seized with malice such as I had never known before. You epicure, you! You're an epicure. You know what's what in food, and in wines, probably, and in women too, most likely... And do you still carry my pen in your pocket?

I got control of myself and carried on with table talk in the prescribed rhythm and requisite tone.

"It's an astonishing thing," I said, "how complex the concept of food has become in the course of history, how many arguments over this concept there have been, how many nuances there are in this concept..."

"Oh, yes," he eagerly took me up. "But after all the concept is a very simple one."

"Right. Simple as ABC—that's food. Foooood. The simplest thing, and the most important for man."

"Come now, that's a bit of an overstatement," he smiled.

"No, really. Food and women—the most important things," I continued my disingenuous patter.

"For me, there are other things more important," he said earnestly.

"What?"

95

"My business, for example."

"Oh, that's all a later stratification."

"No, you don't understand..."

He began to enlarge on his ideas. I understood that he did not recognize me. I understood that he would never recognize me, just as he would never have recognized anyone else in our class except Leo and the Cossack. And I understood why: we were not individuals to him, we were a mass, something that just gave him a little trouble from time to time.

"Now how am I to understand you!" I exclaimed rudely, to my own surprise. "Of course food is nothing to you! After all, you're a direct descendant of the Martians!"

He stopped short and looked at me with narrowed eyes. Knots of muscle flickered on his plump cheeks.

"Shh!" he said quietly. "Don't you spoil my appetite, now."

I fell silent and returned to the kabobs. The cognac stood at my place; it would never be too late to spit in it. Just let him eat up, and I would pay.

There was a man sitting next to us; his plaid shirt was cheap but his watch was gold. He had bent his head over his beer and was whispering something. He was very drunk. Suddenly he raised his head and shouted at us, "Hey you! The Black Sea, right? Sevastopol, right? The torpedo boat..."

And again he dropped his head on to his chest. From the depths of his chest came a hollow grumbling.

"Waiter!" said my dinner companion. "Can't this man be removed?" He was pointing not at me but at the drunk. "To avoid a disturbance."

"Let him sit," said the waiter. "What is he, bothering you?"

"Black Sea..." muttered the man. "Torpedo boat... or maybe I'm exaggerating..."

"Do you actually consider yourself a descendant of the Martians, sir?" I asked my dinner companion.

"Why not? We can't rule out the possibility," he said mildly.

"The Martians are a likeable sort," I said. "They have everything normal folks have: arms, legs, the heart on the left side... But you, now..."

"Stop!" he said. "I'm telling you once more: don't you spoil my appetite, sir, don't even try. After all, I can pay, myself."

I changed the subject, and in a few minutes it was all smoothed over, and dinner went on in a brilliant flutter of smiles and pleasantries. So this was how he'd turned out—a real fine fellow, nerves of steel.

"What are we doing being so formal—'sir' this and 'sir' that," I said. "We haven't even introduced ourselves."

I gave my name and half rose, with outstretched hand. He too half rose and gave his name.

It was the wrong name. This was not he, it was a different man.

Dessert was served.

Translated by Susan Brownsberger

96

JAPANESE JOTTINGS

The Mountain.

Now, when I see the dainty Japanese islands strung between steep continents on a map of the world, I find it hard to believe that I spent three amazing weeks on these brightly painted little rocks, that it was actually there that I met such a multitude of different people, that for three whole weeks Japan demarcated my horizon.

For some reason I want to begin this confused account with a description of the Mountain.

We discussed it a lot on the way back to Tokyo from Hiroshima. All our conversations eventually returned to the same point: were we going to see The Mountain? We were fed up with it already, all our jokes at its expense were becoming banal. The final outburst of witticisms was in response to an abject apology from the personnel of "The Morning Breeze" Express for the thick cloud obscuring The Mountain.

We cracked a few jokes and dismissed the matter.

And still we indulged in a little idle speculation as the taxi climbed from the seaside resort of Atami to the mountain retreat of Hakone.

A yellow sun swam in light motionless clouds, our driver was put out, and Hara was distressed that these stupid mists should block The Mountain. Finally someone suggested that we might have better luck next day.

Frankly, by now I didn't care if I saw it next day or not. So much anticipation and so many words had been wasted on the wind, that I feared a let-down. After all, a mountain is a mountain, and this one was not even particularly high. Perhaps it would be better if the mysterious mountain stayed hidden behind its mysterious yellow luminescence, inaccessible to foreign eyes?

Our hotel in Hakone was vast and empty: it was winter and therefore off-season. The only people we saw next morning were three old English-women. A kind of sadness permeated the hotel and down in the hall we found this notice under a photograph of a venerable parrot: "It is with the greatest sorrow that we announce the demise of Bimbo, the old parrot so well known and loved by many of our guests. We thank you for your attachment to this humble creature. The Management."

Sharing the management's sorrow, Hara and I went off to play ping-pong. Emptiness confronted us at every turn: in the bar, the swimming pool and the games room. Our footsteps rang hollow in the empty high-ceilinged corridors. I conjured up the lonely, pathetic life of a millionaire and suddenly longed to be back in Moscow, in my two-roomed flat, or in a group of friends, or a crowd milling around a coffee-machine.

"Takuya, how would you like to have a posh house like this?" I asked Hara.

"Uh-huh," he replied, although this didn't mean that he would like to, but that he had taken in my question, fastened on it, and was contemplating an answer.

My friend Takuya Hara has an excellent command of literary Russian, but was still finding conversation rather difficult, and always took several seconds to answer.

"No, please, I wouldn't," he replied.

We played ping-pong for a while, then had a drink in the bar, watched the cowboys on T.V. and went to bed.

Everybody was very jolly next morning. Valdemar Kristopovich cracked a lot of jokes, so did Irina Lvovna and even Hara and I. Anyway, we broke the staid silence of breakfast and perhaps even slightly shocked the elderly ladies. We slung off at the thick clouds and milky-gray sky.

By the time we were in the funicular carriage we had forgotten about The Mountain and were busy studying other, more accessible mountains, covered by coniferous forest, and the cottages below. We topped one pass after another, joking about the safety of the ropes, prattling incessantly and delighting in the long-awaited rest, crowning our travels through Japan, when suddenly Hara jabbed me in the side and cried:

"Fuji!"

I turned around, and even the "Oh!" was no more than a gasp.

It was completely visible, taking up half the sky. Looming white, it dwarfed the smaller green peaks. Our yellow insect, suspended in the abyss, crawled past it. How utterly incredible, that it should suddenly open itself up for us, and so simply! Our faces lit up with its white glow, and Hara's usually meek face grew triumphant.

This mountain had some ineffable quality. These few minutes were significant and precious. This was the powerful and simple Japanese mountain. Its symmetry and triple summit resolved the whole surrounding landscape and perhaps the whole country. It was what the Volga is to us. Silently and lingeringly we passed Fuji in our comic little carriage, with a store of nuts and "Torris Whiskey" in our pockets.

We saw Fujiama for a second time on the way home, as we took off from Haneda airport for Hong Kong. It was early morning. The Boeing ripped through the clouds, Japan was hidden except for Fuji, snowy pink from the rising sun, towering above the clouds in a lingering farewell. It remained visible for a long time, that we should remember it better.

The Thousand-armed one.

As the train rocks, rattles and sways its way out of Tokyo's stone jungle, the foreign traveler glues himself to the window, to see the Japanese countryside; a few cottages, some rice fields in the moonlight, upturned boats; that is, an idyll. The lights become sparser, then more and more frequent until ten minutes later it seems he has never left Tokyo.

I recalled the vast expanses of my country and the impenetrable darkness beyond the window, when you smoke in the corridor at night. Here it was completely dark outside only twice the whole way from Tokyo to Hiroshima, both times in a tunnel.

Illuminated Japanese characters and Latin letters flickered in our sleeper all night. Mitsura sauces, Mikasa drilling machines, Goncharov chocolates, Esso petrol...

"Sanyo!," "Sony!," "Apollo!," "Santori!," "Mariman!"...! ...! ...! But then, rising from the horizon, the gigantic, floodlit goddess Kannon sailed out of the night, The thousand-armed Kannon, one of the incarnations of Buddha. Hewn out of stone, she towered above the raving night, above all the flickering advertisements, like a mountain, like Fuji. A shining mountain with an ancient inscrutable smile. And at her feet a collection of gas cylinders reflected the deathly glow of the moon.

Gods, Temples, Augury.

We were in a Buddhist temple in the Asakusa region of Tokyo. The altar to Buddha is separated from the crowd of worshippers by a square pit covered with a large grille, into which coins are thrown. The temple is rather noisy; people come and go, they don't talk of course, but they blow their noses and cough, and clap their hands to attract the god's attention. Coins fly over heads and jingle against the grille. The set-up is fairly business-like. It's nothing like Sunday Mass in Catholic cathedrals or an Orthodox liturgy.

The ancient temples have been handed over to tourists. Take the Daibutsu temple in the sacred city of Nara. We approached it from a sacred park, and were pursued by gentle, but somewhat roguish deer, cadging biscuits. One sacred deer pushes a warm, moist nose into your palm, whilst another prods you in the rear, as if to say "I'm here too."

The ticket gave the dimensions of the gigantic Buddha huddled beneath the roof of the temple. The figure was 16.21 meters high, the face 4.84m in circumference, each eye—1.18m, the nose—0.48m long. He was a very grand Buddha, somewhat somber and austere. Photographs were forbidden, but cameras were clicking all around as Japanese, Americans and other tourists assiduously fulfilled their "obligations." So as not to be odd man out, I too trained my "Quartz" on Buddha.

There is a round aperture in one of the temple columns—whoever crawls through it will find happiness. The opening is designed for the dainty Japanese build: a minor catastrophe befell a cocky American, who climbed into the hole, painstakingly tried to wriggle forwards and stuck fast. His shoulders were in the way, and a certain other place didn't help matters either. Everybody there, irrespective of political views or religious persuasion set about dragging him out. "Peaceful coexistence," I thought, as I grabbed an American leg. We hauled the idiot out.

Peddlers ply a lively trade all along the roadside to the Shinto temple on the island of Miyajima. "Buy this remarkable cup, sir!" A maiden in an enticing costume is depicted in the bottom of the cup. You pour in some liquid and—hey presto, the girl is naked. The ancient wooden temple is magnificent. It stands on piles above transparent blue water and its gates, like a Japanese character, extend way out into the sea. Past them sail old-world stylized boats, dragons with diesel engines. A few monks collect money in a business-like manner, selling "omamori"—amulets for seafarers and travelers. Monks are not the most backward in the tourist trade.

One day I decided to obtain some insight into my future. It was in Tokyo, in Ueno park. There were fortune-telling machines in front of the Buddhist temple. The price was a mere 10 yen. I inserted my coin and pulled out a long strip of paper, dotted with small characters. I had really fallen in love with Japanese characters. They were beautiful in their own right, quite apart from what they stood for. It's no wonder that calligraphy is considered an art in Japan. Later on Irina Lvovna kindly translated the prediction. It began in verse:

> When you come near
> Specks of light from the white hachi flowers
> Dance along your sleeve.
> The flowers give fragrance in the moonlight hours

This was followed by practical advice: You must move quickly, and not lose the moment. If all act together, success will ensue. However, you must exercise caution... Do not go where things are known to be unpropitious. What you have lost is unlikely to return. A journey will be successful and unmarred. In business affairs you will make a profit, but not a large one. In the field of science (art), you will be successful if diligent. An easterly direction will bring you luck. You will win an argument, but should not be overbearing. As regards your employees, you should let things be a while—don't dismiss anyone or hire new staff.

And so on.

Several days later I was walking around Shinjuku in the evening with Takuya Hara and Hiroshi Kimura. An elderly gentleman in a black woolen kimono and round black cap was sitting on the corner under a black umbrella. From time to time he would light a small lantern, a signal that he read palms. Feeling like a diversion I cheerfully stretched out a palm. Tolya (Takuya) and Serezha (Hiroshi) began to interpret.

"You are a foreigner," said the old man. I was struck by his perspicacity.

"You are a writer," he said, and briskly twisting my palm, proceeded to give me advice reminiscent of the automatic oracle in Ueno park.

A strong wind prowled around the crossroad, and paper lanterns and garlands tossed in the narrow lanes of Shinjuku. The wind drove my fate along the lanes of this strange city, and only the tenacious fingers of the old sorcerer prevented me from dashing after it. What was I to do with my employees, and would an easterly direction bring me luck? All the same I hoped that Serezha and Tolya were only having me on.

Buddhism, Shintoism, amulets, automatic fortune-telling machines, anything in some way relevant to man's destiny and soul, flickered in one form or another through the colorful, endless line of our journey. And finally we come to the Stone Garden—sanctuary of the followers of Zen. Zen as a religion exhorts one to examine the depths of one's soul. The Stone Garden is a symbol of eternity. Cast off all egotistic thoughts and desires, listen not to external sounds, think nothing at all, sit and gaze peacefully at the Stone Garden, seek to dissolve in it. The attempt to dissolve into eternity is the Zen act of worship.

And indeed, these stones, scattered like islands, with that lack of affectation peculiar to Nature, the symmetrical lines of gravel, this model of eternity, have some strange effect if contemplated at length. Perhaps my attempt to experience the state of Zen would have come off were it not for the sudden wail of an ambulance drifting across the walls.

The Streets of Tokyo

In the evenings, announcements like this flash across the busiest crossroads of the capital:

"There were 7 people killed in Tokyo today, and 123 injured."

This is peak hour in Ginza. An endless line of gleaming cars stretches past. A train dashes past overhead. Finally the crossing is submerged, as countless hordes of white collars, polished boots, gray and brown overcoats swoop down onto the road. Cigarette smoke floats and dissipates above the crowd. There is the shuffle of feet, chatter, laughter, bubbles of silence....

"Abnai!," which means "danger," rings hoarsely out above the crossroad. This largest of cities is dangerous, vast, magic, swinging, hazy and uneasy, magnetic, surging, a dainty dish, an octupus, a star.

We flew over the sea in the pitch black of night, all the way to Tokyo.

101

And as it appeared below, from the airplane, ten kilometers up, it rather seemed that everything was upside down, that we were flying in to one of the nebulae of Andromeda.

Later, looking down from the overpass, I was struck by the insanity of Ginza's neon lights. "It's insane, like a fair, a whirlpool. How can people live here?" as a friend from Kazan once said of Moscow. But after all, people do live in Tokyo, Paris and Moscow—and don't give a damn. Each has his own circle, his own haven, the bubble he carries through the noisiest crowd.

There are people about in the evening streets, united by something common. Take for example the workers in oilskin overalls and yellow and green helmets. Perhaps they are united by the compressor supplying their perforators with compressed air? Or overshadowed by the long reach of the excavator? Hey, you carefree nimble workers in the evening streets of Tokyo, what is it unites you in your deft labor? What name do you give the unifying force?

And something must unite the bored elegant gentlemen pulling up at nightclubs in their flashy cars. They definitely have something in common, even though each is locked in a sphere of chromed metal and thick glass. What name do you give the threads binding these gentlemen together?

And then there are the girls who greet them, girls in kimonos, bowing in the traditional manner. They, of course, are united by tradition.

The girls from the "Albion" bar, long-legged westernized misses, squeezed into white slacks and jackets... These lovelies are united by the beat of the "twist."

And then you are approached by a lone enterprising shark, cap pushed forward onto his nose.

"Do you like girls, Sir?" he begins in English.

"No."

"Ah! Boys?"

"No."

"Oh! Are you American?"

"No."

"French?"

"No."

"German?"

"No."

"Who?" The shark is utterly perplexed.

"Russian."

"Oh! Oh!" He scampers off and watches after you from a distance.

There is a lone pathetic Santa-Claus with a large placard on his back.

And here is a man with a mike in his hand. He is screaming and wailing; his uncle was unjustly brought to trial. Everybody who loves justice must appear in court to defend his uncle.

Two American soldiers in unseasonably light civilian dress go by, rubbing their blue noses. It looked as if the fellows have shot through a.w.o.l. Candles on the newspaper vendors' trays flicker in the winter wind. The old women shoe-shiners shiver. Nylon Christmas trees are fluttering "Merry X-mas!," "Tra-la-la, tra-la-la"—the honeyed voice of Frank Sinatra.

A crowd of solitaries flows by: tired clerks, elegant revelers, doll-faced girls...

And here I am, a lonely foreigner; Polish raincoat, English boots, Russian suit. I just walk on, comprehending nothing—I came out for fifteen minutes, but have been walking two hours. You may say this city is ill suited to walking. That's quite true. Then why does it draw me further and further into its labyrinth of petrol, soybeans, cigarettes? Perhaps it's the fault of the endless flashing characters, enigmatic as children's constructions from matches? Or is it the paper lanterns, swaying in the narrow lanes? Perhaps this is the capital of Mars? It's not for nothing the contours of the advertizing towers are so outlandish.

And now an amusements street; a continuous row of strip shows on one side, and cinemas on the other. On the right hand side you are menaced by festoons of bared female breasts, whilst countless gangster pistols are trained on you on the left. You could lose your sense of humor completely here. Get a move on, boy!...

Ginza quiets down early. By 11 o'clock there are hardly any people on the street, only rustling rivers of cars flow along the road. Workers warm themselves by open fires. Small smoking wagons appear on the crossroads— they are packed with "yakitori"—astonishingly delicious small shashliks on wooden skewers. This is where the common folk snatch a bite: the vendor puts down a bench, and three or four people take a seat by the wagon. The owner lets down a tarpaulin curtain, closes off an area, and suddenly all that remains in front of you is a candle, the crackling "yakitori," and the tired faces of your table companions. The vendor winks amicably at the foreigner.

I continue along the empty streets. My path resembles the flight of a bat. Where is my hotel?

Suddenly there is music, the howl of hundreds of voices, feet shuffling and I come upon a strange quarter where apparently nobody intends to sleep. Again the shining motor cars, dandies, girls, the wide open doors of countless nightclubs and bars, neon signs, paper lanterns. But a lone cyclist turns off into a side street. He rides unsteadily, locked in himself.

An elderly man in a long peaked cap, all you can see is his nose poking out and the glint of cheap spectacles. He retreated but I wanted to catch him up and run alongside. No, I don't intend to pester him with questions. It is just that he is very close to me, and I understand only too well what it means to transport one's inner world on two small wheels, to ride off into the darkness on brittle spokes. I respect him—that's all.

The Word is "Solidarity"

A group of laughing boys in green nylon jackets and helmets dance along in the wind, carrying carelessly scrawled placards. Irina Lvovna reads the inscriptions:

"Our boss, Makumato—is the biggest shark in Japan! Come to the chief shark's funeral!"

How these lads were enjoying themselves! How they laughed, imagining their boss honored with such a title! They danced along, slapping their sides and one another's shoulders. More and more lads in helmets raced up to join them; their numbers swelled. Tremble, Makumato! There is a word uniting these lads—"solidarity!"

The rapid lifts of the huge Tokyo Tower flew soundlessly upwards. Doll-faced lift attendants thanked the tourists for coming in soft, gentle voices! "Thank you very much, thank you! ("Arigato, domo arigato!") The girls were wearing red bands, inscribed "Solidarity," on their sleeves. This demonstrated their solidarity with the striking miners.

So you Japanese girls are no mere advertizing symbols for superior Japanese service!

The miners had amassed in the capital from various prefectures. A huge demonstration was scheduled to take place in front of parliament, as a sign of protest against the closing down of many mines. Detachments of miners advanced along the road, large detachments of thickset men in oilskin jackets and yellow helmets with red bands on them. And again, on these armbands, was that word: "Solidarity!"

They marched along singing, the older workers smiling with restraint, the young ones laughing outright. I am sure that a restive revolutionary gala mood dominated each man's soul in those minutes.

They marched out of step, swinging their arms out of time, but didn't break up into little clusters or mark time. In that moment they were united not by the piercing whistle of military flutes nor the thunder of intimidating drums, nor subordination, military stripes but by a single triumphant word—"Solidarity!"

Rooted to the spot I watched their movements, and a shiver ran through my skin, the sort of shiver that is produced by beautiful music or verse, or comes to a man in moments of great spiritual elevation.

The crowd on the pavements was silent, and bared radiators in the traffic jams trembled with mysterious emotions.

Pachinko

Suffused in pale blue, forming a crazy abracadabra, the letters "The New Mexico International Pachinko Center" trembled through the dark petrol fumes. A torrent of jazz poured out through its windows. From the street you could see a large hall with long rows of mysterious shining machines. Harsh ringing noises pierced the jazz, and you could hear the clatter of rolling metal balls. Red lights flashed on intermittently. Gloomy men with vacant eyes stood in front of the machines. Each had his right hand glued to a small lever causing metallic balls to shoot out and spin along the labyrinths. Each left hand held a lighted cigarette. Each sported a cap on his head, scarf round his neck, and cigarette butts underfoot.

Pachinko is a form of gambling, brought across to Japan from Hong-Kong. You buy several balls from the cashier and proceed to a machine. Before you is a glass surface with several openings. The idea is to shoot a ball into one of these openings. If you succeed, a bell rings, a red light comes on and the machine spews out a prize at you in the form of a certain number of balls. But more often, after spinning senselessly over the surface and forcing their way through the maze of tiny stakes, the balls disappear into hole zero and you get nothing for your trouble. If you win, you can go to the box office and exchange the balls for cigarettes, tinned foods, sweets or chewing gum. It takes willpower to stop playing this contagious game.

Pachinko is big business. There are countless Pachinko halls in every city and on railway stations. Sometimes they are dirty little dives, sometimes huge institutions like the "New Mexico International Center."

The "New Mexico" was opposite our hotel. One day I found myself in this reckless carousel. I paid for twenty balls and began launching them inexpertly one by one by pressing the lever. A professional worked by my side. A scathing side-glance was all I rated from him. His scornful eye flashed through a cloud of cigarette smoke. His pockets bulged with innumerable balls. No fewer than ten at a time danced under the glass in front of him. His right thumb pressed the lever unceasingly, whilst his other fingers kept sending new balls into the machine. His machine kept up a continuous ring as it threw out prize balls. It was only on the fifteenth ball that I managed to get a small win. Instead of twenty I now had ten in all, but the joy that accompanied a successful hit was so great that I threw myself back into the game. My neighbor worked alongside me to a continuous crash and ring. Suddenly he grew quiet. I turned in his direction. It transpired that he had gone bust in a matter of minutes. My machine rang out and kept on ringing, almost without a break. My pockets bulged with balls. My neighbor watched me with philosophical calm, whilst I lost my head completely. He tapped me on the shoulder: that's enough, mate, go and collect your winnings. But I merely shook my head, kept on pressing the lever, and within two minutes had squandered the lot. My neighbor gave a hoarse laugh and raised his cap. I made my way towards the exit.

Out on the street, I stood for a long while looking in through the window of the Pachinko hall, my neighbor was already putting down fresh money at the box office. Other men were planted obstinately in front of the machines, looking dully ahead, not seeing the spinning balls, swaying slightly to the blare of the music, each engaged in this activity in utter solitude.

Hiroshima and Guernica

"Japan is a sad country," the poet Kusaka remarked one day.

We were taking a walk along the narrow lanes of Shinjuku. A monstrous hoarding for Turkish baths hung over us in the green evening sky.

I remembered the baseballers' yells and the swing of their bats, the firm step of the gay demonstrators, the flashing advertizements, Japan's wild commercial fury, the amazing automation in the factories, and again the baseballers, and the wrestlers' hoarse cries of "smo"...

"Sad? Why?"

"A sad country," repeated Kusaka and glanced away.

The poet is short and sturdy, with a business-like crew cut and business-like spectacles.

"You're a poet, Kusaka, you look for sorrow."

He didn't answer. What could he explain to me, a foreign tourist? Poets know where to find sorrow, but that is their secret.

I remembered what I had been told of Tokyo's immediate post-war days. A huge smoldering ruin out of which hosts of fireproof boxes rose up—all that remained of people's homes. It was among these boxes that life began to reappear—dugouts were built and tiny gardens fenced off. Now look how life has sprung up in this steel, ferro-concrete and aluminium city, this feverishly businesslike city. Where would you begin looking for sorrow?

But our train was drawing near the Japanese center of sorrow, the universal center of sorrow, Hiroshima. We came straight from the station to the hotel, the strikingly modern "Hiroshima Grand Hotel." It was a bright sunny day, so we set off along the seething streets of Hiroshima to the place where the shadow of a man, incinerated instantly, had engraved itself on the wall of a bank.

We stood in a crowd of tourists before this shadow. Movie cameras whirred all round. Le Corbusier's creation, the Atom-Bomb Museum, a glass pencil case on ferro-concrete legs, was visible in the distance. We went up and laid a wreath on the monument. A few hawkers were touting picture postcards and souvenirs right alongside it.

There was much agony expressed in the strange gloomy tunnel of the monument, in its outer and inner spheres, but still one could not quite believe that a lethal flame had once raged on this very spot. Perhaps the bright sun was to blame, and the clumps of bright foliage, the view of the city with its neon towers, but you had to constantly remind yourself that it happened here, here, here, right where you were standing just now.

106

On the way back from the Peace Park to the hotel we passed a baseball stadium. The roar of Hiroshima's supporters came floating out.

I left that city with strange emotions. If I had been shaken by Hiroshima, it was by its wholesome amnesia.

Under a bright sun in the elegant avenues of the park, the noisy city of 300,000 exhibits the last traces of its agony to countless tourists.

The taxi driver told us his story. Yes, some relatives of his had perished here, but at the time he himself was in the Kwantung army. Very few witnesses of the explosion had survived, mostly newcomers lived here now.

"Art reminds us more powerfully of mankind's most terrible days than any material evidence," I thought, remembering "Guernica," the Picasso exhibition in Tokyo's Ueno park.

Picasso's terrible mourners and weeping horses, reminiscent of Lorca, the whole human world, torn, destroyed by the bestial force of Fascism, all the Guernicas, Coventrys, Kievs and Warsaws stared at us from the huge panels, the innumerable études of the great master.

And the memory of Hiroshima lived on in the upturned faces of young Japanese students.

That is perhaps as it should be: forget—and live, devoting only significant minutes of loneliness to the terrible memory. For when you gaze at "Guernica," you are completely alone, no matter how dense the crowd.

Writers

The writer, Kaiko, who is the same age as myself, is one of those people who knows about sorrow. Suede jacket, thick sweater, sharp voice, abrupt laugh, head thrown haughtily back. In some strange way his life has been connected with the production and distribution of alcoholic beverages. In his impecunious stage he worked in the advertizing section of a firm making whiskey and sake. During that time he invented a strange, quaint little man, a sort of Japanese Parnok,[1] an eccentric bungler, and great devotee of the firm's product. This little fellow became extremely popular on advertizements and in newspapers. Now he leads his own, separate existence, quite independent of Kaiko. His texts are written by others.

"Rivers of whiskey and lakes of sake are the source of my pessimism," said Kaiko.

"But are you a pessimist?"

"What do you think? The best years of my youth were devoted to that dirty business."

"Is it so dreadful then?"

"Yes, terrible!"

"My advice then is to go on the wagon. Perhaps you will shed your pessimism then."

"To your health!" laughed Kaiko.

We were carrying on this facetious conversation with bottles of warm sake in our hands.

All jokes aside, Kaiko describes life in an ordinary Tokyo day. He has access to those parts of town where respectable gentlemen are advised not to show themselves. He is an angry writer with a strong social conscience.

We were sitting in the Wantei bar. A strip of tin plate had been set in right along the counter to form a grill. A young barman greases this with butter for each visitor, then throws on oysters, fine slices of meat, onion, some sort of root, and grills it before your eyes, dexterously wielding the long wooden sticks or "hashi."

Next to Kaiko sat his friend, the extremely young writer Oe. In contrast to Kaiko, there was not a thing out of place about him—neat hairstyle, elegant suit, smiling, polite eyes behind thick glasses. This well-brought-up young man had been courageous enough to write a sharply antifascist novel, commenting directly on political events in Japan.

Everyone remembers, of course, how the General Secretary of the Socialist party of Japan was stabbed to death on the rostrum by a fascist murderer.

Oe wrote about the murderer. In his novel this was a youth of good middle-class family, a pathetic young masturbator, tormented with complexes, striving for self-assertion at any price. He was drawn into the fascist camp by admiration for their strength, bitterness and resolution, and desire to become one of their "supermen."

When the novel was published, these "supermen" made persistent phone calls to Oe, yelling hoarse threats into the mouthpiece.

However, why go on about them, as if there was nothing else to talk about. We sat in The "Wantei" discussing optimism and pessimism, the "new novel," our women and children, the various oceans we had flown over. We had met in Moscow several months back, and now we were sitting together here. It was warm, the strange grill crackled away, Fords and Nissans were tooting outside. The barman turned the radio up, Kaiko was shouting with laughter, Oe smiling... Where then was this Japanese sorrow concealed?

... One morning I woke early and looked down from the tenth storey on a damp, morning Tokyo, covered by motley circles of umbrellas. Umbrellas were running in all directions, their paths crossed, they spun, disappeared, new ones appearing to take their place. Then suddenly I felt sad. Perhaps the old cyclist, my friend, was pedaling towards sorrow? This country seemed close to me, yet at the same time distant and hazy. What could I learn about it in 3 years, ten years? It's possible to learn the language and history to perfection, and possess the most exact statistical data, but one cannot dissolve in another nation. The soul has no "emergency ration," it is all consumed on one's own country. Perhaps that is why one cannot discover the exact nature of another's sorrow.

108

Russian Singing.

One day we were invited to Vaseda University by Professor Kuroda. A great expert on Russian literature, the professor can't converse on any other topic. We were wandering through the university grounds, conducting a literary conversation, when we heard singing. Our astonishment knew no bounds—it was one of our popular songs "Snow, wind, and the stars' evening flight."

On the steps of the Administration building, modeled after Cambridge, was a group of young people singing a Soviet song. Boys and girls dressed in sweaters and jeans, arms around each other, rocked to the music, and a crowd of dark-haired student listeners cheered them loudly. Nearby stood the truck which transported the members of this popular group round the countryside.

Singing is generally very popular in Japan. Sixty-five percent of the population sing. Thare are some bars where you come just to sing and hardly drink at all. These are called "singing bars." Young people collect there, sit with song-books in their hands and sing in chorus. One can judge the popularity of Russian songs from the fact that the most famous bar is called Katiusha.

There is another bar, "The Lower Depths," modelled on the Moscow Arts Theater's stage-set for Gorky's play, and all the inscriptions inside are in Russian. Kuroda took us there one day. There was a Russian stove, beside which the singers sat, throwing logs into the flames. They were singing "The Coachman."

"These people are Russian," as we were introduced to the proprietor.

The proprietor, a young man with a dazzling smile welcomed us cordially, but was probably disappointed that we wore ordinary European dress instead of boots and long-waisted coats. The bar only brings in a pittance, as it's patronized mostly by singers, not drunkards. But he keeps it going as a special interest. The man is apparently quite engrossed in this strange, imitation Russia of blouses, samovars, balalaikas.

We were already experiencing strong attacks of homesickness, so we found this bar pleasant, although many things about it were odd.

There is one strange trait in modern man: traditional notions about other countries, inherited from the distant past, are terribly strong in him! Naturally, every Japanese knows about sputniks and Russian astronauts, but somewhere in the depths of his mind lives the traditional image of Russia as an immense snow-covered steppe, resounding only with the peal of Valdai troika bells.

We're no different, by the way. Before leaving for Japan many a highly intelligent acquaintance slipped me a sly wink: "Geishas, rikisha,—we understand, old man!"

Of course, Japan is the country of geishas, "chocolate-box tea-houses,"

109

the seven samurai and so on.

Need I mention that there is not a single rikisha in Japan, and as for geishas...

Geishas

Genuine Japanese geishas have survived only in Kyoto, in the famous Giyon quarter. If there is anything similar anywhere else, then it is mere imitation, for advertizement purposes. The Geishas in Giyon live their own life, quite apart from americanized Japan, and in the quarter itself, the style and spirit of the seventeenth century are religiously kept up.

We were taken there by Mr. Iyoda, script-writer of the famous film Rashomon. Giyon startled us with its twilight and calm, so unexpected after the neon witches' sabbath of the center. There was not a single neon advertizement there. The only light comes from soft, if electric lanterns, hung over the entrances of the small light houses.

The hostess of the tea-house, an old lady with an astonishingly kind face, greeted us with the traditional bows. Several other elderly ladies bowed in unison with her. We parted from our shoes at the entrance, put on slippers and mounted a staircase. Upstairs we parted from the slippers as well and stepped onto the "tatami" in our socks. We sat down around a low table, about four inches off the floor.

The hostess looked intently at Valdemar Kristopovich and remarked:

"What an intelligent, good face you have."

"Oh, come now..."—our leader was embarrassed.

"How did you endure the journey?" she inquired with indescribable concern.

"Well, thank you," he mumbled, somewhat confused.

The hostess turned to me.

"What an intelligent, good face you have."

I grinned stupidly. "Yeah?"

"How did you endure the journey?" she asked me with the same concern.

"Nothing to it," I mumbled.

Irina Lvovna reacted calmly to the same phrases. She knew that the hostess was quite simply adhering to a seventeenth century ritual.

Two geishas appeared, quite young girls in old-world kimonos, with unbelievably high and intricately towering coiffures. In fact they were not really geishas, but so-called "maiko,"—girls awaiting initiation to the order of geisha. Their toilette and coiffures are much more demanding than those of mature geishas. What wasn't in their hair: flowers, combs, silver clips, garlands of tiny bells.

The girls sat down beside us, poured out green tea and sake, and con-

110

ducted a pleasant light-hearted conversation. "How did you endure the journey? What an intelligent, good face you have!" and so on. However, we gradually departed from the ritual and I told a few innocent jokes. The Maiko-San laughed merrily.

"What an interesting sense of humor foreigners have!" said one.

A second one began sketching and quickly presented each of us with a portrait.

A mature, regally beautiful and majestic geisha appeared. They explained that she was one of the most popular geishas, a television star. Yes, these seventeenth-century girls appeared on television.

Then came an elderly geisha, about ready to go out of circulation. She took up an ancient stringed instrument, a "shamisen," began strumming and sang in a bitter throaty voice. The Maiko-San began to dance. Immediately after, the beautiful geisha danced a solo. We learned later that the dancing was an extra, included out of deference to the Russian guests.

These enigmatic dances contained many barely perceptible movements, full of symbols inaccessible to us crude foreigners. Only Iyoda, a great expert in antiquity, understood it all perfectly and was in raptures. We merely guessed at its importance and significance and could only admire the dancers' old-world grace.

We took our leave when the dances were over. In parting, I kissed the hostess' hand, which somewhat perturbed her.

I stress advisedly the chastity of our visit to the geishas in order to dispel the somewhat inaccurate notions surrounding this institution. The genuine geishas from the Giyon quarter are by no means women of easy virtue, they are artists, who have willy-nilly dedicated their lives to upholding the subtlest traditions of medieval Japan. Their lives are enmeshed in a complex web of ancient superstition, perhaps even feudal order, but that is how they live.

The Tokyo prostitutes, masquerading as geishas, are another matter. They may be seen every evening in the back seats of huge cars with dignified drunken company directors.

The traditions of Giyon are very costly. Iyoda, a man with a hypertrophied sense of hospitality, really let himself go, taking us there. But wealth does not always open the doors of the tea-houses. Rockefeller might push a million-dollar note under the door and be despatched immediately. One must be a friend of the house or have very weighty recommendations in order to see the geisha dances and hear the sounds of the "shamisen."

Besides, there are many traditions in Japan that are accessible to everyone, including Rockefeller.

An Asakusa Festival

One day I happened to witness a gathering of Tokyo firemen. These were no ordinary firemen, but about 15 of the elders and purse-bearers of the guild; they entered the building in black medieval costumes—capes with red heraldic signs on their shoulders, and their thin elderly legs encased in breeches. They were full of solemnity and importance. They sat down on "tatami," tucked their feet beneath them, and sipping coca-cola, proceeded to discuss the forthcoming traditional festival of fire-brigades.

But the most astonishing combination of tradition and modernity was to be witnessed at the pre-New Year popular "hagoita" festival.

Several centuries ago, the Imperial samurai introduced a game something like badminton. They would pass a feather-tailed shuttlecock to one another by means of a bat.

Since then, "hagoita" bats have lost their significance and become household decorations. The traditional "hagoita" fair is held in Asakusa the week preceding New Year. Hundreds of stalls are set up in the square in front of the buddhist temple, where they sell hagoita of all shapes and sizes, ranging from miniature to the gigantic and very expensive. They are usually decorated with portraits of actors from the "Kabuki" theater, or other popular people. In 1961 the most "with it" bat carried a portrait of Yurii Gagarin.

This is where the ordinary folk enjoyed themselves. They roasted "yakitori" nuts, and pink fairy floss swirled out of a slow revolving drum. Rubber crocodiles, dragons, hares, huge round balloons and long sausage-shaped ones floated overhead. At the stalls, vendors in kimonos did a brisk trade in hagoita. "Hai"—they sang out whenever someone made a purchase.

And if you buy the most expensive gigantic sort of bat, the vendors surround you, clap their hands and cry "Hai! Hai! Hai!"

Here of course, you get swarms of television cameramen and press photographers.

Music, music... Japanese songs, the twist, "Katyusha"...

"Tsok-tsok-tsok!"... someone clops by in wooden clogs instead of shoes.

Respectable gentlemen carrying umbrellas.

Teddyboys in leather jackets.

Women in furs.

Poor girls in high heels.

The fortune teller in front of a blackboard, with chalk in hand, like a teacher.

A police notice: "Beware of the black boss! The black boss operates here."

The black boss are three leering thick-set lads.

"Hai! Hai!"

The tower is illuminated. The sky is on fire. You have fairy floss in your teeth, a bat in one hand, a rattle in the other.

Farewell, Japan!

I leave my jottings here, although I could continue for a hundred pages. These are all chance observations, Japan showing me several of its many thousand faces. Some time, I hope, I shall visit this country again. Our neighbor of small islands beyond the small Japanese sea is a strong, business-like, interesting fellow. One should meet him more frequently.

Translated by Rae Slonek

NOTES

1. Character in "The Egyptian Stamp" by Osip Mandelshtam.

IT'S A PITY YOU WEREN'T WITH US

1.

Why they should kick such a quiet fellow as me out of the house, I just don't know. When I was sitting in my room in front of the heater reading books on the art of acting, perfecting myself in my favorite profession, you could hear the tap dripping, or a roast potato sizzling; there were no scenes, no scandals, I didn't bother anybody.

And if I was out late somewhere with the boys, again I would come home quietly, without any scenes, knock quietly and go through to my apartment as noiselessly as a cat.

Anyway, to cut it short, she turned me out. She threw open the doors for me onto the open expanse and chilling air of Zubovsky Boulevard; and tucking my tail between my legs I set off along the empty streets in the direction of Kropotkinsky metro, not knowing where I was going; well, after all, I'm not an eighteeen-year-old, and winter's just round the corner; I only just managed to gather up all my references and my diploma.

I walked along with my briefcase, which contained only my papers and my underwear, my nostrils twitching, and carrying inside me all my grudges and a young stomach ulcer, decaying teeth and healthy teeth, one gold crown and a store of pent-up feelings: nerves, nerves, all sheer nervousness. You know, when you get into the vicious circle of human misunderstandings, nothing can help you—neither sober reason, nor a display of affection, nothing. Not even the court.

"Oh, Sonya, Sonya," I thought.

Anyway, to cut it short, there I am standing alone in Pushkin Square. My overcoat is no longer providing any warmth. "Travel by airplane. You gain time!" This is written above a shop selling light female clothing. An elegant model in a transparent plastic coat. Will I survive till summer?

Then the neon Aeroflot advertizement went out; Alexander Sergeevich Pushkin has his head sunk into his shoulders, a desert whirlwind on the frosty asphalt is two giggling girls; oh, if only I could hold you, just for warmth, just for warmth and nothing more, but no, there's only the gold, orange and emerald letters rolling ceaselessly from left to right on the roof of "Izvestia," warm, happy letters, like the last sparks of summer, the sparks of the last freedom of summer: "Watches on credit in all State Jewelers."

Now there's an idea, I thought. It's high time I bought myself a watch, so as it would tick, you know, and bring peace and harmony to my soul. As luck would have it, I saw the sculptor Jacek Wojcechowsky. Jacek was walking slowly along the other side of Gorky Street, like a big, tired camel. I noticed that he was already wearing winter clothing. From where I was, across the street, with his shawl collar he looked prosperous and sad, like a great artist sunk in reflections on, at the very least, the destiny of the

114

world, and certainly not about tomorrow's bread and butter.

"Jacek!" I shouted. "Jacek!"

"Misha!" he exclaimed, and came to the edge of the pavement, lifted one huge foot, and taking a deep breath, like a big camel, he set about crossing.

Anyway, to cut it short, I moved into his studio. I spent the days rushing around Moscow, and we whiled away the evenings together. We didn't have anything in particular to talk about and in any case we didn't even feel like opening our mouths because of the cold. We sat with our overcoats on, facing each other, looking at the floor, and surrounded by stone, clay, plaster-of-Paris and wooden monsters, and all the rest of his Polish contraptions, and we brooded.

All in all, things were far from great with Jacek: he had muffed up some commission or other, and quarreled with all his bosses. That's the sort of man he was—he'd say nothing for a day, a week, a month, and then all of a sudden he'd say something that would make everyone bristle.

Yes, things were far from great with us. In fact, we had neither fuel or drink, and very little in the way of means of support.

"Today, now, I wouldn't have minded a drink,"said Jacek one day.

"Ah, Jacek, Jacek." I began to tell him about the wines that had been displayed that day in Stoleshnikov Lane.

Those wines— "Cherry-brandy," "Camus" and "Courvoisier," "Bacardi," "Chianti" and "Moselle" in different sorts of foreign bottles, glittered in the windows of this fashionable lane, and there was also the automatic doughnut machine with the amber-colored doughnuts floating in oil, and the snow-fall of light, powdered sugar, and the puffs of steam from the kitchen of the "Arpha" cafe, and the dove-like white table napkins of the "Ural" restaurant, with its glass-walled veranda where the pink faces of my merry-making contemporaries glowed behind the frost patterns,—ah, all that sweet life was beyond our reach for the present.

"Right now I wouldn't say no to a pepper-brandy," groaned Jacek. "Pepper-brandy—cie dobrze."

We fell silent again. Jacek, the king amongst his monsters, sat with his large fingers interlocked, looking at the tiled floor, while his monsters, bearded, stone peasants and big-bosomed peasant women, small ones and large ones, rose up like a mountain behind his back, or just like an army, awaiting only his order to move off on the march and frighten the life out of decent people.

A couple of years ago there was a rumor in the Journalists' Club that Jacek was almost a genius, and that if he continued to work a bit longer he would become one more or less, but right now he was not working, nor even looking at his monsters. He seemed to be in a state of impotence.

I too was in a sort of paralysis these days; however during the day I would rush about the mass meetings and, making use of the high positions of some of my famous friends, I sometimes earned a few rubles. I still remembered that I had to feed both myself and Jacek.

But he never remembered anything; he sat there all day long in his expensive fur coat and looked at the tiles. Only occasionally did he get up to chase the blood around his aging veins. It was only today that he made his comment about the drink, and I was glad at this, even though there was no real hope.

"Maybe we could go and drop in on somebody, Jacek?" I asked. "After all..."

"Out of the question," he said and got up.

I looked up at him from below, and saw how big, almost great, he was, and realized that indeed to "drop in on" someone would not become him. Even I am not a lover of such pursuits. Life's tribulations have not yet broken my individuality. I can do the offering myself when I'm in the money, I'm never stingy, but drop in on someone and beg for some crumbs—no thanks!

But Jacek began to walk up and down, then he moved faster, and suddenly he dived into his stone jungle, into the cave, into that wild temple, and his astrakhan hat flashed across the spacious studio.

He appeared carrying three small figures in his arms like an armful of firewood; each one about half a meter long.

"Here," he said, "let's sell these things."

And he stood one of the figures on the floor. It was of a small woman sitting Turkish-style, with a very long neck, a short trunk, very thick little legs and disproportionately large feet.

"Early period," said Jacek and coughed into his hand.

Maybe originally this had been a relatively decent sculpture, but after passing through Jacek's various periods it had become dark, blotched and cracked.

Jacek was very excited. He walked round and round the figure, sighing.

"Ye-es," I said. "You don't think you'll sell that, do you?"

"You know," Jacek whispered excitedly to me, "this is a very good piece."

"But it's all cracked."

"Misha, what's wrong with you? That's from the cold. In the heat it'll warm up and there won't be any cracks."

"And why is her neck so long?"

"Now listen," he roared, "I didn't expect this from you!"

"Calm down, Jacek, old friend," I said. "Don't shout at me. I'm probably more interested than you in selling, but the cracks..."

"I'll smear them over right away," he shouted, and in an instant he had smeared over the cracks.

All right, so we set off. We wrapped up the figure in old numbers of "Soviet Culture," and out we went.

We headed for the Frunzensky district as being the most cultured of the capital. The density of the intelligentsia in this district is unusually high. They say that there are as many as two hundred thousand academics alone living in it.

It went something like this: along the quiet moonlit lanes, skipping the noisy main roads, through communicating courtyards which I knew from childhood, and also from my work in the cinema, beneath the gaze of the warm windows of the intelligentsia's homes, with hastened steps past the policemen, phew...

It had happened for some reason that up till now I had not come to grips with sculpture. I knew a bit about music, I could tell the difference between an adagio and a scherzo, and in art between oil and gouache, but in sculpture—clay and alabaster were the same thing as far as I was concerned. I knew only that Jacek was a great man.

"A work by a successful sculptor, a re-emigre from West Bolivia. He has used motifs from the local Peruvian Incas," I told the retired commisary, quarter-master-sergeant, rat-catcher, Bukashkin-Tarakashkin[1]—a sly-looking little old man. "Imported," I told him. "Wouldn't you like it? You can have it for a fiver."

Tarakan Tarakanovich[2] stood the woman with the touched-up cracks on a rug in the entrance-hall, crawled around it and said:

"Looks like an early Wojcechowsky."

"Jacek!" I shouted, ran out onto the stairs, dragged my friend in and pointed to the crawling old man through the open door.

"Where have you brought me, Misha," babbled Jacek weakly, "that's the academician Nikanorov."

Yes, we had landed on a academician, and what's more he was a specialist in art. And blow me if this academician doesn't throw on his overcoat and demand to be taken to the studio.

At the studio Jacek began to turn his stone offspring this way and that, and I helped him, while the academician Nikanorov sat in an armchair on the dais like King Lear.

"I've been meaning to come to see you for a long time now," he said, "for a long time. For a very long time. Oh, such a long time. For a very, very long time."

He winked delightedly at me and gave a secret, friendly nod towards Jacek, and my heart positively bubbled over with pride.

"These are all old things," said Jacek and took off his astrakhan hat. "I haven't been working for a year now."

"But why aren't you working?" asked the academician Nikanorov.

"I just don't want to, so I don't," answered Jacek, leant his elbow on the head of one of his peasants and began to look at the ceiling.

The academician Nikanorov shook his head in delight, winking at me.

"But where's your self-discipline, Wojcechowsky, eh?" he suddenly asked sternly.

"What about it?" said Jacek. "If I don't want to work, I don't work. If I start wanting to work, I start working. Tomorrow even."

"How blue the moon is tonight," said the academician Nikanorov, looking out of the window.

2.

So. Life began to return to normal. Heating, food. The academician Nikanorov and his colleagues bought up a whole series of works from us. Jacek had still not begun to work, but he did begin to flex his fingers more often, obviously thinking over some idea. In the meantime I bustled about doing the housekeeping, like the washing, minor repairs to clothing, preparing meals, tidying up; what with this and that there was plenty to keep me going.

Suddenly one day he shook himself, stamped his feet, stood up and said:

"Misha, let's go to a restoracja. You and I are art workers and are duty bound to spend our evenings in conversation over dinner. Press my suit for me," says he.

I couldn't believe my eyes—Jacek takes off his fur coat, his jacket and his trousers, and begins to do physical jerks.

At once I burst into feverish activity. I quickly ran the iron over our suits and ties and darned our socks. We got all dressed up and set off for the Artists' Club.

This restaurant is very smart: red and black are set side by side, but the main color is blue; it has rustling bamboo curtains like in the tropics, but modest birches to rest your eyes; they serve you in a friendly way, as though you were part of the family, and shake the crumbs off the table; and no one barks at you, "go home and get dressed properly!"

To some extent the closeness of the elbows at the long table, the passing round of the simple hors d'oeuvres, then a sirloin or a Suvorov fillet, the measured flow of conversation and the pompous repartee, the communal glass and the shuffle of familiar, friendly feet beneath the table— all this is to some extent necessary for the nerves. Otherwise you find your nerves playing up towards evening, and you start counting something, whether it be years or hurts...

I'm thirty-five, but to look at me you'd give me forty. Friends that I haven't seen for a long time say: "You simply wouldn't recognize Misha Korzinkin. He's gone funny." That's just talk, but you know, I often catch myself with strange thoughts. For example, a group gets together over dinner of people of my own age, or else of some much younger men, and they're talking of things I know and understand, when suddenly I catch myself feeling like a child in their midst, feeling that they all know something I don't

118

know. Only one thought consoles me: what if every one of them also feels like a child in society and is only pretending, exactly like me? Maybe each one is simply inflating his own importance, banking that the ground won't be taken from under his feet?

The first person we caught sight of in the restaurant was Igor Barkov, and Jacek and I went over and joined him.

"How are things?" asked Igor, twisting in his chair, his eyes flashing from side to side.

"May we congratulate you?" I asked him.

The week before Igor (he's a film producer) had been in San Francisco to receive the "Golden Gates" award, and had flown home a laureate.

"Yes," said Igor. "Thanks Jacek," he said, "I don't suppose you'd lend me a fiver, would you? Ye gods!" he shouted, "Irka's here!"

Through the rustling bamboo, beneath the curved mirrors and the decorative rocks came Irina Ivanova, our world-famous film-star, a tall, beautiful girl, swivelling through the air. She spent no unnecessary words as she walked, only her skirt swayed on her hips, "Hi," "Hi," and that's all.

Seeing Barkov, she came and joined us, and Igor introduced us.

The year was drawing to a close. Was it going to end up looking like this then: from biting snow-storms to the spring slush, then to the swish of the cycling club on the dried-out road, from the stuffiness of our rented dacha and the quagmire of the pond, from the autumn passion for Sonya to my recent eviction, from misery and humiliation to friendship with Irina Ivanova?

"I want to do a sculpture of you," said Jacek to Irina.

"Go ahead," said Irina, and turned to me. "And are you that same Korzinkin?"

I don't know what came over me, but I just could not stand mockery from Irina Ivanova.

"What do you mean 'the same'?" I exclaimed. "What does that mean— 'the same'? That's all lies! I'm nothing of the sort the same! I'm my own master, without anybody else, I'm not 'the same' at all!"

"Calm down," Irina whispered right into my face, right into my eyes, and stroked my cheek. "Misha, what's the matter with you?" She got up and said aloud: "I'll be back in fifteen minutes, and I would like you, Misha, during that time, to alter your opinion about me for the better."

She left.

"What's she like?" I asked Igor.

"What's wrong with you, are you blind? She's first class."

"Yes, but what's she like?" repeated Jacek anxiously.

"I don't know," mumbled Barkov. "She doesn't excite me."

"Jacek!" I shouted. "Just look at this snob! She excites the whole world, but not him."

Barkov began to laugh.

"No, no, fellows, you've got me wrong. She doesn't excite me from the acting point of view, that's what I mean." He leant over the table and began to whisper, amusingly flicking his eyes from side to side: "You see, the thing is I want to change everything. Everything back to front, you know? Including the female type—back in time, to get away from all these conventions. Like Antonioni with Monica Vitti. Only I want to change that bloke as well, get it? To turn everything upside down."

"Who are you going to film now, Igoryok?" I asked.

"I don't know yet, but Ira Ivanova doesn't excite me at the moment. In that way."

He began to tell us how he was leaving in a few days with his group for the southern coast of the Crimea and was going to begin filming something so astounding, hitherto unseen, something so... he himself still didn't know what.

"Film me, Igoryok," I requested.

He laughed.

"You'd be better joining me as an administrator, Misha."

"No," I said, "there's no question of being an administrator, but on the contrary you'd be better filming me in some role or other."

Igor laughed again, but Jacek took offense on my behalf.

"And why don't you want to film Misha?" he said. "In what way is he any worse than the rest? I for one intend to do a sculpture of him."

"All right," laughed Barkov. "I'll film you in a small part. You won't have time to open your mouth before I've filmed you."

"You're wrong to think that way about small parts," I reproached him. "You should look at Fellini. What small parts he has!"

"I'll film you brilliantly," said Igor. "And I'll show Fellini a thing or two."

Irina came up and sat down next to me.

"Huh," she said, "you could at least have made me a sandwich, Misha."

I quickly threw together a salmon sandwich for her and put on top a slice of hothouse cucumber and a little green leaf for decoration.

"And pour me some water," she requested.

I poured her some Borzhom and put a thin slice of lemon into the tall glass. She looked at me in surprise and suddenly came out with something which almost made me choke over my cognac.

"How cleverly you do all that, Misha," she said. "You should be my husband."

Barkov laughed, while Jacek and I just stared at her.

"I go hungry all the time," complained Irina. "I kicked out my husband and quarreled with my father-in-law, but I'm such an idiot that I can't do a thing for myself."

She burst into tears.

Barkov was smiling.

120

But Jacek and I almost went mad.

"Irina, what's wrong? Tell us! Don't make us suffer."

"My husband's an idler, my father-in-law a pedant, and I'm an idiot, left all on my own," she complained through her tears. Then she got up and said to Jacek and me: "Take me home, friends. Misha, if you can, wrap up that steak in a serviette for me. Thanks."

The three of us went out onto Gorky Street. Immediately all the sharpies fixed their eyes on Irina and trailed along behind us, keeping their distance like a pack of cowardly wolves. They know there's no messing around with Korzinkin.

"How strange life is," Irina was saying, "that a person who is beautiful, intelligent and famous can be lonely."

As she said this she turned one alert eye on me.

"Show me your leg, please," requested Jacek, "lift it up just a little."

"Ups-a-daisy," said Irina and raised her leg like a circus horse.

"Interesting," said Jacek, with his genius taking in the features of her leg in an instant. "Very interesting. It's got something. You can put it down now."

We walked on.

"Listen, Irina, eh, I don't know your patronymic," said Jacek ceremoniously, "Irina Oskarovna, I have a concrete proposition to make. Come along every day to our studio. I'll sculpture you and Misha will look after the food. Naturally, our food isn't refined, but he'll fix up something from tins. There won't be a day when you won't be satisfied."

"A brilliant idea!" shouted Irina delightedly. "God sent you to me, friends. Especially you, Misha," she whispered to me.

We came to her huge, gloomy house, built at the time when the personality cult was at its height. The whole building was in darkness except for one little window up on the eleventh floor, and even that had its blind down and curtains drawn—this was her father-in-law, the study-inhabiting rat, the tormentor, the spider, engaged in his scholarly activity.

"Good-bye, see you tomorrow," said Irina. "Oh, by the way, Misha, give me my steak."

What a boob I was—I nearly forgot all about the steak! Convulsively I snatched it out of my pocket and held it out to her. She put it in her handbag.

"Thanks for everything," she said, and went off towards her house, a ground-wind clearing the snowy footpath before her.

3.

The next day Irina came to the studio and from then on began to turn up every day.

121

She would sit in an armchair on the dais, her legs stretched out, and her hands occasionally moving as she turned the pages of a book.

And Jacek in his canvas robe would wander around the dais, carefully scrutinizing the details of her body, go back to the gigantic block of clay, hit it with a chisel, and then do some more turns around Irina, murmuring:

"Bardzo ladne, bardzo dobrze."

In the meantime I bustled around doing the housework. I cooked the tinned foods till they were jumping in the frying-pan. I even invented a wonderful sauce of my very own. I don't mind passing on the recipe. Suppose you've boiled a chicken; no need to pour out the stock, but put in five teaspoons of arrowroot, five teaspoons of sugar, five teaspoons of salt, five teaspoons of pepper, two glasses of tomato juice, a very thinly sliced lemon, a glass of milk, a small pot of mustard, a couple of bay leaves, add a small tube of herring-paste, bring the mixture to the boil, throw in a handful of olives, and the sauce is ready.

In the course of my life I've changed professions quite a bit. For example I've been a cabinet-maker. If you ask me what sort of furniture I made, let me tell you that already in 1946 I was doing modern stuff, I had a flair for it. I've also been, for example, a port equipment engineer in Riga, and all sorts of other things. I've been successful at everything, just as I am now at the culinary art. I could have been untouched by worries had I not decided to dedicate my life to art, and more specifically to that most complicated and important branch of art—the cinema.

"Misha," says Jacek to me in the middle of his work, "don't get carried away. You're going to suffocate us with your aromas."

But Irina simply gave me a tender smile from the dais. In the studio she behaved as quietly as a dove, ate everything and didn't put on any performances.

"I've never been so happy as I am now," she would say in the evenings, as I saw her home.

We were already having those silent, frosty, moonlit evenings, and Irina and I walked slowly and calmly through December in Moscow.

Usually she would say something like this:

"How are we to understand the relationships between people, Misha?" Can you tell me? I think a lot about the relationships between people, between a man and a woman. Have you never thought about that, Misha? For example, what's the basis of love—is it respect or physical attraction? In my opinion, neither. In my opinion, the basis of love is intuition. What do you think?"

And I would say something like this:

"One person is united with another just as, say, the banks of a river are united. You know, Irina, the rapprochement of minds is as inevitable as the collision of the earth and the sun. Men are not at each other's throats, that's a profound error over there in the West. People are like seagulls, Irina..."

Once she turned her round-eyed, attentive gaze on me and said:

"Misha, you're a real gentleman."

"What do you mean?" I said, taken aback.

"The way you behave with me," she said dolefully.

"How?"

"Can't you be a little, just a tiny little bit... well... well just a bit different with me?..."

We were standing at the window of a baker's shop, and suddenly I caught sight of our reflections. I saw her shadow, tall and slim, topped by the massive outline of her imported sheepskin hat, and my own small shadow, the outline of Jacek's old hat, and the semicircles of my ears...

And you know, it was just then that I was pierced by an unpleasant thought: Irina is making fun of me!

How else can one explain our relationship? Let's look the truth straight in the eyes. Physically I'm not endowed with any special beauty, my position in society is somewhat peculiar, my clothes get more dilapidated every day, my health is lousy, what am I for her? I was suddenly afraid that all this was a prolonged leg-pull on the part of some of my heartless friends.

That night I ran back to the studio and told Jacek I couldn't go on like this any longer and that this week I must get away somewhere: either I sign on to go to the Arctic, or to Africa, or I go off to Tselinograd, where a friend had been inviting me for ages, having found his happiness there.

I gasped for breath every time I thought of all Irina's fantastic treachery.

Jacek fussed around me, and even put the coffee on the gas. He tried to persuade me to take a sedative and have a sleep, and said that Irina loved me, and she had managed to see in me a real man, but what consolations were these for me?!

"Here's a telegram that came for you, Misha," said Jacek as though my whole salvation lay in that piece of paper.

The telegram was from Barkov, from the south coast of the Crimea.

It read: "Come for tests role Konyushka Big Swing group Barkov."

That's what it means to have friends, I thought, collapsing in an armchair. That's what it means to have a real friend like Igoryok, when he says something he means it. He promised to call me and he did. That's the strong friendship between men. I showed Jacek the telegram.

"Well, congratulations, Misha!" he said delightedly. "Maybe this is a start, eh?"

For half the night we discussed my imminent departure and the role of Konyushka. What sort of role was it? It must be the role of "a small man," beleaguered by fate, but preserving in his soul his knightly ardor and nobility.

"Tomorrow we'll go round the shops together," said Jacek, "you've got to get equipped. You certainly can't go to the south looking like that."

In the morning, on my instructions, he phoned Irina and told her that the sessions had to stop temporarily for artistic reasons.

"How is Misha?" over Jacek's shoulder I heard Irina's distant voice, as though from outer space. "He was strange yesterday, and I behaved stupidly."

Believe me, I felt like tearing the receiver out of Jacek's hand and shouting to Irina to stop her jokes, that I wasn't taken in by the sad luster of her big eyes, I knew she was an actress, but I was no fool either, why did she have to make me suffer, why, she should go back to her lover-boys from the Artists' Club, I wouldn't see her again, or perhaps only after my Konyushka was known throughout the world and...

"Misha will ring you tomorrow," said Jacek and hung up.

In the evening I left for the Crimea. It turned out I was alone in a four-berth compartment. I stood sadly in the corridor of the near-empty carriage and looked down onto the platform where Jacek stood stamping his feet. He was putting on a brave front and smiling, while I was wondering with acute sadness how he would get on, left here all on his own, who would look after him.

I pulled on the window and it gave unexpectedly.

"You're off traveling like a prince," said Jacek with a plaintive smile.

"Jacek," I said, "when you're making pelmeni, turn them over. There's nothing to it—you pour them into the frying-pan, put in a piece of butter, a pinch of salt, and that's it. The important thing is to turn them over."

We both burst into tears.

"And don't say a word to her," I shouted. "Not a word!"

The train moved off.

4.

Wondrous things awaited me in the Crimea. In Simferopol a strong frosty wind was whipping along; there wasn't one flake of snow, but it was colder than in Moscow. At the station about fifty taxi-drivers bore down on me. They were obviously all from the south coast, for their teeth were chattering, they whistled through their noses as they breathed, rattled their throats loudly in complaint, swore, and offered their services.

Holding my briefcase out in front of me I forced my way through their barrier and got on a trolleybus.

The trolleybus cut across the town (Simferopol), then across an immense plain, and climbed into the mountains. It climbed steadily higher and higher, and on the ridge it drove into a really thick mist, as though it was not just a normal city trolleybus but a long-distance bus.

Still in the mist, I sensed that it was now going down, like an airplane.

It crawled down and down, till suddenly the mist dropped behind us, and below opened up before us, at full width, like a panoramic film, paradise on earth.

It was simply amazing: the blue sea almost to the sky, and the green mountain slopes, familiar from postcards. The sun immediately heated up the glass of the windows to such an extent that you almost felt like taking off your coat. Shortly after there appeared below the roofs, slanting at various angles, and the massive white blocks of the all-union sanatoriums. Very quickly now we dropped down and were soon bowling along city streets, which is more fitting for a trolleybus, past glass-fronted restaurants specializing in shashliks, chebureki,[3] broths and pirozhki,[4] all completely deserted, which was equally amazing.

When I got off the trolleybus my head began to spin: the air here smelt so strong and pleasant. It was certainly not nearly so warm as it had been in the trolleybus, in fact it was quite chilly, but the sun was shining, the sea was crashing somewhere nearby, and luxuriant trees of some sort were covered in blue flowers.

In a news-agent's stand were displayed some photographs of film stars. I went up and had a look at them as though they were close relatives of mine. Misha Kazakov, Lyuda Gurchenko, Kesha Smoktunovsky—all my friends and colleagues. My heart missed a beat, but nevertheless I asked:

"Have you got a photograph of Irina Ivanova?"

"Ivanova was sold out last week," said the saleswoman angrily. "The cadets from the sailing-ship 'Vitiaz' bought up our entire stock of Ivanova."

"So," I thought, "the cadets from the sailing-ship 'Vitiaz.' Billy the Kids. Naval cadets. I fell in love with a sailor from a blue, blue ship... So."

And, putting the whole thing out of my mind once and for all, I burnt my bridges and boats behind me and strode off easily along the clean, quiet streets of the town. The cloth of my Jordan trousers rubbed pleasantly against my legs.

The day before with Jacek I had bought myself a unique item in a second-hand store—Jordan trousers. I'd like to know who else has trousers like these. Only Misha Korzinkin goes around in Jordan trousers. It's true that the seams of these trousers are on the weak side, but on the other hand, in front they have a zip, no less, and none of your common buttons.

A tall, fat old woman in high heels was coming towards me.

"Excuse me," I said to her, "would you by any chance know where the film group "Big Swing" is quartered?"

"Oh, tch-tch-tch," she said, pouting her lips at me, "just you take a couple of little steps clip-clop, little man, and you'll walk right into them."

I quickened my pace and looked back. The old woman was looking after me laughing and shaking her head in affectionate reproach, as though she had caught me up to some mischievous prank.

Now a dog came running towards me, scraggy and black as night, its long, ungainly legs going up and down, and its eyes meant to look submissive, but in fact looking false and insidious.

"Don't be afraid, doggy," I said, "I won't hurt you."

"Rrruf," said the dog to me as it passed.

"Rex, let's go!"[5] came the old woman's voice.

The dog went off after her on its hind legs, like a monkey.

"Who said 'ruf'?" asked a fat jeweler, poking his head out of his stall. "You, young man? Eh? Can we mend your watch? Do you need a room? How much for your Jordan trousers? Will you sell them?"

Everything in this town was as romantic and enigmatic as in an Andersen fairy tale.

I soon came out onto the sea-front, where the sea was crashing and splashing up to about five meters above the parapet. On the front, too, there were few people, only one or two blue jackets and green cardigans wandering about, but reinforcements were on their way: at this moment the Greek liner "Herostratos" was coming into port with Turkish tourists on board.

On a bench sat a solitary young man with a book, by the looks of it a correspondence student.

"Excuse me," I said to him, "would you happen to know where the 'Big Swing' film group is quartered?"

"Sit down," he said, after giving me a quick glance.

I sat down next to him.

The student opened his book and became absorbed in it, at the same time moving his elbow in a strange way. Now and again he would cast a lightning-swift glance at me, then sink back into his book again.

"Swing?" he asked. "Big?" he repeated the question a minute later. "The 'Big Swing' film group, was that what you said?" he inquired amiably after another minute and held out a sheet of white paper folded in two, on which was pasted my profile. "That'll be fifty kopecks," he smiled.

"Are you an internal or external student?" I asked as I handed over a heavy fifty-kopeck piece.

"External, of course," he said. "I'm preparing for my exams. But the 'Big Swing'—that's their crowd over yonder."

"I'm an actor, I've come to take part in a film." I said.

"A-ah, really," he said, having by now lost interest in me.

The "Big Swing" were thronging around the entrance of a hotel. At this moment they were not doing any filming, but only quarreling fiercely about something, waving their arms, pointing at the sky, the sea, the sun, the mountains, and at the "Herostratos." Barkov was standing with his hands thrust into the pockets of his jeans, sniffing, and obviously singing to himself.

"Look who's arrived!" he shouted, noticing me. "Mishenka's arrived. Well, now we'll get somewhere—Misha Korzinkin is here!"

126

And they all began to applaud me and smile, after which I shook Igor's hand firmly, man to man, and whispered:

"Thanks, Igor, you have no idea what a scrape you got me out of." Then I asked him in a louder voice: "When will you give me the script to read?"

Barkov smiled and, his eyes flicking from side to side as usual, he said quickly:

"Whenever you like. This evening. But right now I've got a special job for you, Mishenka. Go to the local motor depot and ask them for an open ZIL, see? They've got one there standing doing nothing, we need one, but they won't give us it. Sheer cussedness, you understand? Get the papers from Reiman and off you go. Reiman has already been there, but they showed him the door. You're our only hope."

I decided to come to Igor's help and drove off in our "Gazik" to the motor depot.

The manager of the depot turned out to be an army mate of mine, from the landing parties, Felix Sidorykh. At one time we used to sit next to each other on the dural bench in the "Li-2." We used to jump together, me first, then him. Sometimes I'd be already hanging on the straps when Felix would drop past me like a stone. He loved doing free falls.

Now Felix had become a robust red-faced boss of near two hundred pounds. He threw my papers into a desk drawer and roared:

"I don't give a damn about your papers, Misha! You'd do better to admit what you want the thing for, eh? Well, own up! You can't fool me, so come on! Tell me the truth and you'll get it. Eh? What do you want it for? Well? Well? I can see right through you."

I winked slyly, and he burst out laughing in satisfaction.

"I knew it! I know you! I knew that was it! He should have said it right away. If he'd said it right at the beginning he'd have got it without any fuss. O-oh, you rascal! Mishka, Mishka, where's your smile?! Go and take the tank, if it'll start, that is."

I drove up to the hotel on the back seat of the huge open car, which was as tall as a bus. The 'Big Swing' could not believe their eyes and began to hoot with delight.

For the rest of the day and the whole evening Igor and I drove around in the open car taking note of location for the filming. Igor would stand up in the car, with one hand placed above his eyes and the other at nose level, in this way closing the open spaces into wide-screen perspective.

"Our filming is going to be simple, Misha," he said, "simple but elegant. Light gray, wth just a touch of color."

We stopped in the narrow streets of the town and went into the backyards, those little wells with half-rotten balconies, palm-trees growing in tubs and underpants hanging on strings.

"Nice, but not quite right. Not quite right," murmured Igor.

"That's it!" he suddenly shouted.

Against the background of the sunset, high up between the houses fluttered a pair of blue panties.

"This is the one we'll take! Tremendous!"

I took up residence in a room along with the deputy director of the film, Ivan Henrikovich Lodkin. He was a man of slender, elegant build, but very coarse in his manners.

"Korzinkin!" he would yell at me. "Are you sitting around picking your nose again? How about nipping down and getting some beer, you great oaf!"

"You should be ashamed of yourself, Ivan Henrikovich," I would say to him. "You're as vulgar as a cab-driver."

Every day I had special jobs to carry out for Igor. Without me everything would simply have got out of hand in the "Big Swing."

"You see, I've got to organize a mass gathering of old men," said Igor, "but only of genuine old men with long white beards."

And I rushed about the town like a madman in search of old men like that. I found twenty-seven. Luckily I was helped by the president of the local council of pensioners, who was my Aunt Anya's second husband.

Another time he needed six cellos and five double-basses. This time I had to work on the director of the Philharmonic Society, whom fortunately I knew through my earlier cultural work.

The days passed in pursuits such as these, and I got very tired, and could not even find the time to take the script from Igor and get the feel of the part of Konyushka.

"Don't worry," Igor would say, "in a week everything will be settled and then you'll have the time."

Towards evening on the third day I went back to my room. Fortunately Lodkin was not there, and I collapsed onto my bed like an enfeebled colossus.

I was hellishly tired and thought I would fall asleep right away, but my head was still spinning with the merry-go-round of old men, cellos, drums for open-air cooking, telephones, receipts, order-forms and what to do with the amoral make-up man Chashkin.

I had buried my face in the pillow when suddenly the door was jerked open and in came Ivan Henrikovich whistling. He slapped me on a certain spot and said:

"Hey, fat ass, get up! Irina's arrived, she's looking all over town for you."

I jumped up and looked savagely at Lodkin. He was already sprawled in an armchair manicuring his fingernails.

"It's a real circus," he said, "a comedia dell'arte."

"Where is she?!" I shouted.

Lodkin shrugged his shoulders. I ran out of the hotel.

It was Sunday evening and the esplanade was crowded. Everyone was calm and happy, but I raced like one possessed from one end to the other, there and back, from the hotel to the pier, in and out all the shashlik and cheburek cafes, and the broth- and the pie-shops. Irina was nowhere to be found. I was becoming desperate.

Suddenly I saw her. She was sitting on the shingle below the parapet. She was alone, the whole beach was deserted, and in front of her was nothing but the troubled ancient sea and the gulls; she looked like Iphigenia in Aulis.

How could I have acted the way I did with her? What a swine I am! Why couldn't I have understood her? Why did I degrade her like that? How could I? I was thinking all this as I flew over the parapet, over the beach, circled over her and landed.

"Misha, how could you?" she asked quietly in such a voice that my blood stopped circulating.

"Can you forgive me?" I asked.

"Don't even mention it," she said, getting up. "Let's go for a walk. I like it here. It's wonderful. How sensitive you are..."

You know, maybe I'm being too frank, but at that moment her hair was fluttering in the wind, her eyes shining and her teeth flashing: I'm prepared to swear that she was happy at that moment of our meeting.

We went up onto the esplanade and walked silently along it. I took the liberty of taking her arm. Very lightly she pressed my hand to her with her elbow.

Along the esplanade elegant Greek sailors walked affectedly, leading by the arms timid Turkish tourists, frightened by the Sunday noise of this town.

The sun was constantly striving to set behind the mountain, but each time it would pop up again, getting caught on the cypresses. Finally, sideways, it set, and immediately all the lights of the huge "Herostratos" blazed, as also did those of all the smaller vessels, and on the crane-tops and poles, and in the shop windows and open cafes the lights went on.

Shortly after that we met a relative of mine, my Aunt Anya's second husband. I introduced him and Irina to each other, and we stood talking at the parapet.

The old fellow kept winking approvingly at me and then whispered in my ear:

"But what about Sonechka? Eh, Misha?"

"Sonya turned out to be an unscrupulous person," I whispered in reply.

The old fellow nodded in satisfaction, turned half away from us and, still looking at us, began to work quickly with a pair of scissors. A minute later he held out our profiles to us.

"Half a ruble a piece," he said, "one ruble all told. I wish you luck."

The sea was heaving more and more violently and crimson stripes would flash on the crests of the waves, then disappear; it got dark quickly and from the black depths of the elements came only a dull, growing, animal-like growl; in the dark the lights of the little fishing-boats danced, and even the lights of the "Herostratos" at the terminal rocked slightly.

Two lads in duffle-coats stopped alongside us and looked at the lights dancing in the darkness.

"The sea will keep us lively today," said one of them, and they went off towards the pier swinging their cases.

"How amazing all this is, Misha! How wonderful!" said Irina. "Don't you think that sometimes life can be wonderful?"

"Yes, I do," I replied.

Shortly after we met Felix Sidorykh. When still quite a distance away he spread his arms wide, filling almost half the esplanade.

"Let me introduce you, Felix. This is my friend Irina," I said.

"Oh-ho-ho!" Felix began to laugh, embracing Irina and me together. "Now everything is clear! Clear once and for all! Completely clear! Perfectly obvious!"

He swiftly cut out our profiles and held them out to us.

"What does this mean, Felix?" I mumbled in some bewilderment. "What does it all mean?"

"It's a local pastime," laughed Felix. "Here we all cut out one another's profiles. The one who cuts the fastest gets half a ruble. That'll be a ruble."

We said goodbye to Felix and went into a restaurant.

"Let's go wild, Misha," proposed Irina. "Let's have a real slap-up dinner, and tomorrow I'll get some money with a letter of credit."

We ordered champagne and red caviar. It turned out there was no red caviar, so we ordered crab. It was explained that the crab, too, was finished, but there was a "riviera" meat salad, so we took that.

"Dee-dum-dee-dum, and to the ceiling, there gushed a stream of comet wine"[6] said Irina, and stretched her hand over the table to me.

A small band was playing in the restaurant—three young fellows on trumpet, bass and accordion, and an old fellow on the piano. The young ones were always being drawn towards improvisation, but the old boy, brought up in the strict health-resort style, did not like this and when they began to improvise he would get all worked up and stop playing.

Finally they began to play a tune which was obviously to the old fellow's liking. He began to thump his instrument and to sing with tremendous enthusiasm, winking at us and smiling:

"The time has come and I'm the pilot," sang the old fellow at the top of his voice.

We watched him enthralled, and when he finished we invited him to our table. The old boy jumped softly from the platform. It was obvious that his whole life had been spent in restaurants. Although he was wearing a tie, he also had felt carpet-slippers on.

"It was you I was singing for," he said as he took the glass. "I see a cultured young man sitting in a pair of Jordan trousers, and I think to myself, let's sing for him and the little lady. And what's more, I've a surprise for you. One ruble, please."

He held out to us our two profiles pasted nose to nose onto white paper, with two kissing doves drawn above them. How he managed to do all that while he was playing the piano and singing, I never did find out.

I became very embarrassed in the face of this indiscreet allusion, but Irina put it in her handbag with an enigmatic smile.

At that moment, to the thundering accompaniment of all the instruments playing a piece of bop, Igor Barkov came into the room with a broad-shouldered, slow-moving man, very well dressed. They came over to us, walking in time with the music.

"Ah, Irka has arrived," said Barkov.

"I came for Misha, not you," retorted Irina.

"Of course, for Misha," Barkov had no intention of arguing. "Misha's my prized possession."

"Take a seat, Igoryok," I invited, "and you..." I looked at his companion, not knowing how to address him—"comrade," "citizen," or "mister." "And you, signor, take a seat."

"Allow me to introduce you, friends," said Barkov, "this is the Italian producer Rafael Ballone. He and I drank a martini together in Mar-del-Plata two years ago, and a year ago we had a beer at the plane connection in Dakar. He's a great friend of mine, and a progressive artist."

"Pleased to meet you. Rafik," said the other and stared at Irina, while Irina, in the very best film-star style, looked at him, then at the end of his nose, and then looked away—she performed the most expressive of operations with her eyes alone.

I did not like that one little bit.

Igor asked Irina to dance, and while they were dancing Rafik, sitting a pair of spectacles on his nose, looked her up and down.

"Oh, what a marvelous girl," he turned to me, "I want to marry her. She will be my groom. That is, no. A female groom, what's that in Russian? Ah, yes, a bride, thanks. She will be my bride, and I the groom. Have you noticed the proportions of her body? No? Very interesting—absolutely ideal proportions of length of arms, legs and body, and the shape of the frame is just as perfect. Only there is one defect—a little here, how do you say? The enkle, the enkle is just a little thickish."

"You'd better think carefully about her ankle," I said sarcastically, "after all, you have to live with it for the rest of your life."

My heart was beginning to pound. Could it really be that she would marry him, this man from the world of capitalism?

131

Irina and Barkov came back, Rafik took off his glasses.

"Irina," he said solemnly, "I have seen you on every screen in the world in black and white, and now I am seeing you in full dimension and in color. I propose that you become my wife. I'm a progressive artist, but I also own four film companies and five villas in different health-resort regions of the world."

Silence reigned around the table; everyone realized that this was in earnest. Irina was silent for along time, then she snapped her fingers and winked at me.

"Misha, may I marry him? Everything depends on your decision."

"No, you may not," I snapped. Irina began to clap her hands delightedly.

"This character!" shouted Rafik. "What do you see in this character?"

Irina laid down her fork and straightened up. Her eyes flashed angrily.

"What do I see in him?" she uttered slowly. "This man has never offended my honor!"

Barkov burst out laughing.

"She fixed you nicely, Rafik!"

"Well, all right, all right," grumbled Ballone, "let's drop it. Let's order something hot."

When the hot dish had been brought Igor reminded me of what had to be done the next day, that I had to go to the furniture factory to get the material for the background shots.

"When is this going to stop? What am I, your manager or administrator or something?" I asked, though I was already trying to think what relative or friend I had at the furniture factory. "When am I going to start rehearsing Konyushka, and what sort of part is it anyway?"

"Yes, what sort of part is it, Barkov?" asked Irina, too.

"Nothing special," faltered Barkov, "a general part."

"Not of a small man?"

"No, on the contrary."

"I'm convinced that Misha will be able to play any part," said Irina. "He's got talent and, more important, a big heart. Not like some people," she added.

After the restaurant I saw her to her hotel and to the noise of the surf I kissed her hand. Oh!

5.

The next morning I was awakened by the silence. Our windows looked onto the sea, and there was always the roar of the surf, but today there was complete silence, and Lodkin was not puffing in his sleep as he usually did nor blowing bubbles.

132

I went over to the window and saw the following: the sea was dead calm, its surface moving only very, very slightly, as though it were being stroked; only here and there little bumps rippled the surface like goose-pimples; the horizon was not visible, hidden by a distant limpid haze in which the sails of a vessel which had anchored in the roads overnight appeared decidedly dark blue.

"Good morning, Misha," Lodkin said quietly behind my back. Clearly the calm had affected him too.

"Any idea what that boat is, Vanya?" I asked quietly.

"It's the training sailing-ship 'Vitiaz,' " he answered and suddenly burst into terrifying, booming laughter, then began to cough and blow his nose as he got back to normal. He did not notice me quivering. The "Vitiaz!" That's the one which bought up all the pictures of Irina. Now we can expect some trouble!

Getting washed and dressed any old way, I rushed out onto the esplanade. Along it, through the puddles which had not yet dried out after the stormy surf, Irina was hurrying from her hotel to ours. Behind her, their mouths gaping in youthful joy, strode a detachment of cadets from the "Vitiaz." A launch from the "Vitiaz" steered a parallel course in the sea. I raced forward.

"Misha, Misha!" shouted Irina. "Fans! A whole frigate full of them!"

"A barque. It's a barque, not a frigate," I said, seizing hold of her cold, frightened hands.

"But that's not the important thing," Irina said quickly, "I've just met Barkov, and he's let the cat out of the bag. Misha, it's a trick, it's a plot!"

I saw Igor running along the esplanade towards us. He had his finger pressed to his lips in a beseeching gesture, and was pulling at his head. Irina glanced at him, biting her lips vindictively. The cadets stood not far off, tender smiles rippling through their group.

"Misha, I grabbed the script from him, and immediately understood everything. It's a trick! Konyushka isn't a small man, he's a horse!"

Barkov had reached up by this time, and was standing next to us, breathing heavily.

"Yes, a horse," went on Irina, "this wretched modernist has it walking amongst water-melons as though they were heads. It's a horse."

Always in life's difficult, fateful moments I become a man of iron. Inside everything is trembling, I'm all pain and tears, but on the surface I'm a man of iron.

"That's cruel, Igor," I said coldly and calmly. "How could you do this to me?"

Barkov started towards me, but choked with emotion.

"Let's go, Mishenka," wept Irina, "let's get away from here. What right have they got to insult you like that?"

133

Towards evening on the same day we arrived at Simferopol station. The square in front of the station and the roofs of the cars were covered with snow. Irina was wrapped in her light suede coat and quivered now and again, still living through the injury done to me. I was carrying her suitcases, and she my briefcase.

The station towered gloomily above us, and before its enormous portico, its tall spire, and its long colonnades we appeared small and miserable. The taxi-drivers followed us with ironic gazes.

We bought tickets for the Moscow train and deposited our things in a left-luggage locker.

There were still about two hours before the train was due to leave. We remembered that we had not eaten since morning.

"I don't want to go to a restaurant," said Irina, "even the thought of how everyone will look at us when we go in is repulsive."

I looked at her—such a fashionable little thing in high boots with stiletto heels and with a short little coat, frozen and red-nosed from the cold, and here she was showing me her devotion and delicate understanding. It was a miracle, pure and simple, I thought, and suddenly felt happier than I had ever felt before. Don't think I'm making it up, it was all just like that.

We went out of the station and all at once saw, beneath the colonnades which had seemed so endless, a high counter with a large inscription over it: "All-in Meals."

"That's what we want," said Irina and took me by the arm.

We clambered up onto the high, uncomfortable stools and our legs dangled in mid-air.

Behind the counter a puffing and panting old dear bustled about; her gray locks kept slipping out from beneath her cap and she pushed them back with her elbow. She opened the lids of huge saucepans and columns of steam rose up as though from the nether regions. She dipped a ladle into the saucepans and with a somewhat bitter, malicious motion scooped out portions of an all-in meal. Behind her back, on the white doors of a refrigerator, was written in beautiful letters: "Soups, sauces, compotes, blancmanges."

Strictly speaking the meals were not all that cheap—77 kopecks. They included barley broth, barley pilaff and a cup of white coffee. True, there was a lot of meat in both the broth and pilaff, but it could be that we just happened to be lucky in the ladlefuls the waitress served us.

As Irina and I ate, some dogs circled beneath our feet, as beneath those of all the other customers: a pedigree greyhound bitch with drooping udders, a big black dog of doubtful parentage and several little ones. People threw them bones from the counter and shook barley off the spoons for them. Customers came and went, there was a constant ebb and flow, then suddenly Irina and I were left alone at the counter, and the waitress stopped moving

134

and froze, her ladle resting on her hip.

I looked at Irina as she ate, Irina looked at me as I ate, we smiled at each other, I raised my head and looked up at the vaults of the colonnade. The pillars were not round, but had sharp edges; they were very tall, and it was dark at the top; their capitals were not visible, but a bustling bird-life was going on up there with lots of commotion, rustling and whirring of wings.

The setting sun suddenly burst out from behind the clouds, and its heat was so unexpected and powerful that the snow at once began to melt, puddles formed, water began to drip from above and Irina and I seemed to be sitting behind a screen of straight, ringing streams of water.

The sky promptly became blue, then red, then green, and a biting, spring-like wind rushed into the colonnade.

"I want some blancmange," said Irina.

"We never have any blancmange," snapped the waitress.

"What if you had a look for some?" I asked.

"Don't argue," Irina stopped me and smiled at the waitress.

The latter suddenly smiled back at her and shouted into the shaft down which the urns containing the all-in meals were lowered to her from the restaurant kitchen above:

"Vitek, one blancmange!"

"Hu-u-u-r-r-ach!" came down the shaft.

"It'll be here in a minute, dear," the waitress said to Irina.

Throwing aside the curtain of melting spring snow, three cadets from the "Vitiaz" came up to the counter.

"Ah, so here you are!" they shouted. "We've been looking all over the station for you!"

They settled themselves on the stools next to us and fixed their young, insolent eyes on Irina.

"We're headed for Murmansk," they said, "and from there to Freedom Island. Do you want to come with us, Miss Ivanova?"

"May I go with them, Misha?" asked Irina.

"No," I said. "Under no circumstances."

"Who's this guy, your husband?" asked the cadets.

"Just the man I love," answered Irina.

The cadets merrily began to bang their spoons and demand food.

The waitress got up a head of steam, all the while uttering grunts of satisfaction.

Through the dripping snow came a tall old woman in high heels. She was wearing a fur with a pointed fox head, slightly worn with age.

After the old woman in came that thievish brute Rex marching on his hind legs.

"Rex, attendez! Allons, allons," the old woman called him and came up to the counter swaying her hips.

135

"Sit down, mum," said the cadets.

"Though apart life is not easy, none the less I love a sailor," trolled the old woman as she settled herself down, "He's a blue-eyed sailor from a blue, blue ship..."

Our dogs at once accepted Rex into their company.

The correspondence-student arrived, also took a seat and set about cutting out profiles.

"I'm going to Moscow for my exams and I need the money," he explained.

A pleasant little group was forming. The atmosphere became merry. The waitress, joining the old woman in song, danced from pot to pot. Empty saucepans went up the shaft, pearl-barley and mutton came down. The cadets drummed a hornpipe with their spoons. Irina gently moved her hands and eyes. The student and I discussed the poetry of Alexei Zaurikh. Rex tried to incite the dogs to jump up onto the counter all together and gobble up everything. The vagrant aristocrat, her bosom wobbling, tried to make him see reason.

It was already dark when Igor Barkov and Rafael Ballone put in an appearance.

"Misha, you've got to forgive me for that little piece of deception," said Igor. "Things weren't going too well with us and I decided to call on you. If you only knew how everyone livened up when you arrived, they raised their heads and found faith in their own strength. You won't come back?"

"No, he won't come back," said Irina, "but we forgive you, Barkov. And you, too," she said to Rafik.

There was a crash and out of the shaft, with a wide tooth-flashing smile, climbed Vitek himself, dirty-faced and carrying a huge punchbowl. Over the bowl flickered a blue flame.

"And here's the blancmange!" he shouted.

"Well, there's a surprise!" laughed the waitress.

The dogs stood up on their hind legs and poked their snouts between our elbows.

And we sat there feasting noisily, like knights and beautiful ladies beneath the smoke-blackened vaults of a Norman castle. We divided up the blue flame and the pearl-barley and threw the bones to our dogs.

God, I thought, all these people are mortal! But it's impossible even to imagine that some day not one of us will be left alive, not even these cadets nor Irina, God! It's impossible to believe that, or even to conceive it. But what are we to do? Maybe we should believe in one another, in what has brought us together here just now, in what it is that's drawing every person in the world over to our counter right now? After all we all have to console and encourage one another, and talk to one another about everyday things and flatter one another just a little with fine words, and organize just such

136

happy hubbub as this, and not to do the dirty on one another or make malicious remarks. But, unfortunately, how often people behave as though they were never going to die, and it's only occasionally that things go off as well as they did just then. It's a pity you weren't with us.

They had already announced boarding twice over the loudspeakers when an open "ZIL-110" drove up to the colonnade and out of it climbed Herostratos. Getting all tangled up in his long Greek tunic, he made his way purposefully along the colonnade. He was carrying a can of petrol.

"Always fame, fame, always this endless quest for fame," he grumbled as he poured petrol over the walls of Simferopol station. "The temple of Athena is not enough for me, I must set fire to this palace too. I've already seen to the ship which is named after me, so now..."

"Hey you, Stratostatos!" shouted the cadets, climbing down from their stools. "Stop playing pranks, you old crackpot! Do you want to be bounced on your head?"

I don't know how the argument between the cadets and Herostratos finished, because Irina and I were already on our way to the train.

7.

We found Jacek in his studio. He was making pelmeni for himself. In the middle of the room towered something huge, covered in wet rags.

"First of all, I'm glad to see you," said Jacek, "and secondly I've got something to boast of myself. I've been given a commission. I'm working on a group called The Peaceful Atom."

He tore off the rags and we saw the group, so far done only in clay. There was a seated woman with Irina's features, next to her an inquisitive-looking young man resembling me, and behind their backs, his heavy hands laid on their shoulders, towered the thinker weighed down with ideas, resembling Jacek himself.

"I'll soon be a great man, Misha," said Jacek, "and I'll set you up in the world."

And that's how it all turned out. Jacek set me up in the world. Irina became my wife. That was a long time ago.

Translated by P.V. Cubberley

NOTES

1. "insect-cockroach," therefore suggests "beetle-like."
2. tarakan = cockroach.
3. Caucasian pies.
4. Russian pies.
5. English in original.
6. Pushkin—Evgeny Onegin

CHANGING A WAY OF LIFE

1

Aviation plays strange tricks on us. When I fly into a place I feel like cursing geography, because it turns out that there is no such thing as the central Russian ranges, forest-steppes or even the ordinary steppes separating the places I have come from and the Caucasian Black Sea coast. All that separates them is several hours' flight. Two grubby numbers of Ogoniok, four smiles from the air hostess, a caramel at take-off and another at landing. It's about time I got used to it. It's silly even to think on these lines, I thought, standing on the embankment in Gagra one evening.

A dull crimson glow hung askew over the dark horizon. In the dusk the sea appeared calm, and so it was strange to hear the waves pounding the concrete like cannon blasts, see them rise ten meters above the embankment, then drop back with a powerful hiss.

There was no wind. The storm was somewhere way out in the open sea, and it only made itself felt here by pounding at the beaches with powerful, if slightly indolent blows.

Holidaymakers were discussing the water and atmospheric phenomena. A middle-aged Georgian was treating an elderly couple to an animated explanation of what causes fluctuations in water temperature in the Black Sea.

"But, Rezo, you are forgetting the currents," said the middle aged lady capriciously, taking pleasure in saying his name.

"Currents?" exclaimed the Georgian, agitated for some reason, and began to talk about currents. He went on about currents, about the Mediterranean, the Straits of Bosphorus and the Dardanelles. He distorted the Russian words heavily, now and again reverting to his own language. One felt that he understood the essence of the matter perfectly, that only the excitement prevented him from explaining it all.

"What, Rezo," drawled the lady absent-mindedly, looking away. "Surely the Mediterranean doesn't flow in here?"

Her husband put in weightily: "Oh no, the Red Sea comes in here from the Pacific." Rezo could hardly bear it. He was practically screaming, explaining something about the Gulfstream, about various currents and the Black Sea. He had a thorough knowledge of his subject, perhaps was a specialist in this field, but was impeded by his excitement.

"From the Great or Pacific Ocean," repeated the elderly holidaymaker delightedly from under his velure hat.

The Georgian bade them an irritable but polite goodbye and disappeared into the darkness, and arm in arm, the couple turned their steps along the embankment. Their air of solidarity gave me a peculiar feeling. They stood behind each other to the last, sharing a single perception of the world.

I set off along the embankment too. The lights of Gagra hung over me. Cottages clambered high up the mountain, but just now its contours were invisible—the mountain had merged with the dark sky, and you could imagine these cottages to be the top floors of skyscrapers, lit up in the night. I passed the tourist buses standing in a row beside the embankment. The Georgian drivers were sitting in their lighted cabins and chatting with cronies, who were crowded around the buses. They were the sort of people you rarely see in our parts. They wore huge flat caps, and talked as if they had gathered to perform some very serious deed.

Glowing cigarette ends floated along the tunnel beneath the palms. I walked towards them, continually forgetting that it was me walking there, under the palms, just think! Me, an old recluse, strolling under the palms. Essentially I was still back there where I had had breakfast in a milk bar, had my boots cleaned by the familiar bootblack and bought my newspapers. Where just an hour before take-off I had slipped into a telephone booth, dialed a number, informed the sleepy voice I was going away, and after long and fretful questioning actually stated where, naming the guesthouse. Where I had come from smelt of exhaust fumes, like the tourist bus stand, but never of luxurious perfume like this avenue of palms.

"A star just fell!" said a woman's voice ahead.

"Make a wish!" cried the man.

"You have to wish while it's falling, it's too late now," replied the woman, with no hint of disappointment.

"Make a hind-wish," advised the man and I saw the heavy contours of a velure hat ahead.

A searchlight passed along the horizon dividing the bay from the open sea. I went off to bed. The night receptionist in the hall handed me a telegram which read: "Just leaving, meet me, such and such a train, such and such a carriage. Together soon." No need to rack my brains, it was from Nika. Rather, from Vera. You see, her name is Veronica. Everybody calls her Nika, which she likes, but I persist in calling her Vera, an additional pretext for constant bickering.

Several years ago this woman, Nika—Vera—Veronica, took it into her head that I had appeared on this earth solely in order to become her husband. At that time we were all mad about the song "Johnny, you are all I need." It played about 15 times per evening, and Veronica would keep joining in with "Genka you are all I need." I thought it was just a joke, but there you are!

The oddest thing was that all this had dragged on for several years already. I would put down the receiver in my studio, while away weeks and even months on a business mission, occasionally meet other women and strike up odd affairs, now and then completely forgetting Vera, completely forgetting her existence, but sooner or later she would phone or turn up in person, beaming, rubicund, obsessed with the idea that I was all she needed, and she was so very beautiful!

"Did you miss me?" she would ask.

"And how!" I would reply.

"Well hello," she would say and come up close.

And I would put aside whatever happened to be in my hands at that moment—a pencil, cassette, folder with materials. And next morning, without so much as leaving a note, move into a friend's empty dacha. Goodbye! Once again I had escaped safe and sound.

"In any case," she would sometimes say, "I free you from certain responsibilities, thereby doing some good for the government."

She would say this cynically and bitterly, for show.

I knew that I should have put a stop to this farce long ago and married her. Sometimes I was seized by an awful depression that I knew Vera could remove with one sweep of her hand. But I was afraid, because I knew that from the minute we left the registry office my life would undergo a radical, and perhaps catastrophic change.

Yes, sometimes I feel pretty cheerless, when I get up from my study table at night, go to the window and see, across the river, a house that has been there three hundred years, but then mankind has gone so far forward that it can permit certain of its representatives not to settle down. And, after all, to hell with "ships, lines, and other long-lived things?" But perhaps the thoughts and emotions of individuals merge with the thoughts and emotions of generations, and are handed on just like genes?

Whereas Veronica never dreamed of aging, she had fallen in love with me when she was twenty, and hadn't changed a fraction since. Perhaps she thinks that it's been only weeks, not years. Noisy, flourishing, she is a child of the technological institute. This is where she gets her various ribaldries and abrupt manner of speaking, whilst at heart she is sickeningly sentimental. I had a feeling she was born in the south, but she says no, in the north.

What the hell possessed me to ring her this morning an hour before leaving, how could I have forgotten, idiot that I am, that she can't stay angry at me for more than an hour? Why, she had put her celebrated energy to work while I was still in the air and probably even contrived to obtain a pass for the same guest house.

"What time does such and such a train arrive?" I asked the girl on duty. She told me and I went up the dark staircase, entered my room, undressed and fell asleep.

I should mention that I am thirty one, past sport, but trying not to let myself go. Morning gymnastics, season's tickets at a swimming pool— those are a must. It's true all this health habit—there is no other word for it— goes down the drain when I get wound up. And since I am constantly on full revvs.... when would I fit in swimming! When I get going I leave the phone off the hook and don't move from my desk, going out only for cigarettes. The landlady brings me lunch and coffee so strong it makes my heart thump.

Most of my friends live the same way.

I used to work in a design office. One wall was of glass and in winter an early moon could catch hundreds of young fellows and girls bent at work over their boards. We all wore check shirts. You were dazzled by Scotch checks as you came into the room after smoke-oh. We made no distinction between the institute and the office, and continued to execute some abstract theorem-like lesson, taken from heaven knows where. To understand what we were working at would require some hard thought, but many of us quickly lost this ability. It seemed to me that the whole world sat in large and small rooms, with one glass wall, tracing out various assemblies and whistling the songs of three years ago, whilst the moon set its price on each one of us.

Then I began to imagine that the whole world sat till morning in the gray vaults of its studios, writhing in the agonies of creation, rather like holding back water, languored by the window, meditating on a woman's love, which is possibly more durable than any house across the river, beginning to cough by morning, and then hey presto, tubercules have taken root in the lungs!

Then you are treated without time off work (injections in the right buttock and powder by the tablespoonful), and there you are that's that.

"Now you are to all intents cured. But are you in order mentally? You know, everything in the organism is connected. You should change your way of life."

"Have you got stuck into the perpetuum mobile or what, Genka? There's a sort of gleam in your eyes..."

"... It's as if you weren't aware, Gennadii, that the organism needs rest."

I hadn't been away anywhere except on business for three years, and here I was in Gagra, sleeping naked in a large room, Gagra stirring inside me, like in a fat reptile with illuminated innards.

In the morning, instead of a window I was confronted by a poster urging me to deposit my money in the savings bank. It had everything: dark blue sea, cypresses placed symmetrically in the corners, a section of magnificent colonnade and the top of a palm tree. I got up against this backdrop and shouted to the whole world: I SAVED MY WAY TO A HOLIDAY! Then I remembered the telegram and began dressing. I looked in the mirror. I wasn't quite poster standard, but everything was ahead of me.

2

There were potted palms on the station. Fresh sheep's blood and melancholy floated from the open windows of the restaurant kitchen. Five middle aged men were pacing the platform out of step, averting their eyes and their bunches of flowers. I found it strange to see them walking out

141

of step. I thought they should get into file and march. Some taciturn Moscow students showed up on the platform five minutes before the train pulled in. Snorkels, slippers and badminton bats poked out of their bags. A first-rate crowd, I must say. Then they were caught up by a real doll of a girl... but the train had pulled in.

A vigorous blond was first to jump out onto the platform. He threw his case on the asphalt, opened his arms wide and bawled out:

"Oh, the palms of Gagra!"

He was indescribably happy. He looked the girl over with some knowledge of the subject, seized his suitcase and set off at a light elastic gait, ready for a repeat of last season's resounding conquests.

The train was still moving. Men in straw hats trotted after it, holding their flowers in front of them like relay batons. I made a leap to the side, bought a bunch of flowers, and ran after them, already catching sight of Veronica, pale with nervousness in the window. She noticed the flowers in my hand and her eyebrows jerked up in astonishment.

"Hello, Nika," I said, embracing her, "you know..."

3

We led an incredible life; ate fruit, swam and sun-baked, and in the evening dined merrily in a nasty restaurant, "the Gagripsh," dancing gaily to outlandish oriental jazz, and everything seemed just as it should be. We watched the hall, where the tone was set by blondes of titantic endurance and laughingly nicknamed the men "Gagers," the women "Gagras," and the children "Gagrettes." Walking to the hills or pacing the evening streets of Gagra we practiced the few accessible eastern words: "madzhari," "chacha," "churchkela"... I called Veronica "Nika" and brought her flowers every day.

She was mad about everything here; the spicy smells in the parks and the melancholy of the Armenian bartenders, churchkela and sulguni cheese, and, of course, the mountains, sea, sun... She would swim way out from the shore in flippers and snorkel, dive down and not surface for ages. Then she wold emerge from the water, lie down about five meters away on the pebbles and glance at me from time to time, her eyes sparkling, as if to say: "You're a fool, Genka. Where else would you find a girl like me?" We didn't talk on the beach, I was considered to be working—I would sit with a scribbling pad, writing, drawing, thinking over new designs. I actually did sit with a scribbling pad and made notes as Veronica emerged from the water: "There you are! Fancy that! She didn't drown. Well, well, not a cloud in the sky. Oh-ho-ho, the train has left... Tu-ru-ru, its gone north... Eho-he, I am hungry... N-o-n-sen-se. Let's have a pear..." and sketched.

142

And so a few pages every day in my scribbling pad. I couldn't work here. Everything prevented me: the glitter, the laughter, the noise and hubbub, and Nika, although she lay quiet. Still I pretended to work, and she didn't encroach on these hours. Perhaps she realized that these pitiful exertions were asserting my right to solitude. Or perhaps she didn't think along these lines at all, and was content simply to lie five meters away on the pebbles, her eyes sparkling. She was probably content with breakfast and lunch, the afternoon and evening, and the part of the night we spent together.

She was completely happy. She found the surroundings quite natural, and apparently the only possible environment in which she should have lived from childhood to old age. It was as if she had never gone to the laboratory, never clocked on, as was now the rule in all big establishments; never huddled up from the cold in drizzling northerly rain, never humbled herself to walk by the entrance of my house, never rung me at night. She had always been happily in love, processing in a bold sarafan down an avenue of palms towards a beloved and faithful man.

"Hi, Gager!"

"Hi, Gagra!"

"Want to kiss me?"

She always asked the same way, knowing that I would kiss her then and there, and present her with a magnolia, and we would set off, almost at a hop, for the beach.

Suddenly she said to me:

"Why do you always wear this shirt? After all, you've got others."

I shuddered and glanced at her. There was a sudden flush of uneasiness in her eyes, but she had already taken the plunge.

"How many shirts have you got?"

"Five," I replied.

"There you are! And yet you wear the same one all the time. Perhaps there are buttons off the others? Why of course! As if your shirts ever had the buttons intact!"

"Yes, there are some buttons missing," I said, averting my eyes.

"Come on, I'll sew them on," she replied decisively.

We went to my room, I dragged out my suitcase, laid it on the bed, and Nika seemed to fling herself into its contents with a sort of lust...

I went out onto the balcony. Everything was as prescribed: a red sun sinking into the blue sea. The colors were very exact, half-tones are foreign to the south; below, immediately under the balcony our games officer Nadiko was performing a dance step in the square.

"The magnificent 'Apple dance'!" she cried, lightly steering her full body across the square.

Amidst the dancers I noticed the man who had been arguing about tides with Rezo, the Georgian, on the embankment the day I arrived. I barely recognized him. A dark tan concealed the flabbiness of his cheeks, he had swapped the velure hat for a tea-coolies headgear. He was jigging with abandon in the uninhibited, merry-making crowd. He thrust out his funny knees, competely incongruous but rather charming; evidently he had clean forgotten for the marvelous instant what was required of him by his post and general situation. At this point I caught sight of his wife. She passed directly under my balcony with two other women.

"You've no idea how sensitive I am," she babbled, "when someone says 'snake' in my presence, I faint immediately."

I stood on the balcony and looked at Gagra, at this narrow strip of flat land, only 200 meters wide, squeezed between menacing, darkening mountains and tense crimson sea. This long narrow Gagra, Dzveli Gagra, Gagripsh, and Akhali Gagra, throbbed timidly but doggedly, street lights were already appearing, large windows were lighting up, buses switched on their lamps whilst the resonant voices of games officers announced to the whole embankment:

"The jolly foxtrot!"

Who could guarantee that the sea would not swell, or the hills belch fire? That was the sensations I had at that moment. Nika's slender hands rested on my shoulders. She sighed and said:

"God, how beautiful..."

"What?" I queried, in a steady voice.

"Just everything," she uttered, barely audibly.

"It's all artificial," I said sharply, and her fingers jerked away.

"What's artificial?"

"The palms, for example," I muttered, "are artificial."

"Don't talk rot," she exclaimed.

"In winter, after the tourists have left, they are painted with a special durable paint. Fancy you not knowing. You gullible child!"

"Idiot!" she laughed with relief.

"Blessed is he who believes," I croaked. "Everything's artificial. Those smells too. At nights they spray the trees with a special solution from an atomizer which is manufactured by a plant somewhere in the Cheliabinsk region. That's where they get soot and tar! The coal and tar are processed..."

"That's enough!" she cried angrily.

"All these subtropics are bogus."

"Well, what is not bogus?" she queried.

"Rain and wet snow, clay underfoot, tarpaulin boots, goods trains, maybe even passenger trains too. Airplanes are bogus. My desk is not bogus, neither is your laboratory."

"Nor are X-rays..." I added after a brief silence.

"I don't get it," she whispered forlornly.

"Why don't you get it? Look, when they were building this place, they carted cement in wheelbarrows, and lifted panels by crane—that was not bogus, but when they do the 'Apple dance' here, that's bogus."

"What a lot of twaddle," she exclaimed. "People come here for a holiday. That's natural..."

"True. But it wouldn't hurt them to think about something else as well on such a narrow strip of flat ground," I said, but she continued her own line of thought.

"After all, your own work is directed towards people being able to have better holidays."

"I work for work's sake," I said from sheer desire to pose, and she immediately cried:

"You're a show-off and a snob!"

I contradicted her, she began again, I answered her somehow, and we had a long argument about nothing.

"Genka, what's the matter with you today?" she asked finally.

"I just want a drink," I replied.

4

The "Gagripsh" was packed full, and after some difficulty we managed to find spare seats at the same table as a couple of young blond fellows in narrow-lapeled jackets. They were complaining to each other that Gagra was "poorly off for dolls and those there were, were already attached (glancing at Veronica), and there was nothing for it, they would evidently have to go to Sochi, where—a small chap put in—these goods came in bulk.

We ordered. The waitress ran past several times, but eventually did bring us something. Grokhachev entered the hall. He passed between the tables, the same as ever, with mock feebleness, a vague smile on his lips. It was an unexpected pleasure to see him there. Grokhachev was a recluse like myself, we worked in the same field, and even traveled together quite often on field trips.

"Hey, Grokh!" I waved to him, and he acquired a chair from somewhere and joined us.

It turned out he had left his wife in Gudauty and was shooting home in proud solitude in his Moskvich.

We began talking shop. This went well with brandy, and we forgot everything else. Occasionally I noticed Vera dancing with one or another of the young blondes. They livened up, apparently thinking their affairs had taken a turn for the better. Then they went off to the lavatory, and after this campaign Vera danced with just one of them, whilst the other made fruitless sallies at the far end of the hall.

Then all five of us went out to the road to catch a taxi. The blond was terribly lucky. He caught a Moskvich, got in with Veronica and his friend, another blond like himself. And a Moskvich, as you know, only seats three. I followed the taxi's disappearing brake lights, and listened to Grokh.

He was recounting his project. Fifteen minutes later he came back to earth.

"Hey listen, my car is a hundred meters or so from here. What did you let Nika go with that scum for?"

"Don't you know Nika better than that?" I said. "She has long since got rid of them and gone to bed."

We found his car, got in and drove off. Grokh asked me:

"Have you two finally got married?"

"Not yet."

"Why do you keep putting it off? Believe me, it's not as terrifying as all that."

"How many kilometers is Gudauty from here?" I asked.

He laughed, and we reverted to shop.

It's odd, a few years back we could chat for hours about anything under the sun, whereas now we invariably get back to work.

Grokh drove me home. I hopped out of the car and straightaway noticed Nika. She was sitting on a bench waiting for me. I turned back. The car still hadn't moved off.

"What time are you leaving tomorrow, Grokh?"

"About midday."

"Do you park the car by the hotel? I might come with you."

"OK, why not?" replied Grokh.

He drove off and I went up to Nika. Laughing, she began telling me about the boys, how they had "conned" her, how amusing it had been. Arms around each other, we walked towards the house, which shone white in the darkness at the end of the cypress avenue. I didn't tell Nika that tomorrow I would be leaving this paradise, where our love might blossom and strengthen, where people exchange heavy hats for a tea coolie's headgear. And it wasn't because I didn't love her that I was going, it was because Grokh was shooting through and would be back in his hole a week before me, if I stayed in this paradise.

5

In the morning I packed my case and crawled safely past the dining room. I left a note for Nika with the girl on duty and went out onto the road. I knew that you could get strong oriental coffee there, and immediately decided to go on the coffee from early morning instead of all the Kefir and cultivated sour milk they treated you to in the guest house. The pie house was under the open sky, or rather, under the sheltered crown of a huge tree. I gulped down the burning black brew with pleasure, feeling my sleepy brain beginning to clear. My case was beside me, and not a soul in the whole world knew where I was at that moment. A man in a coolie hat was eating at the adjacent table. Fat streamed down his chin, he was enjoying

146

the light wine, which reflected the sun. Perhaps his enjoyment stemmed from the same source as mine.

Suddenly he put aside his cheburek and called:

"Chibisov! Vasilii!"

Smiling awkwardly, and shifting feet, a young man in a crew cut and a blue T-shirt and baggy brown trousers came up to him.

"Greetings, Comrade Uvarov!"

"Take a seat. Have you been here long?" asked Uvarov hastily, taking off his white hat and hiding it behind his back.

"Flew in yesterday."

"Well, how are things back home? Have you got the third shop going?"

"Not yet."

"Why?"

"The Industrial Safety Board is holding it up."

"Disgraceful. Always putting a spoke in the wheel."

They began discussing the construction. Uvarov spoke abruptly, embarrassed, whilst Chibisov answered circumstantially and with a guilty smile.

"Bring another glass," Uvarov said crossly to the waitress. She brought a glass and poured some Tsinandali into it.

"Drink up, Vasilii."

"To recovery, then," Chibisov grinned, and raised the glass between two fingers.

"And how do you like it here?" asked Uvarov.

Chibisov drained his Tsinandali.

"It's not bad, but a little strange."

Uvarov rose.

"OK then! When do you have to get back to work?"

"You know yourself, Sergei Sergeich."

"Quite, I know, so see you don't forget. Well, until then. Make good use of your leave."

Chivisov sat at the table, twirled the empty glass in his fingers and cast an uncertain glance around at the sea—its horizon blazing in the sun. His face, neck and hands were red and wind-burned: but further up his arms were white and his forearm displayed a blue tattoo, resembling sclerosis. I felt I wanted to have a drink with this chap and do everything possible to put him at his ease here because he already knew what was bogus and what was not, and knew that paradise was an alien place to man.

I rose, picked up my case and walked down the avenue. Nika was walking towards me. I wasn't surprised. I would have been surprised if she hadn't shown up. This avenue was specially designed for a slender girl, Veronika-Vera-Nika, her teeth, eyes, hair gleaming, to walks towards me. She took me by the arm and walked by my side.

"Is our love bogus too?" she asked smiling.

"It's a magnolia," I replied.

147

Grokhachev caught us up along the road. He braked and asked me:

"You're not coming then?"

"I've still got ten days," I replied, "after all I'm entitled to the leave."

Grokh smiled at us in very kindly fashion.

"So long then," he said. "We'll see each other soon anyway."

GINGER FROM NEXT DOOR

Dedicated to: the Jakovlev brothers,

Boris Mayofis,

Slava Ulrikh

Sergei Kholmsky

Rustem Kutuy

Erik Dibay,

and also to Ginger from next door.

Whether I went into the restaurant that time smoothly or awkwardly, I have no idea. Most likely I again cringed beneath the glances of the regular customers. Yes, yes, now it's coming back to me—I think there was a brief feeling of shame. It was a slight, habitual shame—a result of my absent-mindedness. I almost always forget the rules of the game at the entrance to this restaurant and never go in the way I ought to—it's not that I go in illegally, but just that I'm not playing my own part, so naturally I look absurd.

So, once again I went into the restaurant, thinking about something un-restaurant-like, and it was only in the middle of the Oak Room, when I found myself caught in the interlacing pattern of looks, that I began to get confused and to bustle around, trying to find a spot to squeeze in as quickly as I could. Suddenly I had a stroke of luck: a table in the corner was vacated, and I occupied it, thereby hiding the right-hand side of my body.

The right-hand side of my body was at once transported into unbridled bliss, while the left-hand side tensed itself, already joining in the game, displaying indifference, boredom, weariness, and irony. Here's how I had to look in this place: my face had to look exhausted, and my movements to be sluggish but significant. If I act like that, someone will ask compassionately: "What's wrong, old fellow, did you have too much to drink last night?" and with that everyone will relax; the thing is clear and near and accessible to everyone--the bloke had had too much to drink last night. But if I act any other way, then they're sure to ask: what are you looking so sad about? This question is inevitable if I appear in any way different, and equally inevitable is the burst of fury, although not visible externally, which immediately follows this question. I sat alone for two minutes, then Yura Pozumentshchikov came over.

"What are you looking so sad about?" he asked, leaning his fists on my table.

The fury at once gushed up in me, and I overcame it on the spot, but nevertheless I said something rotten.

"You look as though you've put some weight on again," I said to Yura. He was disconcerted.

"I've just been told I'd lost weight," he mumbled.

"No, no you've put it on, definitely," I said. "I simply can't under-

149

stand why you're getting so fat."

"And you," said Pozumentshchikov in a trembling voice. "What about you—you're as broad as you are tall. You're a horrible square shape."

We both smiled with affected good-will, and he went away.

Sinking still deeper into the corner, leaving only one indifferent foot sticking out, with its heavy, blunt-snouted shoe, I let my eyes rove for the thousandth time around the restaurant's tall oak panels, the creaking staircase up to the mezzanine, supported by a twisted pillar, the mezzanine with its offices and separate balcony, which I had long burned to jump off.

This restaurant, which was always in semi-darkness and imbued with a dull reddish light, like gas, sometimes filled me with unbelievable apathy. Right now I felt as though I was lying on the ocean-bed on my side, like a submarine with flat batteries.

All this does not mean that I'm some sort of inveterate reveller, who never leaves the restaurant. It's just that I'm here too often. I often dine here, they know me and serve me smilingly and efficiently, and I dine in a quick business-like way, or sometimes with the boys, like Pozumentshchikov, while we rapidly and jokingly pass on various pieces of news. But then at other times it might go like this: you come into a familiar place, with its familiar customers, and suddenly the place seems like a terrifying hall and the people a horde of tin- and copper-eyed monsters.

By now the sluggish damp winter had been going for a long time, and we were probably all tired of it by this time.

Suddenly, I don't know why, it seemed as though music had started playing, the music of my by now very distant childhood, and I had the feeling that Ginger from next door was about to come flying into this pagan temple with the mad eyes of spring.

During the war we lived in Kazan, in Karl Marx Street, formerly Great Georgia Street, opposite the tuberculosis center, formerly the governor's palace, in a large wooden house, formerly the private residence of the industrial engineer Zherebtsov. Our garden, in which Zherebtsov's lime-trees still stood, was closed in by a fence on one side and by wood-sheds on the other.

Every spring during the war the lime-trees, strange as it may seem, grew new leaves, and so well that you could sit in their shade and forget about your hunger, and the exhausted adults of your family, and the hard winter.

Ginger from next door used to sit for hours on one or another of these limes, high up on a bough, imagining himself the look-out sailor on the frigate Dumont d'Urville.

As for me, I preferred the roof. From Mr. Zherebtsov's terrace, on which the rotten floorboards gave dangerously under your feet, I used to climb up the carved post onto the roof and sit there on the ridge, imagining myself one of Cook's sailors.

150

From the roof could be seen distinctly all the numerous intricate weather-vanes of the tuberculosis center, the square niches of the House of Specialists, the granite pillars of the technological-chemical institute, and the bright patch of the tiny little garden of that cultured old lady Evgeniya Olympievna next door. The place next door, where Ginger had been born, reminded one of an intricate archipelago, still not completely explored. It was connected to our place by a narrow passage between the outside toilet and the rubbish bins. It had several wooden houses in it, two two-storeyed brick houses, and away at the back there rose a tall good-quality house with wide windows in patterned frames, bronze railings on the balconies, and a great number of dormer-windows, garrets and weather-vanes.

Straits, bays, secret entrances, damp cellars—that's what it was like next door, where Ginger came from.

Ginger would be perched about twenty yards away from me, and slightly higher up, amidst the foliage of the limes.

"Hey there, on the fo'c'sle," he would sometimes shout to me. "Hey, Pat! Have you read 'Mutiny on the Elsinore'?"

The only boy with whom Ginger had more or less human relations was me: we used to exchange Jack London books. The others could not stand Ginger—he terrorized them. Towards the end of the day he would come down from his lime-tree and organize fiendish little games in both gardens, rushing around like a mad ginger tom, or perhaps even like a lynx. In the game "stand still" the ball was thrown onto the roof; for "pitch and toss" the coins and the five-kopeck striker were stolen: in "thirteen sticks," a plank of wood was split in two; twirled around by the tail, a dead cat would fly at the girls. The sailors of the Dumont d'Urville are wild after their lengthy wanderings in Polynesia....

"The catastrophic drop in all interest in art... Do you see what I mean?"

"Eh?"

"Look at that, for example, here comes a real scoundrel."

"Who?"

"Him there, you know him." To the scoundrel, dryly: "Hullo." My dear fellow, what can I say—'a grim monster, savage, gigantic, hundred-mouthed and... 'how does it go again?"

"Bellowing."[1]

"That's it. The cultivation of thought, the realm of emotion... some Borzhom?[2] ... In Europe they've got unification... here's health... Europe has guzzled itself, if you'll pardon the expression, but that's how it is, don't you agree?"

"Yes, in general, but..."

"Now there's a good man just come in. Hullo, hullo! How are things at home? My regards to them all! Do you know him?"

"Pass the cucumber..."

"Of course he's a craftsman, he's a cabinet-maker, and I love carpentry. You know, it's become boring by now, everyone going around with such fashionable things. Don't you agree?"

"Yes, in general, but..."

Somebody with a grand, well-to-do air, perhaps some celebrity, or someone of high rank, speaking as though through a chloroform pad, in search of a waitress:

"Who's serving here... hm, hm, ha-ah... any hopes? How about a look at the stomach book?"

He meant the menu.

... the wild sailors of the Dumon d'Urville, like red cats or red lynxes, rushed about our gardens, flew up onto the wood-sheds, dashed down into the cellars with loud whistles, and jumped up on the trees.

Aska Pokrovsky was playing lapta.[3] Slavka and Seryoshka were trying to hit her with a little hockey ball, but trying to hit her softly, so as not to hurt her. Aska was prancing about happily, enjoying her power over the boys, and thinking herself graceful.

Ginger from next door ran up, grabbed the ball from Slavka—"give it to me and I'll hurt her!"—and hit Aska on the face so hard that she fell.

"The steel glinted in John's hand!" squealed Ginger from next door and vanished in a flash.

"It seems that you've been going around with this Ginger from next door?" my aunt asked me. "Just you wait, you'll both end up in the reformatory."

I thought of Aska standing in the middle of the deserted garden. The spring sunset could be seen through Zherebtsov's lime-trees, presaging the future life through which Aska would walk—over the distant sea, in Polynesia, thick-legged Aska in a mantilla, with a fan—Aska—everything's confused.

"Did you see how I hit Aska?" asked Ginger, coming up.

"Yes. I would have hit her like that too."

"Well it's me who hit her, and not you," said Ginger with a sly smile. "Now we must hand a note to the victim. Will you do it, pal?"

The note read: "Aska, I hit you because you shouldn't lift up your legs. You're a member of the pioneers, and it doesn't become you, little Mary. Tomorrow I'll be in the gully in TPI park all day, at the Podluzhnaya Street entrance. If it's sore you can hit me back there with anything you want, even a brick. May 1744. Aboard the 'Astrolabia'."

Ginger screwed up his eyes, looking at the sunset with a sly smile. Thick-legged Aska figured in his future life too.

Suddenly he started, spun around and tensed himself. The smile gave way to the rapacious teeth-baring of a cornered cat. At the foot of the garden, over the fence were climbing the Jakovlev brothers, Slavka Ulrikh, Seryozhka Kholmsky and Borka Mayofis. In their hands were short wooden swords. Jumping down from the fence, they ran towards us.

"Petka!" they shouted to me. "Hold Ginger! Grab the lunatic!"

Ginger picked up a stick of some sort, and shoved a broken brick into my hand.

"We're back to back at the mast, two against a thousand!" he shouted wildly right into my face.

They surrounded us, and we defended ourselves, whirling over our heads...

"... Eh... *introduce to you my best friend*[4] ... if you like we'll sit here. What do you want?"

"*Please, please, please, please, please,* s'il vous plaît!"

... a brick and a stick, a brick and a stick, a brick and a stick, hell!

"... caviare, pressed, unpressed, or whatever, chicken-tabaka, vodka?"

There followed a series of contacts under the general heading of "internationally famous *Russian strong vodka"*: knowing smiles, winks, aphorisms, until the subject under discussion had been absorbed inside with a slight gurgle, *"all the best."*

"Tell me, is it true that in Loch Ness there lives a not unknown plesiosaurus?"

"Gr-r-r—chicken-tabaka," but with ears cocked at the same time to the interpreter.

"Yes, it lives..."

By now the interpreter, *"my best friend,"* his ears thrust forward, all attention, was already working on the bones, gr-r-r-r-kh-phu...

... a brick and a stick, yes, a brick and a stick...

"*Excuse me,* please translate, I must leave you for a few brief minutes."

In the toilet next to the basin had been scratched the joke: "Barankin,[5] watch what you say! The 68th police department." I knew the author of the joke, but did not intend to start thinking of him. I closed the door firmly and leant against the wall.

... a brick and a stick. Borka, Slavka, Seryozhka and the Jakovlev brothers, fencing skillfully but cautiously, worked us into a ring.

"You too, Brutus!" Slavka Ulrikh shouted to me, although the situation was the exact opposite of the Roman story to which he was alluding, and he was clearly not Caesar, nor were any of them, but Caesar, it seems to me, was the terrible Ginger from next door, whom I was for some reason now defending, and with a heart full of bravery, a heart which had come under the power of a brilliant demagogue: we're back to back at the mast...

"Take that!" Someone thumped me on the cheek-bone. "Take that! And that!"—the swords crashed down on Ginger's bonce.

"Retreat to next door!" he shouted.

We broke through the ring and set off at a run.

Yes, obviously all the fellows had united in their desire to avenge Aska Pokrovsky: in the passage between the toilet and the rubbish bins were waiting in ambush Rustem Kutuy, Erik Dibay and a few others, their swords held out in front of them.

We began to run every way, and only at the last moment did we manage to dart into the toilet and close the door.

"That's it, Ginger, we've had it," I said. "They'll soon break down the door."

"Don't lose hope, friend," said Ginger quickly, inspecting the surroundings with flashing green eyes, and testing the wooden walls with his shoulder. "We're not many, but we're wearing sailor shirts."

Through the chinks in the door could be seen the horde of armed boys. They weren't hurrying. They were standing there gaily and evilly laughing at us for landing such a degrading trap. They had all the advantages on their side—number, arms and, most important, right, justice. There's no point in even trying to recall what they shouted to us.

Then Borya Mayofis came up to the toilet and said quietly:

"Look, fellows, give yourselves up, there's no way out. Petka, we'll let you go, you don't come into this, and Ginger just has to apologize to Aska, and that's the end of it. Do you hear? Hey! Why don't you answer?"

We remained silent, not looking at each other. Mayofis' shiny eye and black, slanting fringe could be seen through a chink.

"A conference!" finally shouted Ginger. "Move away, Borka, we're having a conference!"

"We'll give you two minutes," said Mayofis.

"There's no question of giving up," muttered Ginger fiercely. "Agreed? Now we'll show them, we'll demonstrate to them how real men fight. Apologize to Aska? She's the one who'll come to me, and then I'll see whether I'll marry her or not!"

He pulled two boards from the inside wall and plunged them down the hole.

"Open the door!" he yelled. "Open the door and let them see that men will come out, and not mummy's little boys!"

I threw the door open and we went out, holding the boards in front of us like spades.

We crossed the whole garden obliquely, not even looking at our adversaries but looking somewhere in the azure skies, the malachite skies, the radiant, nautical skies, which promised a great life in Polynesia, and sometimes looking over our shoulders at the third-floor window out of which leant smiling Aska in her blue dress.

We spent the rest of the day in front of the stove laughing like demons...

From the mezzanine the restaurant hall reminded one of a boiling soup, sometimes pea soup, sometimes noodle. That was at the first glance, but then you began to distinguish the flattened chicken-tabakas, the lumps of caviare, the familiar bald patches, the side bald patches, the middle bald patches, the pro-bald patches, the contra-bald patches, the left-hand partings, the right-hand partings, the pro-rectors and the rectors, the sportsmen, the spinsters, the little Anglo-Saxon group at my table and the blissfully happy interpreter.

I stayed a little while on the balcony which I always wanted to jump off, and then began to go back down.

... until my aunt came home from her evening shift, and then we ran out into the garden, flitted around amongst the limes like bats, or rather, like the proud albatrosses of the Atlantic, and then we climbed up a drainpipe and walked along the eaves, along the boom, and threw Aska the note through the ventilation window. And I, fool that I was, felt that this was the night of our victory and our secret, and, bursting with enthusiasm, would not leave Ginger's side, and even now I remember that night, fool that I am, with its cool, rustling wind, and its twinkling stars, as my own.

The next day I couldn't find Ginger anywhere, till I realized that he was in the gully at Podluzhnaya street.

I took my place at the table, showing my appreciation of the growing cultural exchange with smiles and nods. I was waiting for the waitress, to pay and leave, but just then into the restaurant came Ginger from next door.

He came in calmly and surely, except that he rubbed his face, which was pink from the frost, with his hand, in a somewhat familiar gesture. He had become a well-built man with straight shoulders, a provincial technical-school intellectual who had kept well up with the fashion, in fact he even looked quite prosperous. I hadn't seen him for nineteen years, since he had gone off as a lad of fourteen to the Nakhimov Naval College in Riga. Yes, of course—to Nakhimov College! He must be a naval officer who only occasionally parades in this fashionable, well-made suit.

... There, in the gully, amongst the wild undergrowth of ferns, burdocks and buttercups, walked a couple—a ragged Ginger and Aska, the general's daughter. From behind the elders I followed them as noiselessly as

155

Hiawatha, and I wasn't the only one following. Oh, poor girl and boy, you don't sense the trouble that's coming, but three hooligans from rough Podluzhnaya Street in "Captain Kostya" caps, cheeks bursting with cotton-cake, squirting streams of yellow saliva, are already on your trail.

"Heh-heh!" the hooligans stifled their laughter with their hands—"we'll have a bit of fun now, we'll pull Lady Hamilton's pigtails for her..."

I jumped from above onto one of them, and at once everything rolled into one sheet of yellow and green in which now and then Ginger appeared, larger and larger, as he ran up with an insane look on his face, and then everything would spin again, a purple and yellow circle of memories, only occasionally interrupted by flashes of blue during which our lads came running up in a compact group, and then the "Podluzhnys," then ours again, then them again, and Aska would appear for a moment, now her ribbons, now simply her eyes, and punches rained down, and again the purple and yellow clouded my eyes until the dust settled and that wild race ended at the three strange weapons on timber carriages: the three catapults designed by Ginger, and set up by us during the night overlooking the gully.

... My Ginger—was this him? He was gradually losing his initial dash, there wasn't a trace left of his naval—or provincial?—cock-sureness, he was growing somber as he looked around, standing in the middle of the hall, in which there was not one vacant place, and in which, naturally, the speaking movements of the lips, the smiles, the winks and the loud laughs appeared to him to be some secret of the capital, full of profound significance, while I sat glued to my chair, terrified at the thought of a possible mistake; meanwhile the Anglo-Saxons had already got up and the table was vacated.

"Are these places free, comrade?" asked Ginger, coming over right away. "I need two places."

"Yes, of course. Only I'm sorry the table is not cleared yet," I babbled, "but that won't take long. Shurochka will fix everything right away, don't worry..."

He was looking in surprise at this obliging fellow.

"... about it, I'm well known here. Shurochka! It'll all be cleared away and re-set right away, don't worry, but why do you want two?"

"I'm waiting for..."

"A lady?"

"That's right. A lady."

A smile flitted over the ginger freckles.

God, could it be Aska?

"That's fine. That's just great, comrade. But won't I be in your way?"

"Of course not, the table's big," said Ginger tiredly, as though wanting to brush me off.

The lady soon appeared. It was Aska, of course, but there wasn't a trace left of her thick-leggedness or constant sulking. She was a remarkable, tall woman of thirty, rather tired, very sophisticated, and slightly ironic. Her short black (there's a strange thing!) hair, her graceful neck, her slender hand holding a cigarette, her calm gaze—all this was unaffected, natural and beautiful, but how was it that through the lady could be seen so incredibly clearly our dear, affected Aska?

Ginger got up to meet her with a sternness which indicated the complexity and drama of their relationship, stood to attention and in an officer-like way—chair back, chair forward—sat the lady down, while she nodded slightly to me and gave me a faint smile, as a man "of her milieu"—she at once saw in me a man "of her milieu"—and turned her whole body towards Ginger with a quite different sort of smile. The smile and the turn were such that it immediately became quite clear what was what.

They at once began to speak quickly and with muted voices, Ginger angrily, Aska vexedly, while I buried my face in my coffee-cup, stealing glances at them, at one moment wanting to stroke the heads of these children, at the next suddenly becoming again that ragamuffin of old in the presence of strange grown-ups.

They fell silent when Shurochka came up, then placed their order, and then fell silent again... Discord, discord, a disagreement, a "drama," suffering—this is what they were going through, I sensed this and realized that it had been going on for years.

"Hey, comrade," Ginger suddenly addressed me, "Is it true that real celebrities come here? I've been told that if you spit in this restaurant, you'll hit a celebrity."

"Yes, they come here. You were correctly informed," I said, and Aska again smiled at me, as a man "of her milieu."

"Well, where are they then, comrade? Show me just one. I must have something to boast about," Ginger said insolently and impetuously.

"Well, just take a look over there—next to the pillar are sitting X, Y, and Z. There are celebrities for you!"

All three gave a little salute, and Y stood up and bowed towards Aska. Aska nodded haughtily to him.

"Do you know him?" asked Ginger quickly.

"Slightly," she answered.

X smiled in an oval, Z in a half-moon and Y, the dog, in a circle.

"Perhaps you're a celebrity too?" Ginger asked me.

"No, no, not me," I said in fright.

"Now, now, don't be modest," Aska smiled at me.

"What are you then, comrade, if you don't mind my asking, eh?" asked Ginger.

"I'm an artist, but not a well-known one. And what have you become, Ginger?"

"What's that?!" roared Ginger. "Don't be funny, fellow, or..."

"Calm down, my dear Ginger from next door!" I exclaimed. "I know

157

what you've become. You've become a constructor of those terrible catapults with the help of which Hannibal defeated Napoleon's armies and took
the city of Jericho? And what have you become, Aska, the general's
daughter?"

They both leant across the table and stared at me, but their gazes were
unseeing, they were like drills, traveling headlong back into the past, to that
summer morning, when...

... our whole army was gathered at the edge of the gully—the Jakovlev
brothers, Borka Mayofis, Slavka Ulrikh, Rustem Kutuy, Erik Dibay, Seryozhka Kholmsky and another dozen or so lads, and Aska—the Beautiful Lady,
and I, and Ginger from next door said:

"These are the famous catapults, with the help of which Hannibal
defeated Napoleon's armies and took the city of Jericho,"—and burst out
laughing.

All around was garlic sauce, tomato sauce, tartar sauce, tkemali sauce
and nasharbi sauce, seasoned with purslane and Georgian cabbage, winter
tomatoes and cucumbers, along with mushrooms and game fillets, sirloins,
American croquettes, shashliks, sturgeon, perch-orly and chicken-tabaka,
the crackle of pink notes, the gurgle of dry Georgian wines—tvishi, psou,
gurdzhaani—and *"Russian strong vodka,"*[6] with toasts and without toasts,
with raised glasses and without raised glasses, with appetite and without
appetite, and all to the accompaniment of the orchestra.

They were still wandering with their gazes somewhere in the nooks
of "next door," hallooing to each other amongst Zherebtsov's lime-trees,
and diving into the damp semi-darkness of the gullies in TPI park, amongst
the buttercups.

"Hey, aboard the 'Astrolabia,' is there any soup?" I shouted, uniting
the cry of our childhood with this stupid contemporary joke.

"Petka," smiled Ginger. "Petka?!" he shouted. "Petka!"—he burst
into laughter and gave me a punch across the table.

"My god," said Aska, and pressed her hands to her cheeks. "Petya,"
she smiled tenderly at me. "Well, I would never have thought that the artist
Pyotr N. was our Petya."

Then it began: but do you remember, wait, do you remember...

... the "makhnushka"[7] championship... How are you legs? The headquarters in the wood-shed, do you remember? Wait, boys... as usual you
went over the roof... was that when Timur's team was being formed? Yes,
yes... I didn't like the morning exercises... and you... if you please, comrades, Timur's team is a secret society of swift benefactors, and Borka Mayo-

fis... but who was the first to jump off the cliff? Me, me, me... how yellow the water was there, do you remember? How could you know that? Our earnings, from cleaning, shining, polishing, who was the best at beating the drum? You, you, you... we slipped into the cinema to see "Lady Hamilton," I always cried at the bit where she was old... and taking the little bottles to the chemist's? And those frogs in the pools at the river... who caught the most frogs? Me, you, the Jakovlev brothers, we sold them to the physiology department at five kopecks a time, and at the flea market—the millet in German syrup... the packets of substitute sugar hanging on a thread, which Seryozhka Kholmsky's dad brought from Germany... yes, and the catapults?

It has now been proved that all wars on earth, of no matter what sort, had an economic motive. The Crusades, as is well known, were precipitated by the search for new trade routes to the East, and even the war which was started by some voluptuous Khan in order to seize the Georgian princess Tamara for his harem also had a secret economic basis.

So also our war with Podluzhnaya Street was only on the surface a fight for the offended honor of our Aska, and for her right to walk in the gullies with her cavaliers. From interrogation of prisoners it was elucidated that Podluzhnava Street was not at all defending the gullies or the right to uncontrolled brigandage in them, nor even the right to insult little girls in blue bows, but in fact they were defending the stables of the cavalry school adjoining the park. The secret entry into the stables to an unlimited supply of cotton-cake, the company of resplendent cavalrymen, and also the horses, the beautiful horses which they were sometimes allowed to lead by the bridle—that's what was upsetting the lads from Podluzhnaya Street and that.s why we saw their serried ranks that morning at the foot of the gully.

"All right, come one, now, let's drop it—so we don't burst into tears, how terrible—nineteen years, well, what's past is past, whether you like it or not, my dear Aska, let's have a drink, only without any of this false 'to our frequent meetings,' but simply to our reunion; so, have things gone all right, Ginger?"

"The time has flown past," grunted Ginger officer-like, squinting slyly at the chandelier. "But would there be any chance of getting some Jamaican rum with cayenne here?"

"Shurochka, Jamaican rum with cayenne," I said.

"You'll have to wait a bit," said Shurochka.

The drink had a moistening and very softening effect on Aska.

"It's all right for you, boys," she said, "it's all right for you at the prime of your manhood, but as for me... I..."

"You're at the prime of your life too," I said, "and you'll be there for a long time yet. And it was visible even then, in the stars, but it was only a vague hint of what you've become..."

"Are you serious?" asked Aska excitedly.

"Are you serious?" Ginger leant over the table.

"But what's become of you, Ginger," I asked.

"Me?"—a distant beacon lit up in his eyes. "I'm a builder. I'm on an executive committee, in the building section."

"Bravo," I said, "you're engaged in creative work. The spirit of destruction has given way to the spirit of creation."

"Yes," said Ginger, "we're carrying out great feats in the opening up of the North."

"The North?" asked Aska. She turned away from us, smoking and looking at the ceiling.

Ginger raked her with a look of creative burning.

"We're building towns of the future in our far North. Plastic domes, fountains playing underneath, birds chirping, and..."

"Give over," said Aska.

Ginger buried himself in his plate and from there, from behind his steak, as though from ambush, his eyes flashed at me, and he began to wink.

"He's not a builder at all, Petya," said Aska, "he's not on any executive committee."

"I know very well what you are," I said and smiled. "After all, didn't you enter the Nakhimov Naval College? You're a naval officer."

"Is it wrong to dream a little?" said Ginger, smiling and straightening up. "Of course I'm a sailor. I'm in command of a ... hm ...hm ...vessel."

"Bubble-bubble?" I asked delightedly, and delightedly depicted with my hand a weaving (though why weaving?) submarine.

Ginger cast a conspiratorial glance to the right, then to the left and then closed his eyes in affirmation.

"The arctic patrol?!" I exclaimed. "High-speed dives?! Shots from below the surface?!"

"Steady on, friend," Ginger smiled condescendingly. "Not so loud."

He was sitting opposite me chuckling. The captain of an atomic missile-carrier, I would tell X, Y, and Z when they asked who that had been with me. The captain of an atomic missile-carrier is sitting opposite me, and the impressively swollen veins are visible on his freckled hands.

Aska turned to him with malicious, screwed-up eyes.

"Why do you have to act like that?" her voice was raised. "Why all this bragging? Surely you can manage without..."

Ginger pulled out his handkerchief suddenly and sneezed, drowning her last words.

"Where's our rum and cayenne?" he shouted through his handkerchief and from behind it winked to me with the eye further from Aska.

"Here's your rum," said Shurochka. "Viktorina put Malabar in instead of cayenne. It had to be changed."

The rum stirred a gentle yellow fire in us, and we drew nearer to one

160

another, our eyes united.

"I'm a juggler!" said Ginger proudly.

"Now we're getting closer to the truth," smiled Aska, and got up and held out her hand to me. "Let's dance."

I held my hand against her tender back, and we danced slowly. She inclined her head a little and alternately gave me a warm smile, then looked away sadly. X, Y and Z smiled at me like dot-dash-dash-dot-dot-dash and suddenly an unexpected comma. The food was getting cold in front of them, they had completely forgotten about it, being enthralled by our dancing.

"How strange," said Aska, "the artist N. is you, Petya. I've heard of your work and have even seen some of it at..."

Ginger, standing next to our table, was juggling with plates, glasses, spoons and bottles. He was watching us with enormous eyes and barely moving his spread fingers, while over his head hung a ringing arc of dishes flying in various directions.

"I'd like to drop by at your place," said Aska, and I suddenly had the feeling that here was some sort of challenge, some decisive challenge of fate. "I would like to look at your work."

I thought of how she would sit in my studio, her legs crossed, her chin in her hand, while I stood in front of her in my ridiculous cap and my velveteen jacket, and this would be in my studio, surrounded by my favorite objects, in my secluded life, about which few people knew very much, and this visit of hers, her sitting in my studio, would be precisely the sum total, the full stop, towards which I had been heading without knowing it myself...

When they drew near, we saw that they were carrying steel rods, either broken off from rusted bedsteads or forged by the blacksmiths of Damascus, and we saw that two of them were bigger than us, and that our catapults and clay bombs were a mere nothing for them, but the slopes were occupied, and the Carthaginians stood with battle standards raised, and the sailors of the Dumont d'Urville stood back to back at the mast, and Ginger shouted with a sideways glance at the girl who was visible in the distance, at Her Thickleggedness in the blue bows:

"Prepare arms!"

"No," I said, "it's better not to. It's better if you don't come, Aska. It's better if you don't come to my place."

Two or three turns of little steps, with rhythmical swaying of shoulders and hips to the ta-ra-ra-ra of the saxophone, and the bom-bom-bom of the double bass, and it was as though this conversation had never taken place, as though there had never been any challenge of fate.

Ginger pulled a red cockerel from under his shirt with a pitiful smile, and pulled a strip of fire from his mouth. The cockerel, its neck stretched out like a wild duck, shot across the restaurant straight to the kitchen, and

161

the strip of fire trailed after it like a jet exhaust. Ginger began to bow. He bowed and bowed, but there was no applause.

"I'm unhappy with him, Petya," said Aska quietly and sagged in my arms.

At that Ginger, with a burning look on his hard carved face, flew up the staircase with elastic bounds and appeared on the little balcony, which I always wanted to jump off.

"Hey, eaters!" he shouted. "Fat chieftains of the island of Tuamotu! You spend your lazy days in idleness, and nature's gifts drop straight into your arms. But I've come here to you, to your kingdom of Lotus, leaving behind the typhoons and hurricanes, simoons, sandstorms and tornadoes, I, Ginger from next door, have come here, and I would exchange all your food and your whole island for one measly string of beads, for only one tiny little string from the bottomless holds of the 'Astrolabia.' I salute you!"

He flew over the rail and down, and rebounding from ground as though it were a trampoline, turned head over heels in the air.

"Petka, come and join me!" he shouted to me, and I immediately found myself in the air too, turning head over heels right under the ceiling.

We jumped for a long time, roaring with laughter, bouncing up from the floor as though it were a trampoline, and turning somersaults, and then we flew outside with gigantic jumps, doing rolls, cartwheels, and double and triple somersaults as we went.

Afterwards I was told that the restaurant customers had been surprised at our strange behavior, but that the head waiter Adrianich had said:

"Nothing unusual has happened. We were informed in advance. Meetings of childhood friends always finish like that."

1967

Translated by P.V. Cubberley

NOTES

1. Epigraph to Radishchev's 'Journey...'
2. Mineral water.
3. A game resembling cricket.
4. English in the original.
5. Allusion to popular film character.
6. English in the original.
7. A game in which a small hard object is kept up in the air with the foot.

ORANGES FROM MOROCCO

ORANGES FROM MOROCCO

1. Victor Koltyga

Actually, I for one was fed up with it... The "Labor-in-Vain Co-op." We'd drilled this picturesque ravine in two spots and now we were drilling in a third. A losing proposition—there isn't any here. That's a hunch—but still, I've been kicking around in prospecting parties for five years now, I've been up near Okha in Sakhalin, and along the Paronay, and at the mouth of the Amur, and on Kamchatka. I've seen plenty of this terrain!

Not that I have anything against the ravine, it's even pretty here; you could build a ski resort, there's an excellent spot for a slalom course on the west slope, the air here is good, and there might even be some kind of mud for invalids, it's quite possible. A medicinal spring? I can well believe it, go ahead and build your sanatorium; my God, there may even be gold here—this marvelous, picturesque ravine, the best in the world, may be a genuine gold mine, there may be enough to gold-plate all the johns in communist society—but oil there is not!

Of course, I hadn't said anything to Kichekian. None of the guys had said anything. Kichekian was new to us, this was his first prospecting trip. He'd finished Leningrad Miners' that year and come out here to be boss of our party. Now he was practically having a nervous breakdown, and so we had kept quiet. But I felt like saying, "Know what, Airapet-Jahn (or whatever it is the Armenians say), we ought to pack up the whole kit and kaboodle and skip out of here. You know, Jahn (that's it, Jahn), science is science but practice is practice." But we kept quiet, ate our canned goods—there wasn't much we could do.

Night had fallen at four o'clock, and the summits of the sopki glistened like silver in the moonlight. Wisps of smoke had been rising over the kitchen for some time now, and the guys on the next tour were coming down the bottom of the ravine, signaling with their cigarettes.

"Let's go have dinner, Comrade Boss," I said to Kichekian, but he only shook his head. He was sitting on a box eating bread and butter, or rather, not eating but fortifying himself, as they say. In the cold the butter had turned hard as soap. Kichekian cut off thick pieces, put them on the bread, and piled it in. Knots of muscle flickered on his thin, stubbled face. He was small and gaunt, even in a quilted jacket and quilted pants he seemed—I don't know... delicate. From time to time he put down the bread and butter, breathed on his hands, then set to work again. Then he stood up and roared, "Oh Moo-oon, Float on high in the spacious night, Bathe in the sea your rays of light..."

It wasn't easy for him here, of course, being a man of the south.

164

I'm a man of the south too, from Krasnodar, but over these eight years (three in the army and five as a civilian) I've gotten pretty well acclimatized. I may take a vacation this summer and spend it at my mother's in Krasnodar. Everyone knows that Krasnodar has the prettiest girls in the Soviet Union. Now this isn't an ad, but if you just decked our girls out a little finer, then that'd be it—you'd have to put several more railroad lines and highways into Krasnodar and build an international airport. I often think about Krasnodar and the Krasnodar girls, and these thoughts come to me on the bluest days. In '59, at Ust-Maya, when the pass was snowed in and we lay in our tent for three days playing tunes on our teeth, I kept picturing myself on vacation, out walking along in the Krasnodar farmers' market early on a summer's morning, with plenty of jack and not specially hungry, and the evening still ahead of me, when I'd go to the open-air dance floor, where slim girls and strapping girls would stare at me thinking how hip I was, clearly nobody's fool, and independent: altogether, sharp as a tack.

Right now, too, going down to the camp at the bottom of the ravine, I was thinking of Krasnodar, of women, hot beaches, esplanade concerts under the open sky, Oleg Lundstrom's jazz band... I like to think that all this exists, that there's something else in this world besides this terrific, magical, stinking ravine.

In the kitchen we had a good feed and immediately felt logey, ready to turn in. Lenya Bazarevich, as was his habit, went to take a bath, while we crawled into the tent and hoisted our bodies into our assigned bunks.

When the guys on our tour all pull off their felt boots at once, it's more than a saint could bear. A newcomer might put on an oxygen mask, but it's nothing to us, we're reconciled, because we've gotten to be like brothers.

No sooner had Yura, Misha, and Volodya plonked themselves down on their reserved seats than they began honking, singing, snorting. This was just the warm-up. Then came the real thing! When they snore it's like three jackhammers going. And they do a comedy bit: as soon as one ceases to snore, the second one stops, and —Cut!—the third's out. And they start up again simultaneously, too. If I lived in a capitalist country, I'd exploit these three young men fiendishly. I'd exhibit them in the circus and earn a pile of lire or pounds sterling.

I felt sleepy, too, but I still had one little job to do. I switched on my pocket flash and by its dim light began writing a letter to a certain Krasnodar girl who at that moment, can you imagine, was within seventy-four kilometers of me. This girl had an ordinary name—Lusya Kravchenko. I had met her the spring before, when the Kildin brought the summer girls to work at the fish-processing combine. Usually, toward the time the summer girls arrive, all the guys make with the spit and polish, get themselves a ducktail haircut, and hasten to the Port of Petrovo on all forms of transport, or else on their own two feet. And why not? For us it's a sensation—two or three hundred eligible new girls at once!

That time, too, a lot of guys happened into Petrovo. They all strolled along the main street waiting for the steamer, pretending they'd landed here by chance or on business or hung over. But all these wiseguys turned up at dockside when the *Kildin* began to moor. They all watched the girls come down the gangway, and then trooped after them along the main street, and toward evening they all turned up "by chance" at the fish-processing combine.

It was there I spotted Lusya Kravchenko. Well, I circled two or three times and then began to close in. "Where are you from, home-town girl?" I ask. That's a line I use. And she suddenly says—bingo!—"Krasnodar." Huh? I didn't even have to lie. All evening she and I walked. I felt melancholy looking into her dark eyes, and her tanned hands brought back memories of Pioneer Camp on the Kuban and the little song "Mighty John Gray the Rake." And I thought how I was already going on twenty-six, and I had neither house nor home, and all evening I snowed her with talk of space flights and the relativity of time, and then I tried to put my arm around her. Well, she clipped me one.

Then we left on an expedition, and on the expedition I didn't think about her, I thought about Krasnodar girls as usual. But this time for some reason all the Krasnodar girls looked like Lusya Kravchenko. There were a hundred thousand Luse-Kravchenkos looking at me when I, hip, clever, and independent, sharp as a tack, mounted to the dance floor in the park overlooking the Kuban.

In the fall I encountered her at an evening party at the Seamen's Culture Club in the Port of Slush. Frankly, I was amazed. It turned out she'd decided to stay in the Far East, because, she said, one felt the laboring pulse of the nation more strongly here. She was working as a bricklayer and living in a dormitory in the settlement of Cinderblocks. There she was, taking a correspondence course in construction technology, there she was, dancing with the Choreography Club—all very proper. She was dressed fit to kill, and there was a certain little sailor named Gera hanging around her, quite a young kid, maybe born in '42. She had another guy after her, too, a famous "bich" (that's what they call social parasites on the seacoast) from Petrovo Port; his nickname was Root. I had them both beat by a mile. I talked to her all evening about Romania, told her what the grapes are like in Transylvania, what a leap forward the textile industry has made there, and about the writer Mikhail Sadoveanu. Then I saw her home on the bus to the famous Cinderblocks, and I looked sidewise at her profile and it made me melancholy again, and several times I felt my temper rise when she gave me that thin little smile. I don't know what had made her stay here—it may have been the laboring pulse of the nation, but she was obviously not averse to seeing all the men, the whole busload, crane their necks because of her.

Near the barracks I gave her a gentle hug. Well, for the sake of appearances she clipped me a couple of times. Her hands had grown hard by

166

this time. Then it turned out I had nowhere to stay, and I sat all night like a homeless pup on some logs near her barracks. A wet snow started to fall, and to everyone's amusement I contracted an inflammation of the lungs. I spent a month lolling in the hospital in Phosphate City, and then left on this famous expedition under the command of the "brilliant scientist" Airapet Kichekian.

So, I still had one little job to do before I fell on my bunk and started up a fine, delicate, whistle through my two nostrils in counterbalance to these three jackhammers.

I wrote Lusya that she of course might scorn me but she had to respect me as a man, not a dog, and inasmuch as we had already established comradely relations she might at least answer my letters and report on how things were going.

I finished the letter, put it in an envelope, and fell to thinking. Suddenly I was terrified—my God, my life is about to get derailed! My God, and what if there's nothing in the world but this real fine ravine? My God, and what if everything from my life before is only something I dreamed while I slept for twenty-six years at the bottom of the ravine, and here I wake up to find I've been digging into it all this time, the third try already, and not finding anything, and it will be this way now forever? And what if this is some asteroid, mislaid in "one of the extremely remote galaxies," and it has a diameter of seventy-three kilometers; and at the seventy-fourth kilometer, instead of the settlement of Cinderblocks, there's an abyss, a precipice dropping off into black outer space?—This was a first for me. I was frightened. I didn't know what was happening to me, and couldn't address the envelope.

I leaned against our little window, the size of a school notebook, and saw that Lenya Bazarevich was still taking his bath in the silvery snow. He was wallowing in the moonlight without a stitch on, his stout blue legs sticking up out of the snow. What a guy, this Bazarevich, such a nut. He does this every day, and goes out in the cold without a hat and only one thin Chinese sweater on. He calls himself a Walrus and he's all the time agitating us to take up this nice sport. He says that there are Walrus associations in many countries, and he corresponds with a psycho like himself in Czechoslovakia. He and this Czech have a sort of friendly competition and exchange of experiences. For example, the guy writes: "Dear Soviet Friend! Yesterday I jumped into an ice-hole and spent half an hour in the water. On coming out of the water, properly ice-covered, I lay down on the snow and spent an hour in it. Having thus turned into a snowman, I slowly rolled along the riverbank in the direction of Bratislava..." On receiving such a letter, of course, our Lenya strips off his clothes and runs out looking for an ice-hole so as to get a few points up on the Czech. I used to be frightened at first, frankly. You're walking to the tent, there's a blizzard, with wind and sleet, and suddenly you see it: a stout and hairy body prostrate on the snow.

167

Bazarevich got up, stretched, rubbed his ears with snow, and started putting on his pants. I addressed the envelope: "L. Kravchenko, Construction Workers' Dormitory, Fiberboard Barracks No. 7, High Voltage Street, Cinderblocks Settlement."

If she didn't answer this letter either, then that was it—I'd cross her out of my personal life. I'd give her to understand that there were other fish in the sea, that there was in the world the city of Krasnodar, where I had come from and where I would go on vacation this summer, and she was not at all such a hundred percent ideal as she imagined herself, even she had her shortcomings.

Bazarevich came in, and, seeing the envelope on the stool, he asked, "You've already written?"

"Yes," I said, "I've dotted the i's and crossed the t's."

Bazarevich sat down on his bunk and began taking off his clothes. That's all he does in his time off from work, take his clothes off and put them on.

"Terrific tone, Vitya," he said, massaging his biceps. "Listen," he said, massaging his abdominals, "what's she like, your Lusya? Your famous Luse-Kravchenko?"

"Oh, I don't know," I answered, "she comes to here on me, maybe a meter sixty-five..."

"A good height for a woman," he nodded.

"Well, and here she's like this..." I demonstrated. "And she's okay here. On the whole, appropriate parameters."

"Uh-huh," he nodded.

"But even a princess is not without shortcomings," I said challengingly.

Bazarevich sighed. "You don't have a picture of her?"

"I do," I said, fidgeting. "Want me to show you?"

I dragged out my suitcase and took from it a clipping from the district newspaper. There was a photo of Lusya in Ukrainian costume, dancing with some other girls. The caption ran, "Girl construction workers labor gloriously and spend their free time well in cultural activities. In the photo: a performance by the Choreography Club."

"That one." I pointed. "Second from the left."

Bazarevich looked at the photo for a long time, sighing.

"You're a fool, Vitya," he said at last. "She's all okay. No shortcomings. Perfectly okay."

He lay down to sleep, and I turned off my flashlight and lay down too. Through the window I could see a scrap of sky and the glimmering slope of a sopka. I don't know, maybe in my childhood I dreamed of the sopki, these volcanoes crusted with crackling, sparkling ice. Anyway, at that moment the volcano looked to me like Santa Claus's sack. I realized I wasn't going to fall asleep, turned on my flashlight again, and got a magazine. I always bring some kind of magazine along on an expedition and study it from cover to cover. Last time it was *The People's Romania*, this time *Sports*. For the hundredth time, probably, I looked through the photographs and analyzed the plans for attacking the opposing goal.

"Haste... Mistake... Goal!"

"How to Make Your Own Hockey Stick."

"Soon to be enroute to the U.S.A. again, to Colorado Springs..."

"Tricks Up Ray Meyer's Sleeve."

"The Japanese Serve."

I, center forward Victor Koltyga, all-round athlete and coach no worse than Ray Meyer[1] of DePaul University, I set off enroute to Colorado Springs again, carrying a hockey stick made with my own hands... Hmmm... "Can You Play in Goggles?" Aha, turns out you can... In special goggles made with my own hands I advance, a quick play, Koltyga-Ponedelnik-Meskhi-Koltyga;[2] the goalie displays haste, then makes a mistake, and I knock in a goal by means of a remarkable Japanese serve, and Lusya Kravchenko in Finnish national costume comes skating up to me with a bouquet of Kuban tulips.

Chudakov and Yevdoshchuk woke us up. Just as they were, in their hats and sheepskins, their boots clumping on the floorboards, they pulled out their suitcases and roared:

"Rise and shine!"

"Rise and shine, you lummoxes!"

"You guys will sleep through kingdom come!"

With no idea what was going on, but getting the idea that it was a big deal, we sat up on our bunks and stared as the two men kept up their indecent roaring.

"What, did you bring our pay, you eagle?" Volodya asked Yevdoshchuk.

"Like hell," replied Yevdoshchuk. "It was the construction workers that got paid."

That's always the way in Phosphate City: the construction workers get their pay first, and when they've eaten and drunk it all up and the money is back in the treasury, then it's our turn. Perpetuum mobile. But then why were Chudakov and Yevdoshchuk making such a racket?

"What, did you bring a movie?" I asked. "*The Girl with the Guitar* again?"

"Oh sure, a movie, that's a good one!" answered Chudakov.

"What, some compote?" asked Bazarevich.

"Boys!" said Chudakov, and raised his hand.

We all stared at him.

"Quickly, boys, get up and get your dough out of hiding. The *Kildin* has arrived in Slush and brought oranges."

"Here, straighten it out," I said, and stuck out my bent finger to Chudakov.[3]

"Pineapples, perhaps?" laughed Volodya.

"Bananas, perhaps?" smirked Misha.

"Coconuts, perhaps?" guffawed Yura.

"Grandma's pies, perhaps, the *Kildin's* brought?" asked Lenya. "Still warm, eh? Presents from the mainland?"

At that Yevdoshchuk took off his sheepskin, then unbuttoned his quilted jacket, and we noticed that under his shirt on the right side he had like a woman's breast. We gasped, and he thrust his hand inside his shirt and pulled out an orange. It was a big, huge orange, the size of a fairly large child's head. It was lumpy, golden, and it practically gleamed. Yevdoshchuk raised it over his head and held it up on the tips of his fingers, and it hung right under the peak of our tent like the sun, and Yevdoshchuk—who never, I should tell you, talks in anything but four-letter words—was smiling as he looked up at it, and at that moment he seemed to us a wizard of a magician, honestly. It was a dumb-show like the scene in Gogol's play *The Inspector-General*.

Then we came to and began admiring the orange. I am sure that not one of the guys, had that orange belonged to him, would have bitten into it. It had taken a long time growing and soaking up the sun somewhere in the south, and now it was sort of—I don't know... consummated, perhaps, and it was the only one; yet to gobble it up, after all, would only take a few seconds.

Yevdoshchuk explained everything. It turned out he'd acquired the orange in Phosphate City: a shipping clerk named Paramoshkin, who'd just returned from Slush, had given it to him in exchange for a pen-knife. Well, Yevdoshchuk and Chudakov had raced over here to raise the alarm.

One after another we jumped up from our bunks and got busy pulling out our suitcases and rucksacks. Yura clapped me on the back: "Vitya, I'm counting on you for the do-re-mi."

"What do you do, use your money to light the stove?" I asked in surprise.

"Quit it," he said. "I'll get it back to you."

We crawled out of the tent and ran up the mountain to inform Kichekian of the excursion to Slush. We ran fast, now and then slipping off the trampled path into the snow.

"So then I'm counting on you, Vitya!" shouted Yura from behind.

Kichekian was standing on the level ground near the campfire, clapping his mittens.

"Don't try and snow me," he said. "Oranges indeed. What is it, you feel like a drink?"

At that, we all turned and looked at Yevdoshchuk. Yevdoshchuk, with a languid air, glancing nonchalantly at the moon, unbuttoned his sheepskin. Kichekian broke into a grin when he saw the orange. Yevdoshchuk lobbed the orange to him, and he made a one-handed catch.

"Moroccan," he said, clapping the orange with his mitten, and he lobbed it to Yevdoshchuk, who threw it back. They kept it up, passing the orange back and forth.

"It's for you," said Yevdoshchuk, "as a man of the south."

Kichekian raised the orange on high and exclaimed: "May this sumptuous fruit be a sign that today we shall discover oil! Ride on, men. We, too, may show up to celebrate."

We had nothing to say to this, and ran on down. Below, Chudakov was already warming up the motor.

When you drive from our camp to Phosphate City and see the sopki, sopki countless and endless, the snow, the sky, the moon, and nothing else, you can't help thinking: Where is it you've ended up, Vitya my boy, did you ever think, did you guess in your childhood, that you'd end up in country like this? No matter how long I drift around the Far East, I still can't get used to the emptiness, the enormous empty expanses. What I like is trucks, barracks, tents, so jammed with guys you can hardly breathe. Because, when there's one guy snoring, another eating stew, a third telling about some village in the Tambov, its apples and pies, and a fourth writing a letter to some girl, and the radio is crackling and the tuning light is blinking, it seems to be all here, the whole world, and no calamity seems terrible to us, not even atomic horrors or strontium-90.

Chudakov was driving hard and fast, shaking us up but good. We kept jostling against each other, thinking about oranges. I'd eaten oranges more than once in my life. The last time had been in Moscow three years before, on vacation. Never mind, I got properly vitaminized that time.

At last we passed Crooked Rock, and Phosphate City lay open below us—prefab apartment buildings, strings of street lights, narrow gauge railroad. In the center of town, blue in the moonlight, gleamed the skating rink.

So we rolled on down into this "major industrial and cultural center," population all of 5,000, and Chudakov spun along at full speed through completely identical streets between completely identical four-story apartments. I may end up living in one of these buildings, if Comrade Kravchenko finds time to tear herself away from her social activities and reply to my serious intentions. I do not know how I'll find my own house if I drink a drop on pay day. I'll have to put up some kind of mark or inscription: "This Living-Space Occupied. Head of Family: Victor Koltyga."

We shot out on to the highway and went rolling along. It was smooth here: the graders had been at work. Yura was dreaming: "I'll cut it open, sprinkle it with sugar, and eat it..."

"Screwball," said Bazarevich, "sprinkling oranges with sugar is bad form."

"Vitya," said Misha, turning to me, "is it true that there's solar energy in oranges?"

"Right," I said, "three kilowatts apiece..."

"Vitya, so I'm counting on you," said Yura.

"Quit being such a drag," I said. "You're counting, so shut up."

Now there was a Yazik dump truck gaining on us, and instead of a load of dirt or crushed stones it was packed with men. They were laughing, having fun. The dump truck drew even with us, aiming to pass.

"Hey," we shouted, "where are you going, friends?"

"To Slush, for oranges!"

We hammered on the roof of the cab: we were annoyed that the decrepit Yazik had overtaken us.

"Chudakov!" we shouted. "Show your stuff!"

Chudakov got the idea and was about to, but at this point the dump truck swerved sharply and we saw a grader, all covered with guys in black city coats. In a second we too started around the grader, but Chudakov slowed down. The guys were sitting on the grader like jackdaws, rubbing their blue noses.

"Where," we asked, "are you hurrying to?"

"To Slush," they said, "for oranges."

Well, we took these guys into the back of the truck with us, otherwise they'd have made it to Slush on their grader only in time for the talk, the to-do about who'd eaten the most. And besides, they were guys we knew, from the auto repair shop.

Then Chudakov did begin showing his stuff. We scrunched down in the bottom of the truck and just listened to the wind whistling and howling around us. We look and the dump truck is already behind us. The guys there are standing up, pounding on the cab.

"Hi there!" we shout to them.

"Hey!" they shout. "Leave some for us!"

"They'll be all gone!" we shout.

The road began to go uphill, then went along the side of a sopka. Below us, in the thick dark blue of the ravine, we saw a long string of little red lights, the taillights of trucks going to Slush ahead of us.

"Looks like there'll be a real festival today in Slush," said Lenya Bazarevich.

Where the road to the State Fur Farm forks off from the main highway, we saw a thick knot of people. They were standing under the streetlight, right hands raised in hopes of hitching a ride. It was obvious they were sailors. Chudakov put on the brakes, and the sailors jumped in back with us. Now our truck was full up.

"Where," we asked, "are you headed, sailors?"

"To Slush," they said, "for oranges."

They had hitched all the way from Petrovo Port, it turned out. They were the crew of the seiner *South Wind,* at full strength except for the watch. I look and sitting there among them is the same young kid that chased after Lusya at the dance. He's sitting there, has his visored cap pulled down over his ears, his collar turned up, a sad sort of guy.

"Oh," I say, "Gera! Hi!"

"Ah," he says, "whaddaya say, Vitya!"

"Well how," I ask, "are the fish biting?"

"Good enough," he answers.

There we were, he and I, tossing remarks back and forth as though we were buddy-buddy, as if we were good friends; not so much old pals, but just friends.

We rode along, raced along. Chudakov was showing his stuff. We passed all sorts of automotive equipment: trucks, some with sides and some GAZ-69s; tractor-trailers, graders, bulldozers, motorcycles. Hell, all the equipment within a hundred-mile radius seemed to have been mobilized! Good God, we look and there's a dog sled tooling along at the edge of the road. One, another... So the Nanay tribesmen had also decided to get vitaminized.

We sat, smoked. I told the guys everything I knew about citrus crops, and sometimes I looked at Gera. And now and again he glanced at me too.

Just then I saw that a motorcycle with a sidecar was gaining on us. Sergei Orlov was in control, dressed all in leather, with goggles and a motorcycle helmet. He was sitting up straight, holding his gloved hands stiffly apart, like some kind of police escort. Behind him, I saw, sat a guy with a beard—aha, Nikolai Kalchanov. And in the sidecar they had a girl, also wearing motorcycle goggles. These were guys from Phosphate City, intellectuals, but somehow I didn't recognize the girl.

They undertook to pass, drew even with us.

"Hi, Sergei!" I shouted to him. "Nick, whaddaya say!"

"Ah, Vitya!" they said. "Are you rushing for Morocco potatoes too?"

"Exactly," I said. "You guessed it."

"Do you have a smoke?" asked Kalchanov.

I tossed him a pack, and he immediately thrust it at the girl in the sidecar. I look and the girl has ducked down behind the windshield to light her cigarette. Now I recognized her—it was Katya, wife of our Airapet Kichekian; she was a teacher from Phosphate.

Katya lit up, waved a mitten at me and smiled, or at least showed her teeth. When she and her husband came to us from the mainland, no one noticed Airapet himself, his wife was so pretty. A blonde right out of the Polish magazine *Screen*. Panic broke loose among us then too, like right now with the oranges. Everyone was finagling trips into Phosphate City to get a look at her. Well, later on we got used to her.

Man, did Orlov have a beast of a bike! He passed us easily and started to pull away. Chudakov tried to touch him, but not a chance. We did catch up with them at the seventy-third kilometer, they were dragging their bike out of the ditch. Kolya Kalchanov was limping. Katya, laughing, was telling how she'd gone flying out of the sidecar, flown ten meters through the air—

no twenty, well not twenty, but fifteen, actually she flew about five meters, well, okay, five—and landed headfirst in the snow. Orlov, in his helmet, and waist-deep in snow, cut a fine figure. We helped them drag the bike out, and they started driving a little more carefully now, staying behind us.

Actually, the trip was fun, the whole highway was rumbling with dozens of vehicles, and just before Cinderblocks we encountered the bus making the Slush-Phosphate City run. Some comedian on the bus tossed a handful of golden orange peels to us in the truck.

We hit Cinderblocks at top speed, the little houses flicked past my eyes, I got confused and couldn't even figure out which side Lusya's barracks were on, and I realized that in a few seconds it would be left behind, this little settlement, my capital, when suddenly Chudakov braked. I saw Lusya's barracks, hidden almost to the roof in the snow, and the white smoke from the chimney. Chudakov got out of the cab and asked me, "Want to drop in?"

I looked at Gera. He was looking at me. I jumped out of the truck and strode off toward the barracks.

"Only make it fast," Chudakov shouted after me.

At my back I could hear the guys jumping out of the truck. So the stop had come just in time.

Nonchalantly, as if just in passing, I dropped by the room and saw that it was empty. All ten beds were neatly made, as they always are in girls' rooms, and in the corner, hung on a line to dry, there were various little blue and pink things, which I preferred not to scrutinize. But I did look through the notes on the table.

"Shura, we've gone to Slush. Rosa," I read.

"Igor, we've gone for oranges. Nina," I read.

"Slava, sell the tickets and come to Slush. I.R.," I read.

"Edik, I've gone to Slush for oranges. I'm sorry. Lusya," I read.

"Who's this Edik?" I thought. "Not Tanaka? Then it's curtains for me."

Yes, just try and compete with an eagle like Edward Tanaka, Champion of the Far East Zone in the Nordic Combined—the ski-jump and cross-country.

I pulled out my letter, laid it on the table, and left. At the door I bumped into Gera.

"Well, how are the girls?" he mumbled.

"They've gone to Slush," I said. "I guess they're already digging into the oranges."

Together we walked toward the truck.

"You don't know Tanaka, by any chance?" I asked.

"Who, the champion?"

"Uh-huh."

"No, I don't. I've only seen him jump. In the movies."

"He's great at jumping when he's not in the movies, too."

"Uh-huh, he's good at jumping."

174

The snow near the truck was all decorated with intricate yellow designs. We climbed in back and started on.

2. Nikolai Kalchanov

At the Komsomol meeting they suggested I shave off my beard. The meeting was crowded, in spite of its being payday at the Trust. They all knew my beard was going to be the topic, and everybody wanted to have his say on this burning issue, or at least be in on the fun.

For the sake of propriety they talked about the mass-culture and sports programs first, and then turned to the cardinal question on the agenda, which was noted in the minutes under the rubric "The Appearance of the Komsomol Youth."

Yerofeytsev made the report. He said the majority of Komsomol youths had a clean, tidy, and smart appearance during their time off from work; however (but... at the same time... unfortunately, it should be noted...), there were other Komsomol youths who neglected... and among them one would have to include the young engineering specialist Kalchanov.

"I'd understand," said Yerofeytsev, "if Kolya—forgive me Kolya (I nodded)—if he were a geologist and grew his beard in a natural way (laughter), but you, Kolya, forgive me, you're not even an artist or anything, and I'm sorry but this is Fancy Dan stuff and we aren't in any Moscow or Leningrad."

A hubbub arose on the floor. The guys from my section kept shouting that a beard was the boss's own personal affair, next Yerofeytsev would be checking into everyone's least little personal affair; this, they said, was repression, and all that sort of thing. Other people shouted the other view. The girls from Cinderblocks were trying especially hard. One of them was definitely not bad looking. She declared that a man's outer appearance nevertheless bore witness to his inner world. She was a dark little thing, an Italian type, to put it crudely. I winked at her, and she stood up and added that she thought bad examples were contagious.

The vote was taken. The majority were against the beard.

"All right, I'll shave it off," I said.

"Perhaps you'd like to say a word or two, Kolya?" asked Yerofeytsev.

"Oh why no, what for," I said. "It's decided, I mean, that's it. So what..."

Such was the speech I gave. The audience was enchanted.

"We aren't forcing you, now," said Yerofeytsev. "We aren't ordering you, this is something some people have misunderstood, misinterpreted. We know you, you're good at your specialty and stable, actually, in your way of life. We're just making a recommendation, now..."

He was talking to me the way he'd talk to a sick man.

I stood up and said, "Well, okay then, so what. No sooner said than done. I'll shave it off. Think of it as already gone. Come and gone."

That was the end of the meeting.

In the corridor I encountered Sergei. He was walking along with a roll of blueprints under his arm. I leaned against the wall and watched him: tall, just a little heavier now that he was three years out of college, elegant as a big-city businessman.

"What is it, Barbudo, things going badly?" he asked.

This was something he still maintained—the friendly but slightly condescending attitude of the upperclassman to the small-fry.

I straightened up.

"Not too bad, boss," I said. "Not very."

"This is no Cafe Aelita, no hipster hang-out," he said with a warm grin.

"Right, boss. Well taken."

"You don't feel bad? Fess up." He winked and pulled my beard.

"Oh why no, what for," I said in confusion. "Okay then, so what..."

"That'll do," he laughed. "You're all wired up. Coming over tonight?"

"Very gladly, even," I said. "Our pleasure."

"We have a conference now." He glanced meaningfully at the blueprints. "Have to talk shop for forty minutes, an hour or so..."

"Quite! We understand these things, boss, with all due respect..."

He smiled, bopped me on the head with the blueprints, and walked off.

"Ask him about the cement, boss," said my namesake Kolya Markov, one of our foremen.

"Sergei!" I shouted. "How about that cement?"

He turned at the door to the director's office.

"What about the cement?" he asked innocently.

"Try and cut without a knife, you snakes!" I shouted, with a slight note of hysteria.

At Sergei's back I glimpsed the frightened face of the director's secretary.

"We'll have it there tomorrow," said Sergei, and opened the door.

I went out of the Trust and looked at the huge sopki hanging over our little city. The rim of the moon was peeking out from behind one of the sopki, and the sparse trees on the summit were distinctly visible, each little tree separately. I went around behind the building—no one was there—and fell to watching as the moon rose over the sopka, and sharp dark-blue shadows and silvery-azure strips of light came to rest on the sopki and the ravines, and the scene turned into a Rockwell Kent. I thought how many hundred kilometers this terrific relief stretched northward, and how few people were there—there aren't even many animals—and how a couple of meteorologists would be sitting in some weather station stoking the stove, two people who never tired of each other.

Footsteps and voices were audible around the corner of the building. Someone was making arrangements about "a drink and a bite to eat," someone was starting up a motorcycle, girls were laughing.

A group of girls, looking very clumsy and shapeless in their sheepskins and felt boots, came around the corner and headed for the bus stop. They were the girls from Cinderblocks. They passed by me chirping like a flock of birds, but one turned around, noticed me. She started, and stood still. I can imagine how I looked, alone against the background of the moonlit white wall.

She came over and stopped a few steps from me. It was that same little Italian. For some time we looked at each other in silence.

"Why, what are you standing like that for?" she asked in a shaky voice.

"So you're from Cinderblocks?" I asked, without moving.

"You're taking it hard, aren't you?" she asked in a changed tone, derisively.

"What's your name?" I asked.

"Why, Lusya," she said, "but the criticism was very much to the point."

"Sure thing," I said. "Want to go to the movies?"

She laughed in relief. "Shave first, invite me after. Oh—the bus!"

And off she ran, clumsily falling all over herself in her big felt boots. To look at her at that moment you'd never have imagined she had the figure of a Diana. She poked her head out once more from behind the kiosk and looked at Nikolai Kalchanov, who cast a huge and misshapen shadow on the wall.

I came around the corner and started toward Phosphate City's Broadway, where four of our famous neon signs were lit up—"Market," "Cinema," "Restaurant," "Books"—objects of communal pride. Our little town puts on airs, goes all out to have everything like the big cities. We even have taxis—seven of them.

I walked past the cinema. There was a Polish picture playing, *Mother Joan of the Angels?*, which I'd already seen twice, yesterday and the day before. I walked past the restaurant, which was packed. Through the blind I could see a richly framed painting by Ayvazovsky, "The Ninth Wave," and below it the head of the drummer, a Korean from Sakhalin, Pak Don Hee. I stopped to watch him. He was beaming. I could tell that the orchestra was playing something loud. When they play something loud and fast, "Cherry Orchard," for example, Pak beams; but when it's something soft, like "Steppe, Steppe, All Around," he droops—he doesn't like to play soft. This time Pak was beaming like the moon. I could tell they'd given him a solo and he was knocking out this fantastic break with his hands and feet, and the guys from our Trust were watching him open-mouthed, nudging each other and giving the thumbs-up sign. The jazz in our restaurant couldn't be called

177

old-fashioned, it couldn't be called modern; it can't be classified at all. This is a completely original group. These guys have spirit. It's just wonderful when they stand up one after another with a brassiness you never heard the like of and play their solos, and then suddenly strike up all together—it's enough to blow your mind.

After watching my fill of Pak and rejoicing for him, I walked on. My throat was a little sore, apparently I'd caught cold today out at the section when I was barking at the construction hands.

The market was full of people. Our Trust was storming the counters, and the miners, auto mechanics, and geologists were hitting us for three-spots and five-spots. The thing was, today was payday for us, the others hadn't had their turn yet.

Someone I knew asked me for a five-spot, too—a driver from Airapet's party.

"I'll get it back to you," he said.

"How are your people out there?" I asked.

"Still messing around, but there's not much point."

"Say hello to Airapet," I said.

"Uh-huh."

He forced his way into the crowd, and I followed.

"You can mess around out there while longer!" I thought.

I like Airapet and wish him luck, but I just can't bear to look at him and Katya when they're together.

I got two bottles of Checheno-Ingush, and a kilo of candy with the appetizing brand name "Zoologic." I thrust all this into my jacket pockets and went out to the street.

Our "Broadway" runs right up to the sopka, to a thicket of brush from which the transparent forest begins its steep rise—black trunks, dark-blue shadows, silvery azure spots of light. The tree-branches are interwoven. Everything is sharp, precise, rather awesome. I understand why graphic artists like to depict trees without leaves. Trees are truer without their leaves than with them.

And at my back was the ordinary, well-behaved street with its four neon signs, like an ordinary street in a suburb of Moscow or Leningrad, and it was hard to believe that the city did not continue out there beyond the sopka, that for thousands of kilometers out to the north there were no pre-fab buildings or neon signs, that there was a boundless kingdom out there, fully regulated and exact, where if there was nothing to eat there was nothing to eat, if you were alone you were alone, if it was the end of you it was the end. Out there it's bad to be alone.

I stood for a while at the border of these two kingdoms, then turned to the left and went to my apartment building. Our building is the last in the row, and always will be last, because beyond it is the sopka. Or it's the first, if you count from here.

Staska wasn't home. I put the cognac on the table, ate some eggplant caviar, and turned on the radio.

"In Turkey the cost of living is constantly on the rise," said the radio.

I'd heard it already, in the morning. It was the first phrase I'd heard that morning, and then Staska had said, "Where'd that bearded no-good hide my dumb-bells?"

He nearly always dignifies me with this tender name, it's only when he's out of sorts that he says "Kolya," and if he's in a rage I'm "Nikolai."

I don't like coming home when Staska's gone. Sure, he's very noisy and wears his shirts on both sides—prolongs their period of usefulness, so to speak. And at night he chews on gingersnaps, washing them down with water, and goes smack, smack, smack until I pull the covers over my head and sing quietly, inaudibly, "Sna-a-ake, swi-i-ine, if you choke that'll be just fi-i-ine." But still, if he were home now, he'd toss his book aside and ask, "Where'd this bearded no-good come from?" And I'd answer, "From the Komsomol meeting."

And when we had a drink I'd talk to him about Katya.

I got up and closed the creaking doors of the wardrobe tightly, and moved a chair against them, too, so they wouldn't keep opening. I don't like it when the wardrobe doors are open, and I shudder all over when they suddenly open by themselves with their faint, heart-stopping creak. I get the strange sensation that a face may suddenly peer out of the wardrobe, or simply that something bad is about to happen.

I got my design project and spread it out on the table, fastening it with thumbtacks. I lit a cigarette and stood back from the table a bit. It lay before me, the future Phosphate City Center, glass and steel, harmonious and unexpected. Forgive me, but there does sometimes come a time when you can judge your own work yourself. People may tell you different things, wise and foolish and neither one nor the other, but you yourself stand rooted to the ground and say nothing—you know, yourself.

Of course, this isn't my business. I'm a section boss. My business is work details, cement, the concrete mixer. My business is a blue nose and beet-red cheeks, my business is "Boss, let's all chip in on a half-liter of vodka," and then, once we're indoors, "Help yourself, I don't mind, men, it's on the house." My business is to find a common language. But hullo—this is my business. My business is to stand rooted to the ground by the table, smoke, brag, and know that I really have achieved a success.

I'm chicken—I never show my work to anyone, even Sergei. It's all because I don't want to climb to the top. Now if they were to accept my project and reward me with a lower-ranked job, and if I were beset by all sorts of afflictions, then I'd be at peace. I am unable, constitutionally unable, to climb to the top. Everyone looks at your face and thinks, "Well, there he goes, up the ladder." Only Staska knows about this thing, no one else, not even Katya.

I'm in a bad way, my dear comrades. I'm in love. No point in betting blind—I'm in love with the wife of my friend Airapet Kichekian.

I took the bottle, hit the bottom of it twice to knock the cork out, and had a couple of swallows. Someone upstairs turned on a record player.

"Buy my violets," sang a woman's voice, "wood violets here."

Wood violets here, and you all in violets, your face in violets, and you are crushing berries with your feet. Barefoot. Strawberries.

I took another drink and flopped on to the bed. I opened my night-stand and got out some letters that I'd hastily read through in the morning.

My mother had gotten married again, this time to a film director. Inka still loved me. Oleg had been published in a poetry annual, reported Penkin. He'd send me some filter cigarettes in a few days. "Haven't you croaked yet, sad sack?" asked Oleg himself, and he went on with a bunch of absolutely uncalled-for insults. What's this strange tone my friends are taking with me, anyway?

I threw the letters back into the nightstand and got up. I caught sight of myself in the mirror. Should I shave it off right now? But however you shave it, I expect you get your cheeks all torn up. I pulled my ears out wide and winked at the guy in the mirror.

"You're sliding down an inclined plane," I warned him.

"Heh, heh," he replied, and grinned his nastiest grin.

"I like you, you villain," I told him.

He lowered his eyes.

At that point someone knocked. I opened the door, and who should walk past me right into the room but rosy Katya.

She took off her parka and threw it on Staska's bed. Then she went to the mirror and began fixing her hair. Of course she combed it down over her forehead so that it practically covered her right eye. She had on a bulky-knit sweater and blue jeans, and on her feet she wore, as we all did, enormous ankle boots.

"Aha," she said, noticing the bottle in the mirror, "drinking alone? A bad symptom."

I tossed her parka from Staska's bed to mine and went a little nearer to her. I should have cleared my project off the table, but for some reason I didn't, I just leaned back against it.

Katya walked around the room, picking up books and things and putting them down.

"What are you reading? *Private Residence?* Great, isn't it? I didn't understand a thing...

"Is the cognac good? Could I try some?...

"Are these Staska's dumb-bells? Oh-ho!"

I don't know what brought her to me, I don't know whether she felt nervous or gay. I watched her walk around our wretched room, still pink-cheeked, a slender little woman, and I remembered Blok: "She came in from

180

the cold, all flushed, and filled the room with..." How did it go? Then she sat down on my bed and began looking at me. First she smiled at me with friendly condescension, the way Sergei Orlov smiles at me; then just in a friendly way, like her husband Airapet; then somehow anxiously; then she stopped smiling and looked at me from under her brows.

And I looked at her and thought, "My God, what a shame I've come to know her only now, we didn't live in the same building and become friends through our families, I didn't ask her to the skating rink and offer her my friendship, we didn't go to Pioneer Camp together, I wasn't the first to kiss her and I wasn't the one with whom she shared the first trepidations of intimacy."

This whole turn of events was strange for me, unthinkable, because actually she had always been with me. Even back when I used to stand rooted to the ground on the Pioneer Camp playfield, looking at the dark forest wall that seemed carved out of tin, and the green sky and the first star... We used to sing a song:

> Where never howls the blizzard,
> In the southland far away,
> Once upon a time there lived
> A rich man named John Grey.
>
> A mighty man was John, a rake...

I was still an amazing wet-head, actually, and did not understand what a rake was. I sang, "A mighty man was John awake..." Such a ridiculous little kid. And we sang "Young Billy had clenched teeth," too, and "In Capetown Port," and the romance of these ridiculous little songs irrevocably touched our hearts. And this romance was Katya herself, whom I didn't know then, and had come to know only here. Yes, Katya was the infinite romance, the first flush of youth, the... Oh my God, Katya was... Yes, yes, yes. Katya was always "yes" and never "no." And she knew it, and she had come here to tell me "yes," because she sensed who she was for me.

"You might buy a shade of some sort for the light bulb," she said uneasily.

"Ah—a shade," I said, and looked at the bulb, which dangled from the ceiling on a long cord and hung at chest level in the room. When we have to work at the table, we tie the light bulb to the window vent.

"Really, Kolya, you might curtain the windows somehow," she said, a little more boldly.

"Ah—the windows." I looked foolishly at the dark naked windows, then looked right into Katya's eyes. Her eyes filled with fear, they turned dark and naked like the windows. I took a step toward her, and my shoulder

181

brushed against the light bulb. Katya quickly got up from the bed.

"You should buy a lamp," she murmured, "one still has to live like a hu..."

The light bulb was swinging, and our shadows tossed about on the walls and ceiling, huge and strange. We stood and looked at each other. We were separated by the space of a meter.

"Flowers would be nice, too, eh?" I murmured. "Eh?! I should get some flowers in here, don't you think? Paper ones, huge..."

"Paper ones are for funerals," she whispered.

"Well, yes," I said. "We shouldn't have paper ones. Wood violets, right? Wood violets here. Think of them as being here. The whole room is full of them. Think of it that way."

I caught hold of the light bulb and unscrewed it, burning my fingers. For several seconds, in the pitch dark, there were dozens of bulbs leaping about and spreading their stains of light before me, and shadows swayed on the wall. Then the darkness settled down. Then the blue windows appeared, and Katya's dark figure. Then the pale splotch of her sweater emerged and I saw her eyes. I took a step toward her and clasped her in my arms.

"No," she said, desperately tearing herself away.

"That's not right," I whispered, kissing her hair, cheeks, neck, "that's not according to the rules. Your motto is 'yes.' All you can say to me is 'yes.' You know that."

Forcefully, sharply, she turned her face away. In my arms she had become all strong, hard, resilient, overpowering. It seemed to me that I'd made a mistake, that in the darkness I'd caught some forest animal—a she-goat or a doe.

"Kalchanov, you're a crumb!" she cried, and at that I let her go. I understood what she meant.

"Oh yes, I'm a crumb," I muttered. "I understand everything. Why sure... Forgive me..."

She didn't move away from me. Her eyes shone. She put her hand on my shoulder.

"No, Kolya, you don't understand... You're not a crumb..."

"Not a crumb, correct," I said. "A holy terror. Kolya the Daring, the blue-eyed terror... O excellent friend of my youth... Box his ears..."

"Oh," she whispered, and suddenly she nestled up to me, clung to me, hung on me, clasped my head, and she wasn't strong at all, she was utterly helpless and at the same time imperious.

Suddenly she recoiled and, bracing her hands on my chest, whispered in a voice that sounded as if she'd been crying for several hours without a break, "Where were you before, Kolya? Where the hell were you a year ago?"

At this point the door slammed and someone came into the room, tripped over something, cursed. It was Staska. He struck a match and I saw

182

his face, his open mouth. He was looking right at us. The match went out.

"That bearded monster, he's taken off somewhere again," said Staska. Loudly banging his heels, he left the room.

"Turn on the light," said Katya quietly.

She sat down on the bed and began tidying her hair. I was a long time hunting for the light bulb, for some reason I couldn't find it. Then I did, caught it in my hand. It was still warm.

"Yes," I thought, "Katya, Katya, Katya! No, no matter what, regardless and with no looking back, and whatever your face looks like when I turn on the light..."

"What are you standing there for?" she said calmly. "Screw in the bulb."

Her face was serene and ironic. She suddenly looked up at me with a sidelong glance, as if she had just now fallen in love with me, love at first sight, as if I were some cowboy and had just come in off the road in my dusty boots, with a tanned face and a worldly air.

"Katya," I said, but she was already getting into her parka.

She pulled up her hood, zipped her zipper, put on her gloves, and suddenly caught sight of the project.

"What's that?" she exclaimed. "Oh, that's neat!"

"Katya," I said. "Well, all right... Well, my God... Well but what next?"

But she was examining the project.

"What a building!" she exclaimed. "Terrific!"

I hated my project.

"Tap-tap-tap," she laughed. "Here I am, going up the stairs."

"It'll have an elevator there," I said.

"Is this your work?" she cried.

"No, Corbusier." I lit a cigarette and sat on the bed. "Listen," I said. "Well, all right... I can't talk. Come to me."

"Stop!" she said sharply, going to the door. "What are you, out of your mind? Don't be out of your mind!"

"Lost my mind, My heart is thine," I said.

"Are you going to Sergei's?" she asked.

"I'm going to Sergei's," she said.

"Well?"—and there it was again, that same sudden look.

"I'm counting to three, Kolya." She smiled in a friendly way.

"Count to zero," I said, and got up.

"Well, all right, we'll play out yet another evening," I thought. "Yet another farce. We'll play house: wonderful. You poor thing, you *know* our password is 'yes!'"

We went out of the building. She took my arm. She had nothing to say, and kept watching her feet. I was silent too. The snow crunched, and the cognac gurgled in my pockets.

At the corner of the main street we spotted Staska. He was standing there rocking back and forth on his heels, reading the newspaper pasted on the wall. He had his doctor's bag in his hand.

"Hi, folks," he said, noticing us, and jabbed a finger at the paper. "How do you like Bobby Fischer? Going great, the tramp!"

"You've been on call?" I asked him.

"Yes, I was making calls," he answered, looking away. "One scarlet fever, three colds, an exacerbated ulcer..."

"Want to go to Sergei's?"

"Let's go."

He took Katya's other arm, and we set off, the three of us. For about a minute we walked in silence, and I could feel Katya's arm trembling. Then she started talking to Staska. I listened to them gabbing and finally lost the thread, and I was filled with an emptiness like heartburn, like a terrible hangover.

"I just don't think of you as a doctor," Katya teased Staska as she had a hundred times before. "I wouldn't go to you for treatment."

"You need to see a psychiatrist, not me," Staska joked back, as always.

We entered Sergei's building and started up the stairs. Staska went on ahead and left us a whole flight behind. Katya stood still, put her arms around my neck and pressed her cheek to my beard.

"Kolya," she whispered. "I'm so sick of it. Chudakov came by today, and I sent clothes and jam back to Airapet with him. You understand, I..."

I was silent. I'm so damned tongue-tied! I could have told her that I would place at her disposal all the tenderness I felt for her, all the cruelty I could muster, that I was ready to take all blows on myself, if that were possible. Yes, I know that everyone must bear his share in life, that's how it is, but let her try to give her share to me, if she could...

"It has never ever been so hard for me," she whispered. "I didn't even dream it could be like this."

Upstairs the door opened, we heard Sergei's and Staska's loud voices and the voice of Harry Belafonte from the tape recorder. He was singing "When the Saints Come Marching In."

"Katya!" shouted Sergei. "Kolya! Everyone upstairs!"

She hastily wiped her eyes.

"Let's go," I said. "I'm going to cheer you up."

"Are you really?" she smiled.

"Do you hear Belafonte?" I asked. "We'll get to work right now, the two of us."

We ran up the stairs and burst into the beautiful apartment of the Deputy Chief Engineer of the Trust, Sergei Yuryevich Orlov. I walked right through to the living room and plunked my bottles down on the table. I'm used to behaving a little boorishly in this apartment: track in with my huge boots, for example, sprawl in the armchair and stretch my legs out, blow my nose loudly. This time, too, I tramped across the waxed parquet floor (custom laid, not prefab), turned up the volume on the tape recorder and began kicking up my heels. Dollops of snow went flying from my boots. Staska paid no attention to me. He sat in an armchair by the magazine rack, reading the papers. Katya and Sergei had lingered in the hall for some reason. I glanced their way. They were standing very close to each other. Sergei was holding Katya's parka in his hands.

"Have you been crying?" he asked severely.

"No." She shook her head and caught sight of me. "What would I be crying about?"

Sergei turned and gave me an attentive look.

"Come on, folks, let's have a drink," I said.

They came into the living room. Sergei saw the cognac and said, "Checheno-Ingush again? Looks like the great Far East is becoming a subsidiary of little Checheno-Ingushetiya."

"Our brothers in the reborn republic keep us in mind," I said.

Sergei brought glasses and poured the cognac, then went out again and returned with three bottles of Narzan mineral water. He modestly set them on the table.

"My Lord—Narzan!" exclaimed Katya. "Where ever do you get it all?"

"Good people keep me in mind," grinned Sergei.

"Yes, and he has Moscow cigarettes and the books that are hardest to get. The man's fixed himself up an oasis of civilization!"

Staska drank off a glass and became intently absorbed in himself.

"It's on its way," he said, "going along my esophagus."

He meant the cognac.

"Have you seen *Mother Joan?*" Sergei asked Katya.

"Twice," said Katya. "Yesterday and the day before."

"Have you?" Sergei asked, turning to me.

"I saw it with Katya," I said.

"Is that so?" He again gave me an attentive look. "Well, how was it? How's Lucyna Winnicka?"

"Terrific," said Katya.

"It's gone to my stomach," observed Staska in a melancholy tone.

"The Poles aren't fools in their work, by any means..."

"Yes, the Polish cinema today..."

"One film I saw..."

"There's a moment in it..."

"It's being absorbed," said Staska, "being absorbed into the stomach walls."

"Remember the bells? Soundlessly..."

"And the women's wail..."

"Lots of nice touches..."

"But the Italians..."

185

"If you recall *La Dolce Vita*..."

"And it's in the blood, in the blood," sighed Staska. "Lord, what's going on in my blood!"

So we sat there engaged in our usual small-talk. We always gathered at Sergei's. Here, somehow, everything disposed us toward such conversations; but lately these gatherings had begun to be reminiscent of some obligatory exercise to strengthen the tongue, and this prodigious gabble had developed a sort of falseness, just like all the furniture, the modernistic prints on the walls. I think we were all aware of it by now.

I looked at Katya. She was smiling sadly, smoking a cigarette. How I wished we weren't here, but out at a weather station somewhere... Stoking a stove.

"Maybe you oughtn't to smoke so much?" Sergei said to her.

And only in the music was there nothing false—in the metallic sounds, the sharp womanish voice of Paul Anka. I jumped up.

"Katya! Katya baby! Let's go dance!"

Katya ran to me, her boots clumping. "Now how am I going to dance in these clod-hoppers?" She smiled in perplexity.

"Just a minute," said Sergei, and he crawled under the couch.

I was kicking up my heels like mad and suddenly saw that he was pulling Katya's best shoes out from under the couch. He stood up with the shoes in his hands and looked at Katya. He was holding the shoes in a special way, somehow, and looking at Katya with a new, foolishly sad expression that took me by surprise.

Katya gave him her condescending smile and grabbed the shoes.

Yes, we danced. I showed what I was good for.

"Go, go, you bearded beast!" shouted Staska, clapping his hands.

"Watch it, Kolya!" shouted Sergei, clapping too.

I spun Katya around and tossed her up; it was easy for me. I have good muscles, and a sense of rhythm, and malice aplenty. And the dance was unthinkable and false, because this was not the way I needed to dance with her.

When the mad whirl ended, Katya and I fell on to the couch. We lay side by side, breathing noisily.

"It won't be long now before I can't dance such dances," she said quietly.

"Why?" I asked in surprise, sensing that something bad was coming.

"I'm pregnant," said Katya. "Beginning the second month..."

It seemed to me that I was going to suffocate, that the couch had gone riding out from under me and I was already swinging by a single spoke of the wheel, just on the point of being torn off.

"Yes," she whispered, "wouldn't you know... This on top of everything else."

And she stroked my head, and I held her hand. We paid no attention to

186

the fact that Sergei and Staska were watching us. "So life will pass as the Azores passed... So life will pass..." The words spun in my head.

"Well—be cheerful," said Katya. "Why don't you cheer me up?"

"Why don't I," I said.

We started dancing again, but not the same way, the music was different.

Just then the bell rang. Sergei went to open the door and came back with Edik Tanaka. Edik was all white with frost, he must have been hanging around out in the cold a long time.

"Dancing?" he said threateningly. "Dance, then, dance. Thus will you all dance out your time on earth."

Looking at Tanaka, Katya began to smile, and for some reason my heart lifted a little with his arrival. He's always turning up fresh from some special, sporting, robust world. He's very funny, a thickset, well-built little guy with passionate brown eyes. His father is Japanese. Your ordinary Soviet Japanese, but Edik himself is a champion at the Nordic Combined.

"But look here, gang!" he shouted, and out of his coat he suddenly pulled something round and golden.

He grabbed it like a bomb, took a swing at us but didn't throw it, he raised it high over his head. It was an orange.

Katya clapped her hands. Staska froze, open-mouthed, curtailing his observations on his bodily state. Sergei stared appraisingly at the orange. As for me—I don't know what I was doing at that moment.

"Katya, catch!" shouted Edik exultantly, and he lobbed the orange to Katya.

"What are you doing!" she said, startled, and lobbed it back to him.

"Catch, I say!" And again Edik tossed the fruit to her.

Katya twirled the orange in her hands. She was shining all over like the sun.

"Eat it!" shouted Edik.

"How can you! Surely it's not to eat?" she said. "We should hang it from the ceiling and dance around it like idolaters."

"Eat it, Katya," said Sergei. "You need it now."

And he looked at me. What? Did he know? What was this? I looked at Katya, but she was tossing the orange in her hands and had forgotten all else in the world.

"Make ready quickly, men," said Edik. "We have a great race ahead of us. A steamer has come into Slush crammed with this merchandise."

"What is this, a new Japanese joke?" asked Staska.

Without a word, Sergei went to the other room.

"Skeptics will be left without oranges," said Edik.

At that Staska apparently realized that Edik wasn't kidding, and he made a dash for the front hall. He all but took a header on the parquet floor. Katya would have run after him, but I seized her by the hand.

"You mustn't go along," I said. "You *mustn't*. Have you forgotten?"

"Nonsense," she whispered. "It's still all right."

The door opened, and Sergei Orlov was revealed in full motorcycle regalia. He had on leather pants, a leather jacket with a fur collar, and a helmet. He was buttoning the cuffs of his gloves. Another time I'd have built an entire circus around this leather statue.

"Oh Sergei, are we going on the motorcycle?" asked Katya, just like a little girl.

"What are you, out of your mind?" he asked from somewhere on high. "*You* mustn't go. Don't you understand?"

Katya kicked off her shoes and got into her boots.

"Okay," he said and nodded to me. "Let's go, you help me roll out the machine."

He departed, his leather behind gleaming. Edik said that he and Staska would go on his motorcycle, only later. He had to stop in at Cinderblocks, besides, so we should hold a place in line for them. Katya tugged at my sleeve.

"Why are you standing there? Hurry up!"

"Come here," I said. I seized her by the hand and led her into the hall.

"Who got you pregnant?" I asked her point blank. "Him?" and I nodded toward the stairs.

"Idiot!" she exclaimed, pressing her hands to her cheeks in horror. "You're out of your mind! How could you think such a thing?"

"How does he know? Why did he have your shoes?"

She struck my cheek, not with the flat of her hand but with her fist, awkwardly and painfully.

"Cretin! Pervert! Crumb!" she whispered hotly. "Get out of my sight!"

Of course she started howling. Edik would have looked out in the hall, but Staska pulled him back into the livingroom.

I was ready to strangle myself with my own hands. I never had thought myself capable of such feelings. My heart was bursting with pity for her, and such love that... I felt I was going to melt like a jelly, right there on the spot, and all that would be left of me was a loathesome sentimental puddle.

"You... you..." she whispered. "You can just suffer... I was so happy over the oranges, but you... You're impossible... And it's a very good thing there'll be nothing between us. Go to hell!"

I kissed her forehead, took another blow on the cheek, and started downstairs. Idiot—I remembered about the shoes! That was the night the variety show came to town. I was in a tizzy over the singer, and Katya went to Sergei's to dance. Cretin—how could I forget a thing like that?

In the courtyard I saw that Sergei had already wheeled the motorcycle out and was standing by it, enormous and silent like the statue of the Commandant.

3. Herman Kovalyov

The wardroom was piled with sacks of potatoes. We hadn't gotten them all carried into the hold. We were sitting on the sacks eating goulash. Gramps was telling about the time on the 107th when he left the Detachment in the Olyutorsky Gulf, took more herring than anyone else, and then ran aground on the rocks. We were hanging on his every word and laughing.

"When was that?" The chief scratched his head.

"In '58, I think," said Borya. "Right, it was '58. Or '59."

"It was the year they brought the watermelons into North Kurilsk," said the bosun.

"Then it was '58," said Ivan.

"No, the watermelons were in '59."

"I remember I ate two right off," said Borya dreamily, "and kept some for morning, a couple of hefty ones."

"Watermelon in the morning's good for you. Cleans you out," said the bosun.

"You won't believe it, comrades, but I put away eight of those things..." Ivan was shamelessly wide-eyed.

The chief gave the lamp a shove and it started swaying. We always set the lamp to rocking when someone's putting us on.

Ivan's shadow swaying on the walls—mouth open and cowlicks touselled—was very funny.

"You should be ashamed, Ivan," said the engineer. "All they gave us was four apiece, after all."

"You don't know, Gramps, so don't laugh," Ivan snorted angrily. "If you want to know, Zina brought me another four by the back door."

"Yes, the watermelons were pretty good," said Borya. "All sugary."

"You think those were watermelons!" exclaimed the chief. "You boys don't know the real thing! Now the watermelons we have in Saratov—those are watermelons."

"The 107th ran aground on the rocks in '58," I said.

They all looked at me uncomprehendingly, and then remembered how the argument had started.

"How do you figure that, Gera?" asked the bosun.

"That was the year I got here."

Yes, that was the year I failed the exam for the aviation school in Kazan and set off blindly through the hot, dry city—it never occurred to me that I could return home to my aunt's consolations—and, on the wall of the huge, ancient building that we called the Behemoth, I spotted a government poster recruiting for the labor force. Yes, that was the year I sat on the coarse gray grass near the wall of the Kazan Kremlin and realized that I would not see this city soon again, that the boys and girls could count me out, that I might look upon seas somewhat harsher than the "Sea" of our Kuibyshev

Reservoir. And across the river I could see our Kirov district, and there not far from the apartment blocks was my street, overgrown with plantain; my horizontal bar in the courtyard, my aunt's flowerbeds out in front, and her murmuring, "Our garden has long since faded, It's all matted down, overgrown, Still the nasturtiums are blooming, A fiery clump all alone." And the old peeling board fence, which for some reason evoked at times a whole storm of memories of who knows what. Near it, choking with emotion, I had read Lyalya my own translation of some verses from my German text: "In a quiet hour, when the sun runs across the waves, I think of you. And when, in the moon's rays shining, a spark runs..." And Lyalya had asked, turning crimson, "Does this have anything to do with me?" And I had said, "What? It's just a translation." And she laughed: "Old-fashioned junk!" Yes, that was the year I first looked upon the sea, so real, so green, smelling of snow, and realized that I would devote my whole life to the sea. And Root, who was still serving on the *South Wind* then, stuck a herring down the back of my neck. That night in the bunkroom I boffed him in the solar plexus and he beat me up good. Yes, that was the year the seiner was assigned the captain we have now, Volodya Sakunenko, who wasn't about to tangle with Root. Root would get into a shouting match with him and go for his knife, but the captain fired him after the very first voyage. Yes, that was the year I secretly cried in the bunkroom, from fatigue and from shame at my ineptitude. And that means the watermelons were in '58, because they haven't brought any watermelons to North Kurilsk in my time.

Boots clumped on the deck, the watch came into the wardroom and reported that the flour and meat had arrived and that the captain had ordered him to tell us he had gone to the command to finagle a movie for us.

"Ivan, Borya, Gera," said the chief, "finish your meal and go take on the provisions, and the rest of you do you own jobs."

"Dammit," said the bosun, "are we getting underway tomorrow or not?"

"Annh, who knows," muttered the chief, "you know which end they think with over there."

The thing was that we'd finished up a minor repair a week ago, we were supposed to put to sea tomorrow, but the command had not informed us yet where to go—the Gulf for herring, the Coast for pollock, or Shikotan Island again for saury.

Ivan, Borya, and I went out on deck and began hauling flour sacks and lamb carcasses from the dock. I tried to haul the flour sacks. I'm no sissy, but I always get a little sick when I see those carcasses, red with their veins of white, frozen and hard. Once they were fleecy and warm...

The sun went down, and the round peaks of the sopki became clearly visible under the pink sky. The lights were already going on in the streets of Petrovo. Out beyond the breakwater the dusk was thickening rapidly, but the path the tugboats had broken to the port was still visible, and the icebergs and the cracks, like a quaint design on a stove tile. Tomorrow we'd go out by this path, and again there'd be five months of rolling and pitching, the icy baths every day, the painful dreams in the bunkroom, the yearning after her. So I hadn't even seen her during this week since the repairs. Today I'd send her a last letter, with a poem in it that I'd written yesterday.

> The zephyr barely stirs the leaves
> And hastens, rustling, down the steep.
> The sun, hid low behind the eaves,
> Into the mirror-moon stares deep.

> Nor can I tear myself away
> From your sorrowful great eyes...

I had recited these lines yesterday in the bunkroom, and the guys had been terribly moved. Ivan opened a can of compote and said, "Here, poet, fall to. Talent needs juice."

I wondered whether she'd answer me. Only once had she sent an answer to all those letters of mine. "Hello, Gera! I'm sorry I haven't answered in so long, I've been very busy. Things are going all right here at Cinderblocks, we recently turned over a whole housing complex. We live all right, devote a lot of effort to artistic endeavors..." And so on. And not a word about the poems, and no answer to my question. She's a dancer. I once saw her dance, jingling her necklaces as if she'd forgotten all else in the world. She dances before me like that all the nights we're at sea—turning, jingling all over, taking fine little steps in her Moroccan boots. But her eyes are not sorrowful. That's what I'd like, for them to be sorrowful. Her eyes are distracted, and sometimes sort of strange, crazy.

"Hey, Gera—catch!" shouted Ivan, and he threw a lamb carcass to me from the pier.

I just barely caught it. It was cold and sticky. Somewhere far away, beyond the edge of the shore ice, roared the open sea.

Around the corner of the warehouse, heading straight for the dock, came a green jeep, a Gazik. Who was this coming to call on us—the safety inspector? We went on with our work, as if paying no attention to the jeep; but it stopped near our ship. A young guy with a leather bag over his shoulder and a woman in a fur coat and slacks got out and jumped on to the deck.

"Hi there!" said the guy.

"Hello," we answered. We sat down on the gunwale and lit cigarettes.

"So this is the famous *South Wind?*" asked the woman.

Ah—these were correspondents, of course; they keep us in mind. We're used to this audience. It's a funny thing: when you're hoisting the saury net and you're getting soaked from head to toe, and there's all this filthy snow cutting at your face, you don't think about anything at the time, or you think how you'll be relieved soon, have some coffee, and hit the sack; but it turns out that at this moment you're "in a unified-hoist work situation" et cetera. And you'll meet a correspondent in any port, without fail. What they come for I don't understand. It's as if they had to make a special trip to write about a unified-hoist work situation. Writers are something else again. A writer has to have his little jokes. One time some writers took to visiting the seiner fleet. The guys used to joke that soon every ship would have to be fitted with a special writer's cabin. What attracted them to the fish I don't know. We had a writer from Moscow sail with us for a month, too. He spent a week barfing in his cabin, then got better and made his way into our bunkroom, helped out some on deck and in the galley. He wasn't a bad guy, and we all quickly got used to him, only it was annoying the way he was always reaching for a pencil. This was especially irritating to Ivan. Once he told the writer to stop writing things down and to store his observations on life in his head. But this guy said he'd keep writing things down anyway, whatever Ivan did to him, even if Ivan beat him, he was a writer and would write things down no matter what. Ivan reconciled himself.

After a while we even forgot he was a writer, because he stood watch with us and slept with us. When he first showed up on the seiner I stopped reading my poems to the guys, I was a little shy—he was a writer, after all—but later I started in again because I forgot he was a writer, and besides, I didn't believe he was a real writer, to tell the truth. And like everyone else, he said, "Great, Gera," "You've got talent," "Have some compote," and so on. But once I noticed that he hastily ducked his head and smiled and laid two fingers on the bridge of his nose.

That night as he sat huddled in his habitual place on the poop deck, with his glazed eyes fixed on something beyond the horizon, I went to him and said, "Listen, the stuff I write is garbage, isn't it?"

He sighed and looked at me. "Sit down," he said. "Want me to recite some poems by real poets for you?"

He began to recite, and recited for a long time. He would announce the poet's name sort of sternly, as if he were on stage, and then recite the poems. He seemed to have forgotten me. The verses gave me the shivers. They made things all mixed up in my head.

My life was passing gay and hard.
You walked in a snowy overcoat,
the sudden green wind of a man's cologne
and my kerchief stirred against my throat...

No, I could never write like that. And I don't understand "the green wind of a man's cologne." Wind can't be green, cologne doesn't have wind. Maybe you can write poems only when you come to believe in the impossible, when everything is simple for you and at the same time every object even a matchbox, seems to be a riddle? Or in your sleep? Sometimes I make up some pretty strange verses in my sleep.

"But actually you're a fine boy," the writer told me then, "a fine boy, to write things and recite them to your friends without being shy. They need it."

When he left he wrote down his address and said I could come to his place any time I was in Moscow, with vodka or without, I could stay with him as long as I wanted, and he'd introduce me to some real poets. He told us all he'd send his book, but he hasn't sent it yet...

We went down to the bunkroom with the correspondents. The man put his bag on the table and opened it. Inside there was a Reporter, a portable tape recorder.

"We're from radio," he explained. "Central Broadcasting."

"That's a long way," said Ivan sympathetically.

"Are there really six people living in this itsy-bitsy room?" said the woman in astonishment. "How on earth do you make room?"

"No problem," said Borya. "We're, um, portable, so to speak."

The woman laughed and sharpened her pencil as if Borya had presented her with the greatest joke ever. Our writer wouldn't have written down a joke like that. She was making quite a fuss, as if she were trying to ingratiate herself with us. But we were shy, it was somehow strange for us, as it always is when any outsiders, surprisingly unfamiliar, penetrate the bunkroom where we've all been rubbing elbows. That's why Ivan had a scornful smile, Borya kept joking, and I was sitting on my locker with my teeth clenched.

"Well, let's get to work," said the man correspondent. He switched on the tape recorder and held up a small microphone. "Comrades, tell us about your latest expedition for saury, on which you succeeded in making such a good showing. You tell us," he said to Ivan.

Ivan cleared his throat. "There were difficulties, of course," he enunciated in an unnaturally high voice.

"But difficulties don't frighten us," Borya added brightly.

The woman looked at him in surprise, and we all exchanged surprised glances.

"Could you give us a little more detail?" said the woman in a nice, cheerful radio voice.

Ivan and Borya began nudging me: Come on, talk.

"The gale howled, the rain roared," I said. "Altogether it really was a super-stormy situation, and we... ah... and so we... were catching saury... and it..."

"Okay," said the correspondent gloomily. "That's enough tape wasted. So you don't want to tell us about it?"

We were very embarrassed in front of the correspondents. Really, we were behaving like pigs. These people had come a long way in their Gazik to see us, they were probably chilled to the bone, and here we couldn't talk. But actually, what was there to tell? How they lower the saury nets into the water and turn on the red light, and then they heave the line and you mustn't start the winch now, you have to do everything by hand, and the rope burns your palms through your gloves, and then they turn on the blue light and the saury begin writhing like mad, they plump up the water, while on the horizon the dark sky is slit by a cold yellow stripe, and out beyond it is the infinite surface of the ocean, and in the middle of the ocean are the Hawaiian Islands, and farther to the south mushroom clouds rise from H-bomb explosions, and slowly crossing the yellow stripe are the strange shadows of Japanese schooners—we're supposed to tell about this? But this is really very hard to tell about, and does radio really need it?

"You'll have to wait for the captain," said Ivan. "He knows everything, he has all the figures at his fingertips."

"Okay, we'll wait," said the man correspondent.

"But comrades," exclaimed the woman, "you mean there's nothing you can tell us about your own life?! Just tell it to us, not for radio. Why, it's so interesting! You go to sea for half a year..."

"Our job's a small one," giggled Borya. "Catch to the shore, cash to the wife, head out for more."

"Marvelous!" exclaimed the woman. "May I write it down?"

"What are you, a writer?" asked Ivan suspiciously.

The woman blushed.

"Yes, she's a writer," said the man correspondent gloomily.

"Stop it," she told him angrily. "Now comrades," she said bleakly, "we heard there was a poet among you."

Ivan and Borya beamed.

"There sure is," they said.

It soon became clear that I was the poet. The man switched on the tape recorder again. "Recite something you've written."

He thrust the microphone in my face, and I recited with expression:

> I love life's tempests, rain squalls,
> Her seething snow and hailstorm,
> She has no quiet landfalls,
> Life is all a maelstrom.

I thought this poem would be most suitable for radio. Storms, squalls—the romance of the fisherman's work day.

I recited, Ivan and Borya watched me open-mouthed, the woman opened her mouth too, but the man correspondent suddenly ducked his head and smiled just like that writer friend of mine and touched his fingers to the bridge of his nose.

"And you like your comrade's poetry?" the woman asked.

194

"We like it a whole lot," said Borya.

"This Gera's a clever kid." Ivan smiled at me. "He catches on to everything so fast; he's on the job, right?—and next thing you know he's made up a verse."

"A great script," the man said to the woman. "I got it down. Tremendous!"

"You think it will do?" she asked.

"I'm telling you, it's just the thing."

Just then a sound reached us from up on deck.

"The captain's back," said Borya.

The correspondents gathered their belongings and climbed up, with us behind them.

Our captain Volodya Sakunenko was standing with the ship's papers under his arm, talking to the chief. The bosun came up to him just as we did. The bosun had gotten very tired during these days of preparation for departure and you could even see he'd lost a ton of weight. The correspondents greeted the captain, and at the same time the bosun said, "Like it or not, Vasilyich, I've done my job and now I'm going to go get gassed."

Volodya, our Sakunenko, turned red and covertly shook his fist at the bosun.

"What's 'getting gassed'?" asked the curious woman.

We all cleared our throats, but our sharp-witted chief explained, "That's kind of a term, ma'am. An engine-check, a de-gassing, so to speak."

The woman nodded wisely, and the man correspondent winked at the chief, as if to say, "We know you and your de-gassings," and knowingly flicked his finger against his throat. And Volodya, our Sakunenko, turned redder and redder, took his hat off for some reason, ran his fingers through his curls, then recollected himself, put on his hat.

"Tell us, Captain," said the woman, "are you going to sea tomorrow?"

"Yes," said Volodya, "only we don't know where, yet."

"But why not?"

"Well, you see," stammered Volodya, "our senior officers sort of aren't punctual, or what's the word... aren't principled, perhaps... in short... aren't exigent."

And he got all hot.

"Well, we're off, Vasilyich," we told him. "We're going out."

We went down to the bunkroom, changed to clean clothes, and set off for the shore, to the city of Petrovo, our own local Marseille.

Without talking it over we proceeded to the post office. The guys knew I was waiting for a letter from Lusya. The guys know all about me, just as I know all about each of them. It's the kind of job we have.

In Petrovo the main street was crowded. Light from the stores lay on the slippery, ice-coated boards of the sidewalk. Our bosun was already sitting in the blintz room of the Cliff, surrounded by bichi—Root wasn't among them. Near the club we encountered the guys from the *North Wind,* which lay in port alongside us. They were hurrying back to their old tub.

At the post office I watched Lydia Nikolayevna leaf through the letters in the general delivery box. I was terribly nervous, and Ivan and Borya kept glancing at me from under their brows; they were worried too.

"They'll write," said Lydia Nikolayevna.

And we went toward the exit.

"Don't take it so hard, Gera," said Ivan. "Forget her!"

Of course I could have caught the bus to Phosphate City right then, hitched from there to Cinderblocks, and cleared it all up, dotted all the i's and crossed the t's, but I wouldn't do it. My masculine pride prevented me, and besides I didn't want to dot the i's because tomorrow we were going to sea for a long time. Let her stay the same for me, a dancer, in the chiming of her necklaces. Maybe her artistic activities really did keep her from writing a letter.

I walked down the planked footpath, the collar of my leather jacket turned up and my cap pushed down over my eyes, walked with my teeth clenched, and Ivan and Borya kept pace on either side or me, also with turned-up collars and their caps jammed down over their eyes. We walked along detached and taciturn.

At the corner I caught sight of Root. His lanky figure cast several swaying shadows in various directions. He was the last person I wanted to see right now. I knew he'd stop me and ask, gritting his teeth, "Gera, have you got something against me?" That's what he said when we ran into each other last fall at a party at the Seamen's Club in Slush, the party where I met Lusya. It was the first time we'd run into each other since Volodya Sakunenko fired him from the *South Wind.* I thought he was going to pick a fight, but that night he was surprisingly sober and clean, in a tie and street shoes, and taking me aside he asked, "Gera, have you got something against me?" I have a terrible disposition: all you have to do is act human with me and I forget to be mean. That's how it was with Root. For some reason I got feeling sorry for him, and we were polite to each other all evening, as if he'd never stuck a herring down my back and I'd never boffed him in the solar plexus. We didn't even quarrel over Lusya, though we both went all out to get her to dance. We even seemed to feel a sort of sympathy for each other when she was led away from the party by Victor Koltyga. He's a driller, a hip guy and a lot of fun.

"Another time I'd be laying for this Vitya," Root said then, "but not today: I'm not in the mood. Let's go, Gera, my comrade in misfortune—I got a couple bimboes here.

And without even getting the point of what he'd said, I went with him. In the morning I came back to the seiner with the feeling that I'd been rolling in mud.

Since then my encounters with Root have been peaceable, but I try to keep my distance. I can't get that night out of my head. And he's gone to pieces again, he's forever drunk, and he asks me every time, gritting his teeth, "Have you got something against me?" Obviously, everything's all mixed up in his poor noggin.

At the sight of us Root swayed and took an uncertain step.

"Whaddaya say, seamen," he rasped. "Gera, have you got something against me?"

"Go on, Root," said Ivan.

Root wiped his face with his mitten and looked at us with unexpectedly bright eyes.

"You meeting Lusya?" he asked me.

"Scram, Root," said Borya. "Get going."

"I'm going, seamen, I'm going. I'm heading for the rocks. On a steady course for the rocks."

We went on silently, steadfastly. We knew where we were going. It's probably something everyone knows—what you have to do when the girl you love doesn't write to you.

We crossed the street and saw our captain and the woman correspondent. Volodya, our Sakunenko, didn't seem to have cooled down, he was walking along red as a lobster and looking dead ahead.

"Tell me, what are bichi?" the woman was asking.

"Bichi are like... like..." mumbled the captain, "something like navy parasites, that's what."

The woman exclaimed, "My, how interesting!"

She was studying life, you understand, but Volodya our Sakunenko was suffering.

We took a table in the Cliff and ordered some Checheno-Ingush and a bite to eat.

"Don't take it so hard, Gera," said Ivan "You mustn't."

I shrugged and caught Borya's sympathetic glance. The guys were sympathizing with me with all their might, and this was nice for me. It's odd, but I sometimes catch myself enjoying the fact that everyone on the seiner knows about my wounded heart. I'm probably a fake and a cornball.

The orchestra began to play "Carramba Signore."

"Look, we may be going to the Coast, then we'll call at Vladik, and you know what girls they have there, Ivan!..." said Borya, looking at me.

The man correspondent came into the room. He glanced around and, with his hands thrust into his pockets, started slowly toward us. In his right pocket lay something big and round like a bomb.

"Don't take it so hard, Gera," said Ivan imploringly, "I can't stand to look at you."

"May I join you, fellows?" asked the correspondent.

Ivan pulled out a chair for him.

"Listen, correspondent, you tell this dope what kind of girls there are

197

in the world. Tell him about Moscow."

"Ah," said the correspondent, "Checheno-Ingush?"

"I can't stand to watch him suffer," Ivan went on in a groaning voice. "You're a dope, Gera. Why there's more of them than us. We're the ones that have to choose, not them. Isn't that right?"

"Exactly," said the correspondent. "The census proved it."

"What did I tell him? You jerk, they have the figures at their fingertips to prove it to you..."

"For a poet, every figure is a zero." The correspondent smiled at me. "Pass me the knife, friends."

Borya passed him the knife, and he suddenly pulled his bomb out of his pocket. It was an orange.

"Good grief!" breathed Borya.

The man spun the orange and it rolled across the tablecloth, across the salad stains, knocked over a wineglass, and bumping against a plate of lamb chops it came to a stop, shining like the sun.

"What's this, a present from the mainland?" asked Ivan cautiously.

"Why, no," the guy answered, "we came in on the *Kildin*—or rather, not here, but to Slush."

"And the *Kildin?* Pardon me, but what'd it do, come to Slush from the Fiji Islands?"

"A steady course from Morocco," laughed the correspondent. "But what's with you guys, you fall out of the skies? The *Kildin* came from Vladik crammed with this merchandise. Have I ever had my fill!"

"Hey, waitress! The check!" bawled Ivan.

We ran like sprinters from the Cliff to the dock. We raised the alarm on the seiner. The boys dragged off their gear in a panic and pulled on clean things. Within minutes the whole crew had jumped out on deck. The watch, Dinmuhammed, was cursing his luck. Borya told him to stand watch vigilantly and we would keep him in mind. The guys from the *North Wind*, when they found out where we were headed, howled like crazy. They still had to take on salt and vegetables and get the old tub cleaned up for inspection. We promised to hold a place in line for them.

At the edge of town near the railroad crossing we put up our hands to hitch a ride. It was a tough spot: the trucks going by were full up with people. Word of the oranges had already reached Petrovo. Finally a MAZ came along, a flat-bed trailer truck with some huge construction panels tied on to it, prefab units that had been delivered from the mainland. It was going to Phosphate City. We stormed the trailer like an amphibious assault force.

I held on to some sort of iron thing. Borya and Ivan hung next to me. The trailer kept jouncing and sometimes tipped sidewise in the snow while we dangled over the ditch like bunches of grapes. My fingers grew numb with cold, and sometimes I thought I was on the point of being torn off.

In Phosphate City we switched to a pick-up truck. The sopki swept past us, moonlit, covered with sparse forests. The sopki were weird, and the tree-cover gave them such different shapes that different poetic images kept coming into my mind. Here was a sopka like a king in an ermine mantle, and here was a round little sopka that looked as if it had a crew cut... Sometimes in the ravines there were glimpses of solitary lights in the thick blue shadow. Who was it that lived in such desolate gorges? I looked at these solitary lights and suddenly wanted to escape from the trade I loved, quit sailing, become a driller, and live in a southern-style shack at the bottom of a ravine with Lusya Kravchenko. She'd stop treating me like a child. She'd understand that I was older than her; she'd understand me there. Lusya would understand my poems and what I couldn't say in them. And she'd understand me always from the slightest word, or elese completely without words, because words are poor things and express very little. There may be words I don't know that express everything faultlessly, there may be some somewhere, only I doubt it.

The truck took us as far as the fork at the State Fur Farm. Here we started trying to hitch again, but the trucks kept going by and there were shouts of "Sorry, friends, we're full up!"

Red taillights kept moving away, but there were new headlights rushing toward us from above, from the sopki, and we waited. The orange spinning on the tablecloth had filled me with hope. The road to Slush lay through Cinderblocks. Perhaps we could stop there, perhaps I could drop in at her dormitory—if, of course, my masculine pride would let me. Anything could happen.

4. Ludmila Kravchenko

The way things worked out it was an idle sort of evening. They'd postponed the meeting of the Committe on Cultural and Personal Affairs, rehearsal wasn't till tomorrow. I was bored.

"Girls, there's some nice hot water waiting for you," said I.R. "Say thank-you, now, I've got everything ready so you can do your wash."

That woman! She's forever bringing up all sorts of unpleasant facts and boring duties.

"I'm not doing any laundry," said Marusya. "I won't have time, anyhow. Styopa has a pass today."

"Maybe Room 5 would let us have tomorrow?" Nina suggested.

"Sure they would, just wait and see!" said I.R.

Nobody felt like doing laundry, and we all felt silent. Nina dragged out her gala costume—a wool blouse and a velvet skirt with huge pockets, her nylons and dressy shoes—and spread it all on her bed. Getting ready for a night out is much nicer than doing laundry, of course.

"No really, girls," I said, "let's at least get our personal things washed."

I may have been the one who felt the least like washing, but I spoke up because I'm convinced a person must learn to govern his wishes wisely.

"Come off it, Lusya!" pouted Nina, but she got up anyway.

We changed into our bathrobes and went to the boiler-room. I.R. really did have everything ready: the big Titan boiler was hot, washtubs and basins stood on the tables. We hooked the door shut so the boys wouldn't come sneaking in with their vulgar jokes, and set to work.

Clouds of steam immediately filled the room. The lamp on the ceiling looked like a spreading yellow stain. The girls were laughing, and it seemed to me their laughter came from somewhere far away, because they were hardly visible through the thick yellow steam. All I could see clearly was Nina's thin, bare little shoulders. She kept looking at me. She's always looking at me in the boiler-room or the bath, as if she's making comparisons. I have pretty shoulders, and Nina's glances embarrass me, but I'll never let on, because I know a person is characterized not so much by outer as by inner beauty.

Sima floated past me, pink, half-naked and huge. She set a basin under the tap and began to rinse some stripey things. I couldn't tell, right off, but they were sailor shirts. So Sima's snared herself an admirer, I concluded. A strange girl, Sima: whenever she has a crush, to put it mildly, we find out about it in the boiler room come laundry time. Sima is a living survival of medieval domesticity. She humbles herself before men and thinks it's her duty to do their washing. She even takes a certain satisfaction in it, but as for me... I read recently that before long everything necessary for the emancipation of women from day-to-day chores will have been invented and brought into use, and women will be able to play a greater role in the life of society. The sooner the better! If I ever get married...

Sima spread out a shirt.

"What arms your boyfriend has!" exclaimed Marusya.

"One hug from a guy like that, and rock away baby!" laughed someone, and they all laughed.

It had begun. Now they'd jabber about you-know... I just don't know what to do with them.

This time I resolved to keep still, and while the girls jabbered about you-know-what, I said nothing, and under my hands the white and pink and blue undies were heaving, squelching, squeaking like a living thing, the water gurgled, the soapsuds turned to rainbowed bubbles, but my head was spinning, everything was dark before my eyes. I felt sick.

I was remembering the time in Krasnodar when Vladimir took off that blue tradesman's smock of his and went to make a pass at me. There was nothing he didn't try, twisting my arms and bending me back! I might have screamed, but I didn't. That would have been degrading, to scream because of a pig like him. I struggled with him, so choked with indignation and anger that had a dagger come to hand I could have killed him, like a Spanish girl. And only just for a moment I got a sick feeling, the same as now, and everything went black, my knees buckled, but in a second I got hold of myself. I ran out of the office. Sveta and Valentina Ivanovna hadn't noticed anything; the tables were already all set. A train was just going by the windows, the tall wineglasses were rattling, sunbeams were dancing on the ceiling, and the silver shone in perfect order—but all you'd have to do is open that door over there, and the crowd would come surging in from the waiting room, the sunbeams would leap around on the ceiling in a panic, dark spots of beer would creep along the tablecloths, and by the end of the day—good Lord!—filthy little heaps of salad with stubbed-out cigarette butts in it... I shuddered; it seemed to me I was plastered from head to toe with this vile night salad. Behind me the door creaked—that would be Vladimir coming out, still hadn't caught his breath yet. I tore off my cap and apron, and without a word to Sveta and Valentina Ivanovna I walked across the dining-room and stole away. They'll see no more of me, Sveta and Valentina Ivanovna, and I'll see no more of them. It's a shame; they're nice people. But, I'll see no more of Vladimir's greasy puss, either—the hard-drinking, gut-stuffing, loose-living no-good! I'll have to start life over, I thought as I walked up and down the city. I sure didn't finish school just to wait on table. The pay is good, of course, but then every Fancy Dan has to try and make a pass at you.

"Hey now, what're you crying about?" someone said right by my ear.

It was a man. I scuttled away from him, went running off like a madwoman. At the corner I glanced back. He was young and tall; in his mouth he had a leaf from a plane tree, he was looking at me in amazement and twirling his finger at his forehead. Maybe I should link my fate with his, thought I—but maybe he's just like Vladimir? I turned the corner, and the tall blue-eyed boy was gone from my life forever.

There was a young people's program on the radio. They were singing my favorite song:

> If it's friends you want to find,
> Come with us, and now's the time!
> Come with us! The journey's long,
> Only don't forget our song...

Away! Away! To the virgin lands, and Bratsk, and the Abakan-Taishet construction, or I could go even farther, to the Far East; now here was an advertisement, seasonal workers needed for a fish-processing combine. I remembered the many movies, and songs, and radio programs about young people going off and doing great things out there in the East, far from their old haunts, and a final resolve ripened within me.

Yes, out there in the East, my life would go differently, and I'd find there a use for my strength and energy. And there, perhaps, I'd suddenly catch sight of a tall blue-eyed sailor; he'd be a long time deciding to come over to me, and finally he would; he'd introduce himself, he'd quake and blush, and at night he'd sit under my windows; and I'd combine a job with my studies and my Komsomol work, and somehow I'd put a certain important question to him myself, and I'd kiss him myself...

"Never mind!" shouted Sima. "I am not mad at my Misha!"

And I saw her big pink body stretching in the haze.

"Huh!" I couldn't restrain myself. "How come you aren't ashamed, Sima? Today Misha, yesterday Tolya, and you do laundry for them all."

"You should talk, Lusya!" Sima, with the striped shirt tied around her middle, walked over and put her hands on her hips. "You'd better sing a different tune or I'll go and tell your Edik about your Vitya, and your Vitya about your Gera, and have you forgotten about the tall guy from Petrovo Port?"

"Yes, Lusya, don't be a fake," Nina added. "You flirt with everyone, you were even flirting with Nikolai Kalchanov at the meeting."

"I was not flirting, I was criticizing him for his appearance. And if you happen to like that hippy Kalchanov, that doesn't give you the right to go making things up, Nina. Anyhow it's one thing to flirt but it's another thing to... wash their underwear. I just have a comradely relationship with the boys. It's not my fault they like me."

"But isn't there anyone you like, Ludmila?" asked Marusya.

"That's not what I came here for!" I shouted. "There are plenty of boys on the mainland!"

True, that's not what I came here for.

The first thing I saw from on board the ship was a lot of fellows on the shore, but honestly, they were the last thing on my mind. I was thinking I'd work here a while, get my bearings and maybe stay on, not for the season but a little longer, and maybe acquire a good specialty here... well, and I was thinking just a little, very remotely, about the tall blue-eyed fellow who had probably decided I was a madwoman, who was gone from me forever. That same evening I met a driller named Victor Koltyga. It turned out he was from Krasnodar too. That was very strange, and I spent the whole evening with him. He's a lot of fun and very well-read, only a little undisciplined.

"Why are you ganging up on me?" I shouted. "All you have on your mind is boys! No self-respect!"

"You're a dope, Lusya," laughed Sima. "At that rate you'll be an old maid for all your good looks. This one's undisciplined, that one's undisciplined. Tell me, what's wrong with the Japanese fellow? A champion, dresses smartly, has a good specialty—he's a radio technician."

"Oooh, you!" Practically in tears, I walked out of the boiler-room.

I'd had it with those damn girls. I went to our room and began hanging up my laundry. I guess I was crying. Maybe so. But what do you do when all the fellows really are undisciplined? Instead of talking about something interesting they always have to be pawing at you.

I hung up my bras and panties with clothespins and felt the tears running down my cheeks. What was I crying about? What Sima had said? No, that wasn't my problem, or rather, it was secondary.

I wiped my face, then went to my nightstand and rubbed my hands with Amber Cream (cream or no cream, I can still crack a nut in my bare hands), combed my hair, I don't believe in wearing lipstick, took out a little volume of Gorki, and sat down at the table.

I don't know, what a strange sort of evening it had been. It started out with me almost weeping at the sight of Kalchanov alone by the corner of the building. It was strange, I felt like coming to his aid, I was ready to do anything for him in spite of the way he's always winking, and then—the talk in the boiler-room; I don't know, maybe it was the effect of the steam, the heat, the yellow light, or the effect of the sopki, dark-blue and silver, convex and calm-looking; but I always have the feeling I want to do something unusual, maybe, something wild, I can hardly keep hold of myself, and yet now I looked at my laundry hanging up—not much of a pile, practically nothing— and began to cry again: I was suddenly terrified because I was so small, here I was, here was my laundry, and here was my nightstand and my cot; and all, all alone; my God, how far away, and what a strange sort of evening, and the shadow of Kalchanov on the white wall. He would have understood me, this bearded Kolya, but the sopki, the sopki, what was hiding in the sopki and what were they urging us to? Soon Edik would come, and again there'd be talk of love and pawing around, sheer torture, and all the fellows *were* sort of undisciplined. I hadn't written to Vitya, or Gera, or Valya. I was a proper good-for-nothing, I didn't have anyone, and I'd be an old maid. And my sister back there with her little kids, how was she? Oh! Did I cry!

Steps were already sounding along the corridor, and the girls' laughter, and with an effort of will I got hold of myself. I wiped my eyes and opened Gorki. The girls came racketing in, but when they saw I was reading literature, they started talking a bit more quietly.

Fortunately I happened on a good quotation right away. I went to my nightstand, took out my diary, and wrote down this quotation: "If I am only for myself, then why am I?" Not a bad quotation, in my opinion. It helps one to understand the meaning of life.

Just then I noticed Nina looking at me. She was standing there, silly thing, in her velvet skirt, with her blouse over one shoulder. She was looking at my diary. Not long ago she'd burned her own diary. There's a story behind that. She'd left her diary on her nightstand and the girls started reading it. On the whole Nina's diary was interesting, but it had a major shortcoming: there were only petty personal experiences in it. The girls were all quite touched and were struck by what a clever girl our Nina was and what a pretty style she had. They especially liked Nina's poetry:

> Eighteen!
> Who can know
> the virgin soul?
> My heart yearns,
> my glance burns
> With a dream.

I said that although the verses rhymed nicely, they were still narrowly personal and did not reflect the mood of our generation. The girls started to argue with me. We were arguing very noisily when suddenly we noticed Nina standing in the door.

Just as we turned to her, Nina burst out crying and ran right across the room to the table, snatched the diary from I.R.'s hands and, clutching it to her breast, ran back to the door. She ran, and she was crying loudly.

She burned her diary in the firebox of the Titan. I looked into the boiler-room and saw her sitting right on the floor in front of the firebox, watching the diary's cardboard covers twist in the flames. The blotter on its blue silk ribbon was still dangling out of the firebox.

Sima made red whortleberry jam for Nina, fed her some tea, and the rest of us stayed awake all night, secretly watching from our beds while Nina and Sima huddled together drinking tea by the night light and whispering.

Soon it was all forgotten and everything was as before: we kept on poking fun at Nina, at her skirt too—and now, catching her glance, I remembered how she had run and how splendid she'd been. I invited her to sit down beside me, and read her the splendid quotation from Alexei Maximovich Gorki, and showed her other quotations, and let her read a little from my diary. I wouldn't have gone and cried if it had been my diary they were all reading, because I'm not ashamed of my diary: it's the typical diary of a young girl of our era, it's no narrowly personal diary.

"Your diary's a good one," sighed Nina, and she hugged my shoulders. She put her arm around me uncertainly, probably thought I'd move away, but I knew how much she wanted to make friends with me, and today I somehow felt like doing something nice for her, and I hugged her thin little shoulders too.

Arms around each other, we sat on my cot, and Nina softly told me about Leningrad, where she came from and where she'd lived all her eighteen years; about Vasilyevsky Island; about the Marble Hall, where she used to go to dances; and how after the dances the gaping boys would stand in a dense crowd by the palace and scrutinize the girls as they came out, and how their nylon shirts would show white in the darkness, and, strange to tell, that was how he had come up to her, and they had met five times, eaten ice cream at the Frog Pond on Nevsky Prospect, and once they'd even drunk a Greetings cocktail, after which they had kissed for two hours in the front entrance, and then he'd disappeared somewhere; his friends said he had been expelled from the university for something and had gone off to the Far East to work as a specimen-collector in a geological party, and she had come here, but why here, exactly? Perhaps he was wandering around in Sakhalin or on the Coast?

" 'Mountains never greet,' " I told her, " 'but friends...' "

"May I, girls?" We heard a sharp voice, and into the room came Marusya's Styopa, a sergeant first-class.

We were carried away by the sight of him. He walked down the aisle between the cots, smart as always, his belt pulled in tight, and as always, made jokes.

"Up! Rollcall!

"How goes it on the military and political-training front?

"Any claims? Personal requests?"

He was playing the general, as always. Marusya watched him silently from her corner. As always her eyes shone, and as always, her lips curved in a smile.

"Private First-Class Rukavishnikova!" Styopa said to her. "Prepare to carry out a special mission. Uniform—winter full dress. Is that clear? Repeat!"

But Marusya said nothing and went behind the screen to change.

While she busied herself behind the screen, Styopa strolled about the room, his boots shining like piano legs and the nameplate gleaming on his belt. He had on some sort of new uniform today: a short warm jacket with the hood thrown back to show its blue artifical fur.

"How handsome you are today, Styopa," said I.R.

"A new uniform for our branch of the service," said Styopa, adjusting the folds under his belt. "By the way, girls, I'm flying to the mainland tomorrow."

"You sure have gotten to be a terrible liar," said Sima. She scorned men like Styopa, short trim musclemen.

"It's so, girls. I'm going. Phosphate to Khabarovsk on an IL-14, and from there a jet to the capital, and then..."

"What are you saying?" said Marusya quietly, coming out from behind the screen.

She had already put on her holiday dress and all her sparklers. That was her weakness—assorted sparkly things, huge clips, beads, brooches.

"Yessir, I'm going," Styopa said, his voice suddenly very quiet, and looked around the room. "My mother died. Passed away, I mean. There was a telegram day before yesterday. So the command is giving me leave. They've issued my travel orders, expenses. Everything's in order."

Marusya sat down on a chair.

"What are you saying?" she said again. "You'll have..."

Styopa took out his cigarette case.

"Do you mind if I smoke?" He clicked open the case and glanced at his watch. "In two days I'll be there. Yesterday I sent my folks a telegram not to have the funeral without me. It's all right, they can wait, can't they, girls? Even if the weather's too bad to fly, all the same. What do you think, girls? It's wintertime, they can wait a little with it, can't they?"

Marusya jumped up, grabbed her fur coat, and pulled the sergeant by the sleeve.

"Come on! Come on Styopa, come on!"

She went out of the room first, and Styopa, pausing in the doorway, saluted. "Good luck, girls! And I'll give your regards to the capital."

We were all silent. The head resident, I.R., was setting the table; it was time for supper. On her bed, wrapped in mountain of pillows, stood the kettle. I.R. removed the pillows and set the kettle on the table.

"Never mind, he'll make it," said Sima. "It really is wintertime, they can wait."

"Of course they can," said I. R. "Summer's a different matter, but in winter they can."

"How can you talk this way?" Nina practically screamed. "How can you all talk this way?"

I said nothing. Styopa had staggered me. This time he had staggered me by his habitual smartness and the whole look of him—"at the ready"—that voice of his, penetrating, even slightly shrill, the whole splendor of him, the click of his metal-trimmed heels, and the cigarette case, and the new uniform, and then his suddenly quiet words; and Marusya's sparklers seemed not funny now but strange: when she stood before her fiance, a yellow ray of light went up from the brooch, up to the ceiling.

"We're out of butter," said I.R. "Someone will have to go for the butter, girls."

"Rosa, will you go?" asked Sima sweetly.

"Uh-huh," said Rosa, and stood up.

"Rosa went for the sweets yesterday," intoned I.R.

"Oh well, I'll go," said Sima.

"Why don't I just run and do it," suggested Nina.

I got my coat on fastest of all and went out. At the end of the corridor there were two tipsy concrete-workers dancing together. The door to one of the rooms was open, clouds of tobacco smoke were rolling out. I heard music and the fellows' loud voices. They were celebrating payday.

"Ludmila, the queen!" cried one of the concrete-workers. "Come here!"

"Hey, the culture committee! Let's have some culture!" shouted the second.

I flung open the front door and burst out into the searing cold. The door slammed behind me and immediately all was quiet. It was like an entirely different world after the stuffiness and noise of our dormitory. The moon stood high above the sopki in a huge black sky. Above the low roofs of the settlement, the square columns of the club showed white in the moonlight. Somewhere there were soft footsteps squeaking on trampled snow.

I started down the path and suddenly heard weeping. On a snow-covered log, with their backs to me, sat Styopa and Marusya. They were not sitting close together but at a distance, two quite small figures in the moonlight, their long shadows swaying slightly. Marusya was sobbing, Styopa's shoulders shook. I had to walk past them, there was no other way to the store.

"Don't cry," said Styopa through his tears. "You mustn't cry, now. I wrote her about you, she knew about you."

"And don't you cry. Don't cry, Styopa dearest," lamented Marusya, "you'll make it all right. It's wintertime, don't take on so."

I don't remember my own mother, or rather, I almost don't. I only remember her spanking me for something. It didn't hurt me—just my pride. When our aunt died two years ago, I grieved and wept very hard. My aunt I remember very well; my aunt was like a mother to my sister and me. And where is our father now? Where is he wandering, what is he working at? Someone saw him in Kazakhstan. How can I look him up? I'll have to look him up, I thought—who knows what might happen, an emergency or an illness.

I walked fast—I knew the shortest way through the tangle of lanes, streets, and blind alleys—and soon came out on the square.

The huge white humpy square lay before me. Sometime, and it may be soon, this square will be leveled and the wind will raise twisters of snow on its asphalt; around it will be tall handsome buildings, and in the center will stand a big granite monument to our Lenin; in summer there'll be young people here carrying on, but for now the square has no name, it's humpy like the end of the world, and deserted.

Somewhere off in the distance loomed the only human figures, and on the far side shone the lighted windows of the grocery store and snack bar.

I practically ran along the tractor rut, I was in a hurry to get across the square. In the middle, where a few saplings and a gray cement statue of a Pioneer bugler stuck up from the snow, I stopped and looked at the ridge of sopki. From here you can see the Muravyovsky Ravine and the headlights of the trucks following the highway down toward our settlement.

This time there was a whole string of lights moving down the highway; some caravan from afar, it seemed, was coming to our settlement. I love to watch the truck lights descending toward us from up there, from the glimmering darkness of the mountains. And in bad weather, in a blizzard, when the sopki are melted into the sky, they look like airplanes coming in.

At the edge of the square some blackened pillars stick up from the snow. People say these pillars used to support a guard tower. They say that once long ago, back in Stalin's time, there was a prison camp on the site of our settlement. It is hard to imagine that here, where we now work, dance, go to movies, laugh at one another, and cry, there once was a prison camp. I try not to think of those times; to me they are utterly incomprehensible.

The store was full of people: payday. Everyone was buying a lot, and the very best. I reserved a place in the butter line and went to the confectionery department to see what I might get the girls for tea, today being payday. And no chipping in. It was my treat today, out of my own money. A surprise for them.

"May I?" A middle-aged woman of thirty-five touched my shoulder. "Could I take a look? How much is this? I don't see very well. And this? And this?"

She butted in first one place, then another, pressing her nose right against the glass display case. A strange sort of woman; she had on a kerchief, and over the kerchief a city hat, a little old, but high style. She was flittering around me so, I couldn't make my choice at all.

"Shall we have a compote? Do you like compote?" she asked, bending down, and I saw she was holding by the hand a little boy, or a little girl, all bundled up with only its nose sticking out and its red cheeks.

"Uh-huh," said the child.

"Give us three hundred grams of compote," the woman said, turning to the saleslady.

The saleslady began to weigh out the compote, alternately layering dried apricots, apples and prunes in the scoop, while the woman impatiently marked time, glancing at the saleslady, the scales, the display case, me, the child.

"Now let's be getting home, Borya," she decreed. "We'll cook up our compote and eat it, shall we? The lady will wait on us now and we'll go home..." And she smiled a sort of uncertain, nearsighted smile.

Suddenly everything inside me ached with pity for this woman and her little boy, just ached, I don't know why, there probably was no reason to pity her, she may not have been unhappy at all, on the contrary, she may simply have been dreaming of her warm room, of how she'd eat hot compote with Borya, but Borya will soon grow up and go to school, and then—time flies—before you know it he'll have finished school... I didn't used to understand why people said so meaningfully, "How time does fly!"—why these words were never empty ones but always carried sadness, or indomitable desire, or God knows what, but now it suddenly struck me that there was a revelation for me in this aching pity for the funny little bundled-up pair dreaming of compote.

I just don't know what was happening to me today. Maybe it was because I turned out to have so much idle time today; the committee meeting was postponed, no rehearsal till tomorrow, Edik hadn't come yet. I just don't know, I've gotten to be a sort of crybaby and a ninny. I suddenly

208

wanted to have a little Borya like that, and walk home with him, and carry a little paper bag with three hundred grams of compote.

Loaded down with my purchases, I came out of the store. A truck was going by, filled with roistering fellows. I heard the ones in the back hammering on the roof of the cab with their fists. The truck braked. Fur-lined boots flashed through the air, and before me stood a tall young fellow, smiling from ear to ear.

"Greetings!" said he. "Dear prima ballerina, never fear! A small gift in honor of your talent, from some ecstatic devotees!"

And he held it out to me—good Lord—bigger than big, more golden than gold, as real as could be, utterly delectable... an orange.

5. Root

I'd been carrying a couple cans of cod liver around with me since morning. I had a gut feeling how things might turn out.

Warehouse Five was way the hell out beyond the lumberyard, near the abandoned docks. You'd have to say it was not a pleasant place to look at. Wander out there sometimes and you practically feel like howling: not a soul, nor man nor dog, only piles of rusty iron and crooked pillars. The scuttlebutt was that the docks were slated for modernization. And sure enough: not far from the warehouse stood a crane with a cast iron ram, and a four cubic meter excavator, and two bulldozers. But operations apparently hadn't started yet, and for the time being everything here was as before except for this equipment. For the time being, they'd sent us over here to clear out the metal scraps and trash from Warehouse Five.

A bright guy, I am. I didn't go wrong on those cans of cod liver. Towards three, Vovik—our foreman, like—said "Knock off, seamen! C'mon get warm! I've got a surprise for you."

And he takes two "geese" out of his knapsack, two of those friendly little six-bit black bottles. A grand man, Vovik. Only where does he get the jack for the grand style?

We sounded retreat, dragged some old mattresses and a ragged auto seat into a corner, barricaded ourselves with boxes—all told, we had ourselves a first-class railway compartment.

Vovik opened his bottles, I set out my cans, and Petya Sarakhan dragged a crumpled package of Novo processed cheese out of his pants.

"It's good stuff," he said. "Doesn't stink."

In short, the three of us had things arranged just great, had ourselves a campfire fit for engineers. We're sitting around drinking, snacking. Vovik, of course, feels like a king.

"Yes, seamen," he says, "and then there was the time I commanded the Liberty Ships out of San Francisco, hauling powdered eggs for you wet-heads."

"Go on," says Petya and I, "tell us."

A hundred and five times already we'd heard about the time Vovik drove the Liberty Ships, but why not give the man the satisfaction one more time? Besides, Vovik's tremendous at doing a put-on. We had a kid on the lumber mission up the Nera, he used to spin yarns for us at night about spies and actresses. Well, so Vovik's at least as good, honest. You could just see Vovik carousing around San Francisco with a couple of babes—one brunette, the other even darker—you could just see these Liberty Ships, understand, going through the La Perouse Strait without lights, and the Jap samurais laying mines under their side.

I don't know whether Vovik actually crossed the ocean, maybe he didn't, but he tells a great story. Wish I could.

"... and an explosion of terrible force shook our ship from keel to mast-trucks. In the menacing darkness there came the wail of sirens." Vovik's eyes sparkled like lanterns and his hands shook. He always got nervous toward the end of the story and had a great effect on Petya, and on me too—I'm not kidding.

"Bastards!" shouted Petya in the general direction of the samurai.

"Bastards is right," hissed Vovik. "You see how they observed neutrality, the SOB's?"

"Go on," I said, barely containing myself, though I knew what would happen next: Vovik would dash into the hold and cover the shell-hole with his body.

"So here's what happened next," said Vovik in a brave voice, and he went to light a cigarette. Right at this point he always takes a long, long time lighting a cigarette, really plays on your nerves.

"Here they are, just look!" We heard a voice and right above us we saw Ostashenko, the inspector from the port authority. He had with him the engineer who'd ordered us to the warehouse.

"So it's like this, is it?" asked Ostashenko. "Well then, like this? In this, well, manner?"

I have no love for chracters who ask such foolish questions. What's with him, can't he see for himself in what, well, manner?

"We're on our smoke break," I said.

"You're indulging in a little, well, vodka, you low-lifes? Fixed yourselves up a wardroom?"

"Stop asking questions," I said. "What do you want?"

"I, well, trusted you, didn't I? And this is, well, the way you..."

At that point I stood up.

"Or is this work for sailors?" I cried advancing through the boxes toward Ostashenko. "Is this any way to use skilled personnel, you mother?"

The engineer turned pale and Ostashenko turned purple.

"Don't you start a shouting match with me, Kostyukovsky!" he bawled at me. "Don't you pull any of your demagoguery on me, you parasite!"

And he was off. "Took a notion to go on a ship, did you? No seiner of ours has room for the likes of you, understand? No seiner of ours has anything but outstanding comrades. And everyone's fed up with your scenes, Kostyukovsky. So watch out or we'll fire you from the reserves, too..."

"You're not being very tactful," I said, trying to play him for a sucker.

Oh boy, did that get a rise!

"We've shown you plenty of tact, and what good has it done? You don't understand it when a body treats you decent. All's you want is to drink yourself cockeyed. They fired you from the *South Wind,* from the tender, too, you didn't even last three months on the schooner *Flame...*"

"Okay, okay," I said, "easy, boss."

I didn't want to remember the schooner *Flame.*

"You think that business with the sea-otters is just going to blow over?" Ostashenko lowered his voice, and his eyes grew narrow.

"My, my—you remembered!" I whistled, but to tell the truth, I suddenly got a sour feeling at these words of his.

"We remember everything, Kostyukovsky, absolutely everything, keep that in mind."

Vovik came over.

"Excuse me," he said to the engineer, "you gave us three days and three nights to clean these Augean stables, didn't you? Isn't that so?"

"Yes, yes," said the engineer nervously. "Three work shifts, that's all. But I have no doubt that you... It was Comrade Ostashenko who decided to check on..."

"It will be clean here tomorrow by the end of the day." Vovik made a sweeping gesture. "That's all. Agenda concluded, you can go."

When the bosses left, we went back to our "compartment," but the mood was already totally spoiled. We ate and drank the next round without any inspiration.

"What's with these sea-otters he threatened you about?" Vovik asked dully.

"That was a certain incident we had on the schooner *Flame,*" I mumbled.

"But what're sea-otters?" asked Petya.

"A kind of a little sea animal, understand? Not a sea lion and not a fur seal. A very valuable animal, if you want to know. A sea-otter collar costs eight grand, old money, understand? Well, me and this Tatar shot a few of the creatures. Thought we'd fence them in Vladik."

"So you got caught?" grinned Vovik.

Here it was, it had come. It had struck. I got a hot feeling, and rapture entered my heart.

"You guys want me to tell you what happened?"

It seemed to me I'd be able to tell it all, in detail and precisely and full of expression, like Vovik. How the Tatar and I talked in the bunkroom at night, and his eyes shone in the dark as if he had the moon revolving in his head. Then—how in the morning the schooner lay all in fog, and all you could see was the rosy peak of the island up above. How we untied the skiff, and so on, and how these little sea-otters float paws up, and what their eyes are like when you stick a twenty-two in their ear.

"You guys want me to tell you my life story?" I cried. "From the beginning? Like it was?"

"Let's go, Root," said Vovik, "you can tell us on the way."

He stood up.

I don't hit my own buddies, even for petty grossness. For grand grossness they get it in the kisser, but for petty grossness I let them off. Actually, I'm a nice guy. That's probably why they call me Root. After all, roots are humble and nice, right? Well, let's go, let's go, seamen! We're heading for the rocks, my hearties! Want me to tell you? Well, okay... I, Valentin Kostyukovsky, was born in the year nineteen hundred and thirty-two, think of it, men, in Saratov...

We went out of the warehouse, and arm-in-arm we strode off past the warehouse toward the highway. It was already dark out and so cold that all my rapture slipped away without a sound.

Vovik left us in town, escaped to some happy hour of his own. Me and Petya, without thinking too long, made a simultaneous turn for Stesha's. Several guys we knew were standing by Stesha's shop, but with a contingent like that we realized right away we'd never talk our way in there. We walked along by the fence then like we weren't even going to Stesha's, so these wimps would see we weren't going to Stesha's at all but were just out walking off a hangover or maybe we were in the money.

Around the corner, we climbed over the fence and went to the shop the back way. Stesha opened to our knock, and I pushed into the shop first and grabbed her around the waist.

"Valya," was all she whispered and she, well, came at me to kiss me. "Are you coming tonight? Are you?" she whispered.

The boys outside had already been banging on the glass with coins for about a minute, and now someone began drumming with his fist.

"Hey, Stesha!" they kept shouting out there.

And Petya creaked open the door, stuck in his nose—the pest—and giggled at this scenario.

Stesha lifted the curtain a little and called, "Wait a minute, sailors! I'm delivering a package!"

And she was at me again. Now Petya couldn't resist and came on into the shop.

"I beg your pardon! Comrade Root hasn't had the honor of dropping in here, has he? Ah, Valya, it's you, my friend! Fancy meeting you here!"

Stesha moved away from me. We sat down on some boxes and looked at her.

"Stesha, how about a drink for me and my comrade?" I asked.

"Oh, you!" she said.

"Honest, Stesha, let us have a drink, huh?"

She took off her kerchief, wiped her face (which was red from my kisses), and more or less recovered. As Vovik would say, she came back down to the sinful earth. She laughed. "But all I've got today is applejack."

"Deal us whatever you've got for a meal!" I said.

And Petya cheered up. "I for one will take applejack," he announced categorically.

"Kolyma, oh Kolyma, A marvelous planet you are..."[4]

What do you know, small-fry? Where have you been, outside of these shores? You're keeping toasty in a warm current, aren't you? The Japan Current—you are the Japan Current, yourself. Want me to tell you about the road, about the cabin at Myakit? Want me to tell you my life story from the very beginning? Well, let's go. Stesha, little one, your hands are fish-hooks in my flesh. Arrive-derciroma! Cold? You think this is cold? What have you seen, outside of this rotten shore? Ah, there she lies, the *South Wind*... Get this, Petya, the oustanding comrades earn their living on her, but for us— no way... Gera's there, a wet-head, like, but a man. What a blow he hit me in the solar plexus one time! Some kind of a guy... Has something against me, and with reason. Anyway—my early childhood was spent, think of it, in the city of Saratov on the great Russian artery Mother Volga... What happened there? Stuffed myself on chocolate one time. There was a garden you could see from the window, thick trees (and yellow sand beneath them), like clouds when you're flying in an airplane, only green. Understand, Petya? There was a kind of a game—"barnyard," you know? And a wind-up clown on a swing; and a popgun with a rubber popper. You shoot at the ceiling and the popper sticks to it, and then someone drags out the table, sets a chair on it, and climbs up on the chair himself and gets the rubber popper down. Maybe that was my father, huh? Or maybe it didn't happen, maybe it was all a dream... This sure is enough of me wasting your time, Petya, I'm going now, buddy...

"Where are you going, Root?" asked Petya.

"Cinderblocks, that's where."

"You ain't going. You ain't going to Cinderblocks today," Petya started in. "Why, where can you go like that—you got no nice boots, no tie, no scarf. You ain't going to Cinderblocks, Valya."

"When am I going to get there, huh?" I shouted. "When am I going to get there, Petya?"

"You will later. Only not now. I'm telling you like it is. You'll get yourself some threads and then go. But why go like this, for nothing? Got no boots, no scarf... Let's go home, sleep till tonight."

213

"Here on our bunks we lie, Keeping a watchful eye!" Petya, did you ever drink Pantocrin? Whatever you've got it'll cure. We drank it in '52 in Magadan before the steamboat. We flaked out afterwards in the steam hatches and, well, cooled it with Pantocrin. It's made of reindeer horns, a tincture of alcohol. You've seen reindeer, haven't you? Haven't seen a friggin' thing; you've seen dogsled teams, but you've never had a look at reindeer. You should see how the Chukcha goes tooling along on his reindeer, and the snow goes flying out from under him like a fan. What! Of course I didn't drive Liberty Ships over the ocean, but I'll tell you, the cold here is nothing to what it is on the Nera. Tomorrow's my birthday, if you want to know—thirty even, understand? Tomorrow I'll go over to Cinderblocks. But why should an old buzzard like me be going over there? What I need now is a widow of some sort, a Stesha. It's only my Polish pride that keeps pulling me over there. You know I'm a Pole, don't you? A funny thing, isn't it? Me—suddenly a Pole. Root—a Polish squire. Squire Kostyukovsky. It was my gaffer told me I was a Pole; I didn't even know, in the orphanage they'd registered me as Russian. And should I tell you, Squire Petya, how I landed in the pen? Should I tell you or not? I didn't drive Liberty Ships, of course, but... So should I tell you? Oh—you've already dropped off... Well, sleep then...

It was in '50, in St. Pete, I was there taking Factory Training. Anyhow I won't be able to tell this right. What a night it was—a fancy dress ball! Whose big idea was it? Mine, maybe? We were repairing the sanitary facilities in a basement on Malaya Sadovaya Street, and at night, after work, there it was in front of us—the Eliseyevsky Shop, behind its huge window panes, just burning with a million lights. Probably it was my idea, because every time I walked past the Eliseyevsky I imagined myself there at night, inside. It probably was me that came up with the idea because, of all us Factory Trainees, I was the closest to being a JD. Anyway—we began digging an underground passage from the building next door, from the cellar, and came right up under the floor boards of the store. We removed the ceramic tiles and crawled inside, all six of us. Oh, hell—it's impossible to tell about: several lamps were shining in this huge chandelier, and a mountain of bottles reflected many-colored highlights, and in the far corner a pyramid of lemons glowed yellow, and sausages thin and thick hung from hooks, and we sat on the floor in the stillness and were as quiet as if we were in church.

The others were young kids, most all of them born in '36, but I—the dolt, numbskull—we should have stuck to work, but out of fear I went straight for the bottles, and the kids followed.

Anyhow I never had such a night in my life, and never will. We lay on the floor and swilled chocolate liqueur, and gobbled caviar right from our hands, and the whole place was sticky, and sweet, and it was a regular fairy tale, not a night. And so we all fell asleep right there on the floor, and in the morning they caught us there, warm and snug.

And off I went from St. Pete to master the Far North, Petya. My life has been full of adventures ever since I can remember; but what age I remember myself from, I myself don't know. Sometimes it seems to me that the guy I remember wasn't me. And anyway, what we drank today in the warehouse, that's already gone; here I put out my cigarette, and that's already gone, and there's darkness ahead, and where am *I?*

At this point such a sleep came over me that I woke up at the knock like I was off my nut, like someone had ambushed me with a sack of dirt, and I was afraid, kind of, and ready to run.

"Hey, Root, a summons came for you," they said from the corridor.

They had to be kidding. How else could you take it—a summons coming for me, at the barber's.

"Say, Root! A summons for you!"

"Get out of here with your summons," I answered, "and yell softer, Petya's asleep here."

Or could it be a police summons? They got nothing on me.

I stood up and took the summons. It was a summons to the telephone station, a long-distance call. I don't understand at all, what wonder is this?

I went into the lavatory and stuck my head under the tap. The stream beat on the crown of my head, my hair hung over my eyes, I felt chilly and good, I could have sat there all evening under the tap.

Then I read the summons again: "Your presence requested for a call from Moscow." And now I understood. This was my Dad's doing. Oh no, Professor, what have you cooked up! Letters and telegrams aren't enough for him so here's what else he thought up—a long-distance telephone call.

My Dad was found a year ago, or rather, he found me himself. Honest, Petya, I had no idea before that I had a gaffer anywhere. I just didn't even imagine I had anyone—Dad there or anyone else.

Turns out he's alive, my Dad, Professor by title, member of some sort of Society, apartment in Moscow—understand? He got sent up in '37 and, well, he did sixteen years in the stir in Kolyma. We were, well, near each other for three years—me on the Nera, and him somewhere near Seimchan. I didn't used to like these counter-revolutionaries. The bastards, I thought, why they wanted to sell out their motherland—the snakes—to the Japs and Fritzes. Turns out there'd been a little mistake, Petya. The Cult of Personality had committed a plain old mistake. Well, for my old man it was a plain old stabwound. Justice miscarried, the mother-effer.

Petya went on sleeping. I put on my coat and started for the post office. I had to stop in the corridor—met a seal-hunter from the schooner *Flame.* He took me to his room and offered me a drink.

"So how are things on the schooner?" I asked.

"We received a prize," the hunter answered. "Too bad you weren't there, Root, you'd have received it too."

"Those sea-otters—the devil made me do it!"

215

"Yes, that did you no good."

And he offered me another little drink.

"Know what, I'm going to the post office. My father's calling me long distance."

"Tell me another, Root."

"My father's a sauerkraut professor."

"That's a good one, real good."

"Well, so long! Say hi for me on the schooner."

"So long!"

"Listen, what is it, you don't believe me? Want me to tell you my life story? The whole thing from the very beginning? I didn't drive any Liberty Ships, of course, but..."

"Sorry, Valya, I'm just about to play chess with the geologist. We'll talk later, okay?"

The moon was floating over the sopki like a trim little ship under golden sails. Past the island of Buyan to the land of great Saltan. There's a little fairy tale something like that, in verse—who told it to me? They say there's some flying saucers have started, that fly through the sky with terrible force. Wish I could mount one of those saucers right now and be in Moscow in a flash. Wish my old man wouldn't strain at the receiver, wish his hands wouldn't shake, wish I could just sit down with him at the table and discuss the issue of the moment over a half-liter of "Capital."

Annh, hunter, all you want is to play chess, you don't know anything about my fascinating life. You should try getting yourself a daddy when you're almost thirty, a daddy who's a sauerkraut professor. And a heap of aunts. And a cousin, a first-rate beauty. You should try sitting at the same table with them. You should try and snow them all evening with your heroic deeds and successes in production. But then, what's it to you—you're a hunter with the schooner *Flame,* you're receiving a prize.

And you know how to be alone in an apartment at night with a professor like that—with, you understand, a member of a society for the dissemination of miscellaneous knowledge. Here you call me a bich, but I bet he doesn't even know there is such a word. I wish I could tell you, hunter, how he asked me, "So you're a sailor, Valya? It turns out you've become a sailor?"

Yes, I'm a sailor, I'm a fisher, I'm an effin' mother-kisser. Whaddaya want me to tell him—how they kicked me off the seiner and how they kicked me off the tender? Maybe I should tell him about the Eliseyevsky Store?

"Oh, Valya, Valya, what is happiness?" my father kept asking, and he'd recite some sort of poetry.

But hunter, what is happiness for me? Getting lit to the gills on chocolate liqueur and making a scene with the caviar?

"You really don't remember anything?" asks my father. "Our apartment in Saratov? You don't remember me at all? Or Mama?"

216

What do I remember? Someone would drag the table out and set a chair on it, climb up and get my rubber popper down. The ceilings were high, that I remember. Wait, hunter, here's something else I remember—a portable phonograph. "Kakhovka, little rifle mine! Burning bullet, fly!" But I don't remember Mama. I remember a cop in a white helmet, and ice cream that was wrapped around a sort of a little drum, with a round waffle set on top. And I remember we had pillow fights in the orphanage, pillows flew in all directions in the bedroom like geese at a dacha. But geese don't fly. Hunter, I bet you've never even seen mainland geese, white and fat like pillows.

"When are you coming, Valentin?" my father keeps asking. "Move back here with me. You know motors, machinery, you'll get established in a job. You'll get married..."

And now he's endlessly writing me: Come back. But how can I when I have no tie, no boots, and no friggin' jack?

If I had a couple suitcases full of threads, and a nest egg, and a classy girl, a girl like that Lusya Kravchenko, then I'd go, hunter.

Good Lord—what did he find me for, why the hell did he, this professor, find a baggage like me?

Now there's who he should've found—Gera there, a friendly wet-head like that, a poet, is who he should have found. Look at you—striding along, you eagles! A regular communist labor crew.

"Whaddaya say, seamen!" I said.

Hell—will wonders never cease! How far is it from here to Moscow—ten thousand kilometers, at least, and here I was, hearing my old man's voice and getting hoarse for some unknown reason.

"Hello, Valentin," he said. "Happy birthday!"

"Hello, Father," I said.

"I have a nice surprise. I'll be with you soon."

"What for?" I choked and thought, "Have they nailed him *again?*" I broke out in a sweat all over.

"I've received a travel assignment from the Society and from a journal. I'm flying out tomorrow."

"But Father!"

"Don't call me 'Father'! What foolishness!"

"Don't fly, Father! What for? You're too old."

"You underestimate my capacities," he laughed.

"But we're going to sea, Father. Why come? I'm going to sea."

He fell silent.

"But can't you delay?" he asked. "Obtain leave from the command?"

"No," I said. "There's no way."

"That's sad..."

And he fell silent again.

"I have to come anyway," he said.

217

Oh, you—Professor Sauerkraut! Oh, you—devil take you! What *is* this?

"Okay," I said, "I'll try, Father. Maybe I can get leave."

The moon was running under full sail like the sealing schooner *Flame*. As if she were carrying me away from all my troubles and my hassles, out to where it was smooth sailing.

I was wild for a drink, and I had a ruble in my pocket.

Well, so you'll come, Father, and you'll find out about everything. I also advise you to consult Comrade Ostashenko in the personnel office. The devil made me do it—going after the sea-otters with that Tatar! I had almost become a man, got me some threads, wasn't drinking...

A ruble—that's a tenner, old money, I figured.

The bosun of the *South Wind* was carousing in the Cliff. He'd already bought drinks for four guys and everyone was coming to sit by him.

"Go on over, Root," the waitress told me. "You'll be satisfied."

I pulled out my ruble and laid it on the table.

"Here," I said. "Serve me what it's worth, Raissa."

She brought me a hundred grams of vodka and a sea cabbage salad.

"This is it," I thought. "I'm through making a spectacle of myself."

I look and Vovik's walking into the restaurant all bright-eyed, without even leaving his things in the coatroom, still in his sheepskin and cap. He comes over to me.

"Root," he says, "all hands on deck! Round up all the guys you know, we're going to Slush."

"Go on, get out of here," says I. "Let a man eat his supper."

"All hands on deck," whispers Vovik. "A steamer's come into Slush with Moroccan oranges."

"Go on, get out of here!"

"Here, take a look."

And Vovik opens his coat and shows me something wonderful—an orange.

"You can touch it."

I touch it—an orange. Hell's bells, an orange!

"What the hell do I want with an orange?" I say. "My finances are tight right now."

But Vovik's fidgeting all over me.

"This," he says, "is on the house. Come on," he says, "round up the guys."

6. Nikolai Kalchanov

"Where's Katya?" he asked.

"Coming right down."

He bent over the motorcycle. I went a little closer, and all of a sudden he practically threw himself at me, seized me by the jacket, by the shirt-front.

"Listen here, Kalchanov," he whispered, and even if his rage and malice were counterfeit it sure was well done. "Listen, you leave her alone. I know you, you little beatnik! Quit your college-kid tricks. I won't let you, you'll get your knuckles rapped."

And just as unexpectedly he let go of me, leaned over the motorcycle. Katya ran up.

"I'm ready, Comrade Captain." She saluted Sergei. "Sidecar passenger Pirogova is ready for the start."

He tucked her into the sidecar with his sheepskin coat, the "work" sheepskin he usually wore in the field, for driving out to construction zones and for putting in appearances at our site too. All the building sites of Phosphate, Cinderblocks, Petrovo, and Slush know Comrade Orlov's sheepskin. The whole seaboard is familiar with it, and even up north, even in Uleikon, it's famous.

"Nobility," I said as he walked around the motorcycle and brushed by me with his creaky leather. "Nobility plus nobility and again nobility."

He didn't even glance at me, mounted the bike. There was a resounding roar, and the motorcycle was enveloped in blue exhaust smoke. I was suddenly seized with fear and couldn't move. I watched Sergei ride slowly away from me, motorized and armed with every logical advantage, watched the light reflecting dully from his egg-shaped head, watched him carrying Katya away from me by means of irrefutable proofs.

Katya hadn't time to glance around before I ran and jumped on the back seat. We rode out of the gate. She glanced around—I was already sitting at Sergei's back like his faithful page.

"You are noble, my dear fellow," I whispered in Sergei's ear, "a gentleman to the marrow of your bones. And an excellent friend. Walk a hundred miles around, a better friend could not be found."

I don't know that he heard this with his helmet on. He made a sharp U-turn and, already, speeding, raced past his building. I barely had time to wave to Staska and Edik, who were standing on the porch.

Within a few minutes we were on the highway. Sergei was showing his stuff—speed was just what we needed! The moon trembled above us, and when we flew up out of a ravine into a mountain pass she would jump for joy, but when we hurtled downwards without reducing speed, she would fall behind the sopki in horror.

Roaring, whistling, and terrible wind in my face. I held the grabrail and scrunched down behind the broad leather back. Even so, the wind blew right through me.

"A marvel!" I shouted in Sergei's ear. "Speed! The twentieth century, Sergei! Step on it, you're getting near home! You're the pride of our era!

A stern man, and a gentleman! And even here, in the wilds of the Far East, we do not lose touch with civilization! You have everything the contemporary burgher needs! Everything for his self-esteem! Speed and pocket music! You don't even get lost under water—an aqua-lung! Tape recorder, cocktail shaker, the whole modernist bit! And you're a damn good-looking guy!"

"A da-a-amn good-loo-ooking gu-uy!" I sang it over and over.

Of course he couldn't hear anything with his helmet on, and at that speed, besides. All the same I wouldn't have had the nerve to say such things to him if he had heard.

Katya was huddled behind the windshield. Suddenly she turned and looked at me. She smiled, her teeth flashed. I couldn't see her eyes—her goggles were full of reflections. She took off the goggles and held them out to me: she must have noticed that I was all white with frost. I batted her hand. With an angry expression she again held the goggles out to me. Sergei took his hand off the handgrip and knocked the goggles away from me, poked a leather finger at Katya: Put them on!

"You're our pride and joy!" I shouted in his ear.

Of course he didn't hear.

Katya put on the goggles and signalled to me with her hand—I want a cigarette. I slapped at my pockets—Don't have any, I forgot them. She nearly stood up in the sidecar to get at Sergei's pockets. At that we both took fright and shoved her into the sidecar.

"Joint effort, Sergei!" I shouted. "Joint efforts bring success!"

But he didn't hear, of course. He was towering over me, he was defending me against the wind, he was rushing me into the unknown future, to the land of Orangiya.

One after another we overtook trucks full of people, and still there were red taillights glimmering ahead of us. Someone waved at us from one of the trucks. When we pulled even with it I recognized Vitya Koltyga, a driller from Airapet's party.

"Hi, Vitya! You in a rush for Morocco potatoes too?" I shouted at him.

He nodded, beaming. He's forever beaming and cracking jokes. When he comes back from an expedition and shows up in town he poses as an awful hippy. Calls himself Vic and me Nick. He's fun.

"Got a smoke?" I asked.

He held a pack of cigarettes out to me. Sergei poured on the gas and we spurted ahead. I held the pack out to Katya. I could tell by the way she'd looked at Vitya that she didn't know he was working with Airapet now. And she hadn't noticed Chudakov in the cab, that was certain.

Katya took a long time fussing with the cigarette behind the windshield. The matches kept going out. Finally she got it lighted, but she carelessly poked out from behind the windshield and the cigarette was blown to shreds in the wind, large sparks came flying back from it. She had to light another.

We had taken a steep rise and now we were rushing down, into the Muravyovsky Ravine. Below us we could already see the dotted lines of the street lights in Cinderblocks.

Katya was sitting sort of sideways, glancing now at me, now at Sergei; her goggles were full of reflections, I couldn't see her eyes, but her lips were grinning, and from them dangled the cigarette, and it all made this girl of mine seem like some alien and altogether unreal, make-believe heroine in some make-believe alpine pageant, she was locked behind seven locks, and only her chin and the tip of her nose were mine. Mine—ha-ha, mine... What's happening, and how am I to find the way out? They say a cybernetic rat will make his way unerringly through the labyrinth. Then program me, cyberneticist lads, and maybe I'll find the way out. Maybe I should hurl myself backwards right now—and put an end to the matter? I saw a leather hand reach out, snatch Katya's cigarette from her mouth, and throw it on the highway.

"My pride and joy!" I shouted at Sergei. "Friend to pregnant women!"

Abruptly he turned his face to me. His huge goggles had no reflections in them, and there in the depths I saw his eyes go glassy with fury.

"Are you going to shut up or not?" roared Sergei.

The motorcycle lurched, went flying to one side. A jolt—and uncomprehendingly I saw above me Katya's flying boots and felt that I myself was flying, and at once I was scalded by snow, and Sergei's leather behind landed on my face.

I threw Sergei off, we both instantly jumped to our feet—waist-deep in the snow—and before we had time to be frightened we spotted Katya, playing in the snow and laughing.

The motorcycle lay on its side—in the ditch, with the sidecar up—and shook with barely controlled fury. Sergei somberly pulled up the cuffs of his gloves.

"Idiot, cretin," I told him, "why'd you let Katya into the sidecar?"

"How come you didn't say anything?" he said gloomily, but without anger. "Your tongue works all right when it doesn't have to."

"Boy, would I love to belt you one!"

"And would I ever take pleasure in..."

He walked off toward the motorcycle.

Katya came toward me, stroking through the snow the way you stroke through the water when you're swimming.

"And I'm just getting up to bean Sergei when suddenly I feel I'm flying!" she laughed.

"Isn't this funny?" I asked.

"Marvelous!"

This idyllic adventure under the windless deep sky against the background of the picturesque sopki—it really had set an alpine, resort-like mood. It was hard to fight the combination, Katya's startling cheerfulness.

"Why did we get ready so fast, why did we so quickly and decisively go riding off to hell and gone?" I thought. "To get oranges, right? Well sure, what we needed was to get out somewhere, get away to this frosty wide-open country, go flying out of our seats, feel like mad wayfarers on the highroad."

I began brushing the snow off Katya, swatting at her back, while she twirled before me and suddenly, after glancing back at Sergei, pressed her cheek to me. We stood like that for a second, no longer. I watched as the film of her goggles extinguished her eyes.

"Kolya, come here!" shouted Sergei.

We set about dragging the motorcycle out of the ditch. Chudakov's truck pulled up and stopped beside us. Vitya Koltyga and a few other guys jumped out and helped us.

"How are things going for you out there?" I asked Vitya. "Will there be any oil?"

"Hell no!" He shrugged. "Jahn Airapet has dug his heels in. We're already drilling our third well in that damned ravine."

"But is there any oil at all there?"

"There's supposed to be, according to science."

"Science, old buddy, is mucho hocum."

"You said it."

Sergei was already sitting on the motorcycle, Katya in the sidecar. I ran over and climbed on back.

"You stay behind them, eagle," I said to Sergei. "It's already clear to everyone you're an eagle. Orlov—even your name means eagle."

"You're talking nonsense, Kalchanov," said Sergei, stepping on the starter and wresting thunderous sounds from his motorcycle.

"Stay behind the truck," I said. "Show some concern for children."

"Bear in mind," he said, "our conversation isn't over yet."

I laid my head trustingly on his shoulder.

Nevertheless, he stayed behind the truck, and all the way to the sea it loomed ahead of us, full of a motley crowd. Victor Koltyga apparently felt he was the star among them, a Milanese opera singer.

The sea opens up unexpectedly here, ten kilometers from Slush. In summer or fall it dazzles you with its green light, unexpected after the mountain road. It's never calm, the sea in our part of the world. The rolling heavy mass of green water and the bird cries carrying through the din, the everlasting strong wind—this is the true sea, it's no lagoon. A sea like this could have a dinosaur come crawling calmly out of it.

The sea was not visible now. In the darkness the ice-shelf glowed white along the shore, but the line of it died out long before the horizon, and out there, in the pitch darkness, you could still hear the waves' dull roar.

A branch of the warm current comes in here, right to the port of Slush. Navigation continues here almost year round—admittedly, with the help of small ice-breakers.

By now we had already entered Slush and were rolling along its main—properly speaking, its only—street. The original hick town, not much to speak of. On one side there are three-story apartments; on the other, behind the low warehouses, there stretches a line of moorings, with lighted ships large and small lying at anchor. This street is forever packed with people. The crowd saunters and scurries back and forth on some mysterious business of its own. When you arrive here late at night, it seems this is some Liss or Zurbagan, or maybe even a Gel-Gyu. I had been here twice before, and it had seemed to me that something surprising and unexpected would happen to me here. But both times I had left here with the feeling that something had passed me by.

7. Victor Koltyga

In Slush the whole street seemed to be permeated with the smell of oranges. Here and there in the crowd citizens with impassive faces could be glimpsed peeling this sumptuous fruit, as Kichekian had called it. Obviously they couldn't hold out till they got home.

We fought our way slowly down the traffic-clogged street. The boys in our truck were dancing with impatience. Just what was going on with Yura, no one knew. I suspect that he'd never once tasted oranges at all. As for me, I was keeping a watchful eye on the passers-by to see if Lusya wasn't among them. Gera was watching too. So he and I were rivals, then. Like a couple of Spaniards; all we lacked were cloaks and swords.

There was a truck unloading near the nursery school. Brightly papered crates in which these very oranges lay side by side, one like the other, were being carried into the school. All the nurses were standing out on the porch in their smocks, arms folded, ceremonially following this procedure. The nursery school windows were dark: the children on the overnight schedule were peacefully pounding the pillow, never suspecting what awaited them tomorrow.

The street was brightly lighted as if it were a holiday. But then, it's always light in Slush, because the ships are docked along one side of the street; the work goes on and bright lights shine there around the clock.

"Eyes right, boys!" I shouted. "There she is!"

Over a warehouse roof we could see the superstructure and mast, and sticking out from around the corner was the bow of the perpetrator of this celebration, the modest steamship *Kildin.*

"Hooray!" shouted my friends. "Long live this ship!"

The sailors from the *South Wind* grinned ironically. We drove up to the food store at just exactly the right moment. Just exactly the moment when, with the help of the police, it was closing for the night. The crowd near the stored clamored, but not very violently. Obviously the majority had satisfied their citrus requirements, within reason.

Yura was simply awful to look at. He turned very white and fastened his paws on my shoulder.

"Relax, Yura. Don't make a cult out of food," I told him. I had heard Sergei Orlov talk that way—a witty fellow. "Oh come on," I comforted him, "all for some dumb little oranges. Now watermelons—they're something else! Have you ever eaten watermelon, Yura?"

"I've had watermelon," said a hulking kid, one of the sailors.

Actually, we were pretty down.

The doors to the cab opened, and Chudakov's and Yevdoshchuk's heads began bobbing around over the back of the truck on either side.

"Some ride, huh?" said Chudakov.

"Some ride," Yevdoshchuk summed up, adding a word or two of his own.

"Panic on shipboard?" I asked in surprise. "Stand to! Now hear this! Head that way"—I pointed—"to the restaurant-type eatery Lighthouse!"

"Victor, you're a genius!" shouted Chudakov.

"....................!" shouted Yevdoshchuk.

And they both darted into the cab.

The motor roared up.

I'd guessed it—the restaurant-type eatery Lighthouse was selling oranges to go. Around the long one-story building stretched a somewhat fluid line. Someone was spieling on an accordion, several girls were beating time with their overshoes on the trampled snow. Of course it wasn't Lusya. Lusya wouldn't up and start dancing in front of an eatery, she's not that kind. But maybe she was here somewhere?

The trading was going on some place behind the building, the saleswomen and scales were not visible, but as we drove up to the line a guy with two bags of oranges popped out from around the corner and trotted off toward the front entrance—to celebrate his purchase, I guess.

We leaped out of the truck and lengthened the line by another six or seven meters. Well, brothers, it was an absolute festival of song and dance!

"And our journey is far and long..." vocalized some guys with theodolites. The accordion spieled on. The girls danced, their stony faces blue from the moon and the cold. The racket was awful. Now and then the drivers ran out of the line to warm up their engines. Of course there were games of "fly" going on here and there. Some wise guys were playing soccer chasing three tin cans at once. The Nanay dogs were barking. The Nanay themselves, who really are wise people, were starting a campfire. A round-dance had already begun over there, around the campfire and around the pensive Nanay. Vroom-vroom, the intellectuals came inching up. Katya was off and dancing, and Kolya Kalchanov after her.

"Sergei, start your barrel organ grinding," I begged.

A transistor radio hung on Comrade Orlov's chest.

Some low-life was wandering along the line, his teeth gritting like a gate in the wind. From time to time he stopped, swaying in his tattered floor-length sheepskin, looked at us from under shaggy brows, and growled, "Russian princes, give a veteran a treat!"

Sergei turned on his music. First there was sputtering, crackling, the beep of Morse code (I love that music), then the Japanese mumbled something, and a strong masculine voice struck up a song, "Doo yoo" et cetera. Now he sang fast, now slow, now he stopped—and here the piano would spill forth, and then he'd smoothly moo again, "Doo you" et cetera.

"Frenk Sinatra," said Sergei, turning away and looking up at the moon.

Nearby, Katya and Kolya were dancing up a storm, you couldn't tell whether to the accordion or this Frenk the Senator. Something seemed to have happened between them.

"Somehow Katya's gotten carried away dancing with Kalchanov," Bazarevich whispered to me, "somehow I don't like it, Vitya. Somehow our Kichekian..."

"Quiet, Lenya," I told him. "Let them dance, no harm in that."

I'll go look for Lusya. I have a feeling she's here somewhere. Why shouldn't I be dancing too, with her, in the beautiful cold?

I was on the point of leaving, but just then a GAZ-69 drove up to the line, and several new orange-lovers got out to regale themselves.

"Who's last?" one of them asked.

"We're on the end," I said, "only keep in mind, friends, that someone else has saved a placed here behind us. Keep it in mind just in case. There may be one more cohort coming."

"Someone asked us to save a place, too," said a sailor, "the seiner *North Wind* is coming."

"Sure," said the newcomers, "but will there be enough merchandise?"

"That's the question of questions," I said. "But now where are you from?"

"Uleikon," they answered.

"Well, brothers," was all I said.

A visit from Uleikon—well I'll be! I know those parts, I've been up there. I bet right now it's snowing so hard there you can't poke your nose out! Every morning they shovel themselves out and dig trenches in the snow. We have snowstorms and everything else pretty often here too, but how can you even compare the Coast with Uleikon?

"We were here getting some new equipment," the guys said, "we look and there's oranges..."

Up there they drink this murk made from the stunted trees to keep from getting scurvy. It helps. Furthermore, they mess around with multiple-vitamin candies.

"Come on, friends," I told them, "come on, come on."

My buddies caught on, and they too pushed the guys ahead.

Around the corner of the building, right on the snow, lay some empty orange crates. Two old ladies, all wrapped up and wrapped again, were bossing things at the scales. One was weighing out and the other was taking the money. There were a few fatheads keeping order.

"My beauties!" I roared. "Will there be enough merchandise for everyone?"

Instead of answering, one of the saleswomen shouted, "Tell them in back not to stand there any longer!"

"Wait here, brothers," I said, and plunged into the crowd.

"Listen," I said to the line, when I was right up near the scales, "here are some men come from a long way away, from Uleikon..."

The line was tensely silent, swaying slightly. Clearly, once you got this close you had other things on your mind than songs and dances. They all averted their eyes when I looked at them, but nevertheless I looked at them with a withering gaze.

"Well and whaddaya mean by that?" said one weak-willed character who couldn't withstand my intent, withering gaze.

"From Uleikon, see? You know what that is?"

"You're not from any Uleikon! You're from Phosphate, I know you," shrilled Weak-Will.

"You jerk, I'll stand in line, don't worry. I'm not taking anything, see?" I pulled out my fountain pen, took the cap off it, and thrust the cap in his face. With these characters you always have to thrust some kind of material evidence in their faces, and then they calm down.

"Uleikonians, come here!" I called, waving.

A roar came up from the line. "Let them take some... So what... What the hell... Shut up, you... Let them take some..."

I walked off to the empty crates. There were labels on them: golden oranges lay against a background of black palm trees, to the side could be seen a white minaret, and in English was written, "Product of Morocco."

I scraped off a label like that with my knife, and stuck it in my pocket. There might or might not be enough oranges, but I would have a souvenir.

When the first Uleikonian made his way out of the crowd with bags in his arms, I went over to him and pulled from a bag a single orange.

"My honorarium, Signor." I bowed to the Uleikonian and looked at him attentively: did he mind very much?

"Take two." The Uleikonian smiled. "Really, we're so grateful to you..."

"Why Signor," I objected, "this is already overstepping the bounds."

I went to my buddies, took Yura aside and suggested that we go have a beer. Across the square from the Lighthouse Eatery there was a shed, which in Slush was proudly called The Bar. Yura agreed, and he and I started off. On the way, Yura kept worrying whether there'd be enough merchandise, probably not, most likely there wouldn't. And I kept fingering the small Uleikonian orange in my pocket.

"Looks like you never even tasted them before, kid."

"What do you mean! Sure I have. I remember..."

"Cut it out! I know your biography."

I held the orange out to him.

"Dig in! Dig in, I tell you, and don't move!"

From the way he touched it, I knew immediately that I had been right.

We were standing on a little rise, and below us was the whole of Slush Bay. The ice that had been ground up by the icebreakers glimmered faintly. Under the searchlights fog rose from the black water. An ice-patrol plane was flying very low over the sea; from here it looked like a bus. In the pitch dark there was a lightship winking, opening its red eye on the count of sixteen: 1, 2, 3, 4, 5, 6 (where's Lusya?), 8, 9, 10 (where is she?), 12, 13, 14, 15, 16!

"Dig in, dig in. I've already had some, the Uleikonians treated me."

The Bar was reminiscent of an old railroad car with its wheels off. Through the little window we could see the press of human flesh. Near the entrance a comparatively small but energetic crowd of stevedores was jockeying for places like kids playing "squeeze out the oil."

"Some doings you have in Slush!" I said to a brawny middle-aged guy.

"Not too bad yet today, there's a chance," he said.

"In Phosphate there's plenty of beer," said Yura, who exuded a fragrance of the sultry south.

"So that's why, you see!" The stevedore squinted slyly. "Because, friends, now it's Phosphate and then it's Slush, that's why."

"Sure."

"This is where the action is," the stevedore said with rightful pride.

"Let's go, Yura, we'd better have champagne, it's easier to get."

1, 2, 3 (where to find her?), 5, 6, 7 (now she'll appear), 9, 10, 11 (on the count of sixteen), 13, 14, 15... There she is!

It really was she. She was standing among some other girls, giving me sidelong looks. She had on a white kerchief and felt boots. Could she really walk in felt boots? 16! She was looking at me somehow uncertainly and perhaps even with fear, she'd never looked at me that way. Maybe she thought...

8. Ludmila Kravchenko

When I saw Vitya I thought, can it really be he? He was standing there so tall and narrow-waisted and blue-eyed, and smiling as he looked at me. He was very much like the man back in Krasnodar who had stood there with the plane-tree leaf in his teeth and twirled his finger at his forehead, thinking I was a madwoman. Could that have been Vitya? He's from Krasnodar, after all. No; he wasn't there at that time. At that time he was "jazzing around" (as he puts it) somewhere in Kolyma.

Perhaps it's an optical illusion, I thought as he walked toward me. Perhaps it's because he's approaching from above and that makes him seem taller? Perhaps it's because it's that kind of night? Perhaps I'm high on the oranges?

How he'll fold me in his arms, how he'll press me to him, everything else will suddenly disappear, how sultry it will be, and the shadows of the plane trees will sway on the ceiling.

He walked toward me, it was just a few steps, but in those seconds my whole future life with him flashed by me like a sudden squall.

Tick-tock, I'd hear the clock at night. Perhaps I'd weep, remembering something lost, something not really worth regretting, but why not weep a little if you're happy? Tick-tock, tick-tock, and suddenly in comes my son, huge and blue-eyed, with a plane-tree leaf in his mouth.

Plunging along knee-deep in the snow, Vitya came up to me.

"Well, how goes it, Comrade Kravchenko?"

"All right, thank you. We'll be finishing up the new school soon. And what about you, Victor?"

"Not a friggin' thing!"

"Aren't you ashamed, Victor? What kind of expression is that?"

"Ekskyooz mee, meess!"

"You've started to study English?"

"A little of everything." He laughed. "English and Japanese."

"Come come! How are you, really?"

"We're sitting in this lous... in this lovely ravine. We're drilling our third hole, and all for nothing. Give me your little hands. Wow—are they strong!"

"What are you, out of your mind? Take your hands off me!"

"And how's that work-study program?"

"All right, thank you. Do you like your specialty?"

"There's something else I like, something else, something..."

"Stop it! Stop it! Take that!"

"Those are some kind of hands! Some kind of hands... And how's the social work going?"

"All right, thank you. How undisciplined you are, Victor..."

"Then everything's fine? Oh yes, how are those dances? 'The maple's

228

green, the leaves are lacy, Lyana...'?"

"All right, thank you. I want to try some classical dances."

"The figure for the classics, sure enough. You, my girl, should have a Graeco-Roman tunic. You should run in your tunic through forest and field..."

"What are you doing! I'll get angry. People are looking at us."

" 'Through forest and field, through gardens, together they fly, like fragrance de-dah, la-de-dah...' You're angry, aren't you? Don't be angry. I'm serious. I love you. You're the only girl for me. When shall we stage the wedding?"

"What are you saying, Victor? What are you saying? Nina, Nina, wait for me, where are you off to?"

"And how are you doing in sports, Comrade Kravchenko? Surely you are engaged in sports? The all-round development of the Komsomol girl must include sports, she must jump farther than anyone, run faster than anyone..."

"This is my friend Nina. May I introduce you?"

"Delighted, Nina baby. Comrade Victor Alekseyevich Koltyga, driller, at your service. You're in A-1 shape like your friend, I hope? So how are the sports going, young ladies? One mustn't neglect this sphere of effort."

"I want to take up skiing."

"That's a good one. The Nordic Combined?"

"Yes, just think!"

"No way, Comrade Kravchenko. That's something that will not go right for you. Perhaps you should try hockey? You could make the hockey stick yourself. Or basketball? There's an idea—basketball! I'll take care of the tactical problems. A personal friend of Ray Meyer's from De Paul University and..."

He began telling us something about basketball, then soccer, then some kind of sports goggles, and something else besides. You might have thought he was a big sports expert. The last time we met he spent the whole evening telling me about Romania as if he'd lived there half his life, and the first time we met he kept saying dreadfully incomprehensible things about the cosmos. He's highly educated; it's a little odd that he's a driller.

We walked slowly across the square to the Lighthouse Eatery. Victor was waving his arms, Nina was looking at him beside herself with amazement, and suddenly I caught sight of Gera Kovalyov.

Gera was standing with two other sailors, and they were all three staring straight at me.

"Hello, Herman!"

"Hi."

"Have you been back on shore long?"

"Not long."

"But what's the matter? Are you sick?"

229

"I'm fine."

"I'd like you to meet Victor..."

"We've met."

"And this is Nina, my best friend. Nina, this is Herman Kovalyov, sailor and... may I tell her?"

"You may."

"... and poet."

"Nina, be sure you don't go home without me. Gera, I'll see you around."

Victor and I were left alone, and he fell silent, stopped talking about sports, began whistling softly, then lit a cigarette, and I think he even blushed.

"Victor, what was it you wanted to say to me?"

"I already said it."

I suddenly lost my head, lost my head, lost everything. Carry me away beyond the forests and mountains, beyond the blue lakes, to the high and far off kingdom. My knees were buckling, and I grabbed him by the shirtfront.

"Say it once more."

"Well then, once more."

"Now once more."

"If you like, once more."

"Vitya... Vitya.. Vitya..."

"Where can we hide?"

"Come here!"

"In there?"

I started to run, and he came tearing after me. We hid behind some sort of sheds, and of course he immediately tried to get his arms around me, but I moved away and then suddenly remembered about the oranges, took the biggest one out of my bag and held it out to him.

"We'll eat it together, all right?"

"Let's, together."

"Do you know how to peel them?"

"Yes," someone said suddenly nearby. "The symbolic eating of the fruit."

There stood Kolya Kalchanov looking at us, and right beside him a very pretty girl in slacks.

"How's our place in the line, Nikolai?" asked Victor.

"It's moving, Adam."

But I wasn't ashamed. I nestled up to Victor and said, "Nikolai, I was wrong about the beard. Wear it, please, in good health."

"Thank you, Eve," said Kalchanov with a bow.

I wasn't even offended by his knowing tone.

Yet she did have sorrowful eyes. Only, her sorrow was not mine. It had literally nothing to do with me.

I watched them approach: Victor was waving his arms, Lusya was giving him sorrowful glances, and this skinny little chick walking alongside was staring at him bug-eyed.

"That's her," I said, "the taller one."

"That one?" Borya stuck out his lower lip. "Big deal. A rank and file comrade."

"There's thousands like her," said Ivan. "In Vladik there's girls like her galore. You walk down the street—one girl, another, a third. It's fantastic."

My comrades snorted as they watched Lusya, but I could see what an impression she'd made on them.

"If you want we can cut in," Borya said to me quietly.

Sure we could cut in. That's what happens at a dance. You call him aside. "Excuse me, may I speak to you a moment? Listen, mate, you better cast off. How come? I don't like your haircut. Go on, shove off. Boys, he isn't getting the point." And his buddies come running and it begins. It's all foolishness. Nothing good ever comes of it. Besides, it's one guy's shame in spite of "sticking together" and "all for one..." And Victor Koltyga is an A-1 guy. Is it his fault that he grew more than I did, and he's a more respectable age, and he has a job on land? Sailors have never been lucky in love.

Lusya lifted her eyes, caught sight of me, and started. She came over and began talking foolishness as if she'd never even received those ten letters of mine with the poems. I answered in a detached way, forcing the words through my clenched teeth. Okay, I thought, the i's have been dotted, tomorrow we put to sea.

And she palmed her girl-friend off on me—the skinny little chick—so adroitly, and walked away side by side with Victor Koltyga.

"Is it true you're a poet?" asked the skinny chick.

"And how!" I said.

A poet, I'm a poet, so who needs a poet?

Lusya and Victor flitted behind the sheds.

Borya and Ivan motioned me toward the skinny chick and gave me the thumbs-up sign: She's a thumbs-up girl, don't clutch.

I took a look at her. She was struggling with the shivers—she was obviously cold in her high-style coat. It was one of those coats like a sack, narrower toward the hem, with a wide half-belt dangling low on the back. Her little face was thin and bluish, probably from the moon, probably we all had bluish faces just now, and she was biting her lips as if she were trying to keep from crying. I got feeling sorry for her and suddenly sensed I had something in common with her.

"You're recently from back west, I guess?" I asked.

231

"I arrived this fall," she murmured.

"And where are you from?"

"Leningrad."

She looked up at me, biting her lower lip, and I immediately realized what was the matter. I wasn't the same to her as I was to Lusya. To her I was a big rangy guy in a leather jacket, I was the same to her as Victor was to Lusya, I was a guy who'd been around, strong as hell, and she was searching for me, trembling all over for fear she wouldn't find me.

It occurred to me that all my poems, if I made some small changes in them, would do for her too, and that she would like them, that was for sure.

"What's your name? I didn't hear."

"Nina."

"And I'm Gera."

"I heard."

"Are you freezing?"

"N-no, I'm f-fine."

"Nina!"

"What, Gera?"

"I have a place in the orange line."

"I already got mine, would you like some?"

"No, I'd rather treat you. Nina, don't you disappear, okay?"

"Okay, I'll run along with the girls now."

"Okay. And then we'll go to the Lighthouse and dance."

"Dance?"

"They have a record player there."

"Really?"

"It's all set, then? You won't vanish?"

"No—oh, no!"

She ran off somewhere, and I followed her with my eyes and thought she would not vanish, that was for sure; I would change the reel of my dream-movies, maybe these dreams would be sweet ones.

I set out for the Lighthouse. When I was still some distance off, I noticed that the line had moved way ahead. Just then I bumped into the man correspondent. He was photographing some Nanay tribesmen sitting by their campfire, and the folk-dance circling around them. I waited until he'd finished and went over to him.

"Lots of impressions, correspondent?" I asked him.

"A carload."

"Well, what do you think?"

"You have it good here." He smiled, somehow shyly, and gave me the thumbs-up sign.

"Good?" I asked in surprise. "What's good about it? Oh—the romance, right?"

"Well, maybe it's not good, but it's... neat. And romance isn't the right word. I'm coming again this summer. Will you take me to sea with you?"

I laughed.

"What is it?" he asked in surprise.

"You're not a writer, are you?"

He frowned. "I'm a minor writer for now, old man."

"You've done a little writing?"

"A little. Not much at all," he laughed. "I expect you've written more than I have, Gera, in spite of your youth."

"And do you know any poets?"

"Some."

"How about Yevtushenko?" I asked, for laughs.

"I know Yevtushenko."

Quit putting me on, I wanted to tell him. Everyone from back west "knows Yevtushenko"—it's a laugh.

Just then I spotted our Sakunenko. He was with the same woman, she wouldn't let him go, kept on questioning him.

"What a dame!" I sighed.

"Yes," said the correspondent gloomily, "she's such a ..."

"Vasilyich!" I shouted to the captain. "What's the word on the cruise?"

He stopped without understanding, and at first he didn't notice me.

"Tell the boys not to worry!" he shouted. "We don't leave till the day after tomorrow."

"Where to?"

"After saury."

"Not bad," I said to the correspondent. "Saury again."

"To Shikotan again?" he asked.

Just then we heard shouting and saw that a scuffle had started in the line.

"*South Wind* over here!" It was Borya's voice, and I broke into a run, pulling off my gloves.

10. Nikolai Kalchanov

Dancing in the land of Orangiya, that must be like dancing in the moonlight, hey my little accordion, saints above, the hopak or the twist—what's the difference, derring-do dances on the Orange Plateau, at the foot of the Orange Mountains, at the ends of the Orange Planet itself, while little satellite-oranges whistle over our thick heads.

If only it were yesterday! How gay and natural this would have been! Good God! Kolya Kalchanov, bearded devil, paired with Katya Kichekian, nee Pirogova, husband's friend with friend's wife, while still another old friend plays a solo on a transistor radio. Ah, what gaiety!

No, no, there wasn't a hint of hysterics. Everything was just fine, it's just that it would have been better if it had been the day before.

Suddenly the dancing stopped. Katya had caught sight of Chudakov.

"Chudakov! Chudakov!" she cried.

He came over and shook hands with her.

"Well, how is it going?" asked Katya.

"Nothing doing," grumbled Chudakov, "we're finishing up our third..."

"Finishing up already?" breathed Katya, and she suddenly glanced back at Sergei and me, took Chudakov's arm, and led him a few steps to one side.

She looked little, next to the tall ungainly Chudakov; there was a campfire burning right behind them, it lighted them up very beautifully. She was gesturing and seriously nodding her head, apparently quizzing him all about her Arik, how he was eating, how he was sleeping, and so on.

My friendship with Arik, with Airapet, was like this: we felt no particular need for one another, but when we did happen to meet, we didn't want to part.

And there was one time—in summer, at night, when all sound had ceased but there was still every kind of filthy smell rising from the asphalt and the doorways, and sticky puddles from the soft-drink machines squelched underfoot, and a forgotten neon sign hung in the bright sky—when I got started talking about my personal feelings, and Arik guessed all, understood all, and was somehow melancholy in a very amicable way. And all my friends were in solid with him, and I with his friends.

Where and when he found Katya I do not know. The first I saw of her was on board the plane. Airapet had called me the day before departure and suggested, "Why don't we fly out together, the three of us?" "The three of us?" I asked. "Yes, three, my old lady's coming with me." "Your old lady?" "Why yes, my wife." "You've sneaked off and got married, eh?" "The wedding will be out there. It's not official yet."

And the three of us made the 13,000 kilometer flight, in three different types of planes: Leningrad-Moscow on a TU-104, Moscow-Khabarovsk on a TU-114, Khabarovsk-Phosphate on an IL-14. They taught me to play canasta and I got so good at it that over Sverdlovsk I started breaking the bank, I was getting the cards, and I was quite fascinated and even quit winking at the stewardesses and was not surprised at Katya's glances but just kept winning and winning and winning.

Over Chita, Airapet went back to the tail of the plane, we put aside the cards, and I said to Katya, "You're some girl!"

"What do you mean?" she said in surprise.

"First class!" I told her. "A great rarity."

And I said something more along the same lines, just to make conversation till Airapet came back from the tail. She laughed; I had pleased her.

234

Actually, this whole thing had begun later. Everything that ended today.

Sergei stood leaning against the wall of the eatery, his hands thrust in his pockets; the Reindeer cigarette dangling from his mouth had gone out, he was looking at Katya from under his brows with tragic gloom. Of course, this was a man. Everything about him said, "I'm a man, things are going hard for me but I'm not going to let a sound escape me, that's the way we are, we men." It was only too bad the transistor was playing something inappropriate at the time, some affected woman was squealing, "Allo! Ah-hah! Oh-ho! No-no!" Funny he hadn't picked himself out some suitable music. Right now what would have suited him was "Sixteen Tons" or something of the sort, something manly.

I walked over and began twisting the tuning dial.

"That better?" I asked, looking him full in the face.

"How spiteful and disagreeable can you get!" I thought, about myself. "Maybe Sergei really is unhappy."

"If you want we can have a talk," he said, without moving or looking at me. "Let's talk while she's gone."

"We already had a talk," I said, "it's all clear..."

"I love her," he murmured, turning his face away sharply.

My heart lifted. I saw it all: sure Sergei was suffering, but how he was enjoying his suffering, how smoothly things were going, without a hitch.

"That's no surprise," I comforted him. "Half of Phosphate loves her, and a third of the whole seaboard, and even in Uleikon I know a bunch of guys who start to drool as soon as you mention her."

"You too?" he asked quietly.

"Why of course!" I exclaimed joyfully.

Just like that. No matter—it got by. We were sliding on the verge of the fake and the cornball, but for the time being...

"You have to understand," said Sergei, turning to me and laying his leather-gloved hands on my shoulders, "you have to understand, Kolya, this is serious for me. Too serious to joke about."

Dear me, what a pity—this was something out of the south. Two childhood friends from one courtyard, and one of them such a strongman, and this southern belle has to go and take his fancy.

But meanwhile I was practically choking with anger. You, I wanted to shout in his face, you're a popsicle on a stick! For you it's serious, but for half of Phosphate, for a third of the whole seacoast, for a bunch of guys from Uleikon it's *not* serious, eh? And even less so for me—*you* know all my college-kid tricks, I'm an open book to you, of course all *I* want is to dishonor the wives of my friends, you're not to be trifled with, only let you do this, what about *me*, *I* don't give a damn about Katya, you do give a damn, now for you it's serious...

235

"Yes, I understand," I said. "It's hard for you, of course."

"That's why I spoke to you like that... back there, old man... You..."

"Well now, what of it, I understand... it's hard for you..."

"But she..."

"But she loves only her husband," I said, just a shade more hastily than I should have.

"I don't know whether she loves him, but she just... *you* know..."

"I know." I lowered my eyes. "It's hard for you, Sergei."

At that he held a pack of cigarettes out to me, clicked his splendid Zippo lighter; its flame illumined our sad faces, the faces of two southern lads from one courtyard, and we lit our cigarettes very theatrically at a most appropriate moment.

"And what do people do in a situation like this, Kolya?" asked Sergei. "Take to drink, perhaps?"

"Either take to drink or bury themselves in work. The latter is generally thought to be of greater benefit."

At that he switched off his radio and looked me right in the eye. Apparently it had gotten through to him that we were boys who were not from one courtyard and he was not the public favorite, that he would get no sympathy from me and all this "manly" conversation was a foolish skit, that I...

I didn't look away and didn't grin, realizing that we would begin talking on different terms now.

When the music ceased—the music that forever accompanied him, his contant absurd background, syncopations or the roar of a motor—in that second of silence we both seemed to realize that our "friendship" had fallen apart, that Katya wasn't the point here at all, Katya wasn't the only point, or maybe she was, maybe only she. Into this zone of silence came the sound of someone fingering an accordion, laughter and the tramp of feet, Katya's light voice and the crackling of the campfire.

"Clear the way, here comes the dung!" someone exclaimed, and a group of preoccupied men came walking quietly past in a cloud of alcohol fumes.

Kolya Markov followed, playing the antic.

"The bichi have come to call from Petrovo Port," he told me. "This is going to be a circus."

The bichi halted at the scales and began to observe the sale. They were self-controlled, slowly smoking their little snipes and spitting in the snow.

The line kept a nervous eye on them. I was keeping an eye out too, and had forgotten about Sergei.

"Sergei Yuryevich!" someone called to him.

A few steps away from us stood a middle-aged man, smiling affably, his hands behind his back. He was dressed like an ordinary Moscow office worker and therefore, in this crowd, looked extraordinary. The harshness vanished from Sergei's face. He waved to the man and went striding toward him, while Katya came up to me.

"How are things out there with Airapet?" I asked her bravely.

"Several men from their party drove in, but Arik stayed out there," said Katya sadly, looking away. "Chudakov says Arik isn't giving up hope."

"Oh?"

"They're going along the ravine from south to north. They've drilled two wells already, and both times they only got sulfur water."

"And now?"

"They're drilling a third," she sighed. "The trails out there are heavy going."

"But still it's not far."

"No, it's not far," she sighed again.

"He can come back sometimes."

"Of course he comes back sometimes. Remember, he did come for three days, not so long ago."

"When?" I asked. "For some reason I don't remember."

"How can you not remember?" she murmured. "He came a month and a half ago. You remember it perfectly well! You do! You do!" she almost shouted.

I worked my way into her mitten and squeezed her cold thin fingers. Of course, I remembered it all. How could I not remember—he went around as if he were drunk the whole three days, though he'd had almost nothing to drink. And she went around as if she were hung over. But then, she was drinking. There were gatherings in his honor at Sergei's, probably he and Edik Tanaka were the only ones who didn't notice the falseness of them.

"Your fingers, little fingers..." I whispered.

"Five cold sausages," she laughed, losing her head and putting her face close to mine. We have only to touch each other and we lose our heads, nothing matters to us any more. This was a dangerous proximity, the proximity of two critical masses. What were we to do?

A sound like a cannon shot shook the air. A second later another shock reached us. It was a flight of airplanes crossing the sound barrier enormously high above us, above the orange-lovers.

We raised our heads, but the planes were out of sight. Preserving its slightly odd calm, confident in its primitiveness and antiquity, the night sky stood over us, decoratively lighted up by the moon.

My head began to spin, and if it hadn't been for Katya's hand I might have fallen.

When I think about jet planes, how they streak across the sky like balls of fire right under old Uncle Cosmos's beard, the earth begins to rock beneath my feet and I feel with special keenness that I dwell on a small planet. It used to be that even though people knew the earth was a sphere, knew it revolved—just think!—around the sun, still they had the feeling they dwelt in boundless expanses of land and water, forests and steppes; and the sky, azure, dark blue, and cloudy, stood over them with warranted calm and silence. But really, no more of this irony—you'll find guys on this earth who are obsessed enough to blow it all to hell, for sport. But really, why complicate matters—in just a few months, in the ocean on whose shores we stand, in warm tropical waters, the big brains will give a command and the sporting lads will accept it, and they'll commence some routine exercises with toys of the category "Earth vs. Death."

And we are waiting in line for oranges. Yes, we're waiting in line for oranges! Yes, damn you, for oranges! You, cretin-brains, and you, wise-guy sports: I, Kolya Kalchanov, want to eat some oranges, and Katya's cold fingers are in my hand! Yes, I build houses! Yes, I dream of building my own city! Screw you! Here we all are before you, we're building houses, and catching fish, and drilling oil wells, and we're standing in line for oranges.

I have a friend, he's a scientist, an astronomer. He has jaws like a bull-dog, and short hair combed down over his forehead. The astrologer's pointed hat would hardly suit him. Once I went to see him on the Pulkov Heights. In the evening we sat in the tower of the main refractor. The sky was cloudy, so my pal was loafing. It struck me that on the whole they do not have a tough job, these astronomers. So here we were, sitting by the main refractor, which resembled a Jules Verne cannon, and Yurka was quietly whistling "The Black Cat" and quietly telling me how biological life like ours here on earth is a phenomenon alien to the universe, to matter. And actually, old buddy, if you follow me, this is all extremely shaky, because from the point of view of modern science a coincidence of favorable conditions such as we have here on Earth, if you follow me, is improbable—a transitory exception to the rules. Well, of course, all this is in universe-wide quantities, for us it's history but there may be thousands of histories, a million civilizations; actually, everything is normal.

"Have you known about this long?" I asked him.

"Not too long, but quite a while—and I don't know, I infer."

"That's why you're so calm?"

"Yes, that's it."

My God, of course I had known our Earth was "a grain of sand in the unbounded expanses of the universe," and the campaigns of Alexander of Macedon, viewed in this light, had somewhat amused me, but the recognition that we were an altogether "improbable" phenomenon left me staggered for some time, and it still staggers me when I think about it. So everything is a wonder of wonders? Innumerable exceptions to the rules, a game of illogic? For example, the marvel of an orange. Accidental interdigitations of impro-bable circumstances—and what grows on the tree is an orange, not a pine-apple-grenade. And man? Think about it, wise guys from the tropic islands. You're the scientists, you know all this better than I do, well, so think about it.

"Katya, you're a marvel!" I told her.

"And you're a marvel-monster!" she laughed.

"I'm serious. You're an exception to the rules."

"I've heard that before." She smiled with relief, shifting into the gay and easy mode we used to use.

"You're the accidental interdigitation of improbable circumstances," I pronounced, a quaver in my voice.

"Quit it, Kolya! You're an interdigitation too."

"Of course. Me too."

"Oh-ho! You've got too high an opinion of yourself."

"Your fingers, little fingers..." I murmured, "improbable little fingers, my darling... I want to kiss you."

"You seem... utterly... you're talking gibberish," she protested weakly. "Kolya, this is indecent, look how many people there are around."

My God, here are two chance occurrences, Katya and I, and chance has brought us together, and by chance we come toward each other like an apple to an apple tree, like dry land to water, like husband to wife, but—here we can't even kiss each other within sight of other people; and this is apparently some other law operating here, no less amazing than the law of chance.

Someone pulled me by the shoulder.

"One moment, Kalchanov," said a stupendous-looking he-man with no hat and no scarf. "Cool it, Kalchanov," he pronounced, looking away and massaging his forearms, "quit driving wedges here, see?"

Now I remembered him—it was Lenya Bazarevich, a driver from Airapet's party.

"I see, Lenya," I told him. "Just don't run me over, Lenya."

I saw that Sergei Orlov was approaching. Two strongmen like that against the one of me—that was too much. I could imagine how I'd look if the two of them got at me!

"Go ahead and laugh, but I'm telling you," warned Lenya, and he walked off.

Screwballs—possibly you're good guys, each of you has his code of honor, but if I can only get control over myself, over my own code, then you can do your stuff, strongmen, you don't scare me.

Sergei walked up.

"How about that!" he said. "My friend there is the director of the Food Trade Organization."

"Now that's clout," said Katya. "Then why don't you get us a nice table in the Lighthouse. I hear they even have cocktails there."

"Right," I said, "I had a good time there once. A Riddle cocktail, the coastal sailor's dream."

"A table—nonsense," said Sergei. "He's fixing us up with some oranges. Let's go." He reached for Katya's hand. "No more standing in line for you."

Katya looked at me indecisively.

"Go ahead, folks," I said, "go on, go on."

"You're not coming?" asked Katya, and she freed herself from Sergei's hand.

Sergei was looking darts at me, but he restrained himself. "You have to understand," he said to me, "it's just that it's awkward for us to be standing here. Lots of our workmen are here."

"Uh-huh," I nodded, "the supervisor's authority, the principle of one-man management, the leadership decides all."

Katya laughed.

"But have you no thought for her?" asked Sergei.

"No, I don't give a damn about her."

Katya laughed again. "Go on, Sergei, and I'll settle up here with this crumb."

"They're using four-letter words here," said Sergei in some perplexity.

Katya let out a shout of laughter.

"Never mind," I said, "she and I are pretty good with four-letter words ourselves."

He left anyway. He seemed to have a strong need to leave. I even felt sorry for him, he wanted to leave so badly.

"He's a funny one, isn't he?" said Katya, following Sergei with her eyes.

"He's in love with you."

"Lord, as if I didn't know."

"You know about all of them?"

"All of them."

"It's not easy for you."

"Of course it's not easy."

"And your shoes? You forgot them the night the Vladivostok variety show was playing at the club?"

"Ah—you remembered! Now that was the night you got a passion for 'genre songs'..."

"But sometimes I have to..."

"My word, what idiocy. Of course you have to. It's none of my business!"

"Katya!"

"We were dancing at Sergei's. It was all so romantic and modern—lighting and all. Later on I got into my clod-hoppers and forgot my shoes. He's not so fresh as you."

"I'm fresh, eh?"

"Of course you are. Ask Vladivostok, they'll tell you what you are."

"But he's sincere, is he? You confided all your sorrows to him, didn't you? Such a kind, noble strongman."

"Kolya! But how can I go on?"

"Let's take a walk."

We stepped out of the line and climbed up on a knoll. From here we could see the whole Bay of Slush and the town itself, which was strangely like Gagra. It stretched in a narrow shining line at the foot of the sopki. An ice-covered city billowing smoke, a Gagra come to its senses.

"Well I never!" exclaimed Katya. "Really, it's like Gagra, it even has the railroad going through just the same way."

"Only it's a narrow-gauge line here."

"Yes, it's a narrow-gauge line here."

In the pitch dark far out to sea there was a lightship winking; it lit up on the count of 16.

"If we'd only met in Gagra two years ago."

"What would you have done then, Kolya?"

"You and I would have been..."

"Okay, shut up," she said crossly.

We walked slowly, arm in arm. 1, 2, 3, enough of your snickering, 5, 6, 7, she's all knotted up with fear, 9, 10, 11, I can't talk about this, 13, I have to, it's not up to her to talk about it, 15, no I can't, not right now...

We went behind some sort of sheds, and she nestled up against me.

"Do you want me to say it myself?" she asked bleakly.

"No."

"What do you want?"

For the first time I moved away from her myself. She nodded understandingly, pulled out a cigarette and began to crumple it in her hands. I gave her a light.

A girl and a guy came running behind the shed, breathing hard. They immediately flung themselves on each other and began to kiss. They didn't notice us, they weren't noticing anything in the world. I put my arm around Katya's shoulder. She smiled immoderately, looking at the kissing couple. Now I recognized them—it was Vitya Koltyga and the girl from Cinderblocks, the one that had criticized me at the meeting.

We exchanged some pleasantries with them, and I took Katya away from there. We came out of the trees and started slowly toward the Lighthouse, toward the orange-line. It was noisy over there, the line had bunched up, a scuffle seemed to have started, but I still had a groundless glimmer of hope that something would come our way.

"I didn't mean anything by that," said Katya, looking down at her feet. "You do understand?"

"Of course."

"Well, that's that."

I'm in a jam, I thought. I didn't use to offend the girls, and they didn't take offense at me. Everything was simple and light, a bit of romance, a bit of drivel, pleasant memories! I'm in a jam. What to do? They didn't teach me about this. "Love knows no barrier," we read in books. That's foolish-

241

ness; often enough thousands of barriers rise up before love, that too is written in the books. But Katya—she's not love, she's a part of myself, she's my youth, the water of my life.

The crowd had reached a stage of confused motion. Arms were flailing. It seemed someone had already gotten it on the chin. Several guys from our Trust ran past, unbuttoning their sheepskins as they went.

"What's up, men?" I shouted after them.

"The bichi jumped the line!"

"Forward, Kalchanov!" laughed Katya. "Forward, to the attack! The trumpet calls! You're already trembling like a warhorse."

"Know what they called me in school?" I said to her. "Punch Hard-Blow."

"Really?" said Katya, surprised. "Forward, then! Kolya, don't you dare! Kolya, where are you going?!"

But I was off and running.

Boy, am I going to catch it now, I thought. Boy, is the bat ever going to bounce off me now! I'm going to get what's coming to me for all of today's hocus pocus. I plunged into the crowd. They weren't fighting yet. They were still just pushing. There was still a stern conversation going on.

"Do you have a social conscience or not?"

"And have you counted my dough?"

"Why are you talking to him, Lenya! Why try and talk straight to him? Knock his block off!"

"Working stiffs stand in line, but hand the bichi their orange on a platter!"

"But these aren't common bichi, they're royal bichi!"

"Speculators!"

"I'll eat you without salt, you dirty dog, and I won't spit out the buttons!"

"Lenya, why talk to 'im!"

"Leggo of me, I just got off the contagious ward!"

"Back, you beggars!"

"But ain't ya sorry for us? Sorry?"

"Sorry my..."

"I'm gonna eat you without salt, see?"

"Leggo of me, I'm contagious!"

A shaggy tattered bich suddenly gritted his teeth and let out a yelping shout, a squeal: "All non-Russian ethnics out of the line!"

For a second there was silence, then several guys descended on Shaggy.

"Crush the Fascist!" they shouted.

"Come on, boys, let's get them out of here!" commanded Vitya Koltyga.

Of course he was already here and taking over—farewell love in early May!

Fists whistled, voices were stilled, the battling men could only grunt, cry out, get trampled in the snow. I was shoved, tossed, squeezed, several times I got it on the chin accidentally and I'd hear a voice, "Sorry, thought you were someone else." No one could tell whom to hit, the bichi weren't wearing any special uniform. People came running from all sides to join the frenzied heap.

"Do like me!" shouted a pilot to his friends, and they forced their way into the thick of the bodies, cutting the fighting crowd off from the scales, where the indifferent saleswomen stood by, hopping from one foot to the other and blowing on their fingers. I got in behind the pilots and finally received a blow squarely on the jaw.

The tall bich who'd punched me was already flailing at someone else. I noticed Tall's distracted face, he seemed to be operating in a semi-trance. With two blows I brought him down in the snow.

The crowd reeled back and I was left standing over the body stirring about in the snow.

"Give me a hand, Beard!" said Tall peaceably.

I helped him up and took my boxing stance again.

"You hit hard," said Tall.

I felt my jaw. "You're not bad either."

"Want to go have some champagne?"

"Champagne, eh?" I echoed. "That's an idea."

11. Root

Actually, no one on our side was truly interested in oranges, but Vovik had promised to put us each down for a half-liter for the common cause. He needed the oranges for some kind of a flim-flam.

First he by-passed the head of the line to hand some money to a sidekick, who had already waited his turn, and the guy got him four kilos. That's how they were giving out the produce, four kilos apiece. Then Petya went up to the sidekick and he got four kilos too. The line began to push. Vovik's sidekick snarled back at the line and held back the crush. When Ivan-and-a-Half sidled over to the sidekick, the line broke up and we were surrounded. The straight-talk began. Vovik started making like an epileptic. He's such a wired-up guy, this Vovik. It's a losing proposition when you're surrounded, outnumbered ten to one, and the straight-talk begins. It's perfectly clear things are going to blow here, I bet some nice-guy's already gone for the police, and here he has to play circus.

I should have high-tailed it out of there, but I couldn't run out on my own buddies, and they were already flinging themselves at people, Vovik had set them off with his hysterics, and, well, we were just about to have a St. Bartholomew's Day Massacre.

So, I'll have to meet my Dad with a fine shiner on my map. I'll say that I caught myself on a coaming. I'll tell a bunch of lies. But what if I get sent up for fifteen days?

Well I never! This is always the way. Soon as you start making plans for self-improvement, you're instantly plunged into a mess. Shake and squeeze all you please... And with Lusya here, too. I saw her with that guy, with Vitya Koltyga.

I look and Vovik's got someone by the shirtfront, and Ivan-and-a-Half is starting to make like he's contagious. I feel this is it, I'm getting wired up myself. I feel I'm going up to someone. I feel I've slugged someone. I feel someone else's laid a bouncer on me. I feel I'm fighting—scapegrace—and I'm dishing it out right and left. Fear takes hold of me like some other man has gotten inside my skin.

Then I saw stars and landed hard in the snow. Someone had decked me with a one-two punch. Then I came to and all the meanness in me passed off like a flash, vanished in nothing flat.

The guy that'd downed me was even on the puny side, to look at him, but a sport, had a beard like he had to be a big-city geologist. Those guys grow a beard just as soon as they hit our part of the world. He'd knocked me off my pins just in time.

Our gang was already lamming it in all directions like rabbits. Vovik had run away, and Petya, and Ivan-and-a-Half, and the others.

"Let's go have some champagne," I suggested to the Beard.

A man after my own heart, he agreed right away, a fun-loving guy.

"We're off to the Lighthouse, my treat, " I told him.

I didn't have any money, of course, but I decided to sweet-talk Esther Naumovna. Even if she wrote it down on my account, I just had to treat this guy in honor of his good and timely blow.

"Let's go, old man," he laughed.

"Now what year were you born?" I asked him.

" 'Thirty-eight."

"Just a kid, honest to God! I really am an old man. I bet you've put high-school behind you?" I asked him.

"College," he answers. "I'm in construction. An engineer."

Just then a classy girl comes up to us—such a beauty, brothers, a real far-out chick, right out of a picture.

"Katya," says my pal, "meet my sparring partner. Come and have some champagne with us."

"But we won't miss out on our turn, Kolya?" says the girl and offers me her mittened hand.

And I—fool—take off my glove.

"Root," I say, "... dammit, Valya's my name... Valentin Kostyukovsky."

Off we go, the three of us, and this Katya doll takes us both by the arm, understand? No, I'll talk Esther Naumovna into some chocolate candy too.

"Your Kolya lands a mean punch," I say to Katya. "Accurate and hard."

"That's my boy," she laughs.

But I glance at Kolya and he's looking dark. Why, he's so lucky, the snake, and he still looks gloomy. In his place I'd have forgotten what gloom was. Still a kid, after all, and college already behind him, a specialty that's in demand, I bet he has his own Living Space, and a girl like that, God a-mighty.

I noticed Petya in the line. He was trying to get a place for himself and they were driving him away as a disturber of the peace.

"But I honestly want some!" cried Petya. "In turn. Have you guys got any conscience, or didja eat it up? Valya, have they got any conscience?"

"Quit making a spectacle of yourself," I whispered to him.

But Katya suddenly stopped.

"It's true, comrades," she said. "What's the matter with you, he's confessed his mistakes, after all. He wants some oranges too, after all."

"I never had these things in my life," Petya whined. "Have you got any conscience or what didja have for a mother?"

"Okay," they told him, "get in line, there won't be enough anyway."

"But there's hope," Petya said cheerfully.

It was cozy in the Lighthouse, there were lots of people. The record player was putting out light music. It was all as if there was no one fighting outside, as if there wasn't any line there. I reached an agreement with Esther Naumovna right off the bat.

I love champagne, brothers. There's sort of a light spinning of the head that you get from it, and happy little thoughts begin to play in your noggin. I could spend a lifetime under the influence of champagne, but hard liquor, my friends, gives you nothing but grief in the end.

"That's a true observation," said Kolya. "Have you been on the bich long?"

He asked me so nicely, somehow, that right away I wanted to tell him my life story. I had the impression he'd have listened to me. Only I wasn't about to tell him; why spoil people's mood?

Suddenly I saw the captain of the *South Wind,* that old devil Volod-ya Sakunenko. He was standing at the buffet counter buying candy for some dame.

"Hullo, Captain," I say to him.

"Ah, Root," he says, surprised.

"Please, from now on," I say, "it's not Root but Valya Kostyukovsky, see?"

"I see," and he motions the dame over to me. "Here, let me intro-duce an interesting specimen."

"From now on, please," says I, "none of your specimens, see? Seaman Kostyukovsky, and that's that."

And I hold out to Sakunenko and the lady a box of Herzegovina Floras, from a stale batch, sure, they smoke a little moldy, but still—it's a brand name. Whenever I'm in the money, or when I drop in on Esther Naumovna at the old Lighthouse, I get myself some Herzegovina Floras first thing and smoke like a bigshot. I have a real weakness for these cigarettes.

"Listen, Captain," I say to Sakunenko. "When are you going to sea, and where to?"

"After saury again," says the Captain, and he coughs, himself, from the Herzegovina, and gives me a penetrating glance through the smoke. "To Shikotan, in a couple days."

"Oh, Volodya, why don't you want to take me," says the dame, "really, why? After all, it could be done properly, through channels."

"Wait a minute, lady," says I. "What about it, Sakunenko, do you have your full complement now?"

"What about it?" says he, zero attention to the dame.

"What about it, Sakunenko," I ask, "have you got something against me?"

"And what do you think, Valya?" Sakunenko asks in a decent way.

"Sure," I say. "You've got reason."

He looks at me and says nothing, and his dame has piped down, I don't know what there is between them. And suddenly I say to him: "Vasilyich!"

That's what they call him on the *South Wind*, because of his age. "Comrade Captain" is awkward, he's too young for Vladimir Vasilyevich, can't call him Volodya because of his rank, but Vasilyich, now—that's just right between friends and respectful-like, too.

"Of course, Vasilyich," I say, "you understand the champagne is making me lightheaded right now, but could you maybe enter me in the Crew List? I just have to go to sea now."

"Let's go have a talk," frowns Sakunenko.

12. Herman Kovalyov

The bichi were driven off so fast I didn't even get in any good blows. The line re-formed. The accordion began to play again. The girls with the indifferent faces broke into a dance again, and the Nanay sat down by their campfire. On the snow lay a torn paper bag. A few oranges rolled out of it. The bag might have fallen from the heavens, might have been thrown from an airplane, might have been a gift of fate. Great—that would be the theme of my new poem.

I suddenly felt gay and happy, as if I hadn't just suffered a disaster in

246

love. It suddenly seemed to me that this whole evening, this whole thing with the oranges, was an amateur performance at the Seamen's Culture Club and I was playing something more than a bit part in it, and everyone in the place was so kind, we were all buddies, and the sets were quite well done, only a little implausible, like in children's books: the moon, and the silvery snow, and the sopki, and little houses in the snowdrifts; but my entrance was soon, and my partner would soon come running in a stylish little coat and felt boots.

And I had two whole days ahead of me, we weren't putting to sea till day after tomorrow.

I picked up the oranges and carried them over to the scales.

"You nut," said my friends, "gobble them yourself. They're your trophy."

"You nut," said the saleswoman, "them's been paid for."

"What!" said I, "This bag fell from the heavens."

"All the more," said they.

At that I began treating them all, everyone who wanted could take an orange from my arms, things cast down from the heavens are usually not for one but for all. I was Santa Claus, and suddenly I caught sight of Nina, she was fighting her way toward me.

"Gera, are we going dancing?" she asked. The frosty fragrance of oranges wafted from her, and her lips were crusted with frozen droplets of orange juice.

"We'll go right away!" I shouted. "Right away, our turn is coming."

Our turn came soon and we all, the whole *South Wind,* crowded into the Lighthouse. I was holding Nina's arm, with my other arm I pressed the paper bags to my body.

"I can do any dance you like," Nina murmured. "You'll see, anything you like. The lipsi, and the waltz-gavotte, and even," she whispered in my ear, "rock'n'roll."

"They'd give it to you good for rock'n'roll," I said, "and anyway I can't do anything but the tango."

"The tango is my favorite dance."

I looked at her. Of course; all my favorites will be your favorites now, that's clear, and as it should be.

We moved three tables together and the whole crew of us settled down. As always, the chief took over.

"Esther Naumovna," he joked, "the *South Wind* awaits you!"

And the oranges already lay in beauty on the table, a small pile before each of us. Later we mingled them together in one huge pile, shining with inner fire.

The waitress came over and, following the chief's finger, began to make apologies: "We're out of that. And that too, Petrovich. It's an old menu. Out of that too, sailors."

"Then we'll each have two of the main course, and so on and so forth!" the chief shouted cheerfully.

"That I can get you," she said, brightening.

Our radioman, Zhenya, got up from the table and began fussing about the lighting. He had decided to record the occasion in a photograph.

When he aimed his camera, I laid my arm on the back of Nina's chair. I thought she hadn't noticed, but she turned up her sharp little nose—she'd noticed. Everyone seemed to notice. The chief winked at the engineer. But Borya and Ivan pretended not to notice. Lusya Kravchenko, who was walking by at the moment, noticed; she smiled, not at me and not at Nina, just smiled. I suddenly felt ashamed as hell, I broke out in a real sweat all over. "The zephyr barely stirs the leaves"—dammit to hell. Why the hell did I write those poems, much less put them in the mail? When would I give up this pastime, when would I get to be a real man?

I put my arm right on Nina's shoulder, even gave her shoulder a squeeze. What a thin little shoulder!

As soon as the shutter clicked, Nina started up.

"Gera, you're so..." she whispered.

"So... what?" I grinned cynically.

"So undisciplined."

"It's the kind of job I have," I answered stupidly, and blushed again.

The waitress came toward us. She was lugging an enormous tray crammed with bottles and plates. They made such a mountain that you could hardly see her head over it, and her bare arms swelled with biceps that any man would be thankful for. Her hands were soft and fluttery, but her arms swelled with biceps.

The chief poured her a wineglass full of cognac, she nodded gratefully, hid the glass under her apron, went off behind a curtain. I saw her knock back the glassful like a man. Some waitress! Such a tame old biddy to look at her, but she sure can soak it up. Wish I could do that!

I get high quickly. I don't know how to drink; what can you do.

Ivan and Borya were snacking away and glancing severely at Nina. Nina sensed their glances and ate very delicately.

"You write him letters, now," Ivan said to her. "You know how he is. Will you write?"

Nina looked at him, evidently choking back tears. She nodded.

"You'd do better sending radiograms," advised Borya. "It's awfully nice to get a radiogram at sea. Will you?"

"I will, I will," she said crossly.

To her, of course, it was strange that the guys were butting in on our intimate relations. The music began to play. The needle sputtered, scratched, got stuck on the record.

"This is a tango," Nina said into her plate.

"Let's go!" I squeezed her elbow.

I was on top of everything now. I sure did seem to know how to tango now.

We danced—I don't know how well, maybe not badly, maybe wonderfully, maybe better than anyone else. A husky feminine voice sang:

> Speak to me of love,
> Over and over, dear,
> I'm always ready to hear,
> Tum-dum-di-dah...

This refrain was repeated several times, but I couldn't make out the last line at all.

> Speak to me of love,
> Over and over, dear,
> I'm always ready to hear,
> Tum-dum-di-dah...

It irritated me. The words kept being repeated, and the last line kept disappearing in the sputtering and rasping of the worn-out record.

"What's she singing there? I can't make it out at all."

"Play it one more time," Nina whispered.

13. Root

"Vasilyich, want me to tell you my life story?"

And I tell him all about how things have been, understand; about my Dad, and my childhood, and the sealing schooner *Flame*, and I myself don't understand where the flow of words is coming from, I'm spouting like Vovik, and Captain Sakunenko listens to me, smokes cigarettes, and the dame has piped down, we're walking along beside the line.

Now this is what the champagne's doing to me today. I used to drink it like water. I'd have a bottle of demi-sec for breakfast with half a loaf and a cutlet. I don't know, maybe I was taking a chance on my health.

"My God, but that's a whole novel!" sighs the dame.

"My understanding," says the captain, "is that every life is a novel. There are as many novels here as there are people in this line. Perhaps I'm wrong, Irina Nikolayevna?"

"Perhaps you're right, Volodya, but don't call me by my patronymic, we made an agreement."

"Well, but write the novel."

The dame became thoughtful. "No, I wouldn't write about Kostyukovsky, I'd write about you, Volodya. You're a positive hero."

Dames! Out with them! Well, what can you say, huh?

Volodya really didn't know where to hide.

"Could you, ah, leave us?" he asks the dame. "The seaman and I have to have a constructive, perhaps, rather, a colleague-to-colleague, well, actually, a confidential talk is what I should have with the seaman."

"All right," she says. "I'll wait for you in the Lighthouse."

She finally took off. The captain even heaved a sigh of relief.

"Listen, Valya," he tells me, "I understand things have been hard for you, of course, and you're a good seaman, on the whole. And we do have room: Kesha, you know, is going into the army... But none of your crazy ideas! Understand?" he yelled at the top of his voice.

"Okay, okay," I say. "Don't start a shouting match. I know you're a great one for yelling, Vasilyich."

He scratched his head.

"How can we push this through personnel? I'll tell them that we're taking you on for correction. 'We're going to influence him,' I'll say, 'with the power of peer-pressure.' "

"Well, okay, influence me," I agreed.

"Let's go," says he, "our boys are already sitting in the Lighthouse. I'll introduce you to the crew."

"Only, you know, Vasilyich, do it quietly, without fanfare. Say, 'Comrade Kostyukovsky here has the honor of joining the ranks of our glorious working crew,' that's all, real quiet, no speeches."

"You big smart aleck," he laughs. "Well, watch out... The least thing and we put you off on Shikotan."

The first person I met in the Lighthouse was Lusya Kravchenko. She was dancing in the arms of her driller.

"How come, Lusya, you're shining like a buttered blintz?" I said to her.

That's the way I am: as soon as things are going smoothly, I become a high-class smart aleck.

"I have my reasons." She smiled and laid her head on his shoulder.

"I see, I see."

I remembered the taste of her cheek—once I had managed to kiss her on the cheek, but she'd fought like a fiend—I remembered, and smiled at her to show what I was remembering. But she seemed to answer, "Well, what of it? What does it matter?"

But Vitya saw nothing and heard nothing, apparently he was wired up something awful. Sakunenko was already sitting at the head of the table and signalling to me: There's room. But someone buttonholed me and pulled me toward another table. I look and there's Vovik. There he sits, old bright-eyes, at his little table, dining on shishkebab, consuming berry wine, and even has a couple oranges in front of him.

"Sit down, Valya," he says, "Have something," he says, "have a little something to eat, Root, and we'll shove off. We've got business."

"Take your business and get out, way the hell out and then some."

"What's with you, lost your marbles, you piece of a fool?"

"Go on about your business, Vovik, but I'm staying here."

"Villain, are you forgetting? Sailors stick together."

At that I up and banged a knife on the wineglass, shouting, "Waiter! Change my table mate!"

That was the end of my friendship with Vovik.

I went over to the *South Wind's* table and looked to see who was new there and who I knew.

I sat down beside Sakunenko, and they all stared at me, because they all knew me already, everyone based at Petrovo or Slush and everyone from the fish-processing combine as well, and from all the coastal co-ops—I've biched it up and down the whole coast.

"Hullo, men!" I said.

Esther Naumovna came sailing over to me immediately. She's sorry for me.

"What will you have, Valya my dear?" she asks, but herself, poor thing, she's already feeling no pain. I kissed her hard-working hand.

"Whatever you treat me to, Esther Naumovna, I'll accept it all."

"You shall have it," she said, and went reeling off, the seagoing soul. Maybe when the floor rolls beneath her she imagines she's still on the deck of the *Chicherev.*

"A drunken woman," says the dame that's planning to write the novel about Volodya our Sakunenko, "is a disgusting sight."

"You should keep quiet, lady!" I shouted. "What do you know about her? —I'm sorry," I said, catching myself, "it just popped out."

But they weren't mad at me on the *South Wind.* They knew all about Esther Naumovna.

Well, so I seem to have veered at the last minute, seem to have gotten past the rocks, and the record player is playing, and I'm a seaman on the *South Wind* again, and there's oranges on the table in a warm heap, and to-morrow my Dad is supposed to come, Professor Sauerkraut, member of the society for miscellaneous knowledge, he'll probably come tomorrow, if Khabarovsk lets the flight take off—the only thing is, will there be much joy in this meeting?

14. Ludmila Kravchenko

He introduced me to all his friends. I was glad to make the acquaintance of these men, prospectors for our mineral wealth. We took a table in the Lighthouse and crowded in around it, the more the merrier: Lenya, Yura, Misha, Volodya, Yevdoshchuk, Chudakov, my Vitya and I. The room was already jam-packed. You could hardly hear the record player over the roar of voices, but there were lots of people dancing—every one of them probably dancing to music of his own. All my girlfriends were dancing and smiling at me, and Nina seemed to have forgotten all else in the world, forgotten Vasilyevsky Island and the Marble Hall. I had done well, introducing her to Gera Kovalyov. They seemed to have found a common language.

And the oranges lay heaped on our table, bottles stood ready, steam rose from the hot food. The service wasn't top flight, of course, not like ours at the railroad restaurant, but then again, no one here was in a hurry, no one was trying to enjoy all thirty-three pleasures in thirty minutes; everyone was happy, I think, on this amazing evening. The lamps shone above, and the oranges below. And Vitya's hand lay on my shoulder; he looked at me through the cigarette smoke with bright crazy eyes in which everything seemed to have come to a stop. It was even a little improper. I inconspicuously removed his hand from my shoulder, something stirred in his eyes, a spark of humor glinted, and he stood up, glass in hand.

"Hell's bells, men!" he said.

I'll have to wean him from expressions like that.

"Let's drink to Kichekian and to our quest! I've got a feeling we haven't been jazzing around in these Swiss Alps for nothing. Frankly, men, there's a gusher roaring in our borehole right now."

"The gusher's roaring in your noggin!" said Lenya.

"And someplace else," added Yevdoshchuk.

They all laughed, and Victor flared up, shouting, "Bellyachers! My induction tells me! I believe my induction! Want a fight?" He was addressing Lenya. But for some reason Lenya wouldn't fight; apparently Victor had such an effect on him that he believed in oil himself.

I didn't understand at first what "induction" was, but then I got it. "Intuition," probably—I'd have to tell him.

"And we won't be there," said Yura. "That's tough."

"The main thing is for Airapet to be there," said Lenya. "Let him be the first to wash his hands in the oil, that's his right. He's worn himself to a frazzle over this thing."

"And forgotten about his wife, even," Lenya added, looking across the room. "This oil thing may turn out bad for him."

"Yeah, win a few, lose a few," muttered Yevdoshchuk. He glanced at me and choked.

"Let's go and dance," said Victor to me.

It was hard to dance with people pushing on every side, it would have been better just to put our arms around each other and stand in one spot swaying to the music. On our left, Sima was dancing with an enormous man in a pea jacket. So that was whose striped shirts those were. They were so enormous, Sima and her admirer, that they practically seemed like people from another planet. Sima gave me a languid smile and laid her head on her young man's shoulder.

"Vitya, do you like your work?"

"You know the answer to that one—I'm well provided for materially..."

"Oh, not that. Do you like looking for oil?"

"I like finding it better."

"That must be neat."

"When the gusher spurts up? Yes, it's neat. And the gas—it's neat when the gas burns, too. You know, there's flame all over the sky, and we inject pulp to put it out but it won't surrender, the whole place is hot, we're all wet, it's all-out war."

"That's the good kind of war, isn't it?"

"The only kind. To hell with any other."

The record—it wasn't even a record, really, but an X-ray film mounted on cardboard—was screaking away.

> Speak to me of love,
> Over and over, dear,
> I'm always ready to hear,
> Tum-dum-di-dah...

"You know, Vitya, everything's going to change here. You'll find oil, and we'll build beautiful cities."

"Well of course, everything's going to change here. We'll have paradise here, the greenery of paradise..."

"That's right, the climate may even change here. Maybe we'll have our very own oranges growing here."

"Naturally."

"Don't you joke!"

"You don't like it here now, child of the south?"

"I like it now... Vitya! Vitya, you mustn't do that, you're out of your mind."

> Speak to me of love,
> Over and over, dear,
> I'm always ready to hear,
> Tum-dum-di-dah...

"What is it she's always ready to hear? I can't make it out at all."

I couldn't hear the last words either, but I knew what I'd always be ready to hear.

> Tum-dum-di-dah.

I'm always ready to hear your breathing, the beat of your heart, your jokes.

"Go put the record on one more time."

15. Victor Koltyga

I don't approve of guys who like to be photographed in restaurants or these restaurant-type eateries. It would never enter anyone's head to be photographed in an ordinary eatery, but if the prices are marked up and there's cut velvet at the windows and a menu with a hard cover, then that means people are bound and determined to record for eternity the historic moment of their visit to the restaurant.

One time I was sitting in the Ussuri Restaurant in Khabarovsk, just sitting there, peacefully dining, but God knows what was going on around me, you'd have thought it was a flock of news photographers descending on a reception for some kind of African chieftain.

Actually, though, I can understand the guys. When you've been roughing it half the year in a tent or a bunkroom and dining right from a tin can, and suddenly you see clean tablecloths, wineglasses, and a jazz band, obviously you'd want to be immortalized against this background.

But I don't like it, I don't attach great meaning to these events, I've seen plenty of restaurants in my time. True, when I was young I used to pick up souvenirs. I had a whole collection: a menu in three languages from the Savoy in Moscow, a fork from the Golden Horn in Vladivostok, a wineglass from the Northland in Magadan. I was young, I didn't understand. This is all a bunch of nonsense. Still, it's pleasant to have your snack to music, of course.

Lenya took six or seven pictures. The last time I decided I didn't give a damn and just put my arm around Lusya, pressed my face to hers. She didn't even succeed in extricating herself, or maybe she even didn't want to. To tell the truth, I simply didn't understand what had happened to her. The way she was that night, my head was going around, never mind my serious intentions, I simply wanted to love her all my life and then some. Probably the oranges were to blame for all this.

"And I'll make you a double portrait," said Lenya. "Two lovebirds. If you love me as I love you, we shall always live as two."

I just gasped, couldn't even answer him. Damned little oranges, nature's gifts, what are you doing to me?

"Lusya," I whispered in her ear.

She just smiled, pretending to watch Yura.

"Lusya," I whispered again. "They'll give us a room in Phosphate."

And Yura had ordered himself a bowl. He put all his oranges into this artistic green glass bowl, pulled it over close to him and, leaning his forehead on his hands, casting sidelong glances at the golden mountain of oranges, he kept mumbling in a voice thick with emotion: "Now we're going to eat them..."

At last Esther Naumovna made her way to us out of the jolting crowd of dancers. She brought me two bottles of Checheno-Ingush, and while I opened them she stood by, her arms folded across her apron.

"What a nice girl, you have, Vitya," she kept saying. "A very remarkable girl. You have the nicest girl on this shore, Vitya, I'm telling you."

"Only it's the last one, Esther Naumovna, okay?"

"Why Vitya, of course!"

"Promise you won't be back again, Esther Naumovna!"

"May I be so strong."

I poured her a glass and she went away, hiding it under her apron.

"Why does she drink?" asked Lusya in a whisper. "What's wrong with her?"

"She had a son that drowned. They sailed on the *Chicherev* together, she was the barmaid and he was an engineer. Well, she was saved, but he drowned. A kid about my age."

"Good Lord!" breathed Lusya.

She went all white and covered her eyes, bit her lips. Now, I'd never thought she was like that.

"It's a good thing you're not a sailor," she whispered. "I'd go out of my mind if you were a sailor."

"Relax," I said. "I'm not a sailor, you don't drown on land."

You really don't drown on land, I thought. Other things happen on land, especially the land where we lay out our trails. I remembered Chizhikov. He might have been sitting with us right now, eating oranges.

Just then I noticed that Lenya, Chudakov, and Yevdoshchuk were whispering among themselves, from time to time glancing at something quite ominously. When I tracked their tracer-bullet glances, I realized what was the matter. They were obsessed with this Katya. Who knows what the hell these guys had in mind. They didn't know that Katya danced oftenest with Kalchanov even when her husband was there. Kalchanov is a good dancer, and this kind of thing is not our Airapet's strong point.

But then I noticed that they weren't dancing just for fun, but the way Lusya and I had been dancing—only their faces were somber, both his and hers. There was something fishy going on, clearly. But where was Sergei?

Sergei was sitting in a corner, like a machine gun trained on them, the guy was barely restraining himself. Only there weren't enough of our guys here yet.

I made some sort of toast and switched the attention of the audience to Yura, who hadn't even looked at the meat dish and wasn't even interested in the drinks, either, but was only digging into his oranges, wolfing them down.

"Well, Yura!" laughed the guys.

"Have *you* ever stocked up on vitamins! You can figure you've had a vacation trip to the south."

"To Morocco itself," said Yevdoshchuk.

"Hey, Yura, you've got leaves growing out of your ears!"

The place was hot and cheerful. I knew a lot of the people there, yes; but then, all the rest looked familiar to me that night too. What a feast this was in the sultry orangey air. An excellent feast! I selected the biggest orange and peeled it so that it opened like a flowerbud.

"Let's go dance," said Lusya.

She stood up and started on ahead. I purposely lagged behind a little, and when she turned I took note of what she was like, all of her, and thought that Victor Koltyga's life at the present moment was shaping up quite nicely, and if the well came in today and if that made the kind of sensation it usually did, then I would have a week or so to spend with Lusya on the quiet.

For some reason I was sure that this very day, this very night, a gusher would strike in our good old ravine.

"Are you happy?" I asked Lusya.

"I've never been so happy," she whispered. "Such an amazing night. Oranges... Really, isn't it happy when there are oranges? I'd like them to be here always. No, it doesn't have to be always, but at least sometimes, if only once a year..."

> Speak to me of love,
> Over and over, dear,
> I'm always ready to hear,
> Tum-dum-di-dah...

Again I couldn't make out the last words.

"I'm going to put the record on one more time."

"Everyone's already sick of it."

"I have to make out the words."

It wasn't a record but a warped X-ray film. The tone arm was barely coping with it, and in order to make it spin, someone had weighted the middle with an upside-down wineglass.

16. Nikolai Kalchanov

I read the menu loudly: "Goat-meat kabobs with assorted garnish!"

Someone had already drawn a goat on the menu, of course, and written the slogan, "Chew and pass on."

"Riddle Cocktail," I read. "Zoologic Candy."

Katya had thoroughly cheered up.

"Sergei, have you already solved all the riddles?" she asked. "You've probably already eaten the whole goat. I heard that they shoot them on the sopki. They probably rounded up an argali specially for you. Kolya, isn't that what they call those Pamir bighorns—argali?"

Sergei was smiling wanly and warming her hands, holding them in his. He was puffy and gloomy, he must really have had a lot to eat, and a fair amount to drink, too.

When we had dropped into the eatery with the gallant bich Kostyukovsky, Sergei was still fresh. He was having supper with the manager; they were clinking glasses, offering each other cigarettes, and laughing. It was nice watching Sergei handle his knife and fork, touch his napkin to his lips; it's nice to sit at table with a man like that. He waved to us, but we clinked glasses with Kostyukovsky and went back to the line.

I must still be a little kid: it astonishes me the way Sergei can be so spontaneous and familiar with middle-aged men of the traditional boss type. I just clutch up in front of astrakhan collars, I don't know how you're supposed to talk to them, and so I either hold my tongue or start being rude.

Sergei gave a house-warming party right after the three of us came to Phosphate City. He was stunned by the fact that we'd come here, Arik and I, and of course he was stunned by Katya. And what stunned me was the fact that Sergei had become my boss, and it goes without saying that we were all stunned by his apartment—an oasis of modernity in this unsophisticated land.

Of course we were invited to the housewarming. We made a very effective montage, as the film-makers say, with the interior decor. Strangely enough, the bosses and their wives also made an effective montage. I made one mistake: I came in a jacket and tie. Sergei spoke to me directly about this: why so formal, he said, you could've worn a turtleneck. I really should have worn my heavy turtleneck.

Sergei served everyone coffee and poured some kind of exotic cognac, while the bosses—nice men, on the whole—marvelled politely at it all and said: that's young people for you, everything they do is new-fashioned; modern tastes, but that's all right, they're practical young people all the same. Small-talk like that is terribly amusing to me.

When we came back to the Lighthouse, this time with oranges in hand, Sergei was sitting by himself. We went and sat at his table. He was gloomy, smoking his Reindeer cigarette; a half-empty glass stood before him on the table, the radio lay next to it making a quiet strumming sound, and the leather jacket and egg-shaped helmet were jumbled on the floor. God only knows what he thought of himself at that moment—perhaps something very improbable.

He allowed us to gaze our fill of him and then started warming Katya's hands.

257

"Satisfied?" he said to me. "You showed me, didn't you? Rubbed it in, didn't you?"

"Treat me to something, Sergei," I begged.

"Go ahead." He nodded at the bottle.

I took a drink.

"The woman's is poured first."

"My mistake," I said. "Let's do it this way, then: you warm the woman's hand, and I will pour for the woman."

He let go of her hand. "You amaze me, Kalchanov."

Katya raised her glass and laughed, narrowing her eyes. "You haven't seen anything yet, just wait. Today is Kalchanov's day, he's amazing everyone, but tomorrow he'll amaze everyone even more..."

"Katya," I said.

"You may think he's nothing special," she went on, "but he is. He's a man of talent, if you want to know. He's an architect."

I didn't say anything, but mentally I seized her by the hand, I implored her not to perform this vivisection, there was no need to suffer so, quiet now, quiet.

"It only seems that way, that everything's a joke to him," she went on. "He has a serious project, his life's work..."

"Is that really so?" said Sergei, astounded. He was taking pleasure in helping Katya torture herself.

"Of course. He's talented as hell. He's more talented than you, Sergei."

Sergei started.

"Let's go dance," I said. I got up and pulled her by the hand.

"Why are you doing this?" I asked, putting my arm around her waist.

She grinned. "It's my last chance to exercise the right of the beautiful woman. The way I'm going to be soon, you all won't even want to talk to me."

She smelled of orange juice, and she was all ruddy, young, a Pioneer Leader straight out of Camp Artek, and this *femme fatale* tone didn't suit her at all. We lost ourselves in the crush of dancers, no one seemed to see us, no one seemed to be watching over us, and again we were inexorably drawn together.

An upside-down wineglass was spinning on the record player, the edges of the record were bent up like the brim of a hat, but even so the tone arm was picking up some kind of hoarse, strange sounds. I couldn't distinguish either the melody or the rhythm, couldn't make out a word, but we danced anyway.

"Have you calmed down, Katya?"

"Yes."

"There won't be any more of that?"

I moved away from her, as far as the crush would allow.

"Katya, let's set up the checkers all over again, go back to square one.

This variant isn't working out, it's clear."

"Is it easy for you to do this?"

"Why of course. All this is a trifling matter compared with the tasks that... Period. You said it yourself: I have a great project, my life's work."

"And here's an excellent formula for me: 'But I was pledged another's wife, And will be faithful all my life.'[5] And besides, I'm a teacher of Russian language and literature."

"Now that is excellent!"

"Hold me tighter!"

The enigmatic record was repeated endlessly, people kept playing it over and over, as if the whole room were striving to solve the riddle.

"This evening is ours, Kolya; agreed? And tomorrow—it's over. It's not every day that a ship comes in with oranges."

> The flame burns, does not smoke.
> How long can it last me?
> No mercy has she,
> She uses me, wastes me.

I recalled a soft-voiced singer, calm like the astronomer. I felt the easier for the recollection.

> Life is not forever young,
> Time never lingers.
> A gold piece unspent,
> I'll slip through your fingers.

I will build cities and time will go by. I'll shave my beard and become a handsome young man, then a hardened lout, and then... Does it make sense to build on this earth? It does!

> I will darken in the wind,
> Rain will flow past me.
> But lavish is she,
> How long can it last me...

But for now we know no sorrow, we know no weariness, and along the dark narrow shore fly our blinding headlights; and our pot-bellied airplanes, losing altitude, land at the little airport; and amid the murmur of crumbling ice floes, their whistles droning, the icebreakers go to Petrovo and Slush, and in comes the *Kildin*, and Katya and I dance on our first and last evening, and what was here before, in Stalin's lifetime, remember it, remember...

Katya was gay, as if she really believed in this fiction. Laughing, she led me by the hand to our table, and I began to laugh too, and we greatly amazed Sergei.

"You're no gentleman," he said abruptly.

I had to rise and bow in gratitude. What kind of gentleman was I? Sergei isolated himself from us, retired into his shell. Attuning myself to Katya's game, I ceased to notice him, moved close to her, took her hand.

"Do you want to know what this is?"

"Yes."

"If you want to know, this is what it is. It's a stifling summer, and for some reason I'm stuck in the city. I'm standing in the courtyard of a ten-story building hung with laundry. There's sand crunching in my teeth, the wind stirs the ice-cream cups at my feet. I'm forty years old and you're seventeen, you come out from under the archway with the first drops of rain."

"Pardon me, buster." Someone touched my shoulder.

I looked up—there was a big guy standing over me with a bag of oranges in his arms. It was one of Victor Koltyga's pals, one from Airapet's party.

"Good evening," he said, and held the bag out to Katya. "This is for you."

She fluttered her eyelashes in confusion. "Thank you, but I have some. What is this for?"

"For your husband Airapet Nara.. Nara..."

"Narairovich." Katya supplied the patronymic mechanically.

He put the bag on the table.

"There's an induction that he'll strike oil today. Your husband may come into town, and he needs fruit as a man of the south." He um-ed and ah-ed around us a little longer, but Katya said nothing, and he went back to his friends. I noticed that they were watching us from their table. I saw that Katya was all rattled, her alarm signal was pealing, there was no refuge for her anywhere, and I took the blow on myself. I held her hand again and said:

"Or the other way around—rain, rain, rain, a waltz test in the log clubhouse. I'm a senior Pioneer, the kids are ridiculing me for not knowing how to play soccer, and you're a senior Pioneer Leader, you invite me to dance..."

Sergei kicked me under the table. I was a little taken aback: what are you going to do if a man starts behaving in such a spontaneous manner?

At that moment, with shouts and jokes, Staska and Edik Tanaka came jostling their way through to us. They dropped their oranges on the table, and Edik began complaining that his girl had deceived him, she hadn't responded to the champion's feeling, can you imagine, and not only that—she was dancing here right before his eyes with another guy, endlessly dancing to the same idiotic record.

"You understand, I take the record off, and he comes and puts it on again, I take it off, and he puts it on again. I ask him, 'You like it, do you?' And he says, 'I can't make out the words.' And all the rest shout, 'Let it play, what's it to you, give us a break, we have to make out the words.' They're obsessed with those words!"

"Have a drink, men," I said, "a Riddle cocktail."

"A riddle *fatale,*" said Staska after taking a sip. "I pity my insides, men."

Gaiety reigned at the table. Esther Naumovna came and brought some sort of food. Edik and Staska recounted the adventures they'd had driving in, and what the oranges had cost them, and I told them about my heroic encounter with Kostyukovsky. Sergei kept trying to prove to the guys that I was a bum, they agreed with him and were only surprised that he was going to drive his motorcycle back.

And Katya talked softly with Esther Naumovna. I listened in.

"He was the kind," Esther Naumovna was saying, "that all these dances-shmances didn't interest him. He only read books, my Lyova did, and not novels, but all kinds of books on technology. He never even had a girl..."

I didn't know what the conversation was about, but I understood that it was no small matter. Katya was listening attentively to the tipsy waitress, she was pale, her fingers were clenched, I couldn't bear to look at her, and just then, from out of the crowd of dancers emerged the black-stubbled face of Airapet.

Katya jumped up. Her husband came toward us, slowly setting one foot in front of the other.

"Hello there, little girl," he said, and for a second he pressed his check to hers.

"Arik, old pal!" roared Sergei, leaning heavily on the table and looking, strangely enough, at me.

"Hello, men," said Airapet cheerfully, letting himself down into a chair. "Give me something to drink."

I saw that his weariness was heavy as a mountain, that he was practically breaking under his smiles.

"A Riddle cocktail," I said, and moved the pitcher toward him.

"Who do you think I am, the Answer Man?" he joked. "Give me some cognac."

Slowly, delicately, the men from his party came up behind him. They were practically having cramps in their cheeks from impatience.

"Well, Arik?" asked Katya.

"Not a damn thing!" He shrugged. "Sulfur water. All in vain. Tomorrow we start on a new trail."

17. And Tomorrow...

The orange-night has ended. You can be sure they'll be talking about it for a long time. And tomorrow...

The bulldozers will start out ahead, behind them will come the tractors towing the equipment—derrick, drilling rig, pipes... Maybe a helicopter will drop in part of the crew, and they will get busy clearing the taiga for the drilling area. Toward evening the men will crawl into sleeping bags and plunge into their dreams. Maybe Vitya Koltyga will find time to leaf through the magazine *Knowledge Is Power,* and Bazarevich is likely to loll about in the snow a while, and Kichekian will close his eyes and hear a thundering gusher of oil.

The forecasters are predicting calm weather.

"That's a lot of hot air," they're grumbling on the *South Wind.*

The flotilla of seiners will start out behind the icebreaker in a whisper of ground-up ice. The icebreaker will lead them out to the warm current and sound a farewell blast. Gera Kovalyov's hands will be stiff as boards, it will be hard for him to hold the pencil.

"You've got talent, Gera. Dig in, have some compote," Ivan and Borya and Valya Kostyukovsky will tell him at night in the bunkroom.

Amber Cream may help some people, but not Lusya Kravchenko. The bricks flow along the conveyor belt. Higher and higher rise the floors. The crane lowers the containers right into the girls' hands. One more container, one more container, one more floor, one more apartment building, store or nursery, and soon a city will grow up, and in it there'll be a monument to our Lenin, and—after work—Lusya and her lawful husband Vitya Koltyga will walk down Komsomol Prospect to their own apartment on the fourth floor of a prefabricated building. That's what Lusya thinks about.

"Hey boss, you'll get your nose frostbitten!" Kolya Markov will shout to Kalchanov when he's lost in thought, and Kalchanov will start, run down along the scaffolding, needling his workmen.

"Pushkin's Eugene Onegin—prototype of the 'superfluous man,' " Katya Pirogova will dictate as the theme of a new composition.

The orange-night has ended.

Tomorrow everything will be back on track, but in the meantime...

18. Victor Koltyga

All the same it was the best night of my life. Induction let me down, the hell with it. I'd told Lusya that what I liked was finding; I probably had it wrong. What I really like is looking.

"That means you're going away again tomorrow?" she asked.

"What can you do."

"For long?"

"A couple of months."

"Oh!"

"But I'll come in sometimes. It's not far from here."

"Really?"

"But then, better not wait. I'll surprise you. Lusya, tell me, are you a virgin?"

"Yes," she whispered.

We went out and stood for a moment on the porch, arms around each other's shoulders.

The moon hung high above us in the peaceful dark sky. On the square in front of the Lighthouse Eatery, the crowd was devouring oranges, panting in concentration. Golden peels were falling on the pale blue snow. The bichi too had gotten a few.

1962   Translated by Susan Brownsberger

NOTES

1. Ray Meyer: A basketball coach.

2. Ponedelnik, Meskhi: Soviet soccer players.

3. Vitya has in mind an anecdote about a draftee who appears for his physical claiming that his trigger finger is paralyzed in a bent position.

4. Kolyma: A region of Siberia, along the Kolyma River, known for its forced labor camps.

5. Katya quotes the lines Tatyana uses in rejecting Onegin's love. (Alexander Pushkin, *Eugene Onegin,* translated by Walter Arndt. E.P. Dutton, New York, 1963.)